Presented in Memory of
Geannie Rourke Kimball

By
Cyndy and Will Palcich

Catherine saw the uplifted arms of the Joshua tree before she saw him. His soft laughter reached across the yards of sand and rock to stroke her.

For a long minute she held back on the reins of her prancing mount. She still had time to turn back. A war raged inside her . . . and she sat there, helplessly watching as Law kneed his sorrel and slowly moved across the distance that separated them.

His gaze held her immobile as his hands took the reins from her unresisting fingers. And still she could not move when his hands encircled her waist and lifted her from the sidesaddle as easily as if she were a child. The kiss that seared her, reaching down to relieve the torment twisting inside her—this was what she had been waiting for, wanting. . . .

Also by Parris Afton Bonds:

DUST DEVIL

THE FLASH OF THE FIREFLY

LOVE TIDE

SAVAGE ENCHANTMENT

SWEET GOLDEN SUN

DEEP PURPLE

A Novel by

Parris Afton Bonds

With Warmest Wishes
Parris Afton Bonds

Fawcett Columbine • New York

The author is grateful for permission to reprint excerpts from the following:

"I Want You" by Arthur L. Gillom, found in *The Family Book of Best-Loved Poems,* edited by David L. George, published by Doubleday & Co., Inc., © 1952 by Doubleday & Co., Inc. Reprinted by permission of Doubleday & Co., Inc., and Copeland and Lamm, Inc.

"It's Been A Long, Long Time," lyric by Sammy Cahn, music by Jule Styne. © 1945 Morley Music Co. © renewed 1973 by Morley Music Co. International Copyright Secured. All rights reserved. Reprinted by permission.

"You Made Me Love You (I Didn't Want To Do It)," lyric by Joe McCarthy, music by James V. Monaco. © 1913 Broadway Music Corp. © renewed 1941 by Edwin H. Morris & Company, A Division of MPL Communications, Inc., and Broadway Music Corp. International Copyright Secured. All rights reserved. Reprinted by permission.

DEEP PURPLE

Published by Fawcett Columbine Books, CBS Educational and Professional Publishing, a division of CBS Inc.

ISBN: 0-449-90073-8

Printed in the United States of America

First Fawcett Columbine printing: May 1982

10 9 8 7 6 5 4 3 2 1

For
Cathy and Pete Cella
and
My editor, Suzanne Sorice

I want you when the shades of eve are falling
  And purpling shadows drift across the land;
When sleepy birds to loving mates are calling—
  I want the soothing softness of your hand.

I want you when in dreams I still remember
  The ling'ring of your kiss—for old times' sake—
With all your gentle ways, so sweetly tender,
  I want you in the morning when I wake.

I want you when my soul is thrilled with passion;
  I want you when I'm weary and depressed;
I want you when in lazy, slumberous fashion
  My senses need the heaven of your breast.

I want you, dear, through every changing season;
  I want you with a tear or with a smile;
I want you more than any rhyme or reason—
  I want you, want you, want you—all the while.

—ARTHUR L. GILLOM
I Want You

AS a child, a young girl with coltish legs and dusky skin, I spent many anxious hours prowling the low desert and the craggy foothills of southeastern Arizona's Huachuca Mountains—anxious hours not just because I was trespassing on the forbidden Cristo Rey land grant but also because I was searching among the rocks and cactus-stubbled dunes for the Ghost Lady, hoping and praying I could get a glimpse of her and at the same time scared to death that I really would.

The army's electronic proving grounds and the state's futuristic superhighways now desecrate a wilderness that knew only the tracks of the jaguar and coyote, the lonely soughing of the wind, and the gentle whisper of a lover's words. Much has changed since then, yet the tales of the Ghost Lady persist.

The old-timers tell different versions of the woman who rode sidesaddle, sometimes on a blaze-faced roan and at others on a rangy bay. But in every version the Ghost Lady, dressed in a black formal English riding habit with top hat, always appeared first near a Joshua tree.

It is at that point the similarity of the versions ends. Some say she haunted that area of Cristo Rey because she was a tormented wraith looking for the lover denied her in life. And others say she rode the area, its barren deserts and rock-clad mountains and lush, grassy valleys, because her soul was condemned to wander Cristo Rey until the fifty thousand acres—and the Stronghold—were at last returned to her heirs.

Of course, I preferred to believe the latter . . . perhaps because at that young age my childish mind could not conceive of a love so great that it would transcend time and space. I had yet to taste of love's binding passion. But in all likelihood I chose to believe that version of the tale because even then I knew, like my Ghost Lady, my soul would know no peace until I possessed what rightfully belonged to me . . . Cristo Rey.

PART
1

Chapter 1

1863

*T*HE tests are all in, Catherine," Dr. McFarland said.

He studiously wiped a handkerchief over his spectacles' thick milk-bottle lenses, and Catherine realized he was afraid to meet her gaze.

Why, she could not imagine. Surely, after watching death claim the hundreds of men given into his hands by the rapacious War Between the States, one more death could not be that difficult to acknowledge. But then, she reminded herself, the good doctor had been in love with her mother for years.

"Dear Dr. McFarland," she replied as she worked the fingers of her kid gloves onto her hands, "please don't imagine for one moment that I am incapable of shouldering unpleasant news. I have worked at your side too many times during the last year when Death came for its victim."

She laughed then, a laugh husky with rare, humorous insight, and the aging doctor was once again stricken by the transformation—a rather common face made uncommonly beautiful. "But then it was not one of my family Death was seeking those other times, was it? I assume it is pleurisy?"

Dr. McFarland jammed his spectacles back on his bulbous nose. "Interlobular pleurosis, to be exact." His walrus mustache fluttered with the grunt of exasperation he expelled. "But it's not just your mother I'm concerned about. You're wearing yourself ragged taking care of her and working here at the hospital also."

She fixed him with steady eyes that were neither green nor gray. Crème de menthe, her sister called the color. "But that is neither here nor there," she said crisply. She fastened the buttons of her kid gloves. The gloves, like her dress, were meticulously mended so that only the most observant eyes noticed.

"There is no justice in life—isn't that what I have often heard you mutter?"

The doctor had the good grace to flush, realizing Catherine was referring to the times he had resorted to alcohol to alleviate the pain in his soul which no physician could heal. She was right—what man was doing to himself in the bloody Civil War was horrendous. He occasionally half wished he could die along with the men on the makeshift cots that crowded the hospital's wards. Sixty-six years was too old. He had seen too much.

He regarded the woman sitting so properly on the other side of the desk. He was fond of Catherine Howard. Perhaps because of her mother—though twenty-six-year-old Catherine did not seem to possess her mother's exotic delicate beauty as did Catherine's sister. But what Catherine did possess was a strength of will and an unsuspected courage demonstrated in her care for men mangled beyond recognition.

"Well, Dr. McFarland?" she asked, her hands clasped lightly in her lap. "What do you propose? Don't bother to gloss over whatever you have to tell me. By this time I am all too familiar with pleurisy's—effects."

The old man complied. "Then I don't need to tell you about the chills and fever, nor the hacking cough."

"No, all that I know. Tell me rather how much time my mother has left—approximately, of course."

The doctor's shoulders hunched with the weight of the prognosis he had to impart. "No one knows much about the disease. We do know that the patient needs plenty of rest and treatment—what little we can give with our limited medical knowledge."

Catherine rose, drawing the string closed on her reticule as tightly as if she were drawing it on her emotions. "I will see that my mother gets the best care we can give her. Good afternoon, Dr. McFarland."

Despite the frigid March air that blasted through Baltimore's snow-packed streets, Catherine was perspiring as she maneuvered about the attic's dusty boxes where her father's belongings were stored. Then she located the crate with the word *Books* penned across in her father's precise handwriting.

Her father had been a schoolmaster, and it was he who had taught her the appreciation of books and knowledge—of languages and histories; as her mother, the daughter of a wealthy shipbuilder, had taught her the appreciation for the finer things of life. But it was her father, Catherine reflected wryly, who in a way was responsible for the decision she had made that afternoon—the decision to head toward the gold fields of the West, for her father had done the same in 1850, the year after gold was discovered in in California.

He had abandoned the wife who loved him so little, who found a schoolmaster's salary inadequate contrasted to her former way of life. Disinherited by her parents for eloping with the schoolmaster, the pampered woman was left by herself to care for the thirteen-year-old Catherine and the six-years-younger Margaret . . . or rather Catherine was left to care for her mother and younger sister.

The newest gold fields were in Colorado and Arizona now, and that was where Catherine meant to go. That afternoon, when she returned from Dr. McFarland's office, she stood before the long pier mirror and looked at herself . . . the face made pallid by too little sunlight and her body emaciated to a rail thinness by too much work. The mirror told her she had little hope of courtship from war-weary men. No, they would have their pick of buxom, voluptuously curved young women, who outnumbered the men and were anxious for the taste of romance and marriage that the Civil War had long denied them.

It took only a moment to locate the *Encyclopedia Americana*. She began to scan the facts about Arizona, which had been a part of the Territory of New Mexico until only two weeks prior, in February, when the U.S. Congress had established it as a separate territory.

She read about the Hohokam Indians who had come to Tucson's teacup valley long before the Spanish and whose origins were lost in the course of time. And she read about Tucson itself with its watchtowered walls. As a sleepy Spanish pueblo, the Royal Presidio of San Agustín de Tuscon, it was the same age as the American Republic.

When the last light of the afternoon faded·from the small attic window, she put away the thick book with the certainty that Tucson was where she would go—where hordes of men had migrated a decade earlier, where women were few. Out there in that barren territory she could earn the money to see that her mother received proper care. Out there she still might find the husband and children for which her own heart cried out.

Chapter 2

CATHERINE snuggled her hands deeper in the fur muff as Arizona's new chief justice, William Turner, swore in the territory's new officers. It was the last of December, and the snowy chill of a northern Arizona winter enveloped the travelers assembled at the tiny settlement of Navajo Springs, just across the New Mexico boundary line.

"A carpetbag government if ever I saw one," said the stocky old man, the new territorial general surveyor, who stood next to her. Hiram Ogilvee was referring to the fact that all the officials, but for himself, came from Eastern states, most of them lame-duck congressmen.

Catherine couldn't have cared less. She only wanted to climb back into the great blue army ambulance and get warm again; however, she graciously accepted the tin cup of almost frozen champagne and drank to the health of the new Arizona Territory.

The governor, John Goodwin, at last closed the inauguration ceremony with a speech of his hopes for the new territory. Catherine then translated the speech into Spanish for the benefit of the New Mexican soldiers who acted as escorts. It had been part of her arrangement with Goodwin when he agreed to let her accompany the officials to Arizona. She could only think how strange it was that they stood in the wilderness to inaugurate the territorial government, with no citizens of Arizona to greet them.

At last, grimly wondering what had happened to Arizona's famed sunny climate, she climbed back beneath the ambulance's white canvas cover. More than once in the three-month journey she had experienced second thoughts about her decision to come west. But it was too late to change her mind, she told herself firmly. The fact was she *had* signed with the Albert Teachers Agency listing service and as a result was now being bounced most uncomfortably in the ambulance as it lumbered southwestward toward the temporary capital, Fort Whipple.

Her sister and mother had been aghast that she could actually consider accepting a teacher's position in what Margaret called a "godforsaken place on the frontier."

The afternoon Catherine announced she had taken a position as a private teacher near Tucson in the Arizona Territory, her bedridden mother had caught her by the hand. "Catherine, you can't do this. I'll arrange to go to Europe. They've excellent spas there and good doctors. For God's sake, I'll get another opinion before I'll let you go off to some dirty border town. Make her listen, Margaret!"

Margaret, beautifully dainty Margaret, had looked hopelessly from her mother to her sister. She picked up the letter from Don Francisco Godwin that lay on the pedestal table and glanced through it. "It's quite outrageous, Catherine! No well-brought-up woman in her right mind would do such a thing. Papa always did call you his headstrong one."

Catherine poured out a teaspoon of the elixir Dr. McFarland had prescribed for her mother's "nerves." The still-beautiful woman lay pale and gasping with the shock of the news—not the news that her body harbored pleurisy. This malady she had suspected for some time. What she could not come to terms with was losing the almost maternal support of her older daughter.

"If you would both stop to think," Catherine said firmly, "you would realize that for one thing we have no money to go to those 'excellent spas in Europe' and that, working for the Godwin family, I will earn an enormous salary—more than I do working at the hospital."

She turned away, mortified by her false gesture of nobility, and set the medicine bottle on the table. How could she admit to the base, petty jealousy that darkly colored her love for her sister—dear Margaret who had been the most sought-after young woman in Baltimore before the Civil War whisked away the men?

Catherine could remember watching from her mother's upstairs dormer window as the young men came to call on Margaret. And she could remember sitting on the sidelines the few times she escaped her mother's bedside while Margaret danced one cotillion after another.

Oh, Catherine was very much aware of Dr. McFarland's high

esteem for her brave decision to go west in order to earn a living to support her mother and sister. But what Dr. McFarland and her mother and Margaret did not realize was that she stood to lose nothing. For twenty-six years she had marked time, an uneventful, boring process. Even tending the soldiers had added some color, some shading, however drab, to the pale canvas of her life.

Dr. McFarland's prognosis had been the stimulus that had caused her to accept the daring and dangerous challenge offered by the lure of the Western wilderness.

At Fort Whipple, in the central Arizona Territory, Catherine stayed only long enough to eat the roasted wild turkey and plum pudding and unashamedly bask in the attention the soldiers showered on the lone white woman. Then, in order to arrive in Tucson by the date agreed upon with Don Francisco, she had to hurriedly board a privately owned stage line—the only stage that still operated in Arizona since the Civil War had forced the abandonment of the Butterfield Overland. With her traveled the windy old surveyor general who was returning to Tucson after a two-year absence in Washington.

Before the driver cracked his whip over the mules, Governor Goodwin charged Ogilvee to care for Catherine. Tugging at his beard, as if afraid of making some inappropriate remark, the governor said, "You know, Miss Howard, if Tucson is—uh, worse than you expected, write us. We'll somehow arrange for you to return to the States."

She reassured the old gentleman she would be all right, but she had her doubts as the coach, creaking on its leather springs, crawled mile after miserable mile across a desert wasteland that seemed to stretch into infinity. How could land and weather change so abruptly, from snow-blanketed pines to heat-shimmering sands? She dotted at the perspiration beading her hairline with her lace-edged handkerchief and readjusted the porkpie hat's ribbons that were biting into her chin. If hell was hotter than this, she knew she did not want to go there.

For a while she closed lids heavy with the weight of thick lashes to block the sting of the alkaline dust kicked up by the six-mule team. She willed away the tired face of the surveyor general to dwell on the image of the cool green valley of Tuscon's thickly wooded Santa Cruz River. From that point she allowed herself to speculate more fully on the family for whom she would work.

Don Francisco Godwin had explained briefly in his letter that he wished her to tutor his two grandchildren for a one-year tenure and went on to tell her a little about Cristo Rey, perhaps to whet her appetite, for there were no public schools in the territory and private teachers were difficult to obtain. For that one year she would receive a salary triple that of a public-school teacher, a room of her own, and servants to wait on her in that land of perpetual sunshine.

But she drew her own conclusions, both from Don Francisco's autocratic letter and from the bits of information delivered by Ogilvee. She suspected Don Francisco of being an opportunist; for what kind of man was he to have sought his fortune by marrying a widow who had inherited the most prized land grant in the territory—a Mexican woman of aristocratic birth whose lines traced back to El Cid and Burgos, Spain?

"Doña Dominica Davalos was not a bad-looker either," Ogilvee added. And old Don Francisco, Frank he was then, didn't seem to mind when he married her that she already had a son—Lorenzo. Wild as a March hare. Of course, Don Francisco's son, Sherrod, was only four or five years older than Lorenzo, who was six or so at the time. So that helped."

"Oh? Don Francisco was married before?"

Ogilvee's wheezy laugh turned into a coughing bout. "Don Francisco never was unmarried," he said when he regained his breath. "When he married Doña Dominica, he already had a wife."

Catherine's brows rose. "A bigamist?"

"No, madam. Not in the territory, anyway. A Mormon!" He laughed and slapped his knee at the irony. "The old rascal was an elder of the Church of Jesus Christ of the Latter-Day Saints when he set eyes on the delectable widow. Can't say the citizens of Tucson were too happy about the wedding. The men lost out on a chance for a wife that would delight the eye and a land grant that would fatten a bank account. And the women—well, you can imagine how indignant those old crows were at the thought of a man's having two wives. Can't ever help but wonder how the two women felt about sharing their husband."

Catherine's lips curled in a private smile as she joined in the old man's curiosity.

The stage did not arrive in Tucson, or Stujukshon as the Papago Indians had called their village for hundreds of years, until after five in the morning, but there was just enough of dawn's light for Catherine to realize that Tucson was not the paradise Don Francisco had depicted.

Hogs wallowed in the nearby Santa Cruz River. Behind the old presidio's crumbling adobe walls were hidden brown one-story houses that looked like little mud boxes, cheerless but for the scarlet *riastros* of chilies that graced the adobe walls. Garbage littered the narrow dirt streets, and to her amazement a dead burro lay in the middle of the main winding thoroughfare—the Camino Real, the last lap of the Kings Highway from Mexico City. In the Plaza de la Mesilla she saw people sleeping out on the open ground.

"Are there no rooms to be had?" she asked the lawyer with growing concern as the coach halted before what her instincts told her had to be one of the West's notorious saloons.

Ogilvee chuckled. "Nary a hostelry—unless one considers the outhouses the people seek on particularly cold nights. But most of the time, madam, it's too hot to sleep indoors even if Tucson did have a hotel. They call it a Tucson Bed—you lay on your stomach and cover yourself with your back!" He slapped his knee again, laughing at his drollery.

"I'm surprised people bother to sleep," she said, eyeing the many brightly lit establishments that rimmed the plaza. From inside the coach she could hear the army mules braying in the corrals and mixing with the loud music and laughter coming from the cantina. Even at that time of the morning the cantina doors swung constantly with the entrance of miners anxious to spend their nuggets and *hidalgos* reckless with their Mexican 'dobe dollars.

When the Mexican town of Tucson came into the New Mexico Territory with the Gadsden Purchase in 1854, it was known as the Old Pueblo, but to Catherine the plaza about the Meyer Street Saloon in no way resembled a sleepy little pueblo.

"Anyone going to meet you, madam?" Ogilvee asked.

"Yes," she said, looking uncertainly past the doors into the smoke-congested room. "But I don't think they expected me to arrive this late."

He grunted. "I promised the guv'nor I'd see you through. Let's see what we can do."

He led her into the saloon, his hand protectively at her elbow. For a brief second she paused as her senses were assaulted—by the thick, acrid smoke of cigars and tallow candles, by the noisy men packing pistols at their hips, and by sights she had only dimly imagined in her musings.

Games of chance were in full swing with the tables of monte and faro crowded by tense throngs of gamblers. At a bar that she would have sworn was a block long men lounged in tipsy conversation. Beneath an immense gilded mirror a bartender served drinks to a pompous old madam and a stripling.

The surveyor general ushered her over to the bar. The strangeness of the place with so many men pressing about her made the pulse at the hollow of her throat beat a little quicker. The surveyor general had warned her that Tucson was a resort of horsethieves, murderers, and vagrant politicans. "Men who are no longer permitted to live in California or Texas find the Tucson climate congenial to their health, madam." She was beginning to think that Ogilvee knew what he was talking about.

"I don't suppose you have a place the lady could stay?" Ogilvee asked the bartender. "Just for a few hours?"

The squat Mexican rounded his eyes as he glanced at Catherine. Wordlessly he shook his head. "You are making the joke, señor? A lady—here?"

The aging madam whom Catherine had seen with the young cowboy turned to face her, and Catherine could see up close how the rouge clogged the woman's wrinkles. "There's the bath at the back, Emilio," she told the bartender. Then to Catherine, "For a small fee that you pay the darky attendant, dearie, you can even rent a bathtub."

Catherine could think of nothing she would like better than a bath and change of clothes before meeting with her prospective employer. She thanked the surveyor general for everything and, after her trunk was safely ensconced behind the bar, made her way down the saloon's narrow, dark hallway with her carpetbag in hand. The farther she proceeded, the murkier and sleezier the hall became. And when a man staggered through the doorway of a room on the right, she jumped.

She literally had to force her footsteps past the man, who stood so tall his curly yellow-brown hair brushed the low ceiling. He lounged in the doorway now, one arm thrown casually around the flashing-eyed Spanish beauty in paint and finery. His free hand caressed the woman's neck in a sensuous gesture that brought a blush to Catherine's face.

She was well aware of the physical aspects of the male body through her work at the hospital, but of man's baser needs she was totally ignorant. She quickened her steps around the amorous couple only to find a hand suddenly at her wrist. Her bowed head jerked up to encounter dark, slumberous eyes in a beard stubbled, mustached face. The disgusting fumes of alcohol and a woman's cheap cologne washed over her.

"Hey!" the slurred voice demanded, "You that spinster teacher I'm supposed to haul back to Cristo Rey?" The eyes blinked in an effort to focus, and she shrank as far away as the young man's grip permitted. "Coward—no, Howard, that's it, isn't it!" He executed a clumsy half-bow. "Be with you in a minute, Miss Coward—er, Miss Howard."

"Please, there's no hurry," she managed to reply and sped down the hall toward the bathroom with the couple's intimate laughter echoing in her ears.

Chapter 3

SORRY 'bout this morning, ma'am," Lorenzo Davalos said, keeping his gaze trained on the greasewood-stunted terrain that was crisscrossed by wagon tracks.

Catherine lifted one dubious brow, wondering if the man was sorry for his drunken behavior before her that morning or the aftereffects of the carousing night. She could almost believe Don

Francisco's stepson was referring to the latter, for his bloodshot eyes looked out of a bronzed face made a temporary pasty-white. She had to smile despite her vexation with the young man. "It must be a magnificent hangover."

The man, whom she estimated to be about five years younger than she, maybe twenty-one, winced as the buckboard he drove jarred over lava rock. "Murderous is more like it."

After the two-day journey on the stage and no sleep, she decided she probably felt little better than her escort, certainly as stiff as the giant saguaro cacti that stood against the rim of mountains—the Santa Ritas, Dragoons, and Huachucas, names that made a beautiful litany.

She realized she no doubt looked every inch the spinsterish schoolmarm the young man had so ungallantly labeled her . . . the starched white linen waist and somber navy-blue alpaca jacket and skirt, the bland little bonnet that perched like some drab wren on her tightly bound hair.

However, Lorenzo Davalos looked none too appealing either. For a man of so few years, he appeared to already be squint-eyed and saddle-hardened. Muffled in a serape that hid his long wiry figure, he hunched over the wagon's lines, saying as little as possible. A sweat-stained sombrero with a snake of silver bullion about its crown slouched low on his head, shading lazy eyes the color of molasses in a rough-cut face that resembled a relief map. An aristocratic nose—the one redeemable feature about the disreputable-looking man—jutted over the drooping mustache.

With his butter-colored hair that curled riotously beneath the sombrero it was almost impossible for her to accept that he was a Mexican of pure Spanish lineage—and heir to the much coveted Cristo Rey.

"Don't have too much to recommend me to a proper Easterner, do I?" he said, flicking her an amused glance.

He had caught her studying him! She blushed and quickly looked away. "I suppose I am more accustomed to a different mode of people, but then that is why I came west."

"Why?" he asked between teeth clamped on a noxious cigarette butt as his eyes squinted against the glare of the late-afternoon sun. "Why did you come west?"

To find a husband? To live? One simply did not confess such

preposterous reasons. "Why, I suppose like everyone else who comes to the territory, Mr. Davalos—for adventure."

The young man's laughter was short. His gaze now appraised her, swiftly and, she was sure, accurately. Once again color flooded her face, for she knew he had stripped her bare with those eyes that did not seem to miss a thing just as surely as if he had actually removed her clothing piece by piece. And he had no doubt found her lacking—certainly in comparison to the voluptuous woman whose charms he had most likely sampled the night before.

"You'll find it different out here, all right, ma'am. Can't say as how adventuresome you might call it. Lucy, my sister-in-law, finds the territory . . . 'crude and boring,' I think she puts it."

Was he challenging her? "I'm quite flexible, Mr. Davalos. I assure you I will adjust."

He only nodded his head, and she had the suspicion he doubted her. When he returned his attention to the mules, she felt like a pinned butterfly suddenly released—or moth, to be more appropriate, she thought dryly.

She tried to concentrate on the route they were taking, but there seemed to be no clearly defined road. The first and only landmark she noted after leaving Tucson was the abandoned Butterfield Overland Stage station at a place Lorenzo Davalos called Cienega Springs. The station's adobe walls were in ruins and the exposed ceiling timbers had been charred and scorched by flaming arrows.

They stopped long enough at the springs to water the mules. Her escort knelt before the brackish-looking water and dipped his sombrero into it. Rising, he came to stand over her. "Want some?"

She saw the sparkle in the brown eyes and knew once again he was testing her mettle. She took the proffered dirt-stained sombrero. "Most certainly, Mr. Davalos."

"Law," he said, smiling wickedly. "Call me Law. Lawrence or Lorenzo is too much of a mouthful."

"Law," she said, trying the name of her lips. "I can't say that I have ever heard of a more inappropriate name."

A full, genuine laugh tumbled out of the raffish-looking young man. She felt him studying her as she sipped the water, which was surprisingly cool and sweet, from the sombrero's crown.

"You know, Miss Howard, you're not so bad for a bluestocking," he said in what was almost a compliment.

Law turned the wagon due south then, following the Cienega Wash through the lava-chopped Empire foothills. It was difficult for Catherine to imagine that somewhere in the craggy, barren black hills beyond lay the lush pastoral valley of Cristo Rey. But then she had learned that beneath the clear bright-white sky distances could be deceptive.

Just as deceptive as the tranquillity of the late afternoon, for she had heard too many tales from Ogilvee of the fierce warriors, the Chiricahua Apaches, who terrorized the area. She found it inconceivable that citizens actually did walk around armed twenty-hour hours a day against the Indians. Yet slung low on Law's hips were a brace of Navy Colts, and balanced against the wooden seat was a lethal-looking carbine rifle.

After a while she discovered that the quiet of the landscape was deceptive also. For with the man obviously disinclined to conversation, she began to pick up sounds peculiar to the area— the sighing of the heated breeze through the eroded *bajadas* and the rustle of the horse-high chaparral as a black chuckwalla lizard scampered beneath its thorny branches for shelter. And once there came the deadly rattle of the diamondback when the wagon's mules passed too closely.

Then, almost abruptly it seemed, there was a dramatic shift in scenery, from bone-dry cholla wasteland to a sea of knee-high sacaton grass, brown and withered from the shortened winter days. Gradually, as the wash deepened, thickly wooded forests of willow and cottonwoods rose to border it. Mountains, the Whetstones on the left and the Santa Ritas on the right, marched closer now.

When the road suddenly emerged from a narrow shady pass, the sun poured down upon the far reaches of a gigantic basin undulating with hills and enclosed by a ring of lofty peaks. This circular basin with its grassy meadows and oak-clad slopes that concealed canyon after canyon contained the core of Cristo Rey's fifty thousand acres.

After traveling across the raw creosote desert and then the jagged ugly lava hills for five hours—five hours of being impressed by nature's dominance that made mere man seem inconsequential—Catherine was not prepared for her first sight of the Stronghold, nor was she ever able to forget it.

The fortress stood alone in the great basin, competing against the mountains for magnificence. Even at that distance the Stronghold was enormous. Surrounded by walls that bastioned a grassy rise, the house itself, an adobe built in the flat-roof Mexican territorial style, looked impregnable. Atop the roof tiny figures paced a parapet—guards, she later learned they were.

Clustered about the great house, like petals about a stem, were the corrals and outbuildings. Outside the big fortress walls a ranchería of adobe huts nestled among feathery tamarisk and black locusts that fanned out from the Cienega—from Catherine's viewpoint, a thin blue thread that laced the grassy valley.

"After the disappointment of Tucson, I was half dreading the sight of Cristo Rey," she said slowly. "But your stepfather's description hasn't disappointed me."

"Cristo Rey isn't the largest land grant in the territory," Law answered, the reins slack in his hands as he paused to let Catherine survey the view. "But it's the richest. It's watered by two great rivers, the San Pedro and the Santa Cruz. And its soil is veined with gold and silver."

She looked up into the young man's face that was shadowed by the hat brim. "It sounds as if you love it—Cristo Rey."

"No, ma'am. I leave that to my stepbrother. I just have great respect for the land."

He flicked the reins, and the mules began the gradual, twisting descent down into the basin, passing herds of black-horned cattle—remnants, he explained to her, of the herds brought up from Mexico by the Jesuit missionary Father Kino. "But Sherrod's trying to persuade the old man to bring in the white-faced Herefords."

"Sherrod?"

"My stepbrother. It's his children you'll be tutoring."

"Oh, then you don't have any?"

"Not likely, ma'am, seeing how I'm not hitched and all." He flashed her a half-teasing look. Had one corner of his mouth not tilted in a crooked smile, she would never have known he was joking. "We're two of a kind, aren't we, ma'am?"

"Misfits, Mr. Davalos?" she retorted, smiling.

"Law," he reminded her.

The clanging of a bell reached them, and he informed her that the lookouts posted had marked their arrival. They passed orchards

(25)

of pomegranate and peach trees now. "Incredible," she murmured. "After the desert, all the vegetation seems a mirage."

"It's real enough. Sherrod's peons put in too much back-breaking labor digging the *acequias*—irrigation ditches," he translated in a deep lazy drawl that she decided was most pleasant and so did not bother to correct his misconception that she knew no Spanish.

As the wagon bumped down the rutted road through the ranchería, terra-cotta children halted their play in the dirt before curtained doorways and scrawny chickens scurried from the wagon's wheels. A leather-aproned Mexican stepped out of the smithy, and a wizened brown woman looked up from her washboard to watch the wagon's progress. The men in the fields who carried rifles slung on their plow handles halted their work as the wagon passed by.

Law drove the mules between the fortress's two great wooden doors, and Catherine inspected the place where she would live for a year. The dusty yard was bustling with men practicing with firearms (Indian drills, Law told her) and vaqueros working about the nearer of several adobe corrals.

Up close the adobe building was even more formidable, and the rifle-toting guards circling the roof's perimeter intensified the imagery of a bastion. Near the large, hand-carved door a cast-iron bell hung from a wooden frame. Unpainted, the house stood alone with no veranda, no large windows to adorn it—unless the small wood-spindled apertures could be counted as such. Yet there was about the great house, she decided, an aura of strength. It imparted the illusion of having triumphed over the elements, over man and nature.

Could it triumph over the ravages of time and loneliness?

Chapter 4

AT the same time a Mexican youth ran forward to take the reins Law tossed him, a woman appeared in the doorway of the house, then turned back to call out to someone inside. "Lucy," Law informed Catherine. "She's been anxious to talk with a real Easterner. You'll meet the rest of the clan soon enough."

His reference to the clan reminded her of the rumored Mormon background. "I understand Don Francisco is of the Mormon faith," she said, attempting to keep her tone noncommittal.

"You understand right—two wives and the whole bit, though my mother's been dead for some years now."

His voice was coldly emotionless, and she cast a quick but scrutinizing glance at the man as he came around to her side of the wagon. The swarthy complexion—and definitely the drooping sand-colored mustache—lent the young man a feral appearance. A renegade, Margaret would have called him with a sniff.

"That's Sherrod's mother, Elizabeth, at the door with Lucy now," he said with an easy drawl that had the soft resonance of the Spanish tongue.

Catherine's gaze went back to the two women. The younger woman with cornsilk hair bound in fashionable waves about her oval face lifted her hoopless skirts and hurried toward them. "Law," she cried out in a kewpie-doll voice, "you really did bring her!"

Law's rangy leanness was deceiving, and he lifted Catherine effortlessly from the wagon while Lucy rambled on. "Gracious, we were so afraid you wouldn't accept Don Francisco's offer, Miss Howard. Your reply didn't come until four days ago."

"I mailed it back in August," Catherine said as Law released her and picked up her carpetbag.

"The mail service in the territory has been almost shut down," he explained, "what with Fort Buchanan's troops withdrawn to serve in the war's Eastern campaigns and Cochise's Apaches thinking they've won some sort of victory."

A stiff-backed woman in black now approached them. "Law, let the young woman get out of the sun." Her stone-gray eyes turned on Catherine. "The men forget their manners, living out here away from civilization like we do."

Illogically, the diminutive older woman seemed to Catherine as formidable as the Stronghold. Her iron-gray hair was pulled severely back in a bun, and her leathery face wore the look of granite . . . surely the type of pioneer woman Walt Whitman had written about. Yet she moved with all the regal stateliness her Elizabethan name implied. A queen in her castle, Catherine thought.

Law called out an order in Spanish, and two Mexican urchins ran out of the house to heft her heavy camelback trunk. Elizabeth led her through the house's wooden-linteled door past the *zaguán,* the breezeway, into the main room on the left.

Catherine's first impression of the interior was one of cool shadows—three-foot-thick walls and high ceilings braced by hand-carved *vigas* of pine darkened by smoke and age and crossed at right angles by *savinas* made of ocotillo stalks. A smooth, hard floor that she learned was mud mixed with ox blood and cactus juice was covered with several Axminster carpets, and the walls, plastered with laundry bluing, were sparsely decorated with Indian baskets.

A caliche fireplace dominated the room and seemed to be courted by the simple but sturdy furniture grouped about it. The framed painting above the fireplace caught her eye. A fair-eyed, golden-complected woman of madonnalike beauty looked down out of the canvas, her lips forming a gentle smile. Jewelry sparkled at her ears and throat and in the comb that piled high her golden tresses. "Law's mother," Elizabeth said, her voice dry like the crackling of autumn leaves.

Law was already striding from the room with Catherine's carpetbag, and children's shouts rang out from the rooms beyond. "Uncle Law's back!" a boyish voice squealed. And Catherine heard something about candy, then Law's patient drawl, "Yes, I brought the licorice."

"You'll probably want to wash up and rest," Elizabeth said, "then my husband will want to talk with you."

"I'll show Miss Howard to her room," Lucy volunteered. "I'm sure it's nothing like what you must be used to," she said as she led Catherine through the *zaguán* and out into a walled, tree-shaded courtyard paved with uneven cobblestones and surrounded on three sides by tiers of open corridors. "Why, it took me years to get used to rooms that were almost windowless! In Virginia we had such big bay windows. Finally, I badgered Sherrod so, he promised me he would have glass panes, not mica mind you, but real glass, freighted in from Kansas City this coming year."

They passed along the stucco-covered portico that had a number of bedrooms opening off it. Lucy prattled on, hesitating only long enough for Catherine to assure her that the cage crinoline was still in fashion.

"I do so miss following the modes," she continued. "I've heard that the women in the States are wearing—Zouave jackets, isn't it? And Balmoral mantles. As soon as you get settled, you must tell me all the society gossip. I'm so tired of listening to talk of the war and Indian raids!"

At last Catherine stood alone in her own room. Actually Doña Dominica's room, Lucy told her. Slowly she stripped off her gloves as she surveyed the furnishings. Austere was the word that came to mind. And scrubbed cleanliness. A substantial bed stood in one corner with a neat patchwork counterpane. Tacked from the ceiling over the bed, as if it had been a four-poster, were manta curtains. Tin *retablos*, religious paintings, adorned the walls. A pine washstand and bureau and hardback cane chair were the only other pieces of furniture in the spacious room.

Yet there was a peacefulness about the room and it was her room, as Don Francisco had promised. Too exhausted to remove her kid boots, she settled for discarding her hat and jacket before she fell across the bed. Later she would hang up the clothes she had packed away in camphor in her trunk.

A strange loneliness kept her awake. She had deliberately cut herself off from all family and friends. She was wholly alone in the world with her way to make. A terrible sense of uncertainty lapped like cold ripples at her feet. At last her lids closed, but voices, that were not so loud as they were harsh, awoke her. She opened her eyes to find that only a faint light now streamed through the foot-square aperture that served as a window.

Afraid she was late, she quickly poured the pitcher's tepid

water in the porcelain basin and washed her dusty face, then tucked the wisps of hair into the heavy knot at the nape of her neck. She was fastening her jacket's buttons as she hurried outside and not really looking where she was going when the door of the room next to hers opened and slammed shut and she collided with the man who emerged from the room.

She staggered, and firm hands reached out to steady her. "I'm sorry, I wasn't looking—" they both began in unison and broke off, smiling.

"You must be Miss Howard," he said, releasing her.

"And you are—"

"Sherrod—Sherrod Godwin," he finished for her.

Though not as tall as his stepbrother, he still topped Catherine's five-foot-three-inch frame by almost a foot. Even in the dimming daylight his darkly handsome looks were evident, with deep-brown hair and sideburns and a well-trimmed mustache only a shade lighter.

"I can't tell you how much Lucy"— he looked awkwardly toward the door—"how excited she is that another woman her age is here. She's getting ready for dinner, but come on with me. The children are asking all sorts of questions about you—and Father, of course, is demanding to see you."

As he led her inside, he recounted the reactions of the children to the idea of a woman tutor—from seven-year-old Abigail's certainty that Catherine would wear men's trousers to five-year-old Brigham's disgust that the tutor had to be a woman.

Yet Catherine only half listened to Sherrod's voice. The voice in her head drummed much louder. She was much too intelligent, her mind warned, to let herself become attracted to the handsome man—and indeed he was handsome, dressed in nankeens and buff waistcoat. She had half expected him to dress with the same negligence as his stepbrother.

He ushered her past the large dining room and through the enormous kitchen that had copper utensils and clay ollas strung from the ceiling's beams. An old Papago Indian looked up from the bread he kneaded and nodded when Sherrod made the introduction, telling her Loco had been at Cristo Rey for over twenty years.

Sherrod paused before his father's office, his hand on the door handle. "I don't suppose my father told you anything about himself?"

She shook her head. "No. He told me very little about anything."

He sighed. "That's like my father. He suffered a stroke last year, and it has left him weakened. As a result he's rather edgy, but don't let his gruffness frighten you."

"There's very little that frightens me any more, Mr. Godwin, and certainly not mortal man."

He cocked his head. His warm blue eyes quietly appraised her. "I can believe that," he said at last. He smiled then and opened the door but did not enter, leaving her on her own.

She paused with her back to the closed door, while her gaze sought out the old man clad in black. He sat in a cushioned rocker with a book spread on his lap and a cane hooked over the chair's arm. He raised his head and fixed her with an equally studious gaze. Whatever she expected from the narrow face framed by a long bone-white beard, it was certainly not the torment that stared out of the shadowed eyes.

"Come in and sit down," Don Francisco rasped and indicated the scrolled hard-backed chair near the secretarial desk.

She took a seat on the chair's edge, arranging her voluminous skirts as best she could. After a moment the old man said, "Your face possesses the same character your letter indicated."

"I hope that is a compliment, Don Francisco."

"It's a sigh of relief, Miss Howard."

She raised a questioning brow, but he did not elaborate further. He closed the heavy book. "The Mormon's *Doctrine and Covenant,*" he said, catching her interested glance at the tome. For the first time he smiled, a bitter smile. "In my more robust days I often strayed from Joseph Smith's revelations, and I suppose a brush with death has brought me back into the fold again."

Was he speaking of his stroke, or the death that had claimed his second wife? "A brush with death cannot help but affect one's outlook on life," she said, fully appreciating the man's situation. "Tell me how else I can be of help."

The door opened, and Elizabeth came in, closing it behind her. "I was just beginning to tell Miss Howard of her duties here, Elizabeth."

He struggled to lay the book on the desk, and the woman took it and placed it there for him. Locking her hands before her, she turned to Catherine. "What my husband probably has not told you is that we brought you out here to be more than just a tutor."

"Oh?"

"First there's Abigail and Brigham. Sherrod's wife has had a smattering of education, if you consider those silly finishing schools that teach music and needlepoint an education. But the woman doesn't have a lick of common sense. I wouldn't trust her to teach Brigham what he will need to know to run Cristo Rey."

"Of course, when he's older," Don Francisco said tiredly, "he'll be sent off to St. Michael's boarding school in St. Louis, as were Sherrod and Law."

Catherine relaxed a little. So far the objectives did not seem beyond her capabilities. "Then there's Sherrod," Elizabeth continued crisply. "He's carrying a heavy burden running Cristo Rey since my husband's stroke. Sherrod needs to devote his total attention to the place—and Lucy doesn't understand."

"Elizabeth, you're being unnecessarily harsh on Lucy," Don Francisco rebuked. "She's lonely and misses civilization."

Elizabeth's lips folded thin. "She doesn't have the stamina—the strength—to live out here. A crying, whining woman is a millstone my son doesn't need. Lucy has to have another woman to talk to—about the finer things of life. I want you to be her companion, Miss Howard."

"I see. That takes care of everyone but Law—Lorenzo—then, doesn't it?"

"Law," Elizabeth said grimly, "can take care of himself."

Chapter 5

ONE rarely heard days, weeks, or months mentioned at Cristo Rey. There were clocks in the Stronghold, but no one bothered to wind them. If a day was referred to, it was the day Loco burned the bread or Sherrod went to Tucson.

After caring for her sickly mother for so long and then listening to the agonizing groans and cries of suffering men, of smelling the putrefying stench of rotting limbs and festering wounds for a year, that first month at Cristo Rey seemed a preview of heaven to Catherine.

January in Baltimore would have brought subzero blizzards howling through the streets, but at Cristo Rey the sun-splashed days and cool crystalline nights slipped gently into another week, another month.

She fell easily into the routine of the Stronghold, waking at six-thirty each morning when Loco rang the bell, warning that breakfast would be served in thirty minutes. The tutoring of Brigham, who was a five-year-old fountain of curiosity, and Abigail, whose preadolescent plumpness concealed the promise of her mother's beauty, took most of Catherine's day. From eight until noon she taught the children in the courtyard, then recessed for lunch and returned to teach from one to three. Afterward she would sit with Lucy and, mending or helping with the carding of the wool, listen to the young woman's chatter until time for dinner.

Despite having borne two children, Lucy was at twenty-seven still a very beautiful woman, and Catherine could understand how Sherrod could have fallen in love with her. "My parents were very much against my marrying a Mormon," she told Catherine one afternoon. "But they soon recognized Sherrod's honorable intentions and"—Lucy smiled—"his charming manner."

"Does it ever bother you," Catherine ventured, "that Sherrod could take a second—or third—wife?"

The clicking of Lucy's needles halted. A small nervous smile flitted across her porcelain face. "You know how it is when a woman gets married. At first you're too much in love to care. And now . . . now another wife would be nice to help share some of the—duties of a wife to a husband."

Catherine could not conceal the surprise on her face, and Lucy laughed. Her needles began darting back and forth in rapid flashes. "Oh, I know what you must be thinking, Catherine. Honestly, I felt the same way when I first came to the Stronghold and watched how Doña Dominica and Elizabeth attended to Don Francisco."

An impish voice in Catherine dared her to ask what it *was* like, but instead she said, "I understand Doña Dominica was at the Stronghold to begin with—that she was a widow."

"Yes. Law's father had been killed in an Indian attack several months before she met Don Francisco. Sherrod told me that his father came out here in '48 with a Mormon battalion that was on its way to fight the Mexicans in California. After the Mormons took possession of Tucson from the Mexican forces, Don Francisco decided to stay. He sent to Santa Fe for Sherrod and Elizabeth, and, as Sherrod tells me, by the time he and his mother reached Tucson his father had taken Doña Dominica as his second wife."

Once more Lucy paused in her knitting to smile wistfully. "You know, Catherine, Mormon wives call each other 'sister.' I'd love to be able to call you my sister, truly. It's so wonderful to have you here I hate to think of your leaving one day."

Stunned at Lucy's frankness, she could say nothing. Only at that moment did she allow herself to fantasize being married to Sherrod. He would have made the kind of husband she had always dreamed of—warm, intelligent, responsible. "It pleases me that you care enough to want me as—your sister. But Lucy, I've waited this long to marry, so you may be sure that if I ever do, I'll be the only wife or I simply won't marry."

"But what of duty, Miss Howard?" Elizabeth's voice asked from behind the two women.

Turning to look at Elizabeth, dressed as always in black, Catherine dryly wondered if the woman was in mourning for her lost youth. Lucy had told her that Elizabeth was forty-four. But the woman looked years older.

"From so many hours tending farm crops," Lucy had told her. "And then when the Mormon persecution began in Illinois, Elizabeth made that long walk with Don Francisco and Sherrod and the other Mormons bound for Santa Fe. And you know, Catherine, so much exposure to the sun is not good for a lady's skin."

"You certainly seem to be a most practical woman, Miss Howard," Elizabeth was saying. "You're not silly enough to think romance is a lasting thing. If your husband took himself another wife, I'm sure you would see that it was your duty to make the best of it so that everything ran smoothly."

The corners of Catherine's lips curled uncontrollably. "I'd see that it was my duty to keep my husband so happy he would not think of taking another wife in the first place."

Elizabeth's smile was thin. "You speak as an unmarried and inexperienced woman, Miss Howard . . . foolishly, unwisely. My daughter-in-law will tell you that a wife knows that it is not always possible to—please a husband."

Lucy blanched and was inordinately quiet after Elizabeth left the room. The woman's words recalled a conversation Catherine had overheard the first week she was at Cristo Rey. An argument it was really, and only a few words—but revealing words. "What?" Don Francisco had thundered. "You gave Miss Howard Dominica's room? I ordered you to leave that room untouched!"

"Isn't it time you stopped keeping that room as a shrine?!" Elizabeth had hissed.

Catherine had hurried on past Don Francisco's office. Don Francisco was still in love with his second wife!

The day after Elizabeth's stinging rebuke to Lucy and herself, Catherine went to Don Francisco's office in hopes of finding an extra dictionary for Abigail. Once again she could hear the old man arguing. His diatribe was cut short when he bade her enter after her hesitant knock on the office door.

Law was slouched in the armchair across from Don Francisco's desk while the old man limped about the room, still raging. "It's all right," Don Francisco told her. He waved his cane in Law's direction. "I was just telling this rakehell if he'd spend less time in bordellos and saloons, he might make something of his life!"

A suppression of a smile hovered over Law's mouth, as if he

were indulging his stepfather's outrage. It was the first time Catherine had seen Law in more than two weeks. Out of the three months she had lived at Cristo Rey, she could count on her hand the number of times her path crossed his, which was fine with her. There was something about the mocking way the young man looked at her—as though . . . as though he found something about her amusing!

He smiled sheepishly at her now. "Don Francisco and I can't seem to agree just exactly what I should do with my life."

She smiled sweetly. "Why, I'd send the boy back to school, Don Francisco." Before her statement could be challenged, she quickly borrowed the dictionary and retreated from the room's verbal battleground.

When she returned to the courtyard, another battle was in progress between Abigail and Brigham. "He does not!" Brigham shrieked. Catherine caught him just as he picked up a chinaberry to hurl at his sister.

"What's this all about?" Catherine demanded.

Tears spiked Brigham's long lashes. "Abigail," he said tremulously, pointing to his sister, who stood at the wrought-iron gate leading out into the compound, "Abigail says cowpunchers are sissies . . . that they like girls!"

Abigail turned from the gate back to Catherine. "I did not," she said in an adult voice. "I merely told Brig that one of the cowpunchers has been making calf eyes at you. There—see, he's coming back to the stables again—and it's just to get a glimpse of you, Miss Howard."

Catherine wanted to laugh, but she smoothed the dark-brown hair back from Brigham's small, serious face. "You know, Brigham," she said in a solemn tone, "just because a cowboy—"

"Cowpuncher," he corrected.

"—cowpuncher likes to look at something nice doesn't mean he's a sissy. Don't you like to look at tintypes of the pretty steamboats I showed you? But that doesn't make you a sissy, does it?"

Mollified, Brigham at last returned to the letters he had been copying on his slate, and Abigail settled down to her geography.

Catherine knew that the perceptive Abigail was no doubt correct. With the stables sharing the far courtyard wall, there was ample opportunity for the Cristo Rey hands to glance through the gate. Several times she had looked up to find one of the hands standing near the gate—but always studiously engaged with tightening a saddle's cinch or checking a horse's shoe. If she happened to catch him spying, the hand would usually tip his hat and saunter off.

Admittedly she wanted a husband. Too quickly she would be thirty! But the hands were either all stringy, work-hardened old men or youths with peach fuzz still on their faces. An inexperienced youth was not what she wanted. And she certainly did not want someone like Law, an aimless, willy-nilly sort of a man, with none of Sherrod's strong-willed nature.

Sherrod was absent from the Stronghold almost as often as Law. She knew he quite often rode the herds with his vaqueros, and when he was home he would more than likely be found drilling his guards or closeted in Don Francisco's office.

In the evenings the entire family came together for dinner, presided over by Don Francisco, who always asked the Lord's blessing. But afterward, when the family adjourned to the parlor, it would be Sherrod's animated personality that dominated the conversation. Catherine would sit in the chair nearest the fireplace and listen to the affectionate banter between Don Francisco and his son while she sipped at the Mexican chocolate Loco served, for Don Francisco allowed neither coffee nor tea in that Mormon household.

She delighted in these after-dinner family get-togethers, because often guests came, as there was no place in the area to stay except at the Stronghold. The first week in April Don Francisco hosted a Jonathan Stridehope. A balding but nice-looking man of perhaps forty, he was an archaeologist who was working on a dig in the nearby Canyon de Canelo.

The articulate Stridehope talked of artifacts he had discovered in the canyon's cave. Brigham was entranced when he learned that among the artifacts were several mummies and followed up with numerous questions.

At one point Catherine asked, "These mummies, Professor Stridehope—were they found in the same layers as the hand-made rope shoes and broken pottery?"

"You're familiar with the theory of stratigraphy?" he asked, surprise wrinkling his high brow.

"Only slightly. I've read some of the work of the Danish archaeologist Thomsen."

The man's serious eyes came to life. He began to talk volubly with her before the two of them became embarrassingly aware they were monopolizing the conversation. She broke off to find the eyes of all the Godwins on her. Yet it was the warmth in Sherrod's that made her color. She glanced at Lucy, but the young woman seemed in a world of her own. Quickly Catherine excused herself and retired for the evening.

Sherrod was not to let her forget the incident so easily. He came to the courtyard the next day after school resumed at one. She was sitting on the bench next to Brigham, showing the boy how to write the cursive flourishes, when she heard Abigail call out, "Papa!"

Catherine looked up to find the handsome man, dressed in shirt sleeves, coming toward her. He bent to scoop up his daughter, who had flung herself against his waist. Brushing her long pigtails behind her shoulders, he kissed her lightly on the cheek before turning her loose. "Good afternoon, Miss Howard. I hope Abigail has been applying herself."

"She's doing very well with her geography. She seems to have a knack for the European countries. If only she did as well with her French and history, I'm quite certain you would have a world traveler on your hands."

His mouth widened in a rueful smile. "I'm afraid she gets her love of Europe from her mother. Lucy has always wanted to visit all its capitals, and I've promised her as soon as the war is over and the Apache problem under control we'll take off and tour the Continent."

"Is there much danger of an attack on the Stronghold?"

"Not likely. My vaqueros ride guard constantly. Cochise seems to be concentrating more on the lone miners and defenseless settlers. We'd be more apt to be raided by a band of Mexican revolutionaries that plague some of our border ranches."

With Catherine's attention diverted, Abigail and Brigham escaped the routine of their studies and began to chase about the courtyard's trees. Intending to call the children back to class, Catherine made to rise and found herself hampered by her gabardine skirts.

"Here, let me help you," Sherrod said. His hand caught her elbow, propelling her upward, which was a mistake, because it put her within inches of his face, so close the scent of his men's lilac cologne reached her. Her heart seemed to flutter, as if teetering precariously on a limb, then double-beat to catch balance.

She did not know what betraying emotion might have flickered across her face, but something in her expression caught his intent gaze. He blinked away a frown of puzzlement. "You know, you surprised me last night," he began quietly, "when you and Professor Stridehope were talking. I had no idea—"

"So there you are," Law said lightly.

Both Sherrod and she whirled. She could well imagine the guilty expression she wore. What could Law have thought, catching his stepbrother's hands at her waist—seeing the two of them standing so close to one another? She strove to compose herself as Law walked toward them in long, easy strides that had none of Sherrod's quick, decisive movements. "The old man wants to talk with you."

Sherrod dropped his hands with a sigh. "Well, I did want to let you know that I couldn't be more pleased with the children's progress, Miss Howard."

She watched him walk away before she turned to face Law. If there was even a hint of smirk on the young man's face, she would slap him. But Law's countenance was expressionless.

"Good day, ma'am," he drawled, tilting the brim of the sombrero and ambling away.

She told herself that it was her own guilty thoughts which had made her jump to the conclusion that Law would suspect Sherrod and herself of improper behavior. Law's craggy face had evidenced no such suspicion. She really had nothing to worry about. Then what was it about those sand-brown eyes that nagged at her so?

Chapter 6

CATHERINE broke the thread with her teeth and let the hem of her riding skirt drop about her Wellington boots. The lead weights she had sewn in the hem halted the swirl of the skirt and, she hoped, would prevent any gust of wind from blowing it above her boots.

The skirt had become threadbare with use but was still serviceable, at least for the solitary riding she planned. It wasn't as if she were riding in Hyde Park before the *haut monde*, although the way Margaret had acted the day Catherine packed, one would have thought so.

"Now you must let me lend you one of my hair switches," she had said as Catherine folded the riding skirt. "It's the latest thing, and you'll look so much better with a sausage curl peeking beneath your riding hat."

With a smile Catherine held one of the switches about her face. Yes, her sister was right. It did soften the sharpness of her chin. With a sigh, she dropped the switch back in its box. Her hair was thick enough as it was, too thick and heavy to make those fashionable curls about the face. And besides, the switch really matched Margaret's deep-brown hair, which had a beautiful russet sheen. Catherine thought of her own hair as "just plain brown," although she could remember her father teasing her that its shade was as rich as fudge.

She placed the beaver top hat on her head, giving it the forward tilt Margaret insisted was *de rigueur,* pulled the white swiss veil over her face, and took up her quirt. She was ready. Ready? She was excited! It would be the first time in—how long, two, three years?—that she had been horseback riding.

The Civil War had curtailed one of the few things in which she truly took pleasure. And it seemed the perfect opportunity for a ride, since it was Sunday and there would be no classes. And Lucy was taking a nap, as she did quite often—for her headaches, she said.

Catherine meant to take the shortcut through the courtyard to the stable, but at the gate Elizabeth's voice halted her. "You aren't going riding, are you?"

She turned to face Elizabeth, who stood in the doorway, a feather duster clutched in her hands. Catherine wondered if the woman ever relaxed—read or took a nap. Even with the wealth of servants, Elizabeth was forever cleaning the house, her hands running over the woodwork, the adobe stones, the metal fixtures as if the Stronghold were a lover. "Why, yes, I was planning to ride."

"Not on Sunday, Miss Howard! It's God's day."

Catherine smiled. "I thought every day was God's day."

Elizabeth's mouth hardened, and the eyes narrowed. "Be careful, Miss Howard. You're tempting the hand of the Lord."

"I shall be very careful riding, thank you," she said evenly, and, closing the gate on the stone-faced woman, she proceeded to the stables. But the confrontation with the woman had dampened her excitement, and she jerked with annoyance on the straps as she saddled one of the better mounts.

"I'll be cursed if I'm going to let that old witch ruin my day," she told the blaze-faced roan as she rode through the Stronghold's wide, open gates, ignoring the astonished looks of the guards.

The lean, swarthy man slouched in the saddle. The fatigue of three days' hard riding showed in the dust-caked grooves on either side of the mouth and the fine lines fanning out from heavy-lidded eyes. Yet the eyes did not miss anything . . . not the centipede that wriggled through the sand two yards away nor the indolent flight of the vulture in the blue-white sky overhead; and most of all the eyes did not miss the horse and rider whose course he had been following for the past quarter of an hour from his lookout on the hogback ridge.

His breath whistled between his teeth. Damn the foolish female! But she was no more the fool than he was to even entertain ideas about such a woman. She knew nothing of life; instead of drinking lightly from the well, she would be like a thirsty man in the desert. It would destroy her . . . and the man foolish enough to drink with her.

He pulled the bandanna from his neck and wiped at the perspiration that slid from the drenched curls down the high bones of his chiseled face, all the while his gaze fastened on the woman, watching the way her firmly rounded buttocks hugged the sidesaddle. No, he didn't have any good sense at all. Damn the woman and double-damn her.

"Just what in the hell do you think you're doing?"

Catherine pulled up on the roan's reins and turned in the direction of the eroded ridge from where the voice had come. Law sat on a horse that looked as though it had been ridden to South America and back. One of the young man's long legs was crooked around the saddle horn as if he had been sitting there for quite some time. His sombrero sported more dust than his yellow duster.

"I asked you what you think you're doing," he repeated.

Another spoilsport! She sighed. It was obviously not going to be a good day for riding. "What does it look as if I'm doing?"

"It looks like you're getting yourself into a hell of a lot of trouble," he said. He swung his leg back over the saddle and edged the pinto down the ridge toward her. "Cochise and his Chiricahuas are on the warpath not ten miles away and you decided to go for a jaunt?"

She shrugged. "If they don't bother me, I won't bother them."

He reined in alongside of her, and she could see now the irritation in the grim set of the mouth and lowered line of the tawny brows. He rolled his eyes. "Miss Howard, there's nothing better that I would like to do right now than throttle you. If there's anything worse than a foolish woman, it's a determined foolish woman."

"Well, you had better think twice before you do, because it won't be easy. And understand me, Law, I plan to continue riding as long as I am employed here."

"Even if it means your death," he taunted.

"We all have to die sometime."

"But not a thousand times, Miss Howard; which is the way Cochise will have it if he gets hold of your pretty little body."

She drew a deep breath, trying to contain her anger. "I'm not afraid of dying," she said evenly. "But I am afraid of living an imprisoned life—which is just what the women at the Stronghold are doing. Lucy's teetering at the edge of a nervous breakdown, and Elizabeth—Elizabeth couldn't care less that a world exists out beyond the Stronghold's walls. If I die, it's going to be from trying to live!"

He glanced pointedly at the roan. "We could refuse to lend you a mount. After all, if Cochise gets you, he gets our horse, also."

"You can take the cost out of my salary. And if you refuse to lend me a horse, I'll simply walk!" She wheeled the horse around and broke into a gallop, hoping the horse's hooves sprayed the abominable young man with more dust.

Once inside the Stronghold's walls, she let loose the rein of her anger. Her entire day was ruined! She reached the stable and slung her quirt into the hay. She was in the midst of jerking her saddle from the horse when she saw that Law had passed through the gates. Having no wish to talk further with him, she quickly tended the horse and stalked back to the house. She had to pass the adobe beehive oven on the way, and the old Indian cook spoke to her in Spanish. "You have been riding, señorita?"

"Not you too, Loco!"

Beneath the thatch of chalk-white hair, the brown pebbled eyes smiled before moving beyond her to the stable. "Lorenzo does not like your riding?"

She slapped her quirt against her gloved hand. "Lorenzo does not like anything—most of all work!"

Loco placed one doughy disc of bread on the wooden shovel and pushed it inside the oven's mouth. "Ah, but, señorita, he likes my bread." She had the suspicion the old Indian was teasing her, calming her. "And he liked my pies as a child."

"He could only have been a demon!" she snapped.

Loco's eyes met hers. "True. A boy like all boys—stealing the fruit pies I made from the window where I sat them to cool. Taking daring chances that would give the Doña Dominica heart failure."

"She loved him very much?"

"He was everything to her, especially after his father died. Then Don Francisco came and offered Doña Dominica a man's love that the boy's love could not offer. And Don Francisco had his own son—and wife. You can understand Lorenzo felt an outsider in his own home. He ran off. Many times I went to find him living at the ranchería in one of the peon's huts. Then Don Francisco sent him off to school. When Lorenzo came back a man grown, his mother was dead."

The bony shoulders beneath the white cotton *camisa* hunched. "But I am old and ramble too much, no?"

"No, I enjoyed talking with you, Loco." She cast a glance behind her. Law was walking toward the house in that lazy stride peculiar to him. Was there no respite? Quickly she bade the Indian cook goodbye and stalked away.

"Lucy? Are you feeling all right?"

A mumbled reply came from the closed bedroom, and Catherine hesitated outside Lucy's door, unsure whether to knock again. Sherrod had been in Tucson for two days now, and Lucy had made only cursory appearances at mealtimes, returning to her room immediately afterward. She seemed only vaguely aware of the others at the table.

With Sherrod gone and Law back in the hills prospecting, so Don Francisco said with a bitter curve to his mouth, the dinner table that night seemed especially quiet. When Lucy failed to appear, Catherine at once volunteered to check on her. Lucy's chatter was infinitely preferable to looking at Elizabeth's inflexible expression across the table. If Don Francisco had not been at dinner to relieve the stilted conversation, Catherine would have taken dinner in her room.

She knocked once more on Lucy's door. When there was no answer this time, she cautiously pressed the latch. It was the first view she had had of the room Sherrod and Lucy shared. Much the size of her own, the room was dominated by an old but elegant maple four-poster bed draped with tasseled blue velvet. It was there Sherrod and Lucy made love. Catherine had only a fair idea of what the act of copulation entailed, but to merely imagine a man like Sherrod holding her caused her mouth to go as dry as cotton.

Quietly she crossed to the bed. Lucy lay there, in a fetal position, as beautiful as a china doll. A pink print cotton wrapper lay open to reveal the full breasts above the whalebone corset. The curly lashes fluttered open. Pale-blue eyes looked up at

Catherine, and for a moment she would have sworn Lucy did not see her. Then, "Why, hello, Catherine." The glazed eyes shifted to note the little light left in the room. "Goodness, am I late for dinner?"

Catherine crossed to the nightstand and removed the lamp's glass chimney. "They're holding dinner for you now, Lucy." The wick caught, and soft light filled the room as she turned to look at Sherrod's wife. "Are you feeling ill?" she asked with real concern, for Lucy's cheeks were flushed.

The young woman pulled the wrapper tighter about her and looked away. "I suppose it must be that time of month."

Catherine leaned over to touch Lucy's forehead, finding it cool. "Is there anything I can do?"

'I'm fine, really," Lucy said.

Her breath, heavy with an unidentifiable fragrance, drifted up to Catherine. For the first time she noticed the small brown bottle on the nightstand. The preparation, no doubt, accounted for Lucy's unusually sweet breath.

Lucy nodded toward the bottle. "If I could just have a touch more, I'm sure I'll feel like going down for supper."

Catherine looked around for a spoon, but Lucy reached for the bottle and swallowed part of its contents directly from the bottle's mouth. Only then did suspicion worm its way into Catherine's mind.

Lucy handed the bottle back to her. The young woman's eyes possessed a brighter look. She slid down from the high bedstead to pick up the nut-brown daydress that lay crumpled on the floor.

"Lucy, you're not—addicted to laudanum, are you?"

Lucy whirled, the dress clutched before her. "Of course not. I don't know how you could even think such a thing!"

Catherine nodded toward the brown bottle. "It does contain laudanum, Lucy," she said gently.

"Not that much. And besides, I need it." A suggestion of tears sparkled in the faded blue eyes. "Some nights it relaxes me." Her lively voice floundered. "Momma always said I was high-strung, and Sherrod—well, he really is patient with me, but . . . you understand."

Catherine was not quite sure she did. Further, she wondered if Sherrod was aware of his wife's problem. The woman's moods vacillated so radically it seemed impossible for anyone not to notice. "Of course I understand. I'll tell the others you'll be out soon."

Lucy grabbed at her hand. "You won't say anything to Sherrod, will you?"

Catherine bit her lip, reluctant to make such a promise, but Lucy seemed not to notice her hesitancy. "If only Sherrod were like Law," she murmured, her fingers fumbling at the buttons of her daydress. "If only he would take his pleasures at the ranchería instead of . . . he's so patient with me, really he is."

When Catherine returned to the dining room, she felt Elizabeth's hooded eyes watching her as she explained that Lucy would be only a few minutes late. Don Francisco frowned and tugged at his beard. Did either of them suspect Lucy's illness? Probably not, for when their daughter-in-law appeared some minutes later, the table's smoking oil lamp reflected only a woman's shining eyes and gay disposition.

Barely touching her food, Lucy addressed no one in particular. "You know, I think when Sherrod returns, we should start planning for a European holiday."

"Oh, Mama," Abigail exclaimed, "can we go to Venice and ride those boats—what were they called, Miss Howard?"

"Gondolas."

"Of course, darling!" Lucy said. Her face was full of animation.

"And those funny humped-back animals—the mammals," Brigham chimed in.

"Camels," Abigail corrected. "And they don't live in Europe."

"We'll see it all, darlings. I'll talk to Sherrod when he returns, and we'll start making plans at once."

Seeing the silent faces of her in-laws, Lucy's pert mask seemed to slip. In a tremulous voice she said, "It'll be all right for Sherrod to go, won't it, Don Francisco? I mean, Law could run Cristo Rey until we returned. It'd only be for three or four months."

Don Francisco patted his lips with his napkin and cast a glance at Catherine. "I don't think Law has much interest in running Cristo Rey, Lucy. And I don't think Sherrod wants to leave right now while he and Poston are lobbying for a change of capitals."

Emphasizing his wish to change the subject, Don Francisco turned to Catherine and said, "Charles Poston is our territorial delegate and owns a mining company in Tubac, southwest of here. He and Sherrod feel Tucson, not Prescott, should be the territorial capital.

"After all, three-quarters of the territory's population live in Tucson, but because Tucson is predominatly 'secesh,' Lincoln's cabinet refuses to make it the capital."

Catherine managed to make some intelligent response, but the sight of Lucy's dejected face disturbed her. The woman was a younger version of her own mother.

Elizabeth did not help the situation when she said, "Sherrod has no business going to Tucson or Europe. He belongs here at the Stronghold. Cristo Rey needs him."

A cold film slipped over Don Francisco's eyes, and Catherine thought she could almost understand why he would take advantage of the Mormon custom of polygamy. And then there was the fact that Doña Dominica had been a very beautiful woman . . . in addition to possessing a prized piece of land.

The continuous clanging of the bell interrupted the poem Abigail was reciting. "Papa's home!" she cried, and before Catherine could stop them the children were running through the *zaguán* to the front of the house.

Lucy flew from her bedroom, pausing only long enough to say, "It's Sherrod, Catherine! Come on."

Catherine hung back, unwilling to watch Sherrod's reunion with his wife and children. The affection exchanged between the family reminded her too sharply of what she did not have. She knew she had to escape the Stronghold at least for a little while; to ride until she had exorcised the jealous demon that possessed her.

That afternoon she rode perhaps farther than she should have, but it was the only way for her to work off the sight of Sherrod and Lucy entering their bedroom together, Lucy clinging happily to his arm and his gift for her, wrapped in brown paper, clutched in one hand—a miniature Swiss music box.

Catherine urged the roan into a gallop across the rolling hills of the Whetstones. She wanted only to flee the thought that tantalized her. But when she returned to the stables, resting weakly against the stall door to catch her breath, the thought was still with her—like a phantom shadow.

Was she never to know the love of a husband and children?

Chapter 7

JUNE 24. It marked the beginning of a change in Catherine's life at the Stronghold. It also marked the Fiesta de San Juan, the Mexican tribute to John the Baptist.

The fiesta started early in the afternoon with the vaqueros presenting feats of daring in the main corral—riding wild horses and swinging bulls by their tails, which brought hoots of laughter from the ranchería families. Catherine, with Brigham and Abigail in hand, walked down to the banks of the Cienega to watch the cockfights and horseraces. "I could do it, I could do it," Brigham persisted throughout the afternoon, trying to cajole Catherine into letting him race a horse.

Privately, she thought it sad the children were restricted to riding within the Stronghold's two acres. But then Don Francisco, in warning her how dangerous it was to ride outside the walls, had told about Pete Kitchen, a neighbor, whose twelve-year-old son had been killed by the Chiricahuas only months earlier. Catherine had thanked Don Francisco for his concern but continued her riding.

"Perhaps your father will let you ride with me tomorrow if we stay close to the ranchería," she told Brigham now, hoping to brighten his spirits.

His blue eyes, warm like his father's, danced. "All right!" Catherine had no further problem the rest of the afternoon with the children.

Later Don Francisco gave a *barbacoa* followed by an evening of dancing. From beneath a hastily constructed ramada, Don Francisco and Elizabeth looked on while the peones danced the fandango and other lively native dances. Catherine saw the disapproval in the tight set of Elizabeth's lips and wondered if the woman had ever felt any stirrings of romance.

Her own blood stirred as she watched the sinuous movements of the men and women. A passion flowed in the music that was difficult to resist. She glanced at Sherrod and Lucy, who stood shoulder to shoulder, watching the gay performance. Did either of them feel that same surge of unidentifiable yearning?

From the Mexican and Indian women gathered to one side, a short, stolid Indian girl crossed to where four or five men stood beneath a large fig tree drinking the potent *aguardiente*. She selected one of the men to dance. It was only after the couple moved out of the shadows and into the light of the lanterns strung from the trees that Catherine recognized the man with the butter-colored curls.

She closed her eyes with a sigh, hoping that Law would not make a fool of himself before Don Francisco, but a moment later her eyes opened to find Law performing quite admirably. His movements were graceful and lithe as he clapped his hands and stomped his heels in tempo to the Spanish music. And when the young Indian girl laughed up into the rakish face as she twirled about him—when he looked down over his shoulder at her with a teasing smile—Catherine found herself wishing the girl with the whirling skirts were she instead. She, who had never danced, had never felt a man's hand at her waist, moving her with him to the romantic spell of the music.

She did not like the direction her thoughts seemed to be taking more and more often, and she was glad when the evening was at last over and the revelers drifted back to their homes and beds. Catherine herself found no sleep in her own bed that night, for the June heat penetrated even the house's thick earthen walls, and the perspiration-dampened sheets continually tangled about her cotton gown.

Her restlessness only increased as the hours passed. Thus she was awake when the light knock came at the door, followed by a girlish voice. Catherine inched the door open to make out Abigail standing in her nightgown. Excitement twinkled in the child's eyes, reminding Catherine of Lucy. "What is it, Abigail?"

"Oh, Miss Howard," Abigail whispered, "do you know what tonight is? It's very special."

"It's almost morning," Catherine corrected, smiling. "And, yes, I know what was special about tonight—it was the fiesta of John the Baptist."

"Yes, but do you know what happens at four in the morning? If you swim at that time, they say your hair will grow thick and long. And also if it rains tonight the rest of the summer we'll have enough rain—and if it doesn't, we'll have a drought!"

Catherine chuckled. "You don't believe all those superstitions, do you?"

Abigail grabbed her hand. "Come on, Miss Howard. It's getting late. Please, can't we try?"

Catherine would have firmly told the girl to go back to bed, but the loneliness in the girl's eyes—she could understand it. Neither Abigail nor Brigham received much attention from Lucy, who seemed to take only an occasional interest in her children. Amazingly, it was the humorless Elizabeth who paid the most attention to the children, especially Brigham.

"All right, Abigail," Catherine conceded. She tied her blue silk robe about her and slipped into her mules, saying, "I'll watch you wade. Then it's back to bed."

The two stealthily slipped from the house. Catherine half expected the guard at the gate to halt them, but apparently he was too far gone on *aguardiente,* as he sleepily waved them through. Within minutes she and Abigail stood on the willow-laced banks, downstream from the ranchería.

Catherine thought she had to be the most foolish woman in the world to let a child persuade her to go wading at four in the morning. But as she sat on the water-eroded slope with her arms hugging her legs and her chin propped on her knees, she decided that for a few moments it was wonderful to be frivolous.

Outside it was much cooler, and overhead the constellations made their nightly swing across the southern skies. The air was sharply pure, fresh and untouched by human pollution. It was a wonderous night, a night that made her glad to be alive.

Finished with her wading, Abigail trudged out of the creek's shallower pool back to the bank. Her gown was wet at its hem where she had held it above her dimpled knees. She dropped down beside Catherine. "Well, do you think it worked?" One hand lifted each pigtail. "Are they any longer?"

Catherine's laughter bubbled up. "Oh, child, you're delightful! Let me look." She pretended to study each pigtail. "Mmmm, yes, I do believe they are."

Abigail smiled and stretched her pudgy arms in a sleepy yawn. "Just wait until tomorrow. I bet—"

She broke off as pebbles crunched beyond the creek's bend where arrowweed and carrizo, giant reeds, dueled with the cottonwoods and paloverde for space. Before Catherine could scramble to her feet, a tall, rangy figure rounded the reed-shielded bend into view. Catherine sighed with relief when she recognized the wildly curling hair.

She came to her feet, folding her arms before her in a gesture of waiting that was really a useless attempt to cover at least a portion of herself. "Evening, ma'am," Law said, ambling a less than straight line toward her and Abigail. He lifted the wicker-covered bulbous flask he toted. "Care for some lightning? Nectar of the gods, it is, ma'am."

He reeked of the *aguardiente.* "No, thank you, Law. We were just going back to the house."

"We're seeing if it's true your hair grows more if you swim on the night of San Juan, Uncle Law."

Catherine rolled her eyes and sighed. Any idea of escaping the drunken man was quite hopeless, for Abigail was holding out her pigtail for Law to examine. "You wait, tomorrow it'll be longer, I bet!"

"Abigail, we'd better go back now. It's getting—"

"And what about you?" Law asked Catherine. "Did you go wading also?"

"I don't believe in superstitions. Abigail, are you ready?"

Law sighed dramatically, but his teeth gleamed as white as the bright stars in the blue vault overhead. "What a shame. But then maybe I can show you something that will change your mind." He grasped her wrist and began pulling her behind him.

Perhaps she should have been worried, but she sensed Law meant them no harm. And she knew it would never do to make a scene before the child. After all, Abigail and Brigham did adore their uncle.

"All right, Law," she said patronizingly, "we'll look at whatever it is you have to show us. Then we really must return to the house."

She turned to see if Abigail was following, but the child was stretching again. "I'm going on back, Miss Howard."

Catherine hesitated. Maybe it would be better if Abigail did return rather than have the child traipsing through the dead of night behind a drunk. "All right, I'll be along soon."

Already he was pulling at her, and she gave in to his strength and let him tug her along the bank toward the creek's bend. He was singing some Spanish ballad in a surprisingly good voice. She found herself scrambling up the bank's incline in an effort to keep up with his longer strides.

"Wait," she gasped and jerked her robe loose from the spines of a cholla cactus. Law continued on, and she gave up trying to protect her gown to follow the liquor-demented man. Somewhere along the way she heard the thud when he dropped his flask, but he plodded on with her in tow.

"There—there it is," he said, jerking her alongside of him now.

She squinted through the starlit landscape. "There's what? I don't see anything."

"The cactus," he said thickly and pulled her down to her knees beside him.

How ridiculous the two of them must look! Groveling on their knees in the midst of the prairie at four in the morning! But, yes, now that she looked, she saw among the twining green stems of the low cactus a large white flower. She looked at Law, whose face was only inches from hers. "This is it? This is what you wanted to show me?"

She felt her voice growing louder, and Law said, "Sssh! This is a special flower."

She glared at the saturnine face. "Why?"

"Because," he said with an elephantine effort at dignity, "this prickly cactus blooms only one night in the year! The flowers open at sunset and are closed by seven or eight the next morning."

"I see," she said, impressed in spite of her cynicism.

Law carefully broke off the white flower and, to her astonishment, wedged it behind her right ear. She looked into the golden-brown eyes, so close to her own, and for a moment it felt as if her lungs had forgotten to function.

"Beautiful," he said in a quiet voice.

The air rushed back inside her. "I'm not susceptible to flattery, Law Davalos!" she snapped, disappointed, for despite the young man's shiftless ways, she thought she had detected a tenuous thread of integrity.

Law's hands reached on either side of her neck to find the one braid she had plaited before retiring that night. "I wasn't making up to you, Miss Howard," he said, as his fingers slowly loosened her hair from its braid. "Your hair's too heavy to knot it back the way you do." His hands lifted her hair free to let it fall straight and sleek, framing her oval face.

They knelt facing each other, Catherine with her hair mantling her shoulders and the white flower at her ear . . . and Law, his dark face above hers, his hands still buried in her thick mahogany tresses. "You *are* beautiful, Miss Howard."

She swallowed. She knew it was the magic of the night, that she was being totally impractical, but for the life of her she could not turn away when Law bent his head to brush her trembling lips.

At first the drooping mustache tickled. Then she forgot everything—the odor of *aguardiente* on his breath, the gravel grinding into her knees, the fact that Lawrence Davalos was five years younger than she, and most of all that he was not husband material.

The kiss was electrifying. That two people could touch in such a simple manner and detonate explosions such as ripped through her was something that had been beyond her capacity to imagine.

Law raised his head at last. His eyes were shining in the night's darkness. "Guess I sort of forgot myself, didn't I now?"

She cleared her throat. Was her body swaying to some inaudible music? "I think we both did," she said in a schoolteacher's pristine voice. "If you'll help me rise, I'll return to the house before it gets any later."

When he assisted her to her feet, his hands at her arms, she considered for the first time what it really meant to have a man's hands on her—the feeling it stirred in her, not romantic, but a purely physical, almost tangible, response.

Walking apart, they returned to the house. They made no attempt at conversation. Law, with his thumbs jammed beneath his concho belt, whistled softly that same Spanish tune she had heard earlier. He walked along the portico behind her, apparently unconcerned that his spurs clanked loudly in the stillness of the courtyard.

When she reached the door to her bedroom she did not even

turn to look at him. Half afraid he might try to follow her inside the room, she quickly opened the door. "Goodnight, Law."

"Goodnight . . . coward-Howard," she heard him whisper as she closed the door; then came the soft whistling tune that trailed off as he made his way to his own room.

Chapter 8

*T*HE bell began its customary ring, signaling thirty minutes till breakfast, and still Catherine did not move from before the small mirror she had hung on the wall. The wide mouth, the hollow cheeks, eyes that were too large for the small-boned face—and the almost pointed chin her sister kindly described as oval. It certainly was not a face one would call pretty.

Yet Law Davalos had called her beautiful the night before. And he had kissed her. The kiss in itself signified nothing, for she had little doubt that he would kiss anything with a skirt on. A womanizer, her mother would no doubt call him.

But the kiss *was* significant in that it was her first kiss. At twenty-six, no, twenty-seven, for a birthday had come and gone in that timeless land.

And the kiss was significant, for, if Law had found her desirable, if even for a brief drunken moment, then there was hope that some other man might find her desirable also—enough to marry her. She recalled the archaeologist, Stridehope, who had stayed overnight at the Stronghold the first month she was there. He had been rather nice-looking. And once or twice she thought he glanced at her with more than passing interest. She had hoped something might come from that night. The man would have made a good husband, she believed. But he had not come again.

At breakfast she was relieved to find Law was not present. If she had seen mockery in that bronzed face, her newly found confidence in her femininity would have deserted her. Oh, she had been the recipient of admiring glances, but only in her role as the angel of mercy at the hospital—or as the lone available white woman at Cristo Rey. But the night before had been something different. Even now her lips burned from the memory of the kiss, though she told herself it was the spicy hot chocolate Loco served in place of coffee every morning.

"Oh, Miss Howard, can I?" Brigham asked.

She started, realizing she had not been listening to the conversation. She looked at Brigham now, whose blue eyes mirrored his father's intelligence. "I'm sorry, Brigham. What was it you wanted?"

"Could I miss school today to watch the branding? Please, Miss Howard?"

She looked at Lucy, who shrugged prettily. Sherrod patted his napkin about his mouth to hide his smile, but Elizabeth said, "I don't think the boy should, Sherrod. You don't want him to get behind in his learning."

"You watched the fiesta last night," Don Francisco said. "That should be enough."

"You can watch after lunch," Sherrod modified.

Throughout the morning hours Catherine could sense Brigham's discontent, for the boy's mind was not on his spelling. And Abigail's eyelids were having trouble keeping open—the aftereffects of the excursion the night before. When lunch was over, the girl, utterly feminine and whimsical, would have no part of watching the branding and opted for a siesta.

Sherrod was already there, directing the branding. He hoisted Brigham on his shoulders so the boy could see over the corral's adobe wall. It could have been her son, her husband, Catherine thought. For a few happy moments she allowed herself to stand alongside Sherrod, watching the wildly thrashing animals and smelling the harsh odor of singed flesh.

But after a little while she began to feel uncomfortable under the gallant glances of the vaqueros as they one by one sensed her presence. She knew that from among the hundreds or so men who worked at Cristo Rey, she could find several who would be eager to marry her. But just a glance at Cristo Rey's ledgers told her how transient the cowboy's life was—rarely a hand lasted through an entire year at Cristo Rey.

Extracting a promise from Sherrod that his son would return for the afternoon classes, she escaped back to the house. As she passed through the *zaguán,* she paused at the door of the parlor to look at the portrait of Doña Dominica. The woman and Law shared the same sun-kissed hair and golden complexion, but there the likeness ended. Her almond eyes were gentle, her mouth tender. None of Law's fierce features were to be found in the smooth curves of her facial bones.

The woman had known the love of two men. Was she, Catherine, never to know the experience? Would she end up like Elizabeth, a withered tumbleweed?

As if bidden by Catherine's thoughts, Elizabeth came into the room, gliding silently like some giant crow. "I was just noticing the resemblance between the mother and son," Catherine said in an attempt at friendliness.

A semblance of a smile curled the corners of Elizabeth's lips. "The two are alike in more ways than one. The jewelry the woman wears—her son sold it. Just as she sold herself for a bed of lust!"

Catherine's breath sucked in at the woman's venomous words. She was relieved when Abigail's high-pitched voice interrupted them. Limping, the girl came into the parlor, holding one stocking and her ankle-high boot in one hand. "Miss Howard, Mama says that a high arch is a sign of the genteel. Look at mine." Abigail stuck out her small bare foot. "Do you think my arch is truly high enough?"

Elizabeth's hand cracked across Abigail's face. "Pride is a sin, child!"

Tears sprang to Abigail's eyes. The sock and shoe dropped to the floor as with a small cry the girl buried her face in her hands.

Catherine was afraid if she even looked at Elizabeth, she would say something in her anger she would later repent. She gathered the sobbing girl against her, saying, "You mustn't cry. We've got to go back to our studies, and you wouldn't want Brigham to see tears in your eyes, would you?"

At least, Catherine thought, the incident kept her mind from dwelling on the night before—and Law's kiss. She plunged into teaching the afternoon session with a forced enthusiasm she did not feel. The evening was no better. Although the rest of the household had retired, she was too agitated by the unwanted images that crowded into her mind. Foolish notions of the heart.

Of all the worthless scoundrels who walked God's green earth, Law was no doubt the worst. And she had to be attracted to him, a man five years younger. Lucy and Margaret at least had more good sense than she.

Rather than undress and toss restlessly on her bed, she lit her lamp and, with a book as a prop, wrote her first letter to her mother and Margaret. She told them about the impregnable Stronghold, the majestic landscape, and the incredibly beautiful weather. Briefly she wrote them how much better she hoped her mother was and went on to write that a sight draft would be forthcoming and that she hoped it would be enough.

It should. She was sending more than three-quarters of her earnings. Perhaps Margaret would soon marry and help with the financial responsibility. Her sister did not like the idea of earning a living. A lady would never engage in business!

Catherine was sealing the envelope when the light knock at the door interrupted her. She hesitated, afraid it might be Law. Had the kiss he had stolen the night before made him think she was a woman of easy virtue? Was he waiting outside—expecting far more? She would certainly disillusion him!

She yanked the door open. "Well?"

Sherrod stood in the doorway, a surprised expression on his darkly handsome face. His black string tie was loosened and his vest open. "Are you in the habit of greeting people like that?" he asked with a repressed smile.

She blushed furiously. "I'm sorry, Sherrod . . . my mind was on other things."

"I was turning in, and I noticed your light. Are you all right?"

She began to roll down the sleeves of her blouse and button the cuffs. It was too late to do anything about her unbound hair. "I wasn't sleepy and decided to catch up on some long-overdue correspondence."

"Something I should probably have been doing instead of losing fifty dollars on a turn of cards to Law," he said ruefully. "Perhaps I should listen more closely to Mother's sermons about the sin of gambling."

"Law's back?"

"I imagine he's over at the ranchería by now," he said with a dry chuckle. "Well, goodnight, Catherine."

He turned to go and abruptly turned back, as if an afterthought had occurred. "You know, I'm not sleepy either. What do you say to a breath of fresh air? June nights are the best of the year."

She hesitated. Then, "Why not? Just let me pin up my hair, and I'll—"

"No, leave it down. It's very—" He broke off, and she knew that it had only just occurred to him that what he intended to say was highly improper. A man might tell his mother or a sister or his wife that her hair was very becoming left unbound, but never a single female; never could such a thing be said to Catherine Howard.

She made no reply but shut the door behind her and walked with him through the darkened courtyard and *zaguán*. Out in the compound they found a bench, worn smooth with the years. Sherrod, sitting a little apart from her, talked quietly of his plans for Cristo Rey.

"I realize the Stronghold has come a long way from the simple stucco rancho that Law and his mother lived in when we arrived in the territory, but there's so much more to be accomplished. I want to irrigate Cristo Rey's desert area and breed a better strain of cow to improve our herds. But that must wait until the Indian problem is settled. And then there's the house itself—wallpaper, glass windows, things that would make Lucy happy."

Catherine saw the flicker of concern darken the thick-lashed eyes. "Lucy speaks often of how much she misses Virginia."

He hunched forward, his hands clasped between his knees. "Lucy came west with her parents when President Pierce appointed her father territorial attorney for New Mexico. Father and I had gone to Santa Fe because we were having trouble confirming Doña Dominica's land grant, and I met Lucy at one of the dinners given by the governor.

"Naturally, I fell in love with her immediately. But with Tucson five hundred miles from Santa Fe, I despaired of being able to court her. Fortunately, I was able to persuade her to accept my proposal immediately."

Sherrod's interlocked fingers came up to rub absently against his mustache. Catherine thought he was finished speaking, but after a moment, he continued. "I know that life out here has been difficult for Lucy to adjust to. Even Santa Fe had more cultural activities for her than this—" His hand swept the darkened panorama. "That's why I'm so relieved my father found someone as educated as you—and so glad you were willing to come out here. You see, Lucy—well, I guess you can tell by now—Lucy's not happy here at Cristo Rey."

"I gathered that."

"Yes, I'm sure it's obvious. She needs to get away, but I simply can't leave right now. I thought next year, when the children go off to boarding school. Perhaps she could spend a year back East with her family."

Catherine wanted to tell him it would all work out. But she was not certain it would. She said instead, "Tell me, what was it like growing up with two mothers?"

Sherrod looked at her and smiled. "It was marvelous. Can you imagine being spoiled by not one but two mothers?"

She knew herself how difficult it was for two women to live in the same household, even when they loved each other dearly. But two wives, competing for the same man . . . it was beyond her comprehension. "Surely the two wives must have had problems with the—I suppose you would call it their bounds of authority."

"Not really. Mother is a very organized, practical woman. She dealt with the running of the household. And Doña Dominica was a very maternal woman. She saw to the raising of Law and myself. I came to love her as much as my own mother—and Law as I would my own brother, though I don't think I'll ever understand his indifference to Cristo Rey."

Catherine opened her mouth to speak, and Sherrod, laughing, held up a hand. "Don't ask me whose area of authority my father fell under, because I was too young at the time to give much thought to things like that. And when I was old enough to wonder, Doña Dominica died—from some female disorder.

"But enough of the Godwins," he said. "Tell me something of yourself, Catherine."

"I would like to be able to tell you something exciting." She smiled, certain that in the shadows he could not see the wryness that curved her lips. "Such as that I'm a Russian princess fleeing persecution. But the simple fact is that between my father, who was a schoolmaster, and the Excelsior Finishing School for Young

Women, I received an excellent education. Some time ago my mother became ill, and between caring for her and my younger sister and working at the local hospital, too many years have slipped away."

"But what brought you out here?"

"The search for excitement, I suppose."

A muscle twitched in his jaw. "And Lucy wants the East, where she thinks all the excitement is! I keep telling her that everything worthwhile is here—at Cristo Rey."

Catherine sighed. "At this moment the East is filled with destruction and death. There is nothing beautiful about the pall of smoke that hangs over the cities. There are no glorious sunrises or sunsets like what I see above the Whetstones when I wake or the Santa Ritas before I go to bed."

"Why can't Lucy understand that?" he asked tersely. "Why can't she love the beauty of Cristo Rey as you do? I thought she—"

He broke off, and Catherine sensed the embarrassment in his voice. "I don't know why I'm telling you all of this."

She shifted uneasily on the wooden seat. The moon had moved past the Stronghold's earthen roof so that the compound lay in total shadow. But she had the strangest feeling of being watched.

"Catherine," Sherrod said softly, "thank you for listening to me tonight. I needed to talk." He paused. "I value your friendship very much."

She was not even aware of the hand that took hers or the way his arm encircled her waist when they returned to their separate rooms. Her thoughts were still back at the compound remembering the tiny spark of light she had seen in the distant shadows . . . and the noxious odor of Sonoran tobacco that had drifted on the air.

Chapter 9

*T*HROUGH the escape of her daily riding, Catherine was beginning to know the countryside. The twisted mesquite grove that heralded Coyote Wash—an arroyo that would run rabid with flash floods in the monsoon months; the red sandstone boulders that indicated the trickle of water seeping at their base; and the miniature canyons that opened fold on fold, like a desert flower, ever exposing some exotic landscape to delight her aesthetic taste. For her the land held incredible lights and shade . . . intensely sharp colors not to be seen anywhere else.

But now the July heat made it almost impossible to ride. The parched land was a fiery furnace. Blue-green mirages shimmered against the horizon. Life itself seemed stilled, the wind wilting, waiting for those first fleecy clouds to mantle the brooding bulwark of the Huachucas. It was all a part of nature's timeless magic show. And she loved it, despite the perspiration that soaked her armpits and dampened her thighs where they rubbed against the sidesaddle's sweaty leather.

It was these hours she lived for. She cared not where the mount took her and was only half aware of the trail it followed as it picked its way along a rocky bed bordered by the waxy-leafed creosote and the green-barked paloverde. But when it halted suddenly, its small ears erect and the muscles in its barrel twitching, she came alert. Something out of the ordinary moved beyond the range of her own senses. She did not know which she feared worse—the screech of the Mexican jaguar that occasionally roamed the area or the sight of a string of Indians riding toward her.

The long seconds she sat on the roan, straining her eyes and ears, seemed more like minutes. She began to believe she was attributing more caution than the situation warranted when a voice behind and slightly above her said, "Aren't you a little far from the Stronghold, Miss Howard?"

She jerked around in the saddle. "Law!" she gasped, recognizing at once the man crouched on one knee on the bank's high rim. Above the black, dust-coated trousers his lean, brown body was bare. "I'm so glad it's you!"

"Oh?" He rose now and scrambled down between a wedge of rocks, crossing to catch the bridle of the roan, which danced nervously at his approach. He stroked the soft muzzle, and when the horse calmed, looked up at Catherine. "I had an idea you might be happier to see someone else."

She tensed. She forced her gaze to meet those watchful eyes. "Whatever are you talking about?"

His mouth stretched thin in a grimace. "Don't pull one of Lucy's simpering acts on me, Miss Howard. I thought you were above something like that."

He did not wait for her to reply but took the roan's bridle and began to turn the horse about. "You're going up a boxed-in canyon," he explained as he led her back the way she had come, then up a slight ravine hedged by ironwood. Fifty yards away stood the gotch-eared sorrel he rode and a burro loaded with picks and shovels.

"Have you been prospecting?" she asked.

He released the bridle. "Trying to. Not much luck. But then I'm not the superstitious sort." He grinned—not a mocking but a friendly, teasing smile. "Been out wading in any creeks lately?"

So, he had not forgotten that night. She had hoped the *aguardiente* he had consumed had wiped out the memory. "No," she said quietly. "Nor have I been out picking night-blooming flowers."

"Then it's time you did something impractical again." And before she could protest, his hands clasped her waist and lifted her from the saddle.

"Oh, no, Law Davalos," she said as he pulled her along with him, "I'm not about to go traipsing the hills for some mysterious flower."

"It's not a flower this time. It's a tree."

"It's far too hot to be—"

"There," he said, pulling her up before him.

She stared at the tree—a type she occasionally had seen in her rides. The largest of the yucca cactus, it had grotesque branches all pointing in the same direction. And yet there was something weirdly beautiful about the tree.

"It's a Joshua tree," he said behind her. "The Mormons named it so because it looks as if it's lifting its arms to heaven in supplication. The Yaquis and Mexicans tell superstitious lore about it."

She turned her head to the side so that she could see his face. "Like what?"

He shrugged and smiled. "The usual things. Like making wishes."

"Then if I make a wish, will that satisfy you? Can we go back?" She pursed her lips and squinted her eyes, as though concentrating. "I am wishing that you won't drag me off to look. at any more desert plant life."

He laughed. "Oh, no. That won't do, Miss Howard. You can't tell a wish or it won't come true. Try again."

She sighed and turned around to face him. "All right. Let me think a minute." And with her eyes closed there suddenly seemed only one important wish. It overrode even the desire for the return of her mother's health. Love—and marriage—with a man like Sherrod.

Law took her shoulders. "You're a foolish woman, Miss Howard," he said grimly. "The kind of man my stepbrother is would never make you happy."

Her eyes snapped open. So, it had been Law out in the compound the night she talked with Sherrod. "And do you think you would?" she gritted.

For an answer Law jerked her to him. His mouth ground down on hers. It was nothing like the kiss he had given her the first time. She tried to twist away, but he held her fast. When he forced her lips apart, his tongue first teasing, then ravishing, she was shocked. She felt sullied. But out of that revulsion there sprouted a seed of desire to take root in her loins, and it seemed that too soon he released her.

"No," he said, still holding her wrists, "I'm not that man. But then I don't think you'll give any man a chance at laying claim as long as you got Sherrod sitting on that mountaintop."

Anger shot through her, but before she could deliver a verbal blast, he held up his hands. "Wait! Don't get me wrong. I've always admired my stepbrother. Sherrod is every inch the gentleman. What every woman wants. And he's too much the gentleman to violate civilization's code of ethics. Excepting . . ." Law paused, his eyes studying her pale face. "Excepting, Cate, if I wanted something bad enough, you can damn well bet civilization's code wouldn't stand in my way of taking it."

And he took her in his arms again, holding her, bending her so that she could not move—one hand behind her head, the other gripping her waist. His mouth clamped over hers in a long, thorough kiss. At first Catherine, constrained by his arms, remained passive. All she could think of was how cool, how refreshing, his mouth was on hers as the sun beat down mercilessly on them.

Then that ember of passion that her Victorian morals would have denied flared into a flame. Slowly her conscious thought ebbed so that she was aware of Law and Law only . . . his masculine strength, his smell of leather and sweat and tobacco, and the solid thud of his heart that seemed to drum in time to her own.

Beneath her palms his back, warm to the touch, rippled with sinewy muscles. His mustache abraded her lips, and his mouth tasted salty over hers. He was all male, and he was making her very much aware of herself as a female, aware of what her body was meant for.

"Open your mouth, Cate," he said, his voice husky with his want of her.

She knew that a proper lady would never do what she was doing. And yet was not that why she was out there—to live her life to its fullest? Slowly, with great misgivings, her lips voluntarily parted.

Law boldy tasted of her mouth. His teeth nibbled at her lips. Dimly she wondered if he had made love to many women and suspected that his women had been innumerable. Any other thoughts she had wavered like the shimmering heat rising off the caked and crinkled earth as his tongue plundered the hollow of her ear. His sure hands traveled down her spine and pressed her against him so she could feel the hard knot at the apex of his long legs. Her knees buckled with the thirst for something more that raged through her, parching her, leaving her depleted.

When his hand cupped one breast, she was jolted by the unexpected act of intimacy, unprepared. "No!" she rasped.

He paused, his hot gaze piercing her wavering one. "Seems I misjudged you." His eyes squinted. "Are you one of that kind, Cate—the kind that leads a man on?"

She blinked. "What?" Suddenly the meaning behind his words dawned on her. "You insufferable clod!" She stepped away and coolly surveyed the young man. "You are a good-for-nothing reprobate, Law Davalos! A parasite. Feeding off the labor of Don Francisco and your stepbrother!"

A crooked grin eased the angled face. "Yes'm. That I am." The man was obviously enjoying himself. He rested his hands on his hips and settled his weight on one leg. "Anything else?"

The infectious amusement softened her anger. "Yes, there's more." She bit her lip. "I'm trying to be honest, and I find it rather painful . . . but the fact of the matter is I—I liked what you did. The kiss."

Law nodded his head slowly, and she saw that he was striving to keep from smiling. "I admit my naiveté—my inexperience—but I didn't know what to expect until it was almost too late."

His grin faded, and he looked at her as if he was trying to understand. "Too late for what?"

She colored. It was really ridiculous standing there under the scorching sun, trying to explain herself to him. "To make it blunt," she said, crossing her arms defensively, "I want a husband."

His eyes narrowed, and she hurried on. "Oh, I'm not after you, Law Davalos. You'd be a poor excuse for a husband."

He smiled broadly and reached for her, saying, "I knew I liked you, Cate Howard. Not only are you a fetching woman, but you're plain-spoken. Now that we both agree that marriage is not in the book for us . . ." He drew her close, and she put her hands up against his chest.

"You still don't understand, you nitwit! I want a real husband. A real marriage. I don't want to go to my husband . . . tainted."

The corners of his lips twitched. "You just want us to go on—kissing, is that it?"

She glared at the tall man. "No! I'm not that stupid. I'm trying to tell you that though I like the way you make me feel—and I know it is quite shocking to admit it, but you did indicate you appreciate honesty—even though I—your kisses are . . . nice, well, you mustn't ever do it again."

His laughter was uproarious. It echoed throughout the small

canyons about them. The more he laughed, the angrier she became. Her fist doubled up, and she socked him below his ribs in the muscled flatness of his stomach.

Law grunted. A surprised look flashed across his face. He jerked her up against him, and her booted toes swung free of the ground. "I ought to whip you for that!"

Then he bent his head, and he began to kiss her with a ruthlessness that frightened her worse than his threat of whipping her. Physical punishment would only make her angrier. But this, the slow devouring of herself, left her weak and helpless, without any volition of her own. Even now her hands crept up to entwine in the riotous sun-bleached locks, to pull him closer.

He released her abruptly, and she almost fell. "And I'll warn you about something else," he said softly, his gaze scalding her. "You can't help what you feel, Cate. You're a hot-blooded woman, whether you know it or not. And you want me."

Her breasts rose and fell in seething contempt. "You're wrong! I don't want you. I'd have any type of man before I'd have you!"

The mouth eased into a smile, but the eyes were the shade of burnt umber. "No, *you're* wrong, Cate. As sure as you're standing under this Joshua tree, you want me. And you know where to find me. I'll be out here waiting for you. I'll wait—and you'll come."

"You'll wait forever!" She turned on her heel and stalked back to her horse.

Chapter 10

*Y*OU must come to Tucson and make the *paseo*, Catrina," the thirteen-year-old Atanacia said.

Looking at the beautiful young Mexican girl dressed in white flounces, it was difficult for Catherine to believe she was the bride of the big, red-headed Welshman sitting across from Don Francisco. Her husband, Sam Hughes, was thirty-three. Atanacia was a child bride indeed. And yet her black eyes sparkled with adoration for the giant of a man at her side. The couple was returning from a honeymoon in Santa Fe and had stopped over to visit with Sherrod, who occasionally bought whipsawed lumber from Sam. The sawmill in the Santa Rita Mountains was just one of the many businesses the Welshman had his hand in.

"A *paseo* is a stroll—a promenade, isn't it?" Catherine asked.

Sam laughed, and the after-dinner hot chocolate sloshed in the tiny cup held between his ham-hock hands. "It is. But in Tucson the *paseo* is special. Tell her about it, Sherrod."

Sherrod's eyes sought hers. "On Saturday night the men walk in one direction about the plaza, Catherine, and the unmarried women in another. When eye contact is made—and acknowledged—the couple drift apart from the others to walk together."

"It's Atanacia's way of matchmaking," Sam interjected. "Now that she is married, she thinks every single female should also be."

Atanacia said, "Oh, Catrina, *mi esposo,* he has not the tact. I think of the *paseo* because you are so *hermosa* and there are so many *hombres* in Tucson without *esposas.*"

Catherine could have sworn she detected a smothered snort from Law, who sprawled at one end of the camelback sofa. A quick glance beneath her lowered lids showed him hastily sipping the chocolate.

"I'm afraid the children would be very unhappy to lose Catherine," Sherrod put in with a smile, "even if it was to a local wife-hunter."

From there the conversation turned to children, with Atanacia declaring she wanted fifteen. Lucy sat silently next to Sherrod. Her beautiful face was pinched, the lovely lips drawn tightly. Catherine wondered how the woman could be unhappy when she had everything that Catherine wanted—a home, children, a husband. But Lucy was clearly morose, and Catherine could not decide who looked the worse at the moment, Lucy or herself.

It had been almost a week since she had been riding, since that day beneath the Joshua tree, and she could tell the difference in how she felt. With the lack of outdoor exercise, her complexion had reverted to its lackluster hue, making her eyes too large for her small-boned face.

She was indeed the coward Law called her. She could endure the putrefying stench of the rotting limbs and festering wounds of the soldiers she tended, but the mocking eyes and teasing lips of Lorenzo Davalos were unbearable; and thus she was bound as surely as a chained prisoner to the Stronghold, afraid of meeting him on her rides, afraid of actually going to the Joshua tree.

For a week she had not seen him. For a week she had paced her bedroom, walked the small courtyard, and haunted the dim rooms, feeling as if her life were ebbing from her there in the Stronghold. She needed the sun and the wind!

And now Law was back, invading the Stronghold, to taunt her.

Even at that moment she could not ignore him. For the Stronghold's other guest, her traveling companion Hiram Ogilvee, brought Law's name into the conversation. "Yep, I could have sworn it was you I saw in San Francisco last month, Law."

Don Francisco shot a disgusted glance at his stepson. "I doubt Law has that much get up and go to turn up in San Francisco, Hiram. But if you did see him, it was no doubt in one of the Barbary Coast's gambling palaces."

Law crooked a smile. "Now, you know Hiram would never be found in any of those notorious establishments, would you, Hiram?"

The surveyor general blustered, "I should say not! It's the riffraff and deserters from the war drifting into places like San Francisco and Tucson that are encouraging such vices."

"And the lawyers are the worst," Sam said. "They're coming to Tucson like bears that have smelled honey. They hope to make a killing representing the Mexican grandees in substantiating their grant claims before the Department of the Interior."

"I'm just grateful that Cristo Rey's deed has been cleared," Elizabeth said. She picked up the *chocolatera*. "Mr. Ogilvee—Sam—more hot chocolate?"

Hiram held out his cup for the woman to refill, but Sam shook his head, saying, "No, we need to get on to bed. I mean to be on the road early tomorrow before Cochise and his gang hit the trail. You know, don't you, that a band of his up in the Dos Cabezas Mountains butchered up that archaeologist—what was his name?"

"Stridehope?" Catherine gasped. "Not Jonathan!"

"That's a shame!" Don Francisco said.

For a few moments the occupants of the parlor discussed the

tragedy of the archaeologist's death. Catherine could feel Law's lazy, speculative gaze on her. Damn him! He alone had caught her disproportionate distress.

That night when everyone had retired, she lay in her bed, trying to will herself to sleep. Her thoughts churned around Jonathan Stridehope. He had been the kind of man with whom she would be content to spend her life. And yet she had never tried to imagine his lips kissing hers. She smiled wryly, thinking he would probably have gone down on one knee and requested permission to court her. Wasn't that the kind of man she wanted for a husband?

Then why was she possessed by thoughts of Law Davalos? She was as possessed by the want of him as Lucy was by the want of opiates. Law's rangy physique stalked her thoughts during the day and invaded her dreams at night.

Her drifting mind froze as she heard the jingle of spurs coming down the portico. Like everyone else in the Stronghold, she had begun to leave her door open to catch the hot night's faint summer breeze. Now she could see the man silhouetted outside her door, a silhouette so tall that the bent head brushed the door's lintel.

A scratching against the adobe brick reached her ears, then a match's phosphorescent flare illuminated the rugged face as a cigarette was lit. Law's cat eyes looked at her. "Evening, Cate," he said and strolled on off, leaving the horrid stench of his cigarette to remind her he was not some will-o'-the-wisp she had imagined.

Resolutely she turned her back to the door and fluffed her ticking pillow, determined to sleep. Yet Lucy's faint crying reached her from the adjacent room, and a few minutes later Sherrod appeared at her door. "Catherine," he said softly, urgently.

She sat up, clutching the covering before her. "It's Lucy," his shadowy voice said. "She wants you."

"I'll be right there. Let me get my robe."

The young woman was drawn up in the rocking chair. Her bare toes stuck out from beneath her gown's lace hem. The coal-oil lamp cast an unflattering light on her watery blue eyes and shiny red nose. Her flaxen yellow hair looked as dry and stiff as straw.

"I caught her taking this," Sherrod said, passing Catherine a bottle. "Laudanum. I thought I had gotten rid of it."

"Tell him I need it," Lucy beseeched Catherine.

Running a hand through his rumpled hair, he said, "I've talked to her about the laudanum. I've told her how dangerous the habit can be. But she thinks I'm just being cruel to her."

Lucy began to tremble violently, and Catherine said, "Come on to bed, Lucy. You're tired."

The woman rose and clung to her. "Will you stay with me?"

"As long as you want." She tucked the muslin sheet over Lucy and sat on the bed's edge, holding the woman's rigid hand. Sherrod went to sit in the rocker. His dark eyes were shadowed with fatigue.

When Lucy's hand slackened, she said, "The laudanum is easily obtained through the mail-order houses, Sherrod. You must make certain you check all the supplies that are freighted in from Tucson each month."

"But, dear God, why? Why does she need it?"

"Fear."

"Fear," he echoed. "Of what?"

"Of not being able to cope, maybe. And other things. There are lots of fears that men don't understand."

"Cope! She doesn't have to worry about coping, Catherine! She has servants for herself, and a tutor for her children, and my mother carries all the responsibilities of running the house. Lucy has nothing to worry about!"

Catherine rose from the bed. "I think she'll sleep the rest of the night." Before she reached the door, he was there, stopping her. "Why can't she have your strength, Catherine?"

He took her hands, and she said, "Sherrod, no!"

"I've fallen in love with you," he said in a tortured voice. "Oh, not like with Lucy—with her pretty facade."

"Don't, Sherrod. Don't say these things. They only make it more difficult."

He pulled her into his arms. "They've got to be said. I'll know no peace until I do tell you. You're real, Catherine. A woman with depth and feeling and substance. And strength."

She put her hands against his chest and pushed him away. "Strength?" Her laugh was harsh. "I'm weak, Sherrod! Why do you think I came west? I'm running, running from myself." She passed her hand across her eyes. "I don't know what it is about this primitive land, but already . . . already I've done things I never thought I'd do."

She raised her gaze to meet Sherrod's and saw the passion flaming in the eyes that were as blue-hot as a fire's core. She saw that he wanted to hold her, to reach out for her, that he was drowning as she was drowning. "Sherrod," she whispered, "I've always dreamed of having a man like you in love with me. But one thing I won't sink to is adultery. Isn't that what we're talking about?"

She had thought to shock him, but his eyes searched her face. "What I feel for you is more than just desire, lust, whatever my Bible-thumping mother would call it!"

"But it'd still be adultery in the final analysis, wouldn't it?" she demanded softly. "I can't let that happen, Sherrod. It'd destroy me, and it'd destroy Lucy and you. Don't do this to me. Don't do it to us."

He laughed then, laughter that held the hint of painful disappointment. "I don't suppose you'd be willing to become a Mormon, to be a second wife? No, don't bother to look at me like that. I wouldn't let you do it if you wanted to, Catherine. I saw the hell it brought to my father and my mother. And Law and myself. I swore I'd never do that to my family. And certainly not to you. I love you too much. As badly as I want you, I'll say no more."

He released her hands, and she fled to the safety of her room.

Chapter 11

*T*HE wind in her hair, the sun on her face! Oh, it felt so good to be alive! The bay carried Catherine on fleet hooves past the Cienega's tall poplars that waved like gigantic plumes, beyond the ranchería to where the grass thinned out and the high desert rose up to embrace her. It was the desert and the Huachuca's rocky foothills she loved most of all—the landscape's clean, pure lines, its clarity—clarifying even her mind.

Out there, galloping over ancient lava beds and alkaline terrains, she was able to think more clearly . . . to see that the warm feelings she had for Sherrod, the desire she felt for Law, only threatened her true happiness—the permanent lasting happiness of a family. She had only to put the two brothers from her mind for another six months, and she would be at last relieved of her torment.

But always there rose up to mock her the sight of a Joshua tree. It was as if Law, as elemental as the mountains he prospected in, were haunting her . . . so that now the image of those laughing eyes, the softly teasing mouth beneath the sensuous flaring of the aristocratic nose, crowded everything out of her mind, even Sherrod.

There existed only Law. And the ache inside her.

Above the Huachuca Mountains, Stygian clouds burgeoned in seething masses of violent impatience. The hot wind carried the musty scent of oncoming rain. She guided her mount up out of the flatlands where the mountain runoffs could tumble without warning through the parched washes. On the higher ground she would avoid the threat of the flash floods.

Only as her horse picked its way along a barranca's edge did Catherine realize the direction she was headed . . . the spot where she had last met Law. Oh, he really would not be there. He was no spirit that could appear at the moment she summoned him. It was just the mystical allure of the landscape. And that damned Joshua tree. That aimless Lorenzo Davalos was as full of guile and glib of tongue as old Marta of the ranchería, the washwoman who some claimed was a *bruja,* a witch.

Catherine saw the uplifted arms of the Joshua tree before she saw him. He *was* there. Sitting like some phantom on the gotch-eared sorrel, he loomed tall and forbidding. His soft laughter reached across the yards of sand and rock to stroke her.

For a long minute she held back on the reins of her prancing mount. She still had time to turn back. A war raged inside her. Her brain sent out signals to her hands, and yet those appendages remained lifeless, unresponsive. And she sat there helplessly watching as Law kneed his sorrel and slowly moved across the distance that separated them.

When he drew near, so that she saw the golden heat coloring his eyes, she at last bestirred herself. "You know, I don't even like you."

He hooked a smile. His slight uneven teeth gleamed white below the tawny mustache. "That doesn't have anything to do with your gut feelings . . . with what your body wants, does it?"

He slung his leg over the saddle and slid off the horse. His gaze held her immobile as his hands took the reins from her unresisting fingers. And still she could not move when his hands encircled her waist and lifted her from the sidesaddle as easily as if she were Abigail's size.

She did not even struggle as he carried her to the tree but gave into the mouth that claimed hers. The kiss that seared her, reaching down to relieve the torment twisting inside her—this was what she had been waiting for, wanting.

Law withdrew his mouth. A wry smile curved his lips as he set her on her feet. He shrugged out of the duster he wore and spread it beneath the Joshua's scant shade. "You never asked me *my* wish, Cate."

Run, get away, a voice inside her cried out. Yet she stood rigidly before the kneeling man. "I don't want to hear anything you have to say."

He rose to stand over her with that quiet, knowing smile. "You just want to kiss?"

She ground her eyes shut. "Yes." Was that her voice that sounded like a croak?

He took her shoulders and shook her lightly. "Then let me hear you say it. Say it—say that you want me, that you couldn't forget my kisses."

Her eyes blazed open. "Yes! But I don't love you!" Her nose wrinkled with distaste. "Your kind—"

He laughed, loud and full. "Did I say anything about love? I know, I know—your kind is my fastidious stepbrother. But he's already taken, isn't he? So the proper Miss Catherine Howard will have to quench her desire with the loathsome greaser."

His hands settled on her shoulders, and he pressed her down until her knees gave way and she collapsed on the spread duster. Her top hat fell away. She lay there, half reclining, supported by her forearms, as she watched him crouch over her on all fours like some predatory cat.

"You'd think I'd have too much pride to take second place, but, damm it, Cate, I don't care. I want you. Lying out under the stars I've pictured you a hundred times. Those haughty eyes and your mouth—do you know you're a damned beautiful woman when you smile? Then I'd get to thinking about what you must look like—without all that fooferaw, not all gussied up as you are now. And I decided that'd have to be half the fun." His fingers touched the ruffled stock at her neck. "Taking off all these ladylike frills. Like unwrapping a Christmas present."

The indolent voice held a hypnotic quality. The sensuous steady tempo of the words drummed into Catherine so that she was at first only vaguely aware of the thunder that reverberated through the canyon walls with dark Wagnerian intensity. Wind-whipped clouds boiled over the mountains and raced down to shadow the land. White-hot lightning snaked across the heavens, unleashing its fury over the couple below.

She felt a sense of foreboding, that by giving herself to Law, she was dooming her soul forever; yet she could no more alter her decision than she could alter the long, too-slim legs that he revealed as he hitched her skirt up past her riding boots.

She squeezed shut her eyes when she felt his long body stretch out half over hers. Her knuckles went white as her fingers dug into the duster's rough cloth. "Just get it over with," she gritted. *So my wanting will be over with. So I'll be at peace with myself.*

"Oh, no, my girl. This isn't something that we go about like two rutting animals. There's more to it than that."

His forefinger traced the high curvature of her cheekbone, slipped down into its hollow, and came to rest at the corner of her lips. "When it's all over, I mean to have known you, Cate . . . all of you. From that widow's peak—a sign of stubbornness, my momma used to say about hers—to the fine light hairs on your legs."

She gasped, horrified. To even hear her limbs spoken of in such a crude term was almost as shocking as actually feeling his fingers moving along the inside curve of one thigh. She tried to push her skirt down, but Law was adamant, as his fingers worked at the snaps of her riding boots.

And just as surely, as deftly, he removed her black jacket, then her corsage habit-shirt that buttoned down the front. She lay there, looking up at the man who labored over her. His face was intense with desire yet tempered by a patient, almost gentle look, and she wondered both how she could go through with it and how she could wait what seemed interminable moments until she felt those demanding lips over hers and the heat and weight of his body atop her.

She lay clad now only in her riding skirt and the fine lace camisole over the whalebone corset. *"Dios mío,"* Law swore softly, "whatever are you about, Cate—wearing this contraption when you're so slim I could break you between my two hands?"

Her hands clutched at his, stopping the fingers that worked at the corset's laces. Soon her full breasts would be free of their restriction, free for Law's taking, and whatever hope she had left would be vanquished. She forced her lids to rise to meet his fierce gaze. Her voice was almost inaudible under the crackling of the lightning about them.

"You'll break me, if you take me, Law."

He rocked back on his heels. "Dammit, dammit, dammit! This makes twice now, Cate. It's enough to make a man impotent! Get out of here! Get!.

"And if you come near me again," he grated as she rapidly gathered up her clothing, "I *will* take you and break you! I'll make a loving whore out of you, Cate Howard!" He came to his feet with a swearing grunt and stalked off, leaving her to ride back alone to the Stronghold, inviolate.

Chapter 12

MISS Howard," Elizabeth interrupted in her cold, starchy voice.

Brigham halted in midsentence the old edition of the *Arizona Miner* Catherine was having him read aloud from, while Abigail's pen paused in the middle of copying a paragraph from Swinton's *A Complete Course in Georgraphy.*

Catherine rose from behind the dining-room table, where class was held now that the late-summer rains cascaded over the thirsty earth. "Yes, Mrs. Godwin?"

The woman clasped her dry hands, the fingers folded as tightly as her thin lips. "I'd like to talk to you—alone."

Catherine nodded to the children. "Why don't you two have Loco fix you an early lunch, and then you can play awhile before we go back to work."

Delighted at the reprieve, the children scrambled from the room, and Catherine was left alone with Elizabeth.

"I shall get right to the point, Miss Howard. I know you are trying to seduce my son. Oh, don't bother to act surprised," she continued, her voice cracking with anger. "I overheard you and Sherrod in the courtyard the night before last."

Catherine's hands clenched the table's edge. "Mrs. Godwin, I resent both your prying and your accusation."

"And I resent you because you are jeopardizing Sherrod's future."

Elizabeth's blazing eyes met Catherine's in a battle of wills as the woman recalled facing another young woman years before—a young woman who would have taken her husband from her; no, who did take Frank for a while. But fate had intervened, and the other woman had died, leaving Elizabeth her husband once more . . . and Cristo Rey.

"I don't care to continue this conversation," Catherine said.

"But you will," Elizabeth said, moving a step closer. "And what's more, you will leave Cristo Rey. I don't care what reason you give the others. But I want you to leave."

"And if I should refuse?"

"I'm giving you credit for intelligence, Miss Howard. I don't think you'd willingly become a Mormon in order to marry Sherrod and be a second wife. I know what it's like to share your husband, and I don't think your type of woman would like it. And I won't permit Sherrod to divorce Lucy and marry you."

The woman's wrinkled lids narrowed over stonelike pupils. "You see, in my husband's old age he has remembered his duties to the Church, and he would most certainly disown Sherrod if he divorced Lucy. Sherrod might give up Lucy for you, but I'd never let him give up Cristo Rey for you . . . or any other woman. So, Miss Howard, I want you to leave now before this affair goes any further."

"Sherrod has a mind of his own, Mrs. Godwin."

Elizabeth smiled, a sneer really. "Do you think my son or my husband would permit you to stay if they knew you were having an affair with Law? Fornicating beneath the very eyes of the children!"

Catherine's eyes widened. "That's not the way it—"

"It doesn't matter whether it's the truth or not. Sherrod's own child saw Law kiss you the night of the fiesta. I myself overheard Abigail tell Brigham about it. And I saw you two returning from a ride together. Do you think Sherrod or my husband would believe your word against Abigail's and mine?"

It could be worse, Catherine thought, as she swallowed the last of the after-dinner chocolate. By leaving, she was removing herself from Law's tempting presence. Of course, there existed the problem of earning enough to support herself, and her mother and sister, if she taught in Tucson.

As badly as the territory needed teachers, no one but the very wealthy could afford one until the territorial legislature was able to pass a bill funding public schools. With the financial havoc wreaked by the Civil War, the possibility of that funding appeared dim for the near future.

Good Lord, a hundred lawyers in the territory and not one doctor or teacher! Still, she was one of the few white women in the Arizona Territory. Surely in Tucson she would be able to find a husband.

She wished now she had not chosen the time after dinner to tell the family of her decision to leave, for Law was there tonight—sitting opposite her, one booted foot crossed over his knee. He would think she was running from him. Was she?

She sat her empty cup aside, saying, "I feel this is the best time—since all the family is together—to tell you that, as much as I hate to, I am going to have to leave Cristo Rey."

Audible gasps filled the room, and she rushed on. "I feel what I am doing, teaching, would have more impact if I taught as many children as possible. And, of course, there are so many children in Tucson alone that do not even know how to write their names."

She looked now to Don Francisco. The old man, for all his age, was no less astute. She would have to sound convincing. "I know it will be an imposition for you, Don Francisco, after all the trouble you went to in order to bring me out here, but I feel Abigail and Brigham already know so much more than I would have hoped to accomplish with them in just six months. Lucy, if you'll just make them practice . . ."

Her voice trailed off as Abigail and Brigham both jumped to their feet and ran to her side. "No," Brigham said, grabbing at her hand, "you can't leave!"

"Are you certain this is the best thing for you?" Sherrod asked.

Catherine colored. She was sure everyone in the room heard the torture in his voice and guessed he was in love with her. She glanced at Lucy, but Sherrod's wife only looked bewildered and slightly distressed at the suggestion that the responsibility for her children would be hers again. Catherine's gaze slid on over to Law—and, naturally, there was the cynical crook to one side of his mouth. Yes, he obviously guessed Sherrod's secret.

Only Elizabeth wore a satisfied smile. "Of course she is certain what's best for her, son."

"Cristo Rey needs you," Don Francisco said at last, "but I think it is important you do what you believe you have to, Miss Howard. It takes courage to make changes, and you have courage."

"Thank you, Don Francisco," Catherine said quietly. Her arms encircled the two children, who knelt on either side of her. She wished she could protect them from the future, from the apathetic mother and the domineering grandmother. But then she had been no more successful herself in holding her own against Elizabeth. Yet there was such a word as justice. Surely one day it would prevail against people like Elizabeth Godwin.

The change was much easier to accomplish than Catherine had forseen. She had worried about finding a place in Tucson, for every available domicile was requisitioned by officers from the army supply depot at Camp Lowell, just outside the city walls.

Fortunately Sherrod remembered an old adobe—the roof was crumbling over in the kitchen, he warned her. The last occupant, a miner, had abandoned the place for more lucrative veins in Colorado the month before when Sherrod was last in Tucson. Sherrod was sure she could arrange to buy the adobe for a small sum from Sam Hughes, who rented it out. A note would be sent to Sam on the next freight wagon into Tucson, he promised.

He even volunteered to drive her into Tucson, when the time came for her to leave. She saw no harm in it, especially since she suggested that Lucy and the children accompany them. She would have thought Lucy would be delighted to visit Tucson, as provincial as the frontier outpost was. But Lucy pleaded a headache, and only Brigham and Abigail, excited at the prospect of staying overnight in Tucson, went along.

For a while Catherine and Sherrod talked about inconsequential things. He spoke of Tucson's desperate need for water and sewerage and the great potential the territory had if it could ever become a state. "Arizona has the five C's," he said in a forced attempt at lightheartedness. "Cattle, cotton, climate, copper, and citrus . . . but, like hell, it doesn't have water."

Catherine discussed what the children would need to study before they went off to boarding school, but he interrupted her midway, saying in a tight voice, "Catherine . . . are you leaving because of me?"

She glanced at Abigail, who was asleep, her head bobbing on Catherine's shoulder, and Brigham, who lay stretched out in the wagon's bed, his body wedged between Catherine's trunk and carpetbag. "No," she said quietly, "I'm leaving because of me. I want what every woman wants, Sherrod. A husband and children of my own to love. That's something I would not find at Cristo Rey."

Sam Hughes's house seemed as crude as the other adobes that fronted the narrow streets inside Tucson's presidio walls, only perhaps a bit larger viewed from the outside. Inside it was airy and cool with gray jerga rugs on the hard-packed dirt floors and brightly colored blankets piled against the whitewashed walls for sofas and later for sleeping.

Atanacia ran out to greet Catherine and led her into the tree-shaded courtyard. She pressed a glass of *limonada* on Catherine and the children, saying, "Sherrod and Sam, they say they will go to the store, but, bah!" She snapped her small fingers. "They go to the cantinas to drink, I betcha!"

Contrary to Atanacia's predictions, the two men returned early enough to enjoy a dinner of stewed mutton and baked pears prepared quite expertly by the thirteen-year-old girl. It was difficult for Catherine to believe Atanacia was only a little older than Abigail, who still played with dolls.

When Catherine commented on this fact, Atanacia said, "But I am the oldest of eleven children. I had to learn early. At nine I was going to Sam's store and myself cutting a pound of beef from the slabs he hung on the timbers outside his store."

As usual the talk turned to the latest Apache depredations and the Union soldiers' trade that improved business before Atanacia rolled out the blankets for the men, who would sleep in the main room, which was also the kitchen. Catherine and the children would sleep with Atanacia in the bedroom.

The next morning was almost as difficult for Catherine as the day she had parted with her mother and Margaret. She hugged each of the children and gave Abigail a copy of Lewis Carroll's *Through the Looking Glass* and Brigham Washington Irving's *Sketchbook.*

Before Sherrod climbed into the buckboard, he took her hand. That early in the morning, people were already out and teams of freight wagons crowded the streets leading to the plaza and were backed up outside the city's walls. "I don't think you fully realize that Tucson is a virtual Sodom and Gomorrah," he said, his blue eyes dark with concern. "If you looked the world over you couldn't find a more degraded sort of villains than Tucson society, Catherine. Please, be careful."

He lowered his voice then, so Brigham and Abigail would not hear him. "You know how I feel about you won't change, my darling. If you should need me, you know I'll come."

Chapter 13

*I*T was not much, the adobe hut, a *jacal* that faced flush with Calle de la India Trieste, the Street of the Sad Indian Girl. But Sam had let her have the adobe for almost nothing, leaving Catherine still with a little savings.

Though the *jacal* set outside the presidio's walls, thus presenting a long walk to the plaza's stores, it was close to El Ojito, an artesian spring; so she would not have to pay ten cents a bucket for fresh water as the citizens inside the Old Pueblo did.

A long main room in the front of the *jacal* was buttressed by a minuscule bedroom and another room which was really an open kitchen, since there was no roof and only a partial wall on the north side. But it was a beginning. It was her own home.

Together she and Atanacia worked to clear the rubble from the main room, where Catherine would teach her students. Except for the beehive fireplace in one corner, the room was bare. Atanacia had taken her to Solomon Warner's general store to purchase blankets and tinware, and Juan Elias had donated from his store a hemp bed that Atanacia covered with a flax bedspread.

When the hard-packed earth was swept clean with the mesquite brush brooms bought from a Pima Indian woman and burlap was spread for rugs, Catherine stepped back, hands on her hips, and surveyed the first day's work. "It doesn't look half bad, Atanacia. Rather beautiful, in fact, wouldn't you say?"

Atanacia tilted her head to one side, her eyes shining with mischief. "*Sí*, both you and the room."

Catherine blushed and wiped at the dirt on her face, smudging one cheek. She glanced down at the dust on her hands and wiped them on her apron. "I guess I look a mess."

Atanacia studied her new friend critically. The cotton handkerchief about the young American woman's head emphasized the fine bone structure and the large, luminous eyes that dominated the pale, camilla-like complexion. "No, *amiga,* you are *muy bonita,* truly. Why have you never married?" She clapped her hand over her naturally pink lips. "Oh, how *malcreado!* How ill-bred of me!"

Catherine laughed at the screwed-up face, the face of the child Atanacia was. "Honestly, Atanacia, I'm glad someone asked. Always before I could sense the stares and felt people's pity, and no one bothered to ask. The fact is, I have never met a man whom I wanted to marry . . . and who wanted to marry me also. It takes two to make a wedding."

"Burros, the men are! But there are so many *hombres* in Tucson. Look!" She grasped Catherine's arm and pulled her over to the small window, moving aside the fringe of leather strips. "There, see!"

Catherine's gaze swept over the randomly scattered adobes on the other side of the street, their windows like tired eyes closed against the brilliant sun. To the left, past the far cornfield, three Indian women washed clothes in the *acequia* running from the Santa Cruz River. Beyond was Solomon Warner's stone flour mill and Sentinel Mountain.

To the right of Catherine's adobe, two Mexicans, smoking their cornhusk *cigarillos,* sat propped against a wheel of one of the many freight wagons that camped on the outskirts of town, near the Tully and Ochoa corrals.

Directly in front of Catherine, four or five men, adventurers if their scrubby beards and grease-blackened buckskins were any clue, lounged beneath the semi-shade of Juan Bueriel's Mescal Saloon. "What are you talking about?" she asked.

"Idiota!" Atanacia exclaimed with affection. "At this time of afternoon they would usually be asleep under some wagon or up at the plaza drinking the mescal and playing the monte. But no, they are here, waiting for you to come out. To only see a white woman is enough. Soon they will be at your door, courting you."

Catherine pulled the handkerchief from her head with a smile. "Well, in that case, I had better make myself presentable."

Atanacia prophesied accurately, for within the week three men, a prospector and two cavalrymen, called upon Catherine, ostensibly to ask if she needed any help in "settling in."

She politely thanked them while mentally making a file of each man's name and appearance and explained that at the moment she required no help.

Her plans for tutoring were working out just as successfully. Already she had twelve students coming each morning (all Mexicans and all boys), thanks to both Sherrod's and Sam's propaganda. Out of her own pocket she supplied the slates at twenty-five cents each. She charged the parents of each student three dollars a month, which barely covered her cost of living, for supplies in Tucson were ridiculously high because of the cost of freighting from the East.

After one o'clock, when school was recessed for the day, she attended to the myriad tasks that a servant otherwise would have performed—filling the lamps and cleaning their chimneys, buying the scuttle of coal for the day's cooking, and, last, sprinkling the earthen floors with water to keep down the dust that was as fine and gray as talcum.

Often she had dinner with the Hugheses. She never had time to be lonely, for almost daily she would have a gentleman caller who would sit on the crude bench made by Sam and padded with fuchsia cushions sewn by Atanacia. The gentlemen who called would twist their hats in their hands and mumble polite phrases about the nice weather (warm days and cool nights now that October was upon the little mud city). Soon thereafter the gentlemen would make their departures, leaving her in a state of amusement. Not even the beauteous Margaret had ever received so many callers!

With her days filled, Catherine found herself lonely only at night when, after she had reread Sir Walter Scott's *Ivanhoe* for perhaps the fourth time or one of Lord Byron's romantic poems, she went to bed. For a while she lay there, the darkness encouraging her loneliness. She could imagine herself growing old and lonely, the spinster schoolmarm.

And always with that thought, she would think of Law. A bitter taste would fill her mouth—a taste that did not prevent her lips from remembering the pleasure they had known beneath his lips. She really must stop reading that romantic literature!

Every morning she awoke early to find some stranger sleeping outside her doorway. After this happened four or five times, with a different slumberer across the doorstep on each occasion, she began to realize that the male society of Tucson had apparently taken it upon themselves to protect their fair neighbor.

Some mornings she would maybe find an old white-haired Mexican, his face covered by a floppy sombrero and his body draped with a Papago blanket. Other mornings would bring forth a hulking cowboy with a mountain of a hangover. Catherine would awaken her protector, give him a breakfast of bacon and tomatoes or, if he was lucky, potatoes and *chiles colorados* (eggs were almost impossible to obtain), and send the man on his way.

As October passed into November and November into December and the days and the nights turned only slightly more chilly with still the day's bright sunshine, she began to receive two gentlemen whom she actually could consider marriageable material.

One, Lionel McCrary, was an attorney who had read law in Pennsylvania until the lure of the West's opportunities had seized him fifteen years earlier. Though the slender wiry man was almost as old as her father, approaching forty, he was the first man in Tucson she found she could converse with intelligently.

After the first three or four times Lionel called on her, she allowed him to escort her to Tucson's only restaurant comparable to those in the States, the Shoo Fly, so called because the Mexican boys always carried fly swatters with their trays. For Catherine the outing was a special treat, and she found herself laughing at Lionel's anecdotes about the town's citizenry, especially the American men who inhabited the Old Pueblo—twelve Anglos with the exception of the transient army personnel.

"Take Mark Aldrich," Lionel told her over dinner one evening. "He's Tucson's first American *alcalde*—that is, justice of the peace. He's married to Margaret Wilkinson, who is living in your hometown, Baltimore."

"I believe I've heard the name," Catherine said.

Lionel grinned and leaned closer over the table. "But have you heard, Miss Howard, that the sixty-two-year-old Aldrich has a six-year-old daughter, Faustina, by his Mexican wife, the beautiful Theofila?"

Catherine's other eligible caller was Jeremy Rankin, a lieutenant of Company G of the California Volunteers, stationed at Camp Lowell. While not possessing Lionel's extroverted personality, Jeremy was nonetheless a charming companion. Quiet, well-mannered, he treated her with a respect that bordered on the near reverence of a Southern gentleman. And he was, in addition, a rather attractive man of medium height with a handsome set of side-whiskers.

The two men naturally crossed paths as they came to call upon her, each giving only a curt nod of the head to acknowledge the other, though neither ever mentioned the existence of another caller to her.

On Saturday mornings, Jeremy would call to escort her for a stroll. Since Tucson's streets were unpaved with no sidewalks, in order to avoid the strewn garbage, they would walk through the Plaza de Las Armas, sometimes buying a pie from John "Pie" Allen's shop. North American adventurers from everywhere flooded the plaza, lured by stories of free land and mining bonanzas.

On one such Saturday, a beautiful sunny one in mid-December, she was walking with Jeremy and lamenting the fact that Tucson's citizens did not think their daughters needed an education. "Do you know, Jeremy, one father told me when he brought his son to my house that all a girl needed to know was how to cook and sew. Imagine!" she said with an indignant toss of her head. "How would I ever support myself if I had not received an education?"

Jeremy, who looked dashing in his blue uniform with the yellow stripe of the cavalry, took her hand in his. "Miss Howard, you wouldn't have to worry about supporting yourself. It would give me great—" The young lieutenant halted as he realized that she was not listening to his stirring address but was gazing with rapt attention just beyond his shoulder.

"Catherine," Sherrod called, "I was just on my way to see you!" He paused as he noticed the officer standing with her, and she made the introductions. The two men looked at each other in a stand-off.

"Lieutenant Rankin was accompanying me to Sam's store," she contributed in the uneasy silence. "I needed a paper of pins. How is everyone at the Stronghold?"

"We all miss you terribly. Brigham and Abigail are bored

restless, and Lucy is at her wits' end with no one to talk to. Father is even grumpier than before."

"And Law?" she could not help asking.

A frown of confusion clouded Sherrod's deep-blue eyes. "Why, he's in and out of the Stronghold, as always. The proverbial will-o'-the-wisp."

Jeremy rested his hand on the hilt of his curved saber, and she knew he was annoyed at Sherrod for monopolizing her time. "Give my affection to your family, Sherrod," she said, reluctant to end the conversation but knowing to continue would have been impolite to Jeremy.

Sherrod tipped his planter's hat. "Nice to meet you, Lieutenant Rankin."

Jeremy did not press his suit that day, and she realized she was glad. She was not certain she could have accepted, not after seeing Sherrod and being reminded of Law. Sherrod was every girl's dream of a husband . . . as in the fairy tales, tall, dark, and handsome and with the wealth to match. But Law—what was it about him that captured her thoughts? He was so self-contained, so sure of himself with a quiet strength that seemed to belie his lackadaisical approach to life.

She was not surprised to find Sherrod calling on her the next morning when she opened her door. "Catherine," he said, catching her hands in his, "I can't stand it with you here, so far away. I worry about you constantly. And then the sight of that officer—"

She touched her fingers to her lips. "Sssh," she said, stepping out of his reach. Outside the door a bewhiskered miner snored.

Sherrod flicked the old man an impatient grimace and sighed. "All right, Catherine, but say you'll come back with me for Christmas. It would mean so much to the children and Lucy."

"Dear Lord," Catherine breathed, "is it Christmas already?" The importance of time no longer held any significance where everything came *mañana* in Tucson's lazily moving society. She had even ceased wearing the small watch pinned to her dress. "I can't, Sherrod. There's the students."

He nodded grimly. "I suppose it's best." Then, in an outburst, "But God help me, I'm tired of doing what's best!"

He opened the door, and the street dust filtered in. Before he closed it, he half turned. "Catherine, will you marry that officer—Rankin?"

She hesitated while the dust settled on her skirts and suffocated her heart. "I don't know."

Chapter 14

CHRISTMAS of '64; how desolate and lonely a time in Tucson. Catherine put down her pen, wondering if she should worry her mother with such a confession. She nibbled at the pen's tip, then resumed her letter *With nine-tenths the population of Catholic persuasion, Christmas is not celebrated here until January 6, El Dia del Tres Reyes—the Day of the Three Kings. The other tenth spend this time in drunken revelry in the multitude of saloons and gambling establishments.*

Despite such a dreary description, please believe I am quite happy in this little outpost on the edge of the world. Here beneath the eternally sunny skies I believe I have found my niche in life. My health continues good. For the first time this year the Santa Catalinas had a very light drift of snow to mantle their peaks. Tonight I shall attend a New Year's Dance—a baile in one of the older Mexican homes; a very formal affair, I understand.

She finished the letter and, dipping the pen in the precious ink, affixed her signature. Her mother would most likely receive the letter as late as St. Patrick's Day, if she did receive it at all.

With so little time left to dress for the *baile*, Catherine hurriedly slipped into her one ball dress, which did not have the worn appearance of the rest of her clothes. The upper skirt was of white tulle over an underskirt of white silk with puffings crossed by bands of bright-lilac velvet. The bodice was cut very low off the shoulders with a pointed waist and a fall of lace to cover her cleavage and upper arms. The dress still smelled of camphor, and she sprinkled the remainder of an almost empty bottle of jasmine cologne over the material.

Wanting a change in her coiffure for the important evening, she left the center part but divested her chignon of its net; instead she pulled the hair atop her head into a mass of plaits, since curling the heavy tresses was nigh impossible.

Though she was going to the *baile* with Sam and Atanacia, she knew Jeremy would be there. And she knew he would ask her to marry him that night. All day she had been brooding over her decision. She told herself she did not have to accept his proposal. There were many more men now who called upon her—a Mexican *hacendado* from as far south as Magdalena, Mexico, and a merchant named Goldwater who came from as far north as Prescott.

Catherine paused in pulling the fringed silk shawl about her shoulders and put her fingertips to her temples. She closed her eyes to shut out the image of Law's passion-inflamed face hovering over hers. Could she lie in bed the rest of her life with one man . . . while her body ached for another?

Yes, yes, yes! Surely after weeks and months in the arms of her husband, she would forget Law. Tonight she would accept Jeremy's proposal.

The *baile* was held in the home of one of Tucson's first families, Don Esteban Ochoa, partner in the freighting firm of Tully & Ochoa. The large oblong parlor had been cleared of furnishings save the wooden benches about the walls. Surrounding a table were clustered men eager to sample the fiery Mexican brews that were little better than turpentine. For the señoritas and their duennas a blackberry cordial and homemade peach brandy were provided.

Both Mexican and American men who were the elite of Tucson society had been invited—Bill Oury, an ex-Texas Ranger, Hiram Stevens, a wealthy merchant, and Charles Poston and Ross Browne, who had just returned from an exploring expedition of Arizona and the state of Sonora in Mexico. Representing the Mexicans were Jesus Elias, Don Solano Leon, and Ignacio Pecheco—all born in Tucson and now naturalized citizens by virtue of the Gadsden Purchase.

Three mariachis costumed in fine, gaudy velvets were already tuning their guitar, fiddle, and trumpet when Catherine and the

Hugheses arrived. Like each previous guest who passed through the doorway, Catherine was pelted with *cascarones,* gaily colored eggshells filled with cologne or confetti.

"I hope you're prepared to dance all night," Sam told her, laughing as he brushed the confetti from his carrot-colored hair. He ushered her and Atanacia to an unoccupied bench, saying, "It's the men's one chance to hold an Anglo woman in their arms, and I assure you, Catherine, they will not pass it up."

"Or let you out the door until you've danced with *every hombre* here," Atanacia added.

Catherine barely had time to remove her shawl and smooth her lace gloves over her fingers before she was besieged for the next dance—what appeared to be a mixture of the waltz and polka, though her partner, a short, thin soldier, seemed to be doing a variation of the Pigeon Wing.

By the time the sweating musicians paused for potent refreshment, she collapsed on the bench, panting with the exertion of the dancing. "And it's only just beginning, not even midnight," Atanacia said and laughed.

"I'll never make it. My feet have been trampled by the cavalry and all their mounts." She wriggled her toes inside her blue broché silk slippers to see if there was any feeling left. But oh, it was such fun. Her years as a wallflower were laid to rest that evening, and she meant to enjoy every delicious moment as belle of the ball.

She looked up to find several cups thrust before her at once. From among the admiring masculine faces, she picked out Jeremy's and accepted the cup of brandy he offered. "I've missed your company," she said, making no pretense at the art of flirtation.

"Then let me have the next dance," he cajoled in a voice slightly slurred with *pulque,* fermented juice of the maguey cactus. "This is the first opportunity I've had to get near you."

Atanacia, looking lovely in black lace, slyly nudged Sam, and the giant took his cue and asked his wife to dance, leaving room for Jeremy to sit next to Catherine.

She fanned herself and sipped at the brandy, listening all the while as Jeremy told her of the patrol he had been sent on in the Santa Rita Mountains. His words were light and joking, but his eyes fastened on her face with adoration. Nervously she turned her gaze to the dance floor, where Sam and Atanacia danced with nimble feet to the ranchero song "Cuatro Milpas."

Suddenly Catherine's gaze focused on the extremely tall man who came into her field of vision and moved toward her, blotting out all else. Law! She was unaware she breathed the name aloud or of Jeremy's startled glance.

The sight of Law was like a blow to her windpipe. Her fan halted its lazy swishing. The brandy sloshed in her cup. She never expected to see Law again, especially moving among decent, civilized people. But there he was, standing before her, dressed in an all-black charro suit bordered with silver conchos. The thick yellow-gold curls framed his face in profusion, softening its angularities but not the sardonic smile.

"Miss Howard, I was sure you would have long since married by now," he said.

Oh, the nerve! Any reply she could formulate would be extremely embarrassing to her and Jeremy.

"How are you finding Tucson?" Law went on easily with a smirk of amusement creasing his face.

"I find it much to my liking," she said stiffly.

"And dancing?" He held out his hand, and she blanched at the scoundrel's presumptuousness.

"I've enjoyed the dancing very much this evening," she evaded.

"Good! Then you'll dance the next one with me?"

It was really more a statement than a question, and she was about to refuse. But Jeremy, hereto respectfully silent, said, "I believe she's promised the next dance to me."

Only then did Law acknowledge the man. *"Claramente,"* he said, reverting to Spanish. Even his stance altered, though she did not know how to describe the change; it was more of a Mexican caballero's lithe, lazy movement. "But the dance, lieutenant, is a Spanish bolero. Do you perhaps know the steps?

"Ahhh, I thought not," Law continued when Jeremy simultaneously shook his head and opened his mouth to protest. Then to Catherine, "It's time you learned the bolero if you plan to remain in our hospitable Hispanic climate."

Rather than make a scene, she nodded curtly. Her smile counseled patience from Jeremy as she handed him her cup, but his left hand went to the hilt of his saber even as he tossed down her cup's remaining brandy.

She sighed; mixing the brandy with the *pulque,* Jeremy would no doubt be sick before the evening was over and spoil the fiesta . . . if it was not spoiled already, she thought, looking up at the tall blond who led her out onto the floor. She herself felt a pleasant warmth from the brandy.

Only the Hispanics in the room danced now to the repetitious and relentless melody of the lone trumpet, and she hung back. But Law would not release her wrist, instead drawing her into the small circle of dancers. "The steps are not that difficult," he told her as he faced her. "Follow my movements—and remember, you are the temptress. You are dancing the bolero atop a table while the men gather to watch you."

The slow, steady cadence of the music, the mesmeric quality of Law's quiet, firm voice, could almost make her believe she was the temptress, the enchantress, as she tried to pantomime his movements. She, who had never danced before that night, was caught up in the music, forgetting all else, as she swayed and swirled. The music steadily increased in sound and tempo. Her silk gown flared above her ankles. Her arms entwined above her head. Now the guitar and fiddle joined in one long, gradual crescendo. The melody built inexorably, increasing the tension in the spectators.

But there were no spectators. There was only Law's passionate face before her. She danced for him.

The music crescendoed to an unbearable height to be broken by the instruments's sudden shift in key to an abrupt end. The tension in the room was so strong that a breathless silence reigned until applause and shouts of *Bravissimo!* erupted from the spectators.

Glancing about her, she realized the other dancers had at some point retired from the floor, leaving her and Law to finish the sensuous performance. Her hands shot up to her flushed face. About her bare shoulders tendrils of loose hair feathered. Why, she must look like a common streetwalker!

She turned to Law, and the fear that she had made a fool of herself seemed to be confirmed by the quiet anger she saw in the sand-brown eyes. What must he think of her, a woman who gave her kisses so easily? And now this! "You're a most unusual woman, Cate," he said, as he led her back to the others. But she detected nothing of a compliment in his statement.

Whatever disapproval Sam or Atanacia may have felt certainly did not show in their smiles and congratulatory words. Jeremy's gaze, but for the instant it crossed that of Law's, burned with a passion that startled Catherine. In fact, all the men wore that same fervent gaze as they continued to claim dances from her.

She fortified herself with several more cups of brandy to help her get through the rest of the long night. It appeared the revelers would dance as long as the musicians continued, which, she had been told, could well run into the breakfast hour. Her own strength was rapidly ebbing with the approaching dawn. So when Jeremy asked to escort her home, she acceded, not wanting to take Sam or Atanacia away from the *baile.*

Shades of orange and pink already illuminated the Rincon peaks when Jeremy and Catherine reached her *jacal.* "Catherine," he said thickly, catching her by her arm when she would have opened the door, "I won't be distracted from my purpose this time."

"Let's talk later," she said gently. "It's late—or rather, early."

She opened the door, and Jeremy's unsteady weight propelled them through the doorway. She recovered her balance, but Jeremy caught at the rickety table to keep from falling. "Jeremy, you really must go," she said, moving to help him. Her head ached miserably.

". . . just want the privi—right to take care of you," he mumbled. He unbuckled his belt with fumbling fingers, and the saber slid to the floor.

"Jeremy! You're not going to sleep here!"

He wavered toward her. "You're all 'lone, and it's . . . not right." His drink-fuzzed voice fell to a fervent whisper as his fingers clutched at her arms, accidentally tearing the lace sleeve. "You need someone, and I want it . . . it to be me."

She was frightened now. She knew Jeremy meant no harm, but the situation was getting out of control. Where was one of her "protectors" now that she needed help?—no doubt still celebrating the New Year. "Jeremy, get out!" Oh, why had she drunk so much? She was not handling this right at all.

At the fury in her voice, he took a backward step and squinched his eyes as if to focus. "It's that blond-haired Mexican you want, isn't it?" He lunged at her. "It's gonna be me . . . me," he mumbled as his arms wrapped about her in a bear hug.

She tried to wrench free. Jeremy wrestled with her, stepping on her gown. She heard the rip as the two of them fell. They rolled over and over on the dirt floor. A portion of her mind was chagrined at the thought of the white ball gown's being soiled. But another part of her mind was frantic with fear. His hands tore at the bodice. His cold, wet lips groped for her breasts. One hand pawed at her bunched skirts.

She shrieked, and his hand clapped over her mouth with smarting impact. With a violent shove, she shrugged loose and scrambled to her hands and knees. Her fingers touched cold metal. The saber! Her hand gripped the blade in mid-length. "No, Jeremy!" she gasped. She held the blade out before her, trying to warn him off. Still he half crawled, half lurched toward her. Then, incredibly, she knew not how, he fell upon the blade.

His gargled gasp echoed her own small one as the blade's edge sliced her own palm with the force of his fall. She crouched over the suddenly inert body. Tears coursing down her face, she screamed and screamed.

Chapter 15

THE cold February rain plip-plopped in the quagmire that had been Tucson's main street. All up and down Calle de la Guardia the buildings' *canales,* drainpipes, poured water from the flat roofs to add to the deluge that riddled the street.

Catherine could feel the mud weighting her skirts. She knew she should hurry on to Warner's store to make her purchases— purchases that could have been postponed to another day. But she had felt herself going crazy in her small adobe hut. Besides, its roof leaked so badly that she was not that much worse off, standing as she was in the drizzle.

With the rain falling about her, she watched the men—and a few women—who queued up before the mud-brick building across the street. Such activity was unheard of, especially during the siesta hour. A chunky young Mexican woman in braids passed by Catherine, heading toward the line, and Catherine called out to her *"Que pasa allá?"*

The woman explained to her that agents were enlisting colonists for the Arizona Colonizing Expedition to Mexico. "They go to settle Hermosillo, in Sonora," she finished and hurried over to take her place at the end of the line that now snaked past the Ciudad Cantina.

As if controlled by a puppeteer, Catherine's feet took her across the rain-sluiced street to halt behind the young woman. One by one the men in line turned to stare at Catherine as the word passed forward of the white woman waiting behind them.

She paid the incredulous stares no heed. Her bonnet's feather drooped above her brow despite the frilly parasol she carried, and the rain plastered strands of hair to her neck and cheeks like seaweed. Still, as the line moved tediously forward toward the narrow doorway, she remained in her place, politely refusing offers by some of the men to let her move ahead.

She was a cornered animal. Since New Year's Eve—the night she had accidentally killed Jeremy Rankin—she had little by little lost her students. Oh, even the *alcalde,* Aldrich, had condoned the killing, pointing out it was done in self-defense, thus saving her from the least of the punishments that could be brought against a murderer—a day at the whipping post. But that did not alter the attitude of the parents whose sons she taught. The number of her pupils dropped from twenty-three to eleven by midmonth. And by the first of February she had exactly four students left.

Sam and Atanacia had come to her defense, standing staunchly by her. "If the baby I carry was old enough, I would send him to your school," Atanacia told her the third day after Jeremy's death, when seven pupils were withdrawn.

Catherine had buried her face in her hands and wept for the first time since the incident. She wept for Jeremy . . . and herself. For her lost dreams of romance and excitement. She had never meant to take another's life. Just as she had thought she would never have been capable of giving herself out of wedlock. She, Catherine Howard, had too high moral standards! How low she had sunk!

Only the week before, Sam had tried to lend her money. She did not know who was more embarrassed, she or the red-bearded giant. She had, naturally, refused . . . as she had refused Sherrod's offer of assistance that had come by letter a few days earlier.

Now her funds were almost depleted. She could, of course, marry. There were still a few loyal suitors, like Lionel, who had offered to defend her if she was indicted.

She knew the answer was, as always, Law. How could she be happily married when each time she ran into him she felt the magnetism of sexual attraction?

But perhaps away from the sight of him she could forget. The state of Sonora across the international boundary would be as good a place as any to forget him. More important, many Confederate families were flocking to Mexico now that the Union seemed to be winning the war. In Hermosillo she could find employment . . . and maybe eventually a husband.

At last she reached the doorway and stepped inside the small, darkened room. To the right of a makeshift desk of crates sat a swarthy old Indian. After Catherine's pupils adjusted to the dark, she realized the old Indian was Loco. Those wrinkle-bound eyes never changed expression or betrayed that he recognized her. His gaze shifted from her to the mustachioed Mexican sitting behind the desk. Loco addressed the man, whom he called Tranquilino in a rapid-fire dialect of Spanish and Indian words that she had trouble following.

The Mexican looked at Catherine now. "You wish to emigrate to Mexico, señorita?" he asked in a gentle voice that did not quite hide his astonishment.

"Yes, of course. Are there any qualifications or conditions?"

Tranquilino looked to Loco. The old Indian shook his head in the slightest negative gesture. "I'm sorry, señorita," Tranquilino then replied, "but we really have no place in the emigrant train for . . . ladies. Later, you see, we will establish families. But, uhh—we mainly are signing up men who can shoot and fight for now. You understand, the Apaches and Yaquis are marauding Sonora, and it will at first be necessary to set up camps and build a fort. These sorts of things."

The young Mexican, hardly older than Law, talked to her in a very reasonable voice, but she did not want to be reasonable.

She wanted to leave Arizona. "You are taking other women," she pointed out, trying to keep her voice as rational.

"Sí, but there women are *lavanderas*—washwomen—and cooks. They can ride—and shoot, as well, if they have to. They are called—"

"*Soldaderas,*" she said. "Yes, I know the term." A camp follower. "But I can wash and cook and ride. And with practice I can learn to shoot a pistol."

Tranquilino made one last attempt. "But you do not speak the different dialects. It would be very difficult to—"

She stamped her mud-caked foot and pointed to the men lined up behind her. "Three-quarters of these men here don't speak Spanish, much less good English!" She whirled on Loco. "I have to go, Loco! I can't earn a living here—I can't support myself."

"But, señorita," Tranquilino interrupted, "this is a delicate subject, but there are many men who will wish to—to make the love," he finished lamely.

"I have killed a man." She enunciated each word clearly so there would be no mistake. "I can protect myself."

Tranquilino looked at Loco with a shrug.

"Maybe it is better this one goes," the old Indian counseled.

Tranquilino closed his eyes with a sigh. "*Bien,* señorita. If you'll put an X here—ahh, yes, I forgot, you are educated. Sign your name then. You'll need your own bedding and a change of clothing. Nothing more. You'll be assigned a wagon and duties on the morning we leave—February 14."

How auspicious! For the first time since New Year's Eve she smiled.

I know you must think I've taken leave of my senses, Margaret dear, but for the first time in my life I'm doing something really adventurous. Unlike my brief period as a tutor for the Godwins, where I had a roof over my head and a guarantee of food and salary, I have no such assurances to carry with me on the undertaking I am about. I know not what tomorrow may bring. And in a way, it is a most liberating feeling. Perhaps I have more of my father in me than you or mother realized.

I hope your next letter will bring better news of Mother's health. In any case, you will have to find work to make ends meet, and for this, I'm truly sorry.

My love to you and Mother.

She had one more letter to write before she left the next morning. To Don Francisco—to Sherrod, really. But there was so little she could write; only to thank the Godwins for giving her the opportunity to come to the territory and tell them she was emigrating to Hermosillo, Mexico. So little she knew about the adventure on which she was embarking.

She had already made her goodbyes to the Hugheses. Sam had come for her trunk that afternoon to store it until she could send for it. She and Atanacia had clung to each other, weeping, and Sam had given her a gruff peck on the cheek before the couple left.

For the last time Catherine prepared for bed. She did not know how long it would be before she experienced that luxury again. She heated the water in a kettle over the fire and poured it into the tarred wooden half-barrel Sam had fashioned for her. Afterward she donned the cotton night shift and braided her hair before putting on her nightcap. It was a ritual of civilization she might not know for a long time to come.

The fire was banked, the candles snuffed. She slid beneath the light woolen blanket, thinking she would not sleep that night with the excitement of leaving occupying her mind. And she did not, for scarcely less than an hour past midnight, as she rolled to yet another position, a sound like gunfire burst through the small house. She bolted upright in the bed, instantly realizing the sound was that of someone banging open the door.

Concurrent with the realization, a shadow loomed before her, filling the bedroom's doorway. "What the hell do you think you're doing?" a masculine voice snarled before she could scream.

"Law!" she breathed in relief, gathering the blanket up before her. Then angrily, "What do you think you're doing, breaking into my house in the middle of the night?"

In two strides his long legs carried him to her bedside. His large hands caught her about her arms and literally raised her from the bed. With her face on a level with his, she could smell the liquor on his breath. "You've been drinking," she said with disgust.

He began to shake her. *"No vayas con la expedición!"* Then, realizing he had slipped into Spanish, he dropped her back to the bed. "You are not going with the expedition," he said with a thick finality.

"Yes, I am," she told him as he turned his back on her and went to the bureau to light the candle. "And you can't stop me!"

The small light flickered and danced through the room, casting Law's giant shadow over her bed. He advanced on her. "Now you listen to me, Cate," he said in speech as articulate as a sober man's. "This is no pleasure trip. Danger and hunger and death will be—"

She shot up in the bed again. "I'm a grown woman, Lorenzo Davalos. I can handle myself."

"Is that why some Don Quixote is always sleeping outside your door?—for all the good it does you. The one outside now is dead drunk."

Her lips puckered in an impish smile. "I always forget that you're an educated man, Law."

He sighed and ran his fingers through the tousled butter-toasted hair. "There's a lot you forget, Cate." He pulled up the one chair in the room and swung it around backward, straddling the seat with his arms resting on its back. "Cate, I'm an agent for Juárez—and this is no colonization. It's a battalion I've raised to fight the French, who at this moment are knocking on Sonora's southern borders."

"You're not going to Hermosillo?" she asked, incredulous that her plans might be thwarted.

"It's only a stopover on the way to the Gulf, to Guaymas."

She frowned and chewed on her thumb, trying to assimilate what he was telling her. She knew, of course, that Napoleon III had put the Austrian duke Maxmilian on the Mexican throne as emperor—and that it had angered the Americans, who felt the French were violating the Monroe Doctrine. But with the Civil War raging in the United States, the Americans could do nothing about it.

Mexico and its own internal problems seemed so remote that she had never given the French intervention in Mexico's politics much thought. "I don't understand," she said slowly. "With your Mexican heritage, why all this pretense? Why don't you just cross the border and fight?"

"Because," he said impatiently, "the French have well-disciplined and well-armed troops. They're three to one over Juárez. They control three-quarters of Mexico, and they want Sonora now—mostly for its mines. And there's nothing to stop them from taking the state except various bands of guerrillas . . . men supporting Benito Juárez who need additional men and arms.

"And we can't get men and arms across the border to them without violating U.S. neutrality laws. But as emigrants who need to protect ourselves against Apaches and Yaquis marauding on both sides of the border"—he shrugged—"it's perfectly acceptable."

"So that's where you were off to all the time you pretended to be prospecting," she accused. "In San Francisco and those other places—"

"I was purchasing supplies and arms," he concluded, rising from the chair. "Now that you understand—"

"No, I don't understand!" She bounded to her feet to face the man, forgetting that her turgid nipples thrust against the thin cotton shift. Her head tilted back to meet his scowl of irritation. "I don't understand why I can't go. You need women; Tranquilino said so himself."

"But these women, the young ones, will serve the men's other needs. And these aren't the gentlemen—the Jeremys and Lionels and Sherrods—you're accustomed to, Cate." He paced the room with his hands clasped behind his back, sounding for all the world like a tirading teacher. "These men are trained killers, adventurers, mercenaries. Some of them wouldn't think twice about violating a woman."

She blanched but said defiantly, "I can take care of myself. Just let me go as far as Hermosillo with you. I'm sure I can find work among some of the Confederate families who have taken refuge there."

He whirled and faced her, hands on hips. "And if the French overrun the state?"

"As an American citizen I can claim neutrality," she pointed out coolly.

"Dammit, Cate, you can't go. It's too—"

"Law, I've got to go!" she pleaded. "I've no money left to support myself and nowhere else to go."

"Why can't you just be satisfied with getting married like the well-brought-up young woman you are? Wasn't that what you told me you wanted? I'd imagined by now that Jeremy—"

"Jeremy's dead," she said in a monotone. "I killed him."

Law's head jerked up. "You what?"

"The night of the New Year's Eve *baile*—he tried to . . . to rape me. I accidentally stabbed him with his saber." Just saying it scrambled chills up her spine and popped goose bumps on her her flesh.

"Santa María de Jesus!" Law breathed. "I left that night for Santa Fe and just got back. That must've been what Loco was trying to finish telling me when I stormed over here."

Sensing her advantage, she pressed, "Then you'll let me go?"

He rubbed his beard-stubbled jaw. "Somehow, Cate, you manage to get around me."

She threw her arms about his waist. "Oh, Law, thank you!"

Immediately he disengaged her arms. "I'm warning you now, don't you come near me, Cate. After you, I've had enough of virgins to last me a lifetime. Give me a warm, willing woman and a jug of wine and you can forget the promises of heaven."

He turned to go, but at the doorway he looked over his shoulder. "That nightcap—it's the God-awfullest thing I've ever laid my eyes on. Be sure to take it with you—it'll keep my men away." He crimped a half smile. "And save their lives."

Chapter 16

CATHERINE surveyed the plaza by dawn's shell-pink light. Men of all ages and nationalities were everywhere, on horseback and on foot, dressed in the remnants of Union blues and Confederate grays, in serapes and tattered blue-tail coats. Some of the Mexicans wore no shoes. Their feet were as tough and gnarled as the bark of an old tree. The men were armed to the teeth with sabers, unwieldy blunderbusses, navy revolvers, derringers, horse pistols, and knives. A motlier bunch she had never seen.

She told herself that the journey would be no worse than that last month she had spent traveling with Governor Goodwin and the New Mexico soldiers. But this time there were no carriages or comfortable ambulances, just the commissary train, consisting of nine twelve-mule wagons loaded with forage, arms, kegs of ammunition, and camp equipment. Behind the wagons, the pack mules stood drowsily beneath their weighted loads.

That early in the morning, before the desert sun rose, the air was sharp. Catherine buttoned her riding jacket about her and picked up her bundled belongings. Plagued by doubts, she nevertheless crossed the plaza to where Tranquilino stood before the line of pack mules, pad and pen in hand. She would not turn back now.

Law's lieutenant looked up, his gaze resting on the young woman standing before him, her small head held high. Not a beautiful woman, but something about her caught the eye—a spirited woman that would make a man feel like a man. Everyone knew she had worked for the Godwins as a tutor, and thought she had murdered a man. Still, that did not explain why Lorenzo shied like a nervous stallion at the mere mention of her name.

"I had hoped you would change your mind," Tranquilino told the woman now.

Catherine looked past him to see Law riding toward them. Like the other men, he was heavily armed—the brace of pistols at his hips and the knife sheathed at his waist. Beneath the floppy sombrero his eyes were hidden, but his mouth was a rigid line in the jutting jaw. "Apparently you're not the only one," she told Tranquilino dryly.

Law reined in the horse. "These other women," he began without preamble, pointing to the dozen or so women wrapped in woolen rebozos who were scattered about the plaza, "they're seasoned *soldaderas*—and they're fighting for something they believe in. Neither of which applies to you, Cate."

So, he had had time to repent of his leniency. She planted her fists on her hips. "You can't tell me three-quarters of the men here volunteered because they believe in the Juárez cause."

"No, they believe in rape and murder and plunder."

Tranquilino turned away in embarrassment, presumably to check a supply wagon.

"I'll leave you behind at the nearest pueblo if you can't keep up with the expedition," Law continued.

"You'd like that, wouldn't you?" she asked the man slouched in the saddle.

"There's nothing I'd like better."

Her lips curled upward. "Why, Law Davalos, I think you're afraid of me!"

"You bet your grammar book I am. There's nothing worse than a woman hell-bent on marriage."

"Ohhh!"

He straightened in the saddle. A few men turned around to stare. "I'm sorry, Cate," he said in a lower voice. "But it just goes to prove I'm right. You don't belong on this expedition. We're not gentlemen, none of us. Go back to the States, Cate."

She shook her quirt up at him. "I'm going into Mexico with you, you hear me? After we reach Hermosillo, you're rid of me—and, thank God, I'm rid of you, you—you bastard!"

Well, there was another first, she thought ruefully as Law wheeled his sorrel away to disappear among the milling soldiers of fortune. It was the first time she had ever used such unladylike language. Her mother would have washed her mouth out with lye soap, and Margaret—her dear sister would have swooned had she heard her.

The situation became progressively worse when Catherine realized she would not have her own mount but would have to ride in one of the wagons like the rest of the women. Buckle up, old girl, she told herself as she crossed to the wagon to which Tranquilino had assigned her. You're as tough as the next woman.

She passed an old woman smoking a cheroot as she strapped a canvas tarpaulin over a pack mule's saddlebag. Well, maybe not quite as tough.

Catherine's day brightened considerably when she reached her wagon and found that Loco was its muleskinner. "Lorenzo cannot lose you?" he asked with a sly wink.

She laughed. "No. And you, either?"

The old Indian's shaggy white hair swayed about his mummified face as he shook his head. "No, Lorenzo cannot lose me. I fed him and played with him when he was a baby. And I shall no doubt bury him with this madness of his, this foolish *patriota.*"

By midmorning the Arizona Colonizing Expedition had left behind the crumbling presidio walls of the Old Pueblo and the desert floor and was making its way south, gradually ascending the Santa Cruz Valley. They passed the San Xavier Mission—a large white lime-plastered edifice with bell towers and domes that dominated the emptiness around it. It was a splendid monument to civilization—the last that Catherine would see for some time; for upon leaving the mission behind, the expedition passed ranch after ranch that had been devastated by the Indians.

No white man's life was secure beyond Tucson's twelve-foot-high walls. Between San Xavier and Tubac the road was marked with the graves of unfortunate settlers. Wheat fields with torn-down fences; houses burned, the walls lying in rubble. A death-like silence fell on the expedition as it moved through the Santa Cruz Valley, a land of waist-high winter grass and scrub-covered hills that were strangely calm and beautiful in their desolation.

To the left rose the nine-thousand-foot peaks of the Santa Rita range—cold, piny, spectacular in the snappy, sunny wake of winter. To the right, the shoulders of the Tumacacori and Atascoca hills. And the mountains way ahead to the left, Loco told her, were the high and rugged Mexican Sierra Madres that picked up at the ragged end of the Rockies.

Law called camp that evening at the deserted Rhodes ranch, which was knee-deep with weeds and grass. All around, adobe walls crumbled to ruin with fallen-in roofs. Doors and windows had been carried away by Mexican vandals when the garrison at Fort Buchanan had departed at the beginning of the Civil War.

Catherine fell easily into working with Filomena, a pretty woman of Catherine's age whose husband had been working Sylvester Mowery's Patagonia mine four years earlier when he and three others were ambushed by Cochise's Apaches. The woman, with her sloping eyes and bright carmine lips, obviously could have had many men from which to choose a second husband. Yet she had elected to keep her widow's status.

Together the two women assisted Loco in the cooking. Elsewhere, under Law's direction, other campfires sprang up in the twilight. As Catherine stirred the coarse cornmeal and flour in a chipped earthenware dish, she studied Law, easily detecting him from the others by his extraordinary height.

As much as she hated admitting it, she had underestimated the man, labeled him an aimless rogue; yet now he moved among the men with purposeful strides and occasional words of camaraderie. The men seemed to accept his leadership easily, though at twenty-two he was much younger than most of them.

Imagine, an agent for Juárez! She wondered how much Juárez was paying him. She remembered Jeremy's telling her that General Custer had been offered by Carvajao, Juárez's representative in the United States, the astronomical sum of sixteen thousand dollars in gold to command the Mexican forces.

More than thirty men served themselves from Loco's campfire, among them Tranquilino and Law, who was off again as soon as his tin plate had emptied. Later one of the men broke out a Jew's harp, and song and laughter soon dispelled the atmosphere of gloom about the deserted ranch. As the fires flickered lower, the men began to turn in. Catherine and Filomena laid out their bedrolls inside a crumbling adobe hut. The fractured walls smelled strongly of urine, but at least the partially thatched roof covered them from any sudden showers.

Camp broke with the dawn, and the brigade prepared for the march again with all the noise accompanying such an expedition. The mules brayed as they were repacked for the trek, and the horses whinnied and neighed as tin cups and canteens and haversacks of hardtack clattered and bobbed on their flanks. Law rode down the line of men, stopping to speak or point out something before he came to a halt next to the wagon she rode in with Loco.

She still half expected him to tell her to fall out of line, but his glance merely flickered over her attire—the durable riding habit and sturdy Wellington boots that she had heretofore deemed quite serviceable. "At least you thought to wear a hat," he said, casting a derisive glance at the tall black hat and veil trailing behind like some knightly banner.

With narrowed eyes she watched him ride away and vowed she would make him eat his words about old maids. Before he dumped her in Hermosillo she would . . . what? Oh, the injustice in being a woman!

The journey proceeded smoothly, passing near the abandoned

ruins of the royal presidio of Tubac, its mud-brick walls exposed by the peeling pale-cream stucco plaster. Below Tubac the Santa Cruz River bent eastward, meandering through hill country that jutted between two stretches of forbidding desert. From there the river began its gradual climb to the Pajarito Mountains, originally called Pimería Alta (the Pima Indian highlands) by the Spanish explorers.

Law called a halt in the Nogales Pass, named for the walnut trees nurtured there. It was a small, chiseled canyon marked by an unshapely pile of stones which was a monument erected by Colonel Emory in 1855 after the Gadsden Purchase set the new boundary.

A festive atmosphere settled on the camp as the women began to prepare the dinner. Singing could be heard at every fire, and from somewhere floated the strum of a guitar. Filomena explained that the men were jubilant because they had passed from under the authority of the United States. "These men—not all of them fight for patriotism." Her hand swept the camp of wagons and pup tents with contempt. "Some fight for the money and mostly the land that Juárez has promised them when the French are driven from Mexico."

Catherine noticed she said "when." Filomena and the others seemed so positive, already celebrating as if a battle had been fought and won.

When it came time to serve the men from the kettle of stew, an American with a cadaverous face presented himself before Catherine, plate in hand. He said nothing as she ladled out the brown juice and bits of meat, but she could feel his colorless eyes sliding over her. The man reminded her of a slug, and she shivered, relieved when he had moved on and someone else took his place.

Each of the bearded and dusty men who appeared before her and Filomena looked over the two women with speculative gazes, yet the one American had managed to disconcert Catherine. There was something unhealthy about him that hung around him like a funeral wreath. She voiced her opinion of him to Filomena as the two women settled against a wagon wheel to eat.

"Do not let the looks these men give worry you. The soldiers, like this Slovel man you speak of, they are only waiting to see which man the unattached women will choose. It is the way of nature, no?"

"And you, have you picked a man?" Catherine asked, somewhat shocked that such a delicate matter was carried out so simply and unashamedly.

Filomena smiled knowingly. "Sí, but he does not know it yet."

After the two women cleaned and put away the utensils, Filomena disappeared toward one of the larger campfires. Catherine's eyes searched among the men and women for a tall figure, certain that the pretty woman had gone to seek out Law.

"You're the little lady teacher, aren't you?" a gravelly voice asked at Catherine's side. Startled, her glance richocheted from the far campfire upward to the American, Slovel, who stood next to her, seeming to have slid out of the darkness.

She shrugged and turned from him to set the cast-iron skillet in the mess chest. "I suppose I am the woman to whom you are referring," she said with a studied casualness. She hoped by ignoring the man she would put him off, but he closed in on her.

"They say you don't have a man in Tucson to protect you— that you came along with us to find one."

She turned on the man. "What they say is wrong," she said coldly. "Did they also tell you I killed the last man who tried to 'protect' me?"

"Maybe he wasn't the right man," Slovel said. He caught her wrist and pulled her to him. "You gotta have a man, missy."

"Don't touch me," she gritted, trying not to show her uneasiness. Her hands came up to shove him away.

Slovel caught them in one big paw and held her against him, a perplexed frown creasing his sloping forehead. "I'll give you a chance to make up your mind, but I'm letting you know I mean to be the man. I'm a hell of a lot more than those other buggers. You'll be safe with me, missy."

"The woman does not need your protection." Loco crossed into the light of the campfire and Catherine's line of vision. Under one arm he carried his bedroll, and in his hand he held the machete he used in cooking.

Slovel looked at the old man incredulously. "You'd protect her!" He laughed. "She'd choose you!"

"Let the woman go," Loco said, unperturbed. "She is Lorenzo's woman."

"Then why isn't she with him now?" Slovel challenged, still holding her.

Loco shrugged his bony shoulders. "Lorenzo is stationing the sentinels, perhaps. I only know he will come for her."

The American watched the old Indian innocently finger the long, wide blade of the machete, then his lifeless eyes slithered back to her. "Is the old man telling the truth?"

"Yes—yes," she whispered, wishing his cold hands would release her.

"For your sake, missy, I hope you're right." Only then did he turn her loose and brush past Loco as he glided toward the larger campfire.

"Thank you, Loco," she said, closing her eyes with a deep sigh.

The old Indian nodded, and she retreated beneath the wagon to prepare her bedroll. The day had begun so gloriously, and now she could only huddle under the wagon uneasily as the merrymaking continued at the far campfire. It wasn't just the encounter with Slovel that made her uneasy. It was Law.

She knew he would be irritated that she had already provoked discord in the camp, as he had warned her would happen. She did not really think he would leave her behind, for it wouldn't solve the problem. There would be men ready to fight over keeping her with them.

With that thought, that her only safety lay in seeking Law's protection, she laid her head on her drawn-up knees in despair.

Chapter 17

INSTANTLY Catherine was awake. Something hovered over her. She opened her mouth, and a hand clamped down on her lips to silence her scream. "Sssh," Law warned.

Her tense body eased with a fractional movement, and he withdrew his hand. "You've gone and gotten yourself in a hell of a lot of trouble, Cate," he hissed.

"It wasn't my fault," she whispered hotly. "That man Slovel insisted I accept him as my protector or whatever you call it, and there was nothing else to do but go along with Loco's claim that I belonged to you."

His hand gripped her jaw. "Dammit, I warned you what would happen if you came around me again."

"But it's not like that time under the Joshua tree, when I wanted—I wanted you to kiss me." A half-lie . . . or else why was her own body responding to the pressure of the one that partially covered hers?

"The hell it's not! We're supposed to be acting like lovers. And Cate, I'll tell you now, as much as you want to go to the marriage bed a virgin, I won't promise you any such celibacy on my part."

Every so often he would let his education show in a slip of his vocabulary, catching her off guard, and she would have to remind herself she was not dealing with an illiterate oaf. "If you would just sleep beneath the wagon with me. We wouldn't have to—touch."

He rolled from her with a grunt of disgust. *"Ejoli,* Madonna!" he swore. He threw one arm across his forehead. "For your sake—and my sanity—we'd better not be delayed in reaching Hermosillo."

After the warmth of his body on hers, the sudden coolness of the night air enveloping her was like a dousing of cold water, and she huddled deeper into her blankets, listening to the cadence of his steady breathing only inches away and wishing morning would hurry. When dawn did arrive, she awoke to find that he was already gone.

She fell into packing and preparing for departure as if she were a veteran *soldadera* now, although her riding habit still set her apart from the other women. Most of the women rode in the front of the supply wagons. Catherine's wagon contained tinned jellies, coffee, highly salted and smoked bacon, salt pork, molasses, rice, and dried fruit and other delicacies. Filomena's was packed with British Enfield muskets, new French artillery pieces, and whole bushels of gun caps. Another wagon might contain medical supplies, and so on. A few women rode burros, and every so often one would get out of a wagon and walk, tired of sitting.

At first the journey progressed smoothly as the rutted wagon road began the slow descent to the drainage of the Magdalena River, a full day's travel away. The land rippled with lanky grasses and was studded with occasional thickets. Then it gradually turned itself into rounded hills, baked and dusty and bristling with ocotillo, like mounds of dried sticks.

After a while the hills, peppered now with oak, hunched higher and rolled away from the road like tidal waves. And it was at this point, midday, that Catherine was quite willing to exchange her heavy riding habit and top hat for a calico skirt and loose cotton blouse and, dear Lord, her hard boots for sandals. Perspiration soaked her clothes and filled her boots so that her feet itched. How much longer to Hermosillo—seven or eight days, Filomena said?

Like the previous day, Law remained at the head of the brigade, and Catherine, who did not see him until camp was made that night at a rancho favorable to the Juarista cause, did not know whether to be relieved or anxious, for the last thing she wanted was Slovel to challenge Law's lack of interest.

The ranchero's wife and her daughter and daughter-in-law, who were both plump with pregnancy, came out to welcome the brigade as it struggled through the hacienda gates late that afternoon. The ranchero women directed discreet looks at the American woman as Catherine rode by with the *soldaderas*.

As customary, the phrase *Mi casa es su casa* was passed among the women. To Catherine's delight the use of a tub and soap and water were offered for the women who wished to bathe. Even the promise of a festive banquet of food did not sound as good to her as a tub of hot water.

Once again there was celebrating. Servants scurried to bank tables of food set beneath ramadas. *Aguardiente* and three bottles of Kentucky sour mash, provided by an ex-Confederate, flowed freely. Though Catherine did not have to work that evening and was thus free of waiting on the men—Slovel, in particular—she stayed close to Loco, who remained apart from the others as usual.

From a seat on a stone water well she and Loco watched the peones perform their native dances. There was one which Filomena danced with another Mexican using the sombrero, which had to be as large as the wheel of a Mexican *carreta*. Was the pretty young widow dancing for Law? Catherine wondered as her own gaze sought out the honey-colored blond head.

Easily found among the dark, shorter Mexicans, he stood with Tranquilino. The two men seemed to be in serious discussion with the *hacendado,* Don Yñigo, a short, heavyset man with a huge handlebar mustache. Law hunkered on one knee, and the other two joined him. They only half watched the dancing, as one or the other of them took turns marking figures in the dirt with a twig.

Her gaze returned to Filomena, who had finished her dancing with wildly clapping hands and stamping feet and swirling skirts. She stood now, with applause and shouts demonstrating the men's acclaim. A fine film of perspiration covered her olive-complected face. She smiled her appreciation before moving off toward the three men, who now watched with various smiles of approval.

"You'd never know there was a war being waged, for all the continual celebrating," Catherine told Loco in a cynical voice.

The old Indian, who sat with his back to the well, his legs crossed beneath him, said, "It helps the Mexicans forget that the French have sworn death and dishonor to the wives and daughters of those who oppose them."

She had heard of Apache cruelty, but she could not suppose such a civilized nation as the French could be so brutal and inhumane. Yet had not many such incidents been perpetrated by both the Confederates and the Unionists on innocent American women and children?

Even as she watched Filomena laughing with Law and Tranquilino and the *hacendado,* her hands on her hips, her head thrown back to reveal the lovely line of her throat, Catherine was uncomfortably aware of being watched herself. Her gaze shifted back to the firelight and the soldiers. Without finding Slovel's face from among the men gathered there, she nevertheless knew he watched her.

Still, she felt safe enough with all the people about her to take advantage of the offer of a bath made by the ranchero's wife. Catherine made her way across the crowded courtyard and located the ranchero's daughter-in-law. The pregnant young woman expressed delight in being able to accommodate Catherine. "Ahh, *sí,"* she said. "It is not so many *norteamericanos* who pass through our gates—and for us to offer our home to a *norte-americana,* a woman, it is our pleasure."

With her hands folded across her great belly, the young Mexican woman, waddling, led Catherine to what must have been a bedroom though there were no beds, only *petates,* straw mats. The tub was little more than a watering trough, hand-carved, but for Catherine, after three days of dust and dirt and grease, it could have equaled the famed marbled bath of Maximilian's wife, the Empress Carlota, at Chapultepec Castle in Mexico City.

An ancient Indian woman materialized through the curtained doorway to attend Catherine. Her gnarled fingers were in the midst of unbuttoning the myriad rows of buttons at the back of Catherine's cambric blouse when the curtain swished behind them. Both women turned, and Catherine's breath hissed in outrage at Slovel, who stood in the doorway. His pale eyes slid down her like slime. "Get out!" she gritted.

"Vayate," he told the Indian woman with the sibilant noise of a viper and a jerk of his head.

The old woman glanced at Catherine with fear in her rheumy eyes before she edged toward the curtained doorway. Slovel stepped aside and let the curtain drop in place when the woman had gone. *"El Capitán* does not seem to have so much interest in you after all," he said as he slowly advanced on Catherine.

She clutched the blouse that now hung loosely about her shoulders. Fear knotted her insides. The man could attack her and with all the noise outside no one would hear. Dear Lord, was it her fate to attract that type of man?

The hulking ghoul ripped the blouse from her grasp and caught her against him. A repugnant odor assaulted her, not just the mescal and sweat but the fetid smell of decay. Now stark fear galvanized her. She twisted against the grimy hands that held her, thrashing her head as the wet mouth slid across hers like a suction cup.

"Slovel!"

Still holding her, the man whipped around. She saw Law in the doorway, behind him the old Indian woman. Slovel's hand dropped for the long pistol at his hip with a rapidity Catherine would not have believed. Yet Law must have been quicker, for even with the burst of gunfire Law managed to at once dodge to his left and grab the candle from the wall sconce. He drove the molten mass into Slovel's face. Sudden darkness blanketed the room. The heavy silence was lanced by a shriek of pain.

The two men rolled, snarling and struggling like two catamounts. In the darkness she could barely make the two men out, but just the sound of the brutal beating—of one surely pummeling the other to unconsciousness—made her sick to her stomach. A light flared, and Tranquilino stood in the doorway, candle in hand. Behind him were Don Yñigo and a crowd of brigands and peones.

Law staggered to his feet above an inert Slovel. The man lay with Law's knife buried between his ribs. Blood trickled from a corner of Law's mouth, and he wiped it away with the back of his hand before he snapped something to Tranquilino that Catherine did not catch. Then he turned on her. She expected to see bitter anger written on his face, but his eyes mirrored only weariness. "Are you all right?"

Her tongue acted as if it were paralyzed. She nodded her head. He picked up her blouse and held it out to her, shielding her from the curious spectators at the doorway. The people began to disperse, the voices fading off into the courtyard. Her hands fumbled with the buttons at her back, and he stepped around behind her, his fingers working deftly with the small buttons.

"It's over with," he said, as she began to tremble violently. He pulled her against him, and she let him support her, the back of her head limply lying against his chest.

"I didn't like him . . ." Her teeth were chattering. "But I didn't want him dead, Law." Her voice rose an octave. "I never wanted anyone dead, not Jeremy, not anyone!"

Law's lips brushed the vein that beat at her temple like a live telegraph wire. "Hush, Cate. I didn't want him dead either. If nothing else, it doesn't set a good example—two men fighting over a woman. And . . . I don't like killing. I never have." A sigh escaped him. "But somehow it seems to be a part of the life I've chosen."

She turned to face him. "You don't have to choose this kind of life, Law." She clutched at his leather vest. For some reason the thought of him going into battle, risking his life time and again— the thought of him lying dead like the man at their feet—was unbearable. "You could make a life for yourself at Cristo Rey. It's as much yours as it is Sherrod's."

For a brief second lights flared in the depths of the toast-colored eyes, then it was as if shades were pulled over the pupils. One brow arched. "Where's your loyalty to Cristo Rey, Cate?"

She wrenched away, hating the mockery that quirked his lips. Fist on her hips, she glared up at him. "It's not a question of loyalty. It's a question of your life!"

"Just a minute," he said, catching her forearm as she pivoted toward the door. "There are a hundred and twenty other men out there who would willingly take Slovel's place. No matter how much you want to share your bed with your husband first, it's going to have to be me until we reach Hermosillo.

"I know, I know," he said, holding up a palm to forestall her protest, "I'm a worthless scoundrel. But I'm just scoundrel enough to dislike bedding a woman who's got marriage written across her forehead like Cain's mark, so you're safe enough with me, God only knows. Your determination's enough to dampen even a lecher's lust, Cate."

She jerked her arm away. "And you'd be the last man on God's green earth I'd marry, Law Davalos, so *you're* safe enough from me!"

He laughed. "I knew we'd get along famously!" He swatted her on the buttocks. "Let's go bed down."

Chapter 18

AT the nebulous gray of predawn Catherine awoke in the rancho's stables with the sour memory of Slovel's death the night before. She found herself still enfolded in Law's arms, her back against the shielding width of his chest. As if he sensed that she was awake, though she had not moved, his lips nuzzled the hollow behind her earlobe. His mustache tickled, but it was the knot in her belly his kiss aroused that made her shiver.

"You said you liked my kisses," he reminded her in a husky whisper.

She would have been anxious about what could follow but for the note of playfulness in his lazy voice. "Yes," she agreed, squirming away, "but I also told you I didn't want you to kiss me again."

"You say a lot of things I don't think you mean." He sat up, resting one elbow on a bent knee. Chewing on a piece of straw, he watched her as she knelt, straightening her rumpled skirt and brushing the hay from her blouse and hair. "You want a husband. But why did you come out here to find one—to the territory? You're a damned good-looking woman, Cate. You've fine lines that'll weather age well. Surely all the Yankee males aren't that blind."

She smiled wryly. "I take that as a compliment, coming from you, Law—the lines that weather well." She chuckled then. "Oh, that's priceless." She smoothed the wisps of hair back into a knot, rearranging her hairpins to hold the heavy mass. "I told you. I came for adventure."

"Adventure!" He grunted. "Well, you've sure got it now, tramping along with a mercenary army, camping out in open fields. My God, Cate, I must have been out of my mind to agree to let you come along!"

He sprang lithely to his feet, and for a fearful moment she thought he meant to leave her there at the rancho. But he only took her hand and pulled her to her feet. "Well, if you're set on this adventuring, you might as well do it in style."

She trailed behind him as he strode across the courtyard. Somewhere a cock crowed. She picked her way among the recumbent men who stirred with the first shafts of sunlight. A mangy dog nipped at her heels, and she hurried to catch up with Law, who leaned now against an adobe corral where a herd of maybe fifteen horses pranced and snorted in the brisk morning air, their breath steaming. "I'm buying them from Don Yñigo for a *remuda*—replacement horses for the expedition. Pick yourself one."

She grinned up into the rawhide countenance. "If you think I'm going to say demurely that nice women don't accept gifts, you're wrong." She feigned a theatrical grimace. "One more day riding in the cramped wagon, and I think I would almost settle for walking."

"Then make your choice, Cate." He chuckled. Then he added, "But don't consider this gesture that of a courting man."

She settled on a steely blue mustang stud, a descendant of the Arab-Barb horses bred in Spain and brought into the Southwest by Coronado's conquistadores in 1540. It was a superbly built steed with a deep broad chest, small ears, and a silver mane and tail.

The mustang, Sonora (Catherine thought the name most appropriate for the animal's unfettered spirit), was indeed a big improvement over Loco's wagon. Catherine cantered along now in front of the wagons, thereby escaping much of the dust thrown up, but not too far ahead to mingle with the advance guard of soldiers. With the threat of Slovel eradicated, she was able to relax and enjoy herself. And for some reason, she could not pinpoint why, she was content—no, even happy—for the first time in what seemed like years.

Perhaps it was the adventurer in her. But she felt so alive—the air there, unpolluted by civilization, was invigorating; the views, breathtaking colors shading narrow green valleys and orange-red canyons and blue-purple mountains; the people, for the most part men and women enjoying the adventure as much as she, laughing in the day and dancing and singing by the campfires at night. It was almost impossible to conceive that these same people would leave her at Hermosillo and continue on to face possible death, to inflict certain death to others.

It was difficult to think the roguishly likable Law capable of destroying another human being, but she had witnessed his quick, efficient method of killing. The hands had wielded the knife proficiently, just as proficiently as they dealt the horsehide cards in the poker game that broke out that evening after camp was called.

From her bedroll spread beneath the wagon she watched those slender brown hands riffle through the cards with consummate skill. Visions of those hands making love to her arose to pique her imagination. She remembered the way the fingers had slipped sensuously through her hair the night of San Juan de Bautista and the afternoon beneath the Joshua tree when for a brief moment one brown hand had cupped her breast. Her heart had slammed against her ribcage with the memory of the unexpected pleasure he had engendered.

Did those same brown hands make love to some woman in camp each night before he finally came to her much later? Perhaps the very seductive Filomena? The idea perturbed Catherine. With a huffy tug at her blankets, she rolled over in her bedroll, determined to sleep. When at last Law came to her, pulling her within the curve of his long frame, she drowsily wished he would tease her with kisses as he had done that morning.

Yet morning light brought only a vague memory of his warmth and nothing more. The blankets beside her were empty. At a far campfire he squatted, with Tranquilino, drinking a cup of coffee. With an inward sigh she retrieved Law's blankets and rolled them with hers in the tight bundle that would fit behind a saddle. She reflected ruefully that she had become an adept *soldadera* in all ways but one, and that she would not be.

The creek that trickled through the camp provided only enough water to fill the canteens and water the animals, and she had to be content with washing her face. How dirty and sweaty she felt. She sorely regretted the bath she had missed at the rancho. She hoped the expedition would reach the villa of Magdalena that evening. A bed and a bath. How splendid they sounded!

As it turned out, Law gave orders for the brigade to camp outside the villa. He and Tranquilino intended to scout the village alone first. While there was some grumbling from the men, who were anxious to make forays on the cantinas and sample the delights of the dark-eyed women, the camp was grudgingly pitched on a broad plateau cut by the Río de Los Alisos.

Catherine knew she could have performed a meager sort of ablution at the river, but she had so been looking forward to the hot bath that she gathered her courage and approached Law. Crouched beneath a shady sycamore tree, he was studying a wrinkled map with Tranquilino and two Americans. She stood off to one side, waiting for the discussion to end. At last, the four men rose and exchanged a few words more before separating.

Then, though his back had been to her, Law rotated and crossed the intervening yards toward her, as if he had known all along of her presence. He halted before her and hooked his thumbs in his belt. "You wanted something, Cate?"

The frown on his face unsettled her. Did he resent her disruption? "I want to go into Magdalena with you. I want to take a bath, a real bath, Law." She felt so strange, petitioning him for such a favor. Perhaps it was because he seemed a stranger to her, no longer the lazy, aimless stepson of Don Francisco but the fierce leader of mercenaries.

"Do you realize French agents may be there?" he asked impatiently. "That they might decide to shoot first and ask questions later?"

"All the more reason why you should take me," she pointed out. "With my obviously Anglo looks and your fairness, we'd be taken as an American husband and wife. Who would question us?"

She waited while he considered. "All right, get your horse. And Cate—"

She turned around. "Yes?"

He smiled. "Don't get any ideas about the husband-and-wife act."

She squinched her eyes at him and stalked away, his soft laughter following her.

La Villa de Magdalena was a picturesque villa situated on the Río Concepción where the river broke into the open Sonoran desert. Magdalena was famous now, for Padre Kino, the missionary explorer who had proved that California was not actually an island, as the Spanish had believed, was buried there.

The houses, chiefly of adobe, though Catherine did note some of brick, were all stuccoed and whitewashed. Many were colored yellow. They were strung out here and there and, closer to the plaza, grouped in clusters. She half expected Law to make for the nearest cantina, but he halted his sorrel before a *tienda*. The small store appeared empty but for the flies that swarmed about the beef strung from the timbers outside.

He looped his reins about the hitching post and came around to her side. "I'll only be a few minutes," he said, looking up at her. "Try to keep your mouth shut. Don't speak to anyone. Got it?"

"Got it." She frowned, annoyed by his authoritative command. Five years ago she could have been in a classroom rapping the scoundrel's knuckles with a ruler.

Looking around at the villa's indolence—the men who dozed on benches beneath the porticos, the lean flea-bitten curs that slunk through the sun-baked streets—she felt her hopes sink that she would find a place to rent a bathtub. True, Tucson was a slightly primitive pueblo without the Union's military depot to lend it an American flavor. But the Villa de Magdalena looked even less civilized than Tucson, if that were possible.

When Law came out of the *tienda,* his face set in stern lines, she knew there would be no bath. "What is it?"

He swung up into the saddle and looked across at her. "The French—under a Colonel Garnier—took Hermosillo the day before yesterday, Cate. Even now Governor Pesquiera and our republican troops are retreating to the capital, Ures."

A cold sweat broke out on her temples. "What will this mean?"

For the first time the lazy drawl was clipped. "It means my men will now assume guerrilla warfare tactics. It means we'll go into the mountains surrounding Ures. It means we can't take you into Hermosillo."

"I'll go by myself. I'll explain—"

"*Bastada!* Enough! Garcia—the storekeeper—his niece, not even yet thirteen, was raped, her mother and father murdered. The Frenchman, Colonel Garnier, is sparing no one who supports the Juaristas. Do you think the Frenchmen will spare you? To them a woman is a woman. It doesn't matter her nationality."

The sun was beating down on her, but her skin crawled with chill bumps as she considered her alternative—traveling back to Tucson alone. And that was out of the question. A woman alone crossing the countryside was exposed to as many dangers as she was riding into a besieged city.

Her gaze locked with Law's before she hung her head, beaten. "Don't say anything," she whispered. "I know I let myself in for this."

"Let's go back to camp," he said. A muscle flexed in his cheek as he wheeled the horse around.

The expedition's festive spirit evaporated when Law returned with the news. At once preparations began for battle. Beside the campfires that night were no card games or drinking. Men cleaned their guns, sharpened their knives. The women talked in low, concerned whispers.

Filomena, pounding the cornmeal dough into a flat circle, talked quietly of the times she and her husband had fought off both the Apaches and the Mexican *bandidos* who raided their small rancho and burned the *milpas,* the corn fields—horrors that she never got used to—and the final battle when the Apaches caught her husband and three others unaware at the shaft of the mine. His sudden death at the point of a lance. Then the onslaught of the cabin, the baby's brains dashed—her own body violated.

The woman raised her gaze to meet Catherine's. "So now I no longer have anything to lose . . . except . . ." Her gaze slid across the camp to fix on the two men who walked among the *remuda,* stopping every so often to run a hand over the flanks of one horse, pat the muzzle of another. One of them, a blond, was much taller than the other.

In spite of the deep sympathy Catherine felt for the young widow who had suffered so much, a streak of jealousy zigzagged through her. Why, she chided herself, should she care if Filomena was in love with Law?

And she knew it was because she was drawn to the rakehell also. It did her no good to tell herself he was a mercenary, that he had sold his mother's jewelry for guns! It galled her to admit it, but she was succumbing to Law as easily as some frivolous woman to the vapors.

She had misjudged him. Now, watching him move among the horses, she realized there was a strength of purpose as resilient as his knife, as indomitable as the Stronghold. He was as committed to Mexico as Sherrod was to Cristo Rey. It would never do to let herself become involved with Law, for he could offer her nothing.

Yet that night, as each previous night, her body betrayed her as he came to her, lying next to her. The pulse at her temples beat erratically, her breath came in short staccato gasps, and she could only stifle the urge to turn to him, to ask him to kiss her.

Chapter 19

CIVILIZATION'S wagon road fell behind, and the sanctuary of canyon upon canyon loomed before the brigade, which had forsaken the pueblos and villas to follow the Río San Miguel south to Ures. Catherine tried to estimate how many days the brigade had been on the march, how many days since a bath and a change of clothes, but she had lost all track of time. How ludicrous she must appear—the elegant riding habit and top hat, now more gray than black, hanging in tatters on her like castoffs on a scarecrow.

She let Sonora pick his way along the narrow path that skirted the outcrops of black rock while her thoughts dwelled on her predicament—an American woman riding with a band of guerrillas on their way to battle a French army!

"You'll be left behind outside Ures with the other women," Law had told her the night before as he lay next to her but not touching her. "You'll be as safe there as anywhere. After the battle—if all goes well—it will be arranged for you to travel to Guaymas. If the American consul there hasn't abandoned his post, he can see that you are safely put aboard an American vessel."

He rolled over and looked down at her then. In the darkness, the gold of his hair and mustache was the only light. "There is a derringer in my saddlebag, Cate. If we don't return to camp, if we lose—you are to use it. Do you understand?"

At first she did not, and he caught her chin between thumb and forefinger. "I don't think you are a weak woman, Cate. I think you will survive no matter what might be done to your honor. But the Yaquis, who ride with the French—they can make death most unpleasant. The weapon is to be used against yourself only as a last resort," he said with a gentle sadness before releasing her.

She lifted her gaze now, trying to find among the line of soldiers ascending the trail into the mountain heights Law's lean figure. There was a strength about him that reassured her. She could not imagine that he would not return from the battle with the French.

The evening was already blanketing the land, more rapidly there in the mountains, and it was impossible now to separate Law from the line of soldiers that was only a snakelike shadow crawling up the narrow pass ahead. By the time camp was called, a blackness had settled on the mountains, and below the lights in the windows of Ures twinkled as if there were no thought of the French army that would soon descend on the capital of Sonora like Attila's hordes.

A solemn quiet hovered over the camp, as there were only a few hours left before the men were to move down into the pueblo at dawn. The soldiers talked lowly among themselves or with their women, who seemed to keep within a close perimeter of their men while they moved about their chores. The specter of death circled over the camp like a vulture.

As Catherine helped Loco dice the chilies, the onions, and the dried beef, she waited to see what Filomena would do. When a little later the woman wiped her hands on her skirts and left the mess wagon, Catherine's heart sank like a stone in water. She knew then that she loved Law, that she wanted him as the female tigress seeks her mate. Perhaps she had wanted him since that first kiss the night of the fiesta of San Juan de Bautista, perhaps as far back as the first time she saw him there in the Meyer Street Saloon.

As she watched Filomena pick her way among the men, her hopes lifted. Then her hopes soared like a condor, for it was Tranquilino the woman approached, taking his hand and moving into the shadows. So, it had been Tranquilino all along!

But where then was Law?

At her side, Loco said, as he continued to dice the chilies, "Lorenzo is a lonely man. He carries the burden of the Juarista cause on his shoulders. I think he is alone now, with his thoughts. Perhaps there, on that bluff."

"I believe you have read my thoughts," she said, dimples forming at each side of her mouth.

A drooping lid closed in a wink. "There is no need. Your eyes mirror everything, señorita."

She paused only once—at the wagon to search among the supplies. Yes, there it was—a bottle of Rosé Chasselas from California. Her skirts caught on the low-lying cholla and the sharp lava rocks, but she scarcely heeded nature's impediments. She was going to the man who held her soul fast in his grip. She did not know if one would call it love. What she felt for Lorenzo Davalos was certainly not the comfortable, quiet relationship one came to expect in a marriage.

She was well aware of Law's deficiencies, that he had none of Sherrod's stability. She knew that if it were not for the war with the French, it would be something else. Too soon he would become restless in the confines of civilization and move on—and she knew she would go with him, for she could not stop loving him . . . if this wild calling of the heart was love.

By the time she reached the summit of the bluff, by the time she saw that tall, rangy shadow and the honey-colored hair in the bright moonlight, she knew that it did not matter what one labeled the feeling, whether it lasted but a night or through the unwinding of the years. For that moment it was real, and to deny it would be to lose something very precious.

He turned and watched her make her way over the last few yards. A cigarette stub was clamped between his teeth. His wary gaze dropped from her face to the bottle she held in her hands. She held forth the bottle, saying with a tentative smile, "You once said that all you needed was a jug of wine and a warm, willing woman and you could forget the promises of heaven. Will we do?"

He cocked a brow and removed the cigarette from his lips. "What about the ring on your finger and babe in your arms?"

She stamped her foot in frustration. "Must you make it so difficult for me? I'm trying to tell you that I want you, Law Davalos!"

"More than your want of a husband and children?" he pressed.

Her eyes glistened. "More than that," she whispered.

He ground out the cigarette with his boot heel. "I don't understand."

"In Baltimore—it seems like eons ago—I was foolish enough to think time was important. I thought my time was slipping away faster than that of other people's. I had goals, and I thought I had to hurry to fulfill them. Now I know there is only the present. I was foolish, but I'm learning. Show me, Law. Show me everything."

He looked at her for one long moment. Then he took the bottle from her and set it down. Catching her about the waist, he raised her off the ground so that her face was even with his. He kissed her lightly, tenderly. "I've underestimated you, Cate," he said quietly. He sat her on her feet again and began to work at the buttons of her blouse. Her skirt fell about her feet. The corset had long since gone, and there was only the chemise to cover her nudity.

When he began to divest himself of his dust-caked clothing with a naturalness foreign to her, she turned her head away despite the urgency that gripped her. "Open your eyes," he mumbled as he tugged the serape over his head. "There's nothing worse than a woman who insists on turning down the lamps so she won't have to face reality. Take a look, Cate. Am I all that repugnant?"

She slit one lid, her field of vision so narrow that whatever she saw would be screened by the heavy thicket of eyelashes. She had caught fragmentary glimpses of the male body when tending the wounded soldiers but never the exhibition of the complete masculine anatomy—in all its glory.

And those were the words that came to her mind when she viewed the six-foot-four-inch length of Law's bronzed, lean frame. Broad, sinewy shoulders set above the hard torso that wedged at the narrow hips and—yes, they were beautifully formed—legs. Not a spare ounce of flesh clung to the muscle-roped body.

He planted his fist on his hips and threw back his head in laughter as her eyes widened when her gaze ricocheted to the thick yellow-brown hair at the crotch that curled as riotously as the hair on his head.

She would have bolted then, but where to? She grabbed her skirt and yanked it up over her thighs, inadequately trying to shield her full, firm virgin's breasts with her free arm.

He came to her and, taking her arms, gently lowered her to the soft mounds made by their clothing. "Why do the Anglos, especially you Yanquis, see such shame in the body?" he demanded, peering intently into her averted face, as if how she felt about what he was going to do made a difference to him.

(123)

But he did not wait for her reply. His hands cupped her face and turned it toward him as he tenderly brushed her closed lids and trembling lips with kisses that demanded nothing. He stretched out beside her, and his heat began to thaw her chilled body.

"What can I tell you to make it easier for you?" he whispered against her breast. His tongue traced the rose-brown aureole. She quivered along the length of her body, and he raised his head. "I've never taken a virgin before, Cate—only willing women—so I don't understand this pain that women talk about. But I do know that it can be something that'll take your breath away, there's not another feeling equal to it—if you'll only meet me halfway."

She understood then. He was giving her the chance to change her mind. It would be her decision. She met his gaze just as candidly. "Just don't let me think," she whispered.

And he did not. Her body, which before she had considered merely flesh, muscle, and bone, with only defects to her biased eye, became a thing of rare beauty worshiped before some pagan altar. His lips, his fingers, his eyes, his tongue—his words—they did homage to her; they did things to her that she could never have imagined. Through the long night he showed her things she had never suspected.

Only then, toward dawn, did he demand she return the pleasure. Half curious, half fearful, but totally stimulated by his lovemaking, she slid her fingers along his golden-brown length, causing him to gasp with pleasure. She had not known that the male physique could be so beautiful. This was what her body had been yearning for, had been made for. And she showed her gratitude in her loving of him. Later his breathing stopped in a sheer agony of suspension when her lips, made bold by her love for him, brought him to a shattering climax.

When they lay satiated in each other's arms, only then did he permit thought to enter her passion-numbed brain. "Cate," he said quietly, "my wish—beneath the Joshua tree—it was for you . . . you stubborn, irresistible woman."

Chapter 20

CATHERINE prowled about the makeshift camp as uneasy as a cat. From afar there came every few hours the whoomph of cannon that made the rocky terrain vibrate beneath her feet. She trailed the women to the mountain stream, for the first time washing out her clothes—and Law's—one of his bandannas, a pair of red flannel longjohns, a faded blue cotton shirt. Was she not his woman now?

She blushed as she recalled the things she had done the night before. She had not known that the giving of pleasure was so great an aphrodisiac. Yet she felt no shame. Was she sinning, going to Law without the blessing of the Church? Surely as great as her love was it had God's blessing. If not, then she would be held accountable for the sin, but whatever the price, it was worth it.

Toward evening the bark of muskets seemed closer, but Loco told her it was merely the echo of troops skirmishing outside the city below. Evening came, and still the men had not returned. She looked at the faces of the other women mirrored in the light of the smokeless campfire. Pale wraiths, she thought. Even Filomena. And herself. Sleep did not come that night, only the torturous waiting for what the sun would bring.

She knew that Law had instructed Loco to take her to Guaymas, the closest destination that would afford her a modicum of safety, if he should not return. Yet she also knew she would not leave Law's land. She was bound to it, by what she could not ascertain. But she loved the raw, primitive land as much as Lucy hated it.

Over the meager breakfast of tortillas and refried beans she calmly told Loco that she would not be going to Guaymas. "If anything, I shall return to Tucson to make whatever form of living I can." She gave the old Indian a dry smile. "Perhaps even as a *lavandera.* I've become quite good at washing clothes on rocks since I've joined the Arizona Colonizing Expedition."

Loco looked up at her from beneath his fringe of bone-white hair. He paused in eating the tortilla, which he noisily chewed. "The people there, they may not forget so easily the Anglo officer's death."

"If I were to try to teach their children, no—they would never forget." She smiled. "But to scrub their clothes—it matters not who does that."

"You love him much—Lorenzo?" the Indian asked, his faded brown eyes studying her.

"Very much," she said simply. "To my soul's everlasting irritation."

One of those fierce electrical storms peculiar to the Southwest rumbled through the mountains, reverberating over the camp like a clash of cymbals. Beneath the tarpaulin-covered wagon Catherine stirred as the first splatter of rain droplets pelted the thirsty earth. Her hand sought the reassuring hardness of Law's body only to come up empty. Another night, and still the men had not returned.

Something guttural in her cried out at the void beside her . . . and the injustice of fate. Had she traveled so far, endured so much, to finally find what it was she sought from life . . . and lose it before she had ever had it?

Then suddenly lightning zigzagged across the black heavens and illuminated the ghostly horses and riders moving up through the sheered-rock defile. The wreath of yellow curls sparkled in the silver javelinlike streak, and a cry of joy shot through her at the recognition. She was crawling from beneath the wagon, running, her arms open wide.

The lead rider watched the slender woman coming to him. So frail, so delicate . . . so strong, so determined. If he'd let her, she could make for him the kind of home he had never known. No, that was untrue. The home he had known before Frank Godwin arrived. And took Cristo Rey, took his mother for his own. His mother had been strong, but love had made her weak. Would love for this American woman make him weak? So weak that he forgot the need of his people, of Mexico?

Madonna, but he was tired! And the wound hurt! The warmth and softness of Cate's breast would take all that away.

He leaned over and effortlessly swept the woman up into the saddle before him, ignoring the flash of pain when her buttocks brushed the bullet hole in his thigh. He wanted only to feel the welcome of her lips beneath his.

Catherine maneuvered about as he cantered the sorrel back to camp so she could see her beloved's face. "The battle—was it successful?" *Dear God, let it be. Let this be over. Maybe then . . . maybe.* She did not dare let herself finish the thought.

His visage was darkly grim. "Pesquiera fled like a polecat! The governor had over four hundred men, and he retreated to Hacienda La Concepción. Garnier controls Ures."

The rain was landsliding now, the wind screaming, and the lightning streaking a kaleidoscope of colors across the sky. He dismounted and lifted her down, while the heaven unleashed its fury about the returning soldiers. The two of them sought the refuge beneath the wagon, and he pulled her into the folds of his huge serape. "You're shivering," he said.

"You'd think I would be used to the cold after the New England winters, but it's a bitter cold up here . . . and I'm frightened, Law. I'm frightened of what you'll tell me."

He reached beneath the serape and withdrew a flask. "Drink some," he told her. "It'll warm you. And give you courage."

She shook her head. She would face this on her own. "You're sending me away."

He took a long swallow and shoved in the cork. "We're going into guerrilla warfare, Cate. Deep into the valleys and the mountains of the Yaqui and Mayo rivers. Our headquarters will be in the jungles with our Indian allies, few though they are. You won't like it. There will be mosquitoes and rain and a heat that's nothing like Tucson's. It steams you alive."

"And where would I go?" she cried above the roar of the rain and thunder. "There's no place for me but here, at your side!"

He looked down at her before turning his gaze up at the darkened board bottom of the wagon. But he still saw the intelligent eyes, the warm, giving mouth. "Our headquarters, in San Marcial, will be only a day's ride from Guaymas. You're going back to the States, Cate, where you belong—on the first U.S. vessel out of Guaymas."

"No," she said with a calm assurance that he always found amusing. She leaned over him, her hands splayed on his chest. "If you're trying to diplomatically tell me you no longer want me as your—at your side, I'm quite capable of keeping up with your expedition—or *guerrilleros,* as you now term yourselves. And I will. I can fend for myself if I have to, but I will not be driven away."

He sighed. "I fully believe you could convince Maximilian to give up and return to Austria if you had half a chance to talk to him. You're so damn logical, Cate."

She put her fingertip on the full bottom lip. "Dear God, I wish that were so, but it isn't. I can't be logical about you. And there's only one person I want to convince. Not Maximilian, but you. Law, I came to the Arizona Territory with an empty cup, and you have filled it. I will not return to that arid life I led before."

"Then let me fill your cup again." He laughed . . . laughter that died away at the passion shining in her eyes. He rolled her over on her back. His leg half-covered hers, his fingers freed the breasts of their constriction so that his mouth could taste the sustenance it hungered for.

She caught fire, her skin blazing beneath the questing hand that slid beneath the band of her skirt to entangle in the soft, dark down. She moaned as the fingers found that tiny knot of flesh, caressing it, until it spawned an identical knot in her belly that writhed and twisted with the need for assuagement. She was inundated with the aching pleasure that rolled upon her, wave after unbearable wave.

Law's lips deserted the tumescent nipple his teeth tugged at to silence her wild murmurs of ecstasy. It was not the time to make love, with nature's elements shrieking in protest about them, with the wound throbbing at his thigh. But there was a greater throbbing inside him that had to be silenced.

He shoved the skirt up past her arching hips. He could hear her urgent breathing, hear his own ragged breath drumming in his ears. He had to have her. Now. He thrust inside her, forgetting his pain, ignoring her own whimper of pain. He shoved deep. Deeper. And she cried out as her body answered. They moved in unison. Slamming. Pounding. Driving toward that ultimate fusion.

By ridding himself of his seed, he would rid himself of her, his need for her . . . this great ache that consumed him whenever she looked at him with those eyes that burned with wanting. A final explosion. The blaze of colors. The temporary suspension of time and place. And Cate's sweet, sweet lips, moving . . . giving . . . wanting again.

Chapter 21

IMPATIENTLY Law sat while Catherine, kneeling beside him, bandaged the wound. "You should have told me last night," she reprimanded him. "It could have gotten infected."

He grinned down at her from the camp stool which he straddled. "You sound like a schoolmarm . . . Miss Cate. Besides, if I had let you attend the wound, then I wouldn't have discovered what a truly astonishing woman you are."

Blushing, she grinned, a grin that faded as she began to shiver, the second time that morning a spasm of coughing had seized her. Law held out the flask from which she had so recently poured its fiery contents on his ulcerated flesh. "Drink," he commanded. "It sounds as if you need it worse than my leg does. You must have caught a cold in last night's rain."

She hesitated, not liking the bitter, burning liquid. But the adamant set of his lips, beautiful lips she thought, told her he would most likely make her drink the mescal if she did not comply. She took a tentative sip and found that after the initial burning, it did set off a pleasant warming once it reached the stomach.

As the brigade moved out that day, traveling southwest toward the rendezvous with General Morales's Juarista troops, the chills abated, although she experienced periods of great weakness over the days that followed.

From Tucson's grassy Santa Cruz valley the terrain had changed to low brown hills, then a cholla wasteland, and finally rock-peppered canyons. Now the landscape was altering again as patches of green valleys and tree-mantled mountains painted the horizon. The farther south the brigade traveled, the more thickly grew the trees beneath the warmer, more humid sunlight, and vines began to drop like snakes from palm and mahogany branches intertwined overhead, reminding her how her life was intertwined with Law's.

Law at last led the brigade up out of the lowlands into the mountains, where the verdant foliage was less thick and the air not so steamy. She could almost feel the cooler air inflate her shriveling lungs, so that it seemed by the time they reached the Indian ranchería her spells of weakness and chills were waning.

The guerrilla headquarters, hidden in one of the many canyons that twisted and tangled through the Sierra Madre mountain range, afforded an unexpected view of civilization for her. The ranchería was a cluster of thirty or forty beehivelike brush wicki-ups strewn across a tableland high in the mountains.

People were everywhere, mostly men, though a few children played before the wickiup doorways and several women with coarse Indian features talked and joked as they pummeled corn-meal with their *metates*. Yaqui and Mayo Indians, Mexican pe-ones and bandits, American soldiers—even some Germans who had immigrated to the more lucrative Sonora mines after the first flush of the California gold rush had paled—these were the Juaristas who would liberate Mexico from the French invaders.

While Law and Tranquilino met with General Morales—a short but darkly good-looking Mexican—Catherine and Filomena were led off to a lovely evergreen-shaded knoll by a smiling, flat-faced Indian woman with bangs that covered her brows. Through rudimentary gestures and broken Spanish, Meija was able to make Catherine and Filomena understand that the women were to construct wickiups for their men. The Indian women would erect wickiups for those soldiers who did not have their own women or wished for more shelter than that offered by the pup tent some possessed. At a stream nearby, two women wove reeds that would form the thatching for the wickiup's roof, and Meija tried to demonstrate how easily the weaving was accomplished.

Catherine would have liked nothing better than a drink of cool water from the stream, rather than the brackish water Law had offered her from his japanned canteen, and then a nap beneath the shady aspen. But she would not be less of a woman than the other *soldaderas.* While the soldiers fell out to rub down travel-weary horses, she began the task of erecting the wickiup. Actually, she had to admit that she was taking a great deal of pleasure in the work, for it would be the first home she and Law would share.

The actual construction of the wickiup went much more quickly than she had anticipated, and by the time Law emerged from General Morales's wickiup with the general and Tranquilino on either side, she was installing the baskets for dried food and cooking utensils along the inside walls.

She had thought how dirty and disheveled she had to look with the calico skirt and blouse Filomena had lent her stained with dust and sweat and her hair falling from its knot and trailing about her shoulders. But Law crossed to her and took her hand, saying, "You are *muy hermosa,* Cate. Much more beautiful, much more alive, than that stiff young lady I first met in Tucson."

She knew she would never tire of hearing the flowery compliments on his lips. If only he would say that he loved her. She let him pull her inside the wickiup, and though it was but twilight, he lifted her to rest on the soft bedding of evergreens she had made. *"Mi corazón, mi alma,"* he whispered, the true Latin lover now. "I've thought all day long of this time."

She would have rained kisses on the fierce brown face, but he took her fingers, kissing each one softly, and next her palms, her right first then her left. She could not have imagined so much time could be given over to the bringing of pleasure to a loved one. Then he took the pins from her hair, scattering them carelessly on the floor. "Always leave your hair down, Cate," he murmured, burying his face in the cascade of her rich brown tresses.

After that he could wait no longer as a feverish hunger seized him. He did not take his eyes off her while he stripped. He had not thought that the urge to possess her again, that one particular woman, would be so great. Why her, a woman a full five years older, a woman who wanted all the things in life he did not . . . a house and children and a structured life?

By the time dawn's light shafted through the canyon, he realized the two of them had missed the evening meal

*   *   *

Catherine stirred the ashes and lime into the boiling coconut oil. The bubbling mixture certainly did not look or smell like the rose-scented soap she had known in Baltimore, nor the coarser castile soap she had used at Cristo Rey. But the fact that she was making it was a triumph for her.

The obviously pregnant Meija crossed the ranchería, waddling like a duck toward Catherine. Watching the young Indian woman, Catherine mentally counted—five months since the brigade had arrived at the ranchería. That would make Meija due any day now.

Five months! Incredible, she thought. The passage of time in the *tierra caliente* was not to be measured by changes of season. Always the insidious green. Always the enervating heat.

What day was it? It had to be toward the last of September. Or was it already into October? It seemed to her that she measured time by the forays Law made. A week away fighting in the southern part of the state near the pueblo of Alamos. Four days spent disrupting French communications between Hermosillo and Ures. Five days riding to intercept pack trains loaded with silver bullion from Sonoran mines bound for French ships at Guaymas.

Meija approached now, shyly holding out a gift wrapped in a bandanna. *"Café,"* she said.

"Oh, Meija, *gracias!"* Catherine could hardly believe her good fortune. How long had it been since she had had coffee? Almost three months, since Loco's supply had run out. She wanted to say more to Meija—to ask her how she felt, if the baby had dropped—but Meija's Indian dialect made it almost impossible to carry on any lengthy conversation.

Yet the language barrier had not kept Catherine from caring for the young Indian woman when Meija became ill in the first throes of pregnancy. It had been Loco who had recommended giving Meija lemonade, sumac, and powdered dry berries. After two weeks of feeding the nausea-weakened girl, Catherine had finally succeeded in restoring the healthy color to Meija's bronze cheeks.

She opened the knotted bandanna. Inside was not coffee grain but ground corn and parched acorns. She tried to conceal her disappointment. And true, even this substitute for coffee was a welcome change of beverages from the water and fruit juices, or the fermented cactus brew which still flowed freely in the evenings.

She watched the young woman lumber away with something

akin to envy. For a woman to know that she carried a child inside her—and the joyous knowledge that it was the child of the man she loved—surely had to be the greatest experience life could give. The gift of giving. She recalled the night before when she had lain naked in Law's arms and his hands had stroked the smooth indentation of the waist and slid down over her stomach. He had been gone three days, and she wanted him to take her, to make her forget the lonely days and nights without him.

But his hand halted over the concavity of her stomach. "When was the last time you had your flow, Cate?"

Color flooded her face. "Why?" she whispered, fighting back the tears of anger. "Are you afraid I carry your child?" She pushed away from him, so that in the darkness of the wickiup she could see only his thick wreath of yellow curls. "Are you afraid I'll force you to marry me?"

A light flared from a phosphorous match, and Law's sun-goldened body was briefly illuminated, then there was only the soft glow of the rice-papered cigar. "You know that not even a child will force me into marriage," he said softly but with a cool distance to his voice, which had previously been warm with Spanish love words.

"Then it should matter little whether I'm with child or not!"

In the darkness his hand groped and found her wrist, and before she could pull free he tugged her back to his side. "Your health matters to me greatly. This is no place to have a child. Pregnancy can kill a woman, you know," His voice grated low and harsh, though he held her gently in his arms. "Don Francisco's unborn child killed my mother."

She had not known how to respond to the grief in his voice. Instead, she laid her head against his chest, the skin warm and matted with curls, and let her hands show him her love. They had made love fiercely—fighting like two mating tigers. The urgency of death hung over them. He rode her with a smooth fast power. And she bucked and reared, giving him back that scalding, delicious fire that streaked through the two of them at the last.

This morning, as he dressed to leave once more, buckling on the pistols, sheathing the knife at his side, she caught his hands, holding them close to her breasts, away from the weapons. "I'm frightened," she said simply. "Of what tomorrow holds."

He looked down at her. "I think everyone is frightened before a battle."

"Even yourself?" she asked. "Somehow I have the impression you aren't afraid of anything."

He smiled gently. "Me most of all. Sometimes to live when all those about you have fallen—I think it's a torture worse than the quick blessing of death."

She clutched at his arm. "Why then, Law? You don't have to. You have everything you could want at Cristo Rey."

"I don't know," he said slowly. "I myself don't understand why. Cristo Rey, the Stronghold, the cattle, the mines. They're things. Things that will erode and rust and wither with time. But abstractions like liberation, freedom, justice—they've been in my blood like a fever."

He pulled her in his arms against him then and said softly, "Just the same as you're in my blood, Cate. I've told myself a hundred times over there is no room in my life for anything but the Juarista cause. Yet always thoughts of you creep into my mind. The prim, delicate Miss Howard with a strength of will that would defy an army."

She knew it was as close to a declaration of love as she would hear from him, and she gave herself up to his fierce kiss and forced herself to hold back the threatening tears as she watched him ride away.

Chapter 22

CATHERINE tried to stay busy (and she was learning things about survival that no Eastern-bred lady would even think of), because it muted her preoccupation with Law's safety. Each night she went to sleep in their wickiup, she petitioned God to return Law to her. And when she awoke each morning, she secretly asked herself if this would be the day the guerrillas rode in without Law at their head.

Six agonizingly slow days passed before he and his men rode into the ranchería again. She dropped the shirt she was mending and ran outside to catch the bridle of his sorrel. He dropped down beside her. Shadows encircled the tired eyes, and, as usual, his jaw was stubbled with a new growth of beard. He looped an arm over her shoulder and walked with her toward the wickiup. "I missed you, Cate," he said simply, but he did not look at her.

She waited until they were safely inside to ask how the mission had gone. He shrugged. Leaving her at the doorway, he stretched out on the bed of fresh evergreens and blankets. "Little by little the French have taken each major city in Sonora. They control the whole province now and have forced Juárez to flee to El Paso. And they control the Indians now also. More and more Yaqui are going over to the French."

"But why?" she demanded. "Surely they don't think the French aristocrats are going to liberate them?"

"The Yaqui and Mayo did not do so well under the Mexican *hidalgo* either. What would make them think the Juarista government would be an improvement?"

She wanted to point out that the government had to be an improvement because Juárez was a pure-blooded Zapotec Indian, but Law said, "They don't understand that we are trying to drag Mexico out of feudalism and end the control of the Church and military and large landowners."

She went to kneel at his side. "That's not all that's bothering you," she said softly. "What else?"

"We traveled as far north as Arizpe. The loyal Juarista families around there had been executed. Entire villages."

Her breath sucked in. He continued, his eyes closed, his voice low, almost monotonous, as it related the savagery he had witnessed. "It's no longer a battle of armies—of soldiers, Cate. It's a *carnicería*—a butcher's shop. And the worst part of it all is that the Juarista general in charge of the Federal Army of the West, Ramón Corona, has sent in a general called Angel Martinez. My God, Cate, what a name for a butcher such as he—Angel! The bastard commands an army of men infamously known as the *macheteros*."

Law opened his eyes now and looked at her. "Our own men, Cate! I couldn't believe my eyes—the *macheteros* had entered a village loyal to the French ahead of us. And their machetes left nothing whole. A child's head, a man's foot, a baby's hand . . . a woman's breast."

His voice cracked. He buried his head in his hands. "Coming back, I wondered if what I'm fighting for is worth it. The peones— those poor uneducated peasants—are so far from the seat of government in Mexico City that it makes little difference to their lives which side rules from Chapultepec Castle."

Now. Now was the time to commiserate with him. To tell him all the bloodshed was not worth his effort. She knew that this was the moment. She must seize it and turn his shame to her own salvation. She must paint an alluring picture of what their lives could be like together in Tucson.

But she could not do it. Damn all the couples who ever lived and loved and married and had normal lives!

She ran her hands through his curls and tilted his face so that she could see the agony in those eyes she loved so. "You *will* fight though, my dear," she said softly. "You'll fight because someone has to. Men like Juárez and you and Morales will always fight without considering the odds simply because it's the right thing to do. You will not desert Mexico in her eleventh hour."

He wrapped his arms about her and hugged her to him, burying his face in the soft hollow of her shoulder. "It was easier for me before I knew you. Then it was easy to be courageous— to take daring chances. I had nothing to lose." He kissed the center of her hairline where her hair dipped to lend the heart-shaped configuration to her face.

She turned her lips up to his, and he kissed them tenderly, his mouth moving slowly over hers. With great gentleness he lowered her to her back. He pulled the peasant blouse down over her shoulders and took one breast lovingly in his hands. His tongue traced the rose-brown rim of the nipple and licked it to life. A deep sigh shook her body as his hand sought her thighs, his fingers sliding in her womanhood's moist warmth.

She grasped his narrow hips and pulled him down on her, her fingers working urgently at the buttons of his pants. When he was free to enter her, she held him back. "Not yet," she murmured and rose to kneel over him. Her unbound hair fell across his stomach and hips as her lips loved him.

"To hell with the general," he muttered as he drew her atop him. "He can wait. I can't!"

"You were beginning to look like General Custer with all those blond curls falling about your shoulders," she told Law. "Only his eyes are blue and his skin is much paler."

Law cupped her buttocks and pulled her up against him, burying his head against her skirts. "That had better be all you know about General Custer," he grumbled. "You're making me jealous."

She slapped his hands and twisted away. "Stop that, Law Davalos. Everyone will see you!" But she was smiling. She sniped at another curl that persisted in wriggling its way out of Law's newly shorn mass of ringlets, which now barely reached the collarless calico shirt. She stepped back, scissors that Tranquilino had appropriated from one of the raids in hand, and surveyed the work in process.

"Not bad. You're almost as handsome as General Custer, in fact."

Handsome? His looks were sensuously devastating, magnificently masculine! How could she ever have thought his face lacking, except, she thought, by the standards of the effete East?

Law grinned. "I hope you aren't playing Delilah to my Samson."

"If it would make you my captive, I am," she teased. She watched while he brushed at the wisps of hairs that still clung to the bronzed chest, which glistened sleekly in the sunlight. The skin was a beautiful color, she thought A sun color.

Even she was tanned a becoming gold—looking a picture of health if she could not ignore the fever that persisted—not often or high enough, fortunately, to draw his attention. Had she caught some disease? She tried to recall if any of the soldiers at the hospital had experienced similar symptoms. She was certain that if Law suspected her deteriorating health he would forcibly gag and bind her and send her back to Tucson.

Was it really possible she had been gone from Tucson exactly a year? Tucson in February . . . there might be snow capping the Santa Catalina peaks at that moment, but the days and nights would be mild and balmy. In Baltimore, winter blizzards were probably icing the streets, yet there in the Sierra Madres of Mexico the weather was languidly hot, though not as steamy as it would be when summer came.

"Excelente!" General Morales said, approaching the two. "Is there any possibility, señorita, I could enlist your aid as the camp *peluquería?* We need a barber badly." He rubbed at the dark bristly head of hair he cropped himself.

Law stretched out an arm to encompass her waist. "Never, general," he retorted with a mock fierceness. "The woman is mine."

"Continue with your work, then," Morales said, hunkering down across from Law. "I only wanted to let you know the news. One of our agents rode in from Durango an hour ago."

She felt Law's muscle-ridged shoulder tense beneath her hand. Her own nerve endings flickered at the import of Morales's words. Surely something important was about for the general to seek out Law immediately. The news could mean another raid against the French . . . and more torturous days to worry about Law's absence.

"I will begin with the pleasant news, Law. Because of pressures put on Napoleon by the United States Secretary of War Seward and now that their war is ended and Seward can back up his threats—and because of the Austro-Prussian war that has broken out in Europe—Napoleon wants his troops back in France. My agent tells me that Bazaine plans to begin withdrawing the troops by the end of the summer."

"Gracias a Dios!" Law said fervently.

"I don't need to caution you," Morales said, "that it will be months, maybe a year even, before withdrawal is complete. Even then Maximilian will have his own troops and the Indians and Mexicans loyal to the imperialist cause. It will not be easy, but there is a glimmer of hope now in the black tunnel of this war."

"With such news, *compadre,*" Law said, leaning forward to rest his arms on his thighs, "I don't believe there is anything you could tell me that would be unpleasant."

"There is. The Austrian butcher, Lamberg, has been appointed imperial commander of Sonora and joined forces with Alamada and the Indian Tanori at Guaymas to rid Sonora of its *guerrilleros.*"

Law studied the other man while his fingers absently toyed with his mustache. "We expected this sooner or later."

Morales looked pointedly at Catherine now. "I've just learned that Maximilian issued a decree—the Black Flag Decree, they are calling it. All people aiding or belonging to armed bands not legally authorized shall be executed within twenty-four hours of their sentence."

She felt Law's penetrating gaze switch to her as Morales continued. "Tanori knows these mountains like the back of his hand. If just once he should chance on our headquarters while we're away, the señorita here would be given no quarter—American or not."

"And would the other women be given amnesty—Filomena, Meija, and the others?" Catherine snapped. "No, of course not. And I am no different. So why the concern for me?" Fear that Law would no longer be so yielding but would force her to return to the States pitched her voice to a belligerent tone. "I will not leave!"

Law said nothing, which frightened her even more. Morales rose. "*Pues*, it seems your woman is certainly devoted to our cause."

From the top of the creek's bank Catherine watched Filomena wash Tranquilino's hair. The woman giggled when the young Mexican sat back on his haunches and shook his shaggy head, showering Filomena with water. He looked up and saw Catherine and called out, "Come on down, Catrina. Tell this woman of mine that you do not drown someone when you wash his hair!"

Catherine laughed and begged off. She did not wish to interrupt their merriment . . . and then, too, Filomena was very obviously pregnant. As much as Catherine cared for the young Mexican woman, it still hurt her, like wrenching a tourniquet about her heart, to see the woman blossom with the growth of the child inside her—or to see the tiny daughter that now tugged at Meija's breast.

Why could she not be pregnant? Surely then Law would not send her away. He had not said anything yet about her leaving. But he was withdrawn ever since Morales had talked with them the week before.

She turned from the laughing couple and made her way back to camp to find Loco sitting beneath an acacia oiling Law's carbine. She squatted down beside him, Indian-fashion. "You are good with herbs," she said straightforwardly. "I need an herb to conceive. Soon."

The old Indian continued to rub the oil-coated rag over the

barrel's smooth stock. As if he had not heard the urgency in her voice, he said, "You need an herb for the chills and fever that feed on you."

She glanced up in shock. "You know?"

He nodded.

"Does anyone *else*?" she asked breathlessly.

"No. He soon will, though."

She caught the Indian's calico sleeve. "Loco, I must have that herb then. He must not find out I am ill!"

"The herb comes from the bark of the cinchona tree. It sometimes grows in the moist places of canyons." He met her gaze and said, "You should tell Lorenzo."

She sighed then and laid her head against the tree trunk. "I don't think he would understand."

"You must understand him first," Loco said and returned his attention to the gun.

"Then tell me," she prompted.

"You must understand how difficult it was for him to come home from the school to strangers. His mother had died, and there was Don Francisco and his family in the Stronghold. I think that Lorenzo had hoped that, returning as a man, he could do the things for Cristo Rey that Don Francisco had done. The two men, despite their continuing disagreements, have a great respect for each other. Don Francisco and Señor Sherrod are . . ." He searched for the right English word, saying at last in Spanish, ". . . *energicos.*"

"Dynamic," she supplied.

"*Sí.* This Lorenzo admires. But Lorenzo, he has his mother's gentleness and concern for people. This is something that Don Francisco could not find in his wife—in Señora Elizabeth—that is in Lorenzo."

Despite her sadness for the life Law had led, Catherine had to smile. "I think the last thing Law would consider himself to be is gentle."

"Ahh, *sí.* But you must remember Señor Sherrod is a caballero. Law, he is all rogue, no?"

All rogue. That worried her. Would the roguish part of him ever allow him to settle down? She rose to go, saying, "Thank you, Loco. For everything."

She got as far as the perimeter of wickiups when the old Indian called out to her, "Señorita."

She turned. "Yes, Loco?"

"You do not need an herb for the child." He smiled. "One grows inside your belly now."

Chapter 23

CATHERINE lay that evening in the darkness of the wickiup, waiting for Law to leave Morales and come to her. Her hand slid down her belly. There was not the slightest curvature to give away her secret. And yet she knew what Loco had told her was so. True, her flux was only two days late, and she thus had put little hope in the fact. But Loco's words . . . and the nights of love . . . there was no way she could not have conceived! *Oh, dear God, let it be so.*

The blanket over the doorway was pulled aside, and Law's tall frame stooped to enter the darkened wickiup. "Cate," he whispered.

She watched him shuck his clothes, and it seemed the anticipation of his kisses, his arms, his hands was too much to bear. She rose to her feet, letting the blanket slide down around her ankles, and, naked, padded across to him. "I'm here," she whispered and wrapped her arms about the narrow waist.

"You've become a shameless hussy," he said and chuckled.

His hands cupped her bare buttocks and pressed her to him. She could feel the rough texture of his body hair against her thighs and beneath her palms where her hands spread on his chest. And there was his hard thrust against the lower portion of her stomach. Would she never get enough of wanting him?

"If I'm a hussy, then you've made me so," she whispered and, taking his hand, drew him to their bed of fresh-scented boughs that by morning would be crushed by their bodies and damp with the musky scent of their lovemaking.

Dawn in the mountains was a glorious pageant of colors, she thought. She had not slept the few hours left before sunrise but had lain quietly, trying to savor and store away the pleasurable contentment of being held against Law as he slept . . . the warm, rough-smooth texture of his skin and the male odor of his body—sometimes overpowered more by leather, other times gunpowder or sweat or that horrid smell of Sonoran tobacco.

Still, any of these scents or the combination of them all had the power to make her weak with sudden want. How fortunate for her that her body did not give visible evidence of how easily he aroused passion in her—as he quite obviously did—or he would really know how wanton a woman she had become beneath his tutelage.

He stirred now and mumbled at her ear. "Cate, why did you leave the Stronghold?"

She turned her head, trying to see his face in the darkness. "Why do you ask now?"

"It only occurred to me. That night you made the announcement, I thought you were running away from me. Then I saw my stepbrother's face, and I was no longer so sure. You could have been running from your love for each other."

She laughed. "It was a little of both." She felt him stiffen ever so slightly beneath her hands, and she went on. "Oh, not like you think. I *was* running from you. You were a threat to everything I wanted in life. And Elizabeth thought I was a threat to her son's future. She was afraid I would cause him to lose Cristo Rey. So she ordered me out of the Stronghold."

"You know," he said, frowning, "I think my mother and Don Francisco, and Sherrod, I think we all could have been happy were it not for Elizabeth. Her hatred contaminates the Stronghold."

Catherine rubbed her fingertip over his lower lip, feeling in the dark the indentation in its center. "When she dies, the hate will die with her, Law. And then you'll be free to go home."

He nudged the hair that had fallen across her face with his jaw. "Cate, if I were the type of man that settled down, you know—the type to work at a living, like Sherrod— If I—well, hell, you know, wanted children—the family man and that sort. Well, would you consider marriage . . . if I were that type? Mind you, I'm not saying I am."

She thought he was going to rub the skin of her forehead raw, but she did not move or betray her mounting excitement. He continued to nuzzle her, saying, "Well?"

"I'd consider it—if you were that type, you understand. Only consider."

His jaw stopped the grinding, rotating motion. "Why only consider? What more do you want?"

She could hear the frustration in his voice. "Well, there's love. There were several men in Tucson who professed their love for me."

"Why the hell didn't you marry them, then?"

"I was trying to make up my mind when Jeremy's—death—forced me to leave."

She held her breath. Had she pushed him too far, wanted too much? But, dear Lord, it would be nothing without his love. He *had* to tell her he loved her!

"I'm not saying I'm marriage material," he said after a long pause, "but after all this is over—I think we could be happy together, Cate girl."

"I don't know," she hedged. "You are so much younger than I—only twenty-two, isn't it? Marriage is a lot of responsibility to take on for a man who's only a little out of boyhood."

"Dammit, Cate. You know our ages don't make any difference! I want the responsibility of caring for you, don't you understand?"

"And love?"

"Well, that too."

It was good enough. She turned her lips up to his, smiling. "It's about time you're making an honest woman of me."

"Then you will?" She heard the joy in his voice and glorified in it.

Large substantial dwellings lined Buena Vista's streets with so many different-colored plaster-coated homes that Catherine was reminded of Easter eggs. Orange trees and flowering jacaranda filled the courtyard, and palm trees graced the streets.

Despite the tranquil scene, perspiration ran down the cleavage of her breasts. Her gaze swung nervously from side to side as she and Law, with Loco trailing behind, rode through the streets of the colorful pueblo that was located on the Río Yaqui.

Although the Juaristas' fortunes had improved greatly by the middle of that year, 1866, so that the liberals controlled the district of Alamos, the strategic northern villa of Magdalena, and numerous other pueblos, the imperialists controlled Guaymas, Altar, Ures, part of the district of Hermosillo—and Buena Vista.

What she and Law were doing was incredibly risky, entering the French-controlled pueblo to find a padre to marry them—for the Church usually sided with the imperial aristocrats rather than lose its wealth by distribution to the masses, as Juárez advocated. However, every so often a God-fearing padre could be found, and this is what she and Law were counting on, praying for.

Soldiers in the blue-and-red uniform of the French Foreign Legion lounged in shadowed doorways, entered and left the local cantina. Yet no one challenged the three as they made their way toward the *iglesia,* the massive sun-baked cathedral located on the plaza, the center of every pueblo. Its tiled dome roof sparkled in the sunlight, its pockmarked walls reflected the coolness within. The cathedral seemed to bid her and Law to enter its sanctuary.

The nave was indeed cool. A soft watercolor wash of light slipped in from the high-placed windows, scattering fragments of color—brown and ocher and rust. Law spoke quietly with the padre, clad in the brown robe of the Franciscan order, who came forward from the sacristy. After a moment Law beckoned her to join him at the altar.

She said a prayer of thanksgiving that no questions were asked as she knelt with him before the padre. Behind him hung Christ's cross of agony. Her mother had been from a prominent Irish Catholic family in Baltimore, but Catherine had rarely practiced the faith. Now she prayed with the long-unused words, her soul seeming to flow from her as she petitioned for God's blessing on her marriage.

So soon the words were said, the paper signed and blotted with sand. Law's reassuring kiss on her cold lips sealed the padre's genuflection and benediction. There would be no wedding ring, but it was enough when they stepped out into the sunshine and Law took her face between his hands. At that moment his expression was very solemn.

"Cate," he whispered, "ever since my mother's death I have

been confusing love with weakness. You have made me see that love is strength. For this, if for none of your other endearing qualities, I love you." He kissed her softly. "I love you, *mi alma, mi amada, mi corazón.*"

He set her from him then and lifted her up into Sonora's saddle. Holding her hand, he looked to Loco, who waited, mounted, on the other side of Catherine. "I am entrusting her to you, my good friend. She is everything to me. Return her safely to Tucson."

Catherine's eyes widened. Her hand gripped Law's with a tenacious strength. "What are you saying?"

Law looked back to her, his brown eyes luminous in the stark sunlight. "I'm saying that I love you very much, too much to risk losing you—ever."

His voice became more brisk. He took the Arab's bridle, saying, "If you are stopped, let Loco do all the talking. And when you reach Tucson, Loco will ride on to Cristo Rey and take Sherrod my message—that I am selling him my portion of Cristo Rey. The money is to be given over to you."

"No!" she protested. "I won't have you giving up your share. I can take in laundry or something until your return."

"It's what Sherrod has always wanted, Cate—and deserves. He has worked to make Cristo Rey what it should be. We'll build our own Stronghold somewhere." He smiled. "Somewhere where there are plenty of Joshua trees."

She bent low. She had not meant to tell him, to use their child as a piece of strategy. She had hoped after they married she would have time to change his mind about sending her back to Tucson, a day at least. But she had not expected him to send her away immediately. "You can't do this," she pleaded. "I'm carrying our child, Law! You can't send me away!"

Shock registered in his eyes. But he was adamant. "Then that is all the more reason why you must return to Tucson. You must give thought to our child's safety."

She grabbed at his hand. "Law . . . without your love, there is nothing for me."

"There is our child. Cate, you could wheedle your way with me—talk me into letting you stay here. But our child needs a home—a real home."

"What kind of place is a home without the father?" she charged.

"I *am* coming home, Cate. Wait for me there," he said gently. "This war is something I must do. I am the man I am. But afterward . . . now I have some place to go, a home to call my own. Wait for me, *mi amada.*"

Chapter 24

*T*HE doctor, who had traveled all the way from Calabaza's Fort Mason, near the international boundary line, stood over Catherine. A frown etched grim canyons into his rawhide face. From her hemp-strung bed she pulled the often-mended blanket over her. "I already know what you're going to tell me," she told the middle-aged man. "I tried to convince Atanacia that sending for you would do no good."

"You have malaria," he said, the incredulity that a white woman could live under such poverty-stricken conditions making his voice rougher than he intended. "It has weakened you so much that I fear for the child's delivery—and your life, Mrs. Davalos."

"I have a stronger constitution—and will, lieutenant—than most people suspect."

"Even the strongest constitutions won't survive under the taxing work you are doing." He picked up his medical kit. "With less than a month left before the child is due, you can't continue to take in wash. You have friends who want to help. Let them."

She ignored the advice. "How much do I owe you for the visit?"

"Nothing. A friend of yours, Mr. Lionel McCrary, insisted on paying when he learned why I was in Tucson."

Dear Lionel, she thought, after the doctor had taken his leave. He had finally married the daughter of Manuel Orduno, the gunsmith. She was surprised by the concern of her friends, from Sam and Atanacia, who came over to check on her every day, to staunch Loco, who foraged at the marketplace for vegetables and fruit.

The old Indian even spoke to her about bringing in an *arbularía*, a woman with special powers who practiced "giving water"—which, Catherine learned, was forcing the saliva from the woman's mouth into the patient's! "A certain cure," Loco told her.

As a last resort he wanted to go for Sherrod, but she forbade him. "There is nothing anyone can do for me. But I will *not* die, I assure you. My heart beats too strongly for your Lorenzo, Loco, to give up on this weak body now."

"You should let the *patrones* pick up their laundry," Atanacia admonished, as she walked alongside Catherine, helping carry the neatly folded stacks of washed clothes.

"Then I would not have as many patrons. And Quong Chang's laundry would have more." She paused, out of breath. The baby was due any day now, and she found even the simple task of washing clothes on the new scrub board Sam had given her an exhausting chore.

"Then you should stay in *su casa*—and in your bed," Atanacia continued, "and let me deliver the laundry by myself." The young Mexican woman had almost as much difficulty walking as did Catherine. At four months pregnant, she was carrying her third child . . . and she had yet to turn sixteen.

"I enjoy the chance to get out, Atanacia—really."

Catherine looked at her surroundings. Tucson had greatly changed. It was two years ago the month before last—September of '64—when she had left Cristo Rey to come to Tucson. It was a Mexican mud village then, no more than eight hundred people. Now a distinct American flavor permeated the Old Pueblo.

The streets now had mostly Anglo names. Her own street, Calle de la India Trieste, was called Congress Street—for the Congress Saloon, so named because Tucson, which was now the territorial capital as well as the territory's military headquarters, had held its first legislative session in the saloon. At Stone and Ochoa, where the Tully & Ochoa corral had been, stood a long adobe building—the territory's new capitol building.

And Tucson now had its first hotel, the Palace. The Butterfield Overland Stage Coach Company was in operation again over on Pearl Street, which had been Calle del Correo. Then there were

the many Anglo businesses that had sprung up like mushrooms—
Fleishman's Drugstore, Levin's Brewery, Rothchild's Confection-
ary—and even a privately owned bank, the Lord & Williams
Store. All Tucson needed was a newspaper and a Protestant
church, and it would be a full-fledged American town.

In the seven months she had been back, she had come to
realize she no longer knew the city so intimately. New streets
pierced the original walls, leaving them in fragmented ruins. And
the town's population had swelled to nearly fifteen hundred, so
that many people had never heard of Catherine Howard, the
murderess.

But then these adventurers that flocked to the city did not care
about events of the past; nor did they care about what went on
outside Tucson. They did not know or care, as she did, that a
war still raged in Mexico. True, Law's Fabian tactics, along with
Martinez's terrorizing *macheteros,* had forced the French to retreat
to the port of Guaymas, thus freeing the state of Sonora. But the
few newspapers that Sam subscribed to reported that Bazaine's
French troops were still in Mexico City.

Was Law fighting in Mexico City now? Seven months since she
had seen him! Fear clutched at her heart. Did even now his
bones lie along some roadside, bleached by the sun, picked clean
by the vultures? The very thought hurt, stabbing at her as sharply
as a knife, so that she clutched at her abdomen. The tidy stack of
laundry she carried spilled into the dust. "The baby," she gasped.
"I think it's time."

Atanacia's stack of clothing tumbled down to join Catherine's.
The young Mexican woman grabbed her friend about the waist.
"Hurry, Catrina, we return to *su casa. Pronto!"*

It seemed to Catherine that it took hours to follow the narrow,
winding streets back to her *jacal,* which was no longer on the
outskirts of town. Then, as she went into the first stages of labor,
she realized that it had taken only a few minutes, maybe ten, for
Atanacia to lead her back home. It was the labor that took hours.
And hours.

Atanacia bathed her face with a wet cloth, gently urging her to
relax when the pains struck like lightning. Where was Law? Catherine twisted and knotted in the throes of the hard contractions.
Why wasn't he here when his child was about to be born? She
doubled into the fetal position and clenched her fists against her

dry mouth. Law, Law, Law. It was a litany her lips formed in tribute for the child that was already asserting its rights as it squirmed in the birth canal.

"You are very narrow of the hips," Atanacia said, concern shadowing her pretty face. Then she brightened. "But the child, it will come. I know. After two, I know there is the *dolor*. But soon it will be over, *mi amiga*. And you will forget the *dolor*. You will want more *niños*—maybe as many as I do."

Catherine groaned. "That is the last thing I want right now, fifteen children."

At last it was over. Seventeen hours after that first knifelike thrust, Catherine wearily looked up to watch Atanacia lay the baby on the old table and enfold it in the muslin blanket. Catherine thought her daughter surely had to be the ugliest baby ever born in Tucson, but when Atanacia handed the squalling, red-faced infant to her, the maternal instinct fiercely surged through Catherine—equaling almost her daughter's sturdy tugging at her nipple seconds later.

A strong mite, she thought, with Law's thick blond curls and her own heart-shaped face. But the eyes—they were a muddy blue, so it was still too soon to tell their final color.

"What will you name the *bebé?*" Atanacia asked as she knelt beside the mother and daughter to gaze at God's newest creation.

Catherine had considered naming the child for her friend, Atanacia. But at the last second she replied with a mystical smile, "I think I shall call her after my father, Jesse. For in a way he was responsible for my coming to the territory. Jessica Atanacia Davalos."

"Miguel, again—the verb forms for the word 'drive,' " Catherine said.

The shoeless boy began, "Drive . . . drove . . ." and then gave up in hopeless laughter as Jessie crawled across the earth-packed floor to pinch curiously at his dusty toes. The five other students joined in the laughter. Atanacia hurried in from outside, where she had been cooking the noonday meal, and scooped up the child. "No, no, *traviesa,*" she scolded the child fondly.

"It's all right." Catherine sighed, taking Jessie. The child was indeed a mischievous little thing. Yet love for the seven-month-old filled her heart to overflowing, it seemed. The feel of the strong heartbeat in that small ribcage, the tiny dimples in the plump elbows and knees, caused Catherine to feel as if she had performed an incredible feat in giving birth to such a perfect creation. Secretly she had to laugh at her mother's pride.

Atanacia's own daughter, the three-month-old Rosalie Catrina, lay docilely in Jessie's crib each day while Atanacia helped about the *jacal* as Catherine taught school. The baby was never any problem, never demanding and daring as Jessie had been at three months—and still was.

Without Atanacia to help, Catherine could never have begun tutoring again. It was Sam and Lionel who had persuaded some of Tucson's citizens to send their children back to her school. In turn, Catherine had insisted on paying Atanacia, minimal though the salary was, for her morning help. And Atanacia was delighted with her own money . . . her *independencia,* as she called it. Sam teasingly claimed that Catherine's talk of the women suffragists, Elizabeth Stanton and Susan B. Anthony, was giving his wife outlandish ideas.

"Class is dismissed," Catherine told the students. She waited for them to leave before she opened her blouse and gave her breast to the small, eagerly sucking mouth.

"Where is Loco?" she asked Atanacia, who picked up her own daughter and began to nurse.

Atanacia shook her head sadly. "He wanders. I saw him earlier this morning down by the river, but now—I do not know."

Catherine worried for the old man. Since February he had behaved like a shaman on peyote. She feared Loco, like his name, was indeed losing his mind with his advancing years. There were times when she feared she was losing her own mind, especially those first weeks after Jessie was born. She had so wanted Law to be with her.

As the months passed and no word came from him, she became like Loco, moving restlessly from her bedroom to the front room and back and sometimes outside to wander the dusty street until a bout of chills drove her to her bed for rest.

She did receive word from Margaret, who had married, surprisingly, a penniless schoolmaster—a short letter telling of their mother's quietly dying in her sleep.

In late March a shabby-looking American stopped outside her house to pass along the news. Law, serving under the supreme commander of the Juarista forces, General Escobedo, was besieging the city of Queretaro, where Maximilian was making a last-ditch stand to retain his empire.

"Is there any other message?" she had frantically demanded of the threadbare man.

"Nope—he just said to wait for him, ma'am."

With a both lightened and saddened heart, she had fed the man and sent him on his way. Surely then within months Law would come home.

Atanacia went home to feed Sam, who closed the store during the summer's long siesta hour, and Catherine picked up the brown wrapping paper the students wrote on that was scattered about the floor.

Afterward she began to feed Jessie the mashed beans and applesauce . . . which was so expensive now that apples were a dollar a pound. She knew she should be eating something herself. Her weight had dropped drastically since Jessie's birth. She told herself it was the nursing that was pulling her down. Atanacia wanted her to stop. "But who can afford milk these days?" Catherine asked her friend.

A knock on the door interrupted the stale tortilla she was forcing herself to eat, and she called out, "Enter," thinking it was Loco. When the door opened and Sherrod stepped inside, hat in hand, the tortilla dropped from her hand.

"Hello, Catherine," he said quietly.

Suddenly she was glad that the room was darkened. Her feminine vanity came to the foreground for the first time in months, and she glimpsed a mental image of how awful she must look—with clothes that bagged on her and gaunt hollows beneath her cheekbones. "Come in, Sherrod—and sit down," she said, rising to set Jessica on the ground.

"Is it all right—or should I wait for you outside?"

She laughed. "My social life has changed considerably. I'm an old married woman now."

"So I heard—only recently, Catherine."

He took a seat on one of the students' benches, realizing that what he had also heard of her illness was true. She was emaciated, as shriveled as an old woman. Yet when she smiled just then . . . dear God, but he loved her. He held out the gift he had brought for the child. Law's child, if what Sam told him was the truth. "I thought your daughter might like this, Catherine."

She took the brown-paper-wrapped package. "Why, thank you, Sherrod." She tore away the paper to find a yellow stuffed duck. "How perfect! Maybe now Jessie will stop crawling after the chickens outside."

Without thinking, Sherrod said what was on his mind, the one thing that was on his mind. "She should be brought up in a better place," he blurted.

Catherine looked up at him, and his gaze dropped to the straw hat in his hands. "I'm sorry, Catherine. But your daughter—Jessie, is it? She's as much an heir to Cristo Rey as Brigham or Abigail. She belongs there where there's plenty of . . ." His words trailed off.

"Luxuries?" she asked. "Perhaps, but that will be her father's and my decision when the time comes." She changed the subject. "How is everyone at Cristo Rey?"

The hat twirled in Sherrod's hands, and, watching him, she thought again how aristocratic, how handsome, were his looks. No wonder she had been temporarily blinded to Law's extraordinary male mystique.

"Abigail is at Miss Phelps's School for Young Ladies in Chicago, and Brigham's at Markham Academy in Richmond. Father's as irascible as ever. And Mother . . ." His shoulders shrugged. "I never know what she's thinking."

I do, Catherine thought. "And Lucy?"

Sherrod's gaze met hers, and she saw the misery there. "Lucy's dying, Catherine. Cirrhosis of the liver. And her mind's going. We just returned from St. Louis to see the doctors there. I would have been to see you sooner, but we didn't make it back to Tucson until last week."

"Oh, Sherrod, I'm so sorry to hear that. I really liked Lucy."

"And she you. She was disconsolate when you left. We all were."

Not everyone. "It worked out for the best." She smiled, and he was struck again by her unsuspected beauty. "If I had not left, I would never have had the opportunity to persuade your stepbrother to marry me."

They talked awhile longer, until Jessie began to play with the gaiters at Sherrod's ankles. With a laugh, he picked the baby up and bounced her on his knee.

"She's adorable," he said, before he took his leave. "All of Congress Street will spoil her."

After he left, Catherine gave thought to his invitation to live at Cristo Rey. She knew, though, that Elizabeth would make it miserable for her and Jessie there. Still, as the months passed, as June gave way to July, then one season passed into another with the almost insignificant changes of temperature peculiar to Tucson, she thought more and more often about accepting the invitation.

Tucson was becoming every day more of a gunman's town, a roughneck place peopled by all sorts of remnants of the Civil War veterans—outlaws, gamblers, and swindlers—seeking the town's wide-open gambling establishments.

Then, too, there was the financial situation to consider. Even with the laundry business and teaching, her income never seemed enough. She had long since sold Sonora to get her, Loco, and Jessie through the long, slow summer when business dropped off everywhere. "You're too proud," Sam accused her one afternoon when she refused to accept a side of beef he offered.

"Perhaps," she said, smiling. "But pride is all I have left."

In November, shortly before Jessie's first birthday, Loco disappeared one morning and was not seen again. "Sometimes the old ones, the Indian ancients," Atanacia said, "they go off to be alone when they know they are going to die. And he was very old, was he not?"

Yes, Catherine thought, Loco was very old—as old as she felt, and must surely look without Law's love to renew her.

And that was the reality that she had put off facing for so long. The war in Mexico had ended with Maximilian's execution in Queretaro, on the Hill of the Bells, five months earlier.

So why had Law not returned?

Chapter 25

Y OU'RE spoiling her," Catherine said. "Gifts for her birthday, Christmas, even the Feast of San Agustín. Jessie's come to expect them from you, Sherrod."

Sherrod lifted the two-year-old from his knee, where he had been bouncing her in the imitation of a horse ride. "She needs a pony, Catherine," he said, his gaze lingering on the cherublike child. With Law's yellow locks and Catherine's gray-green eyes, though they seemed more green than Catherine's, the child was extraordinarily beautiful. But it was the dimpled smile, Catherine's smile, that charmed the beholder. "She'll never ride as well as you if you don't put her on a horse."

Catherine arched a brow. "And I suppose her next gift will be a horse?" she asked, smiling.

"If you had a place to keep the horse, it would be." He paused, then added, "You do have a place to keep the horse, Catherine. Lucy has been dead six months now. And Jessie needs a father." His words accelerated, as if he knew she would stop him. "With Abigail and Brigham away at school and Father getting feeble, the Stronghold is lonely. He took her hand and would not let her disengage it as she usually did. "Say you'll marry me, darling."

"I'm already married, Sherrod," she said, turning her head away.

He jerked her wrist, pulling her around to face him. "Dammit, Catherine, don't you think Law would be back now if he were alive? Nothing would keep him from you! I know, because I love you, also."

The intensity in Sherrod's voice and his piercing gaze made her at last face the truth she had been avoiding. Her mind reviewed the years—how many, five?—since she had come to

(154)

Arizona to find a husband. Now she was getting a second chance
. . . not just any man, but a handsome, loving husband who also
adored Jessie, not just a home but the fabled Stronghold. Her
decision to come west to the Arizona Territory had been a wise
one. She had truly been blessed in those five years.

Her free hand came up to caress Sherrod's jaw. "Thank you,
Sherrod, for what you're offering me. But Law asked me to wait.
And if I have to, I'll wait forever."

He took Catherine out often, as often as he could come into
Tucson. Elizabeth did not approve, of course. She pointed out
that with Don Francisco bedridden following a heart attack, he
was needed more than ever at the Stronghold. His mother was
right, but, like his stepbrother, he supposed, he could not rid
himself of his love for Catherine.

She continued to teach, even as her health dwindled, and she
would not hear of him taking her to the doctors in St. Louis.
"They will not tell me anything, Sherrod, that any of the other
doctors have not already told me," she would say in that
no-nonsense voice of hers. But he knew the malaria was damaging her heart and lungs.

He had to content himself with taking her and Jessie to the
new open-air restaurant in the Carrillo Gardens for the novel dish
ice cream, or to the Tivoli Theater when special acts came to the
territory.

But most often Catherine asked him to drive her out alone into
the desert, for her hacking cough embarrassed her when she was
in public places. "I think there is nothing lovelier than the desert," she told him. "Especially in the spring. Who could think that
such a barren waste could produce such delicate blooms of
beauty? And the sage—what a wonderous shade of deep purple!"

He would help her out of the buckboard, and they would sit
quietly against a tree, usually a Joshua, if she could find one, and
watch the sunset in all its glorious colors, more brilliant there on
the desert than in any other place on earth.

But by the fall, before Jessie's sixth birthday, Catherine had
become so weak that he had to lift her from her bed into the
wagon and carry her again to sit beneath a tree. She always took
a handkerchief with her now. By the time the sun had set there

would be the faint dark splotches on the material to match those last bright-red shafts of sunlight.

He pretended not to notice, for he knew she wanted no mention made of her dying.

Then one evening, when he had driven her out into the desert and settled her against the solid trunk of a Joshua, she mentioned her death herself for the first time. "I worry for Jessie. I know Sam and Atanacia would take good care of her, Sherrod . . . but they already have so many children—six, and another on the way. And then there is Cristo Rey . . . I want Jessica to know her heritage."

She paused to cough spasmodically into her handkerchief, then continued, her voice more hoarse. "I never told you, Sherrod . . . but your mother forced me to leave the Stronghold. She knew you were in love with me."

He cradled Catherine in his arms so she would not see his surprise at the revelation. He would deal with his mother later.

Catherine grabbed at his hand now. "You must promise me that you won't let your mother force Jessie to leave . . . as she did me."

He caught her thin, bloodless hand to his cheek. "I promise," he rasped.

As if satisfied, Catherine's hand relaxed, and she closed her eyes. He was afraid she had died, so shallow was her breathing. But she opened her eyes again and said in what was hardly more than a whisper, "You know, Sherrod, Jessie asked me if death hurt."

He knew Catherine wanted to talk, and he asked, "What did you tell her?"

"I told her that it was probably a quick little pain. Like a cactus spine in the finger." Her voice drifted lower, lighter, so that he had to bend his head nearer to hear her words. "I couldn't tell Jessie that sometimes one even looks forward to death's sweet pain . . . to the release of the emotional pain . . . the pain that has tormented me a hundred times more than . . . the malaria."

But it wasn't malaria's effects that were killing her, he thought. It was a broken heart. Beyond death, he knew, that's where she would find the release she was looking for. That's where she would find her beloved.

But where would he find his beloved? Too soon Death would

steal her from him. He enfolded her more closely against him, as if to withhold her from Death's talons. Dear God, but he loved her! Tears streamed silently down his cheeks as she began to speak again, slowly, painfully. And he was glad they both were looking ahead and not at each other.

"You know ... when I first came here ... the landscape looked as unreal to me as plants on the moon ... now it's a part of me. Did you ever see the night-blooming flower, Sherrod?"

He was too choked to speak, and she continued, unaware of his agony. "No, I don't suppose you ever did," she murmured. "I've only seen one once myself."

His arm tightened about her waist. Her hair was damp where his head rested above hers. "The sky ..." Her breath, her words, were no more than the mere flutter of a butterfly's wings. "It's really quite beautiful, isn't it ... streaked with purple that way?"

Through shimmering eyes he watched the sunset change through its rainbow of colors before he allowed himself to look at her. How beautiful she was, her soft lips parted, her long lashes lying like fans on her cheeks. There was an iridescent quality in her emaciation.

With an anguished cry he realized he was alone on the desert, and he buried his face against her breasts and wept.

PART
2

Chapter 26

1880

AHH, please, woncha?" Bob Merckle pleaded. "Just once around the rink with me, huh, Jessie?"

Impatiently Jessie knotted the ties of her left roller skate, showing more of the booted ankle than was permissible, to the breathless delight of the teenage boy on the splintery bench beside her. He had slicked back his hair from the middle with pomade in honor of this monthly occasion, when Jessie Davalos came into town with her uncle. Three more boys, just waiting for the thirteen-year-old tawny-haired beauty to come onto the floor, skated aimlessly about the newly constructed rink with the rest of the crowd.

Jessie sighed and rose to her feet. "Maybe later, Bob. I just want to practice skating on my own for a while, all right?" She rolled out onto the floor without even waiting for his reply and with a petulant grimace managed to forestall the other boys who hastened to catch up with her.

The floor was jammed with Tucson society trying desperately to remain erect. The rink had opened only that spring at Levin's Park, but the novel idea caught on as quickly as the sailboat rentals on Silver Lake had five years earlier. People jostled for position on the floor. The enormous room was a din of children's shouts, feminine squeaks, and male laughter.

Jessie found it almost impossible to enjoy herself. She loved the freedom her skates offered, but the noise, the people shoving, and always the ogling of the boys and men—she felt hemmed in, imprisoned. Yes, all in all, she much preferred the wild freedom of horseback riding.

Maneuvering around the couples locked arm in arm, she looked for the sight of Brig's dark head. Jumping jackasses, don't let him be skating with the prissy Fanny Roget! But, of course, he would be. Fanny's parents were staying at the fashionable Ornodorf Hotel, there from Denver to do business with Uncle Sherrod. Her father, some sort of a silver tycoon, wanted to discuss a mining venture, and Brig was stuck with the simpering young woman.

She saw Brig then. His arm was around Fanny's hourglass waist, his dark head bent near hers as they skated just ahead of her. Fanny turned her face up at Brig's and laughed at something he said, and Jessie wanted to pull out the young woman's bright-red hair by its roots. The way Brig smiled that slow, warm smile—he certainly didn't look *stuck* with Fanny Roget.

Why did he have to be so damned handsome, with all his father's dark dramatic looks? And why did he have to be seven years older than she? Brig, at twenty, treated her as his little sister. It wasn't as if they were really full-blooded cousins or anything. She had been in love with him since that first day she had come to the Stronghold when she was six.

Brig seemed to have always been there to take care of her—to pick her up the first few times she fell off the calico pony Uncle Sherrod had given her and brush the grass out of her hair; to help her in the middle of the night with the odious math; and to teach her how to handle a rifle. Elizabeth had protested vehemently to Sherrod about that, but on the next day Brig had merely carted Jessie another ten miles out of sight and sound and resumed pitching the beer bottles in the air for her target practice.

It had been deliciously wonderful being alone with him out on the range, feeling his arms about her shoulders, his breath fanning her cheek, as he demonstrated the rifle's mechanics. Then the summer before, Elizabeth had put a stop to her riding out with Brig. "You're getting to be a young lady," the old woman had said, looking pointedly at the breasts that had just begun to develop on Jessie's coltish body. Under Elizabeth's hooded glare, she had felt dirty about her budding femininity.

But she would not be made to feel dirty about what she felt for Brig, whose own body burst now with manhood. That would be her secret.

Abigail must have suspected. That same summer Abigail married the Jewish merchant Ira Ritz. Jessie always thought of the man as Mr. Big Nose. The day of the wedding Abigail pulled her aside, handing her the basket of sunflowers that Jessie, as flowergirl, was to carry. "You look lovely, Jessie."

"I wish that I looked as lovely as you," Jessie breathed, for to her the twenty-two-year-old bride was breathtaking, with the white lace and silk framing the soft blond hair and creamy skin. Jessie tugged at her own wild honeysuckle curls that tumbled in disorder about her shoulders. "I'll never look pretty with hair like a horse's mane and a body like a picket fence."

Abigail laughed softly and hugged her. "You'll be a raving beauty one day; far prettier than I, with your brilliant coloring." Her smile faded then. "But Jessie, at your age a girl dramatizes everything. You fall in love with everything and everyone."

"I'm not like that," she had protested. "I just love the Stronghold and—"

"I know," Abigail said, when Jessie's lips clamped tight. "But there's such a thing as ill-fated love. Did your tutor ever say anything about such lovers as Tristan and Isolde or Dante and Beatrice?"

Jessie shook her head. "Mr. Franklin never talked about stories like that." The old tutor Elizabeth had hired for her, at Sherrod's insistence, had stuck to the Latin tales of Caesar's conquests.

Abigail's voice lowered. "You don't understand Grandmother Elizabeth, Jessie. Maybe it was because her love for my grandfather was ill-fated, but . . . but after you grow up, Jessie, go away. There's a whole wide world out there. Go away. I'm going. I'm going as far from this territory as the Santa Fe Railroad will take Ira and me."

Abigail had escaped with her merchant husband to the bright city lights of New York. But not Jessie. She would never leave. The Stronghold was her home. And Brig was her love.

In the press of the crowd she skated past Brig and Fanny. Fanny went sprawling headlong. Jessie continued on by. She felt ashamed of herself, letting her skate wheels get in Fanny's way as they had. But then Fanny should know that was one of the perils of roller skating.

Jessie skated once with Manuel Drachman and twice more with Bob Merckle before the afternoon was over. Brig, with Fanny hugging his side, came for Jessie. "We'd better go," he said, giving the Merckle boy only a cursory glance. "Father wants to be at the depot before the train arrives."

"I'll help you with your skates, Jessie," the freckle-faced Bob volunteered.

Only then did Brig seem to notice the teenager. "She can do them herself, Bob. We're in a hurry."

Jessie fumed as she yanked the laces off the skate hooks. Brig was waiting at the door with Fanny. Though the couple was not touching, his head was bent over hers, his hand supporting his tall body on the wall above her head. When Jessie reached them, the two went on outside, talking softly, and she trailed along like . . . just like a kid sister!

Tucson's chain gang was sweeping the dirt street, followed by the water wagon that sprinkled the rising dust, and Brig and Fannie were forced to wait for the convicts to pass. Jessie took the opportunity to slide a look at her competitor. Bright-red mouth, bright-red hair . . . a point for Fanny. Small eyes . . . a point for herself. But Fanny's bosom—at eighteen the girl had more bosom than Jessie would have if she lived to be a hundred. Score another point for Fanny, she thought grimly.

Brig took not only Fanny's arm but her own to lead them across the street, and Jessie had to admit that this was better than nothing. At least she was with Brig. Near him. Touching him. Ahh, sweet torture. How old was Juliet when she fell in love with Romeo—fourteen or fifteen? Was her own love so hopeless, then? She darted another glance at voluptuous Fanny. No doubt about it. Her own chances looked dim.

She followed the couple several blocks past the maze of windmills that seemed to grow like rigid, branchless trees all over town. By running, the three were able to catch one of the mule-drawn streetcars that went as far north as the new university. But they were only going as far as Pennington Street's new railroad depot.

The streetcar stopped several times more for passengers as the street filled with people on their way to the depot. Though it was still two hours until the first train would steam into Tucson, elated citizens were already gathering to welcome it.

Sherrod, along with Charles Poston, was to be one of the town officials who were to speak at the celebration. By the time Brig and Fanny, with Jessie in tow, arrived, the Sixth Cavalry band from Fort Lowell was on the platform along with a cannon. Sherrod was there, deep in conversation with Roget. As darkly handsome as Brig was, his father at forty-one was even more so with the distinguished silver to streak the dark-brown hair and the brooding cast to his face that added an almost spiritual refinement to his strong masculine features.

If Jessie loved Brig, she worshiped her uncle—as he had told her to call him and which unfailingly irritated Elizabeth. To Jessie he was larger than life. He rode out of the pages of her mother's book by Sir Walter Scott. Uncle Sherrod was Ivanhoe (an older Ivanhoe, true), riding to take her, Rowena, away from the shabbiness of the *jacal*.

He had given her a new world there at the Stronghold. Servants, a real bed (not the cornhusk one she had lain on in Tucson), food that mounded the table, though it seemed she could never eat enough nor put on weight, and an education.

Best of all, Uncle Sherrod had given her a family—cousins and grandparents, though she did not remember much of Don Francisco. A few times before his death the year after she came to the Stronghold, he had taken her on his lap, when his heart wasn't bothering him, and told her stories of what it was like when he had first come to the Stronghold—of the fierce Indians that lurked outside the gates and the grass that was as high as a horse's flanks then. And always he would tell her, *you are your father's daughter.*

Only Elizabeth had remained distant, ignoring her as if she did not exist. And Jessie knew it was not her imagination. She remembered clearly that first day Uncle Sherrod had brought her to the Stronghold. He had put her in a room that he told her used to be her mother's and before that her Grandmother Davalos's. It was such a nice room with hard floors and walls tinted the blue of a summer sky. Only the mustiness told of its disuse.

Elizabeth had come storming into the room, demanding of Uncle Sherrod what he was doing, bringing the Howard child into the house.

"She is not 'the Howard child,' Mother. She is Jessie Davalos, your husband's granddaughter—and she has as much right to live here as Abigail or Brigham. I want that understood from this time on!"

That had been the first and only confrontation Jessie had with the old woman, but never since had she been comfortable in Elizabeth's cold presence.

Sherrod spied the three young people crossing the platform

toward him and broke off talking with Roget to encircle Jessie's shoulders, drawing her next to him. "How was the skating?" he asked with a fond smile for the three young people.

Fanny looked up at Sherrod, smiling. "Marvelous."

"Crowded," Jessie said flatly.

Brig grinned at her and tousled her hair with his free hand. "That's because half the boys of Tucson were there hoping to skate with you."

She moved her head out of his reach. How could he treat her like such a child? Couldn't he see she was no longer a little girl?

Sherrod cast a quizzical glance from his son to his niece. She was growing, too quickly. And despite the color of her hair, she reminded him too much of Catherine, with those eyes the cool color of English ivy and Catherine's smile that had enchanted him from the very first.

Jessie, of course, was more headstrong—an unbroken colt still, but nevertheless she had her mother's strength of purpose. There were times when, watching the girl, being around her, got to be too much. Too great a pain. He saw Catherine in her smile, heard her in the laugh. At those times, he would make an excuse for business in Tucson. He would find Gay Alley and release with the "gray doves" there.

Perhaps he should have been more like Law. Instead of playing the gentleman, instead of doing what seemed right, he should have left Lucy and the Stronghold. He should have taken Catherine and made her his. But that he never could have done. She had been Law's from the first.

As a young man he had envied Law and his restless, reckless ways. And it looked as if he would envy him the rest of his life.

"Well, it looks like you're going to have to put your hair up," he told Jessie now. "I've just been telling Hugo you're growing into a young lady and it's time I sent you off to a finishing school in the States."

"Yes," Roget said, peering down at Jessie through his monocle, "I was telling Godwin that Fanny here attended Lady Bertram's in St. Louis. I can recommend it as an excellent finishing school."

Fanny moved her myopic gaze from Brig's face long enough to say sweetly, "It would do a world of good for you, child."

She can't wait to get rid of me! "I don't want to go, Uncle

Sherrod. I know everything I need to know for living at the Stronghold."

"But you won't always be living at the Stronghold," Sherrod said patiently. "One day you'll marry and leave."

"I don't want to ever leave!"

Sherrod chuckled at her vehemence. "Well, it's nothing we have to decide today. We'll talk about it later."

But later never came.

As the small wood-burning engine, puffing clouds of black smoke from its funnel-shaped smokestack and drawing small wooden cars behind it, chugged into the station, as the cannon roared and the cavalry band trumpeted above the hysterical yells of the citizens, as Sherrod cracked the bottle of champagne over the engine . . . he clutched at his left arm and twisted forward to slump on the platform.

It was the end of his life and the beginning of a change in Jessie's.

Chapter 27

DEAD of an heart attack! Incredible, people said. Sherrod Godwin was still so young. But privately Jessie thought it was an old-young. He seldom had laughed, and the eyes had always seemed dolorous.

The Methodist Episcopal Church was filled for the memorial services. Men waited outside the church in the hot sun, hat in hand. The burial had been held the day after Sherrod's death because of the spring heat. But the memorial services were postponed a week for his daughter's train to arrive from New York.

The service was being officiated by an elder up from the Mormon town of St. David. A respectful hush lay over the throng. This was a Godwin being buried. All places of business were closed, including the saloons and gambling establishments.

Never before had so many people assembled for a service. Outside, the bells of the San Agustín Cathedral could be heard crying their mourning. An American flag draped the altar.

All eyes in the church were trained on the Godwin family, who sat at the front. But rather than on the grieving matriarch, Elizabeth Godwin, or the heirs, Brigham and Abigail, and her husband Ira, the gazes were directed on Jessie Howard. Or was it Davalos? There was so much gossip that one never knew what the real facts were, who Jessie's father really was.

It was not just the mystery about the girl that caught the imagination. There was the promise of her wild beauty, though to look at her at that moment, sitting between Brigham and the rigid Elizabeth, one would have doubts about that promise. She was really too tall for a child her age. And the tawny hair fell about her shoulder blades like a lion's mane. Not at all the ladylike prettiness of the young lady on the other side of Brigham, Fanny Roget. Only the pale-green eyes thicketed by black lashes lent any immediate relief to the wrathful-looking creature.

An ungovernable child, certainly, though Elizabeth Godwin never did say so in such terms on the occasional trips she made into Tucson. But then Elizabeth was not the kind to complain. The way she had been made to endure her husband's bigamous love affair with the Davalos woman would have been enough to drive a weaker woman to her grave. But not Elizabeth. The fact that she had survived the Davalos woman's death, her daughter-in-law's, her husband's, and now her son's was testimony to her endurance.

And then Elizabeth was so charitable, taking in the Spanish woman's bastard grandchild. Her husband's own illegitimate grandchild. A wicked strain ran through the Davalos blood. And it would show up in Jessica Davalos! Time would tell.

The memorial service was at last over, and Jessie stood stiffly at Brig's side as the mourners filed past the Godwin family to pay their respects. Her face was bleached beneath the suntan. In spite of the loss Brig felt at his father's death, he sensed the greater need of his cousin. Thirteen was too young to have death come knocking so many times.

In the moment of respite that followed, his hand slipped to her side to squeeze her chilled fingers reassuringly. "It's all right, Jessie."

She glanced up into the face pale with its own grief, a face that looked like a dark angel's. "You won't leave me, will you, Brig?"

"Not for a long time. Not until you're ready to leave yourself and go out to find a husband."

He had misunderstood. "But I don't want a husband," she said, staring now straight in front of her, too proud to let him see what was in her eyes. "I don't want things to change."

Brig sighed. "But things do, Jessie. You're old enough to know that. But our friendship won't change, I promise."

Roget and his wife, who looked to Jessie an older, plumper version of Fanny, accompanied the Godwins as far as Ronstadt's stables. Elizabeth thanked the Rogets politely for their support in the time of bereavement, and Fanny hugged Brig tearfully. Jessie turned away and climbed in the spring wagon's back seat.

On the long trip back to the Stronghold, Elizabeth sat beside a grave Brig, who drove. Her lips pressed tightly against her clenched teeth. In the back, sitting with Jessie, was the stolidly silent Ira, and Abigail, who talked fitfully, as if trying to keep back the tears with conversation.

"I so wanted Father to see his first grandchild," she said, her voice cracking.

Ira patted his wife's shoulder with a clumsy hand. "It's all right, Abbie, you'll bear a child yet."

"But the doctors give so little hope. Three times now . . ." Tears streamed down her cheeks, and she took out her handkerchief to blow her nose.

"You'll have to take to your bed for the full nine months then," Elizabeth said, turning to fix her granddaughter with stone-gray eyes. "There can be no shirking of duty, Abigail. There must be children to keep the Stronghold going."

Privately Jessie thought that Elizabeth made the Stronghold sound like some biblical stone idol that needed a blood sacrifice to be propitiated. And it wasn't! Behind its impregnable walls Jessie found warmth and security. Inside those walls were found treasures not to be found in any of the other homes throughout the territory.

Oh, not the tasteless Victorian bric-a-brac that seemed to clutter the drawing rooms she had occasionally visited with her uncle and Brig, but real *objets d'art* that Uncle Sherrod had purchased for his wife those last years of her life—the Waterford glasses and

Spode and Sèvres porcelain, the antique blackamoor statue, and the first piano in the territory, the Chickering grand piano. And Lucy had added items that reflected her own elegance and good taste—the five-piece Aubusson salon suite, a pair of Queen Anne shepherd's-crook armchairs, and a Venetian three-panel folding screen.

When the grieving family arrived at the Stronghold, Jessie went immediately to the cool privacy of her room. She wanted only to be alone, but Elizabeth summoned her to Don Francisco's old office that had been Sherrod's. Brig was pacing the floor, his hands behind his back. Elizabeth sat behind the desk. "Come in," she told Jessie, who hesitated in the doorway.

Abigail, her eyes red, sat in the hard-backed chair, and Ira stood behind it. Jessie noticed he would not meet her eyes. Brig turned toward her, and she saw the anger burning in the dark-blue gaze. She frowned, not understanding the reason for his agitation.

"I was just telling Brigham," Elizabeth said curtly, "that the Roget family will be coming to stay with us for some months. Mr. Roget and I will be closing the deal that Sherrod initiated before his death. They will, of course, be paying us a large sum for the mineral rights—for the excavation rights to whatever mines are discovered on Cristo Rey."

She addressed her grandson and Ira now. "I don't need to tell you that the initial down payment alone will compensate for the money Cristo Rey has lost in its cattle investments. The drought, cattle rustling, and overgrazing will wipe us out without the Roget money."

Abigail gasped, and Brig mumbled, half to himself, "Father mentioned the problem, but I had no idea."

In the silence that followed, Ira said, "You have to bend with the wind, Mrs. Godwin. You're doing only what has to be done. After all, if I understand it, it's only a five-year lease."

Brig jammed his hands in his pockets and turned to pace the floor. Abigail fidgeted with her handkerchief. Jessie was beginning to wonder why she had been included in this family council when Elizabeth said, "I have decided that Doña Dominica's room"—and Jessie noted how Elizabeth's voice seemed to hiss like water on a hot stove when she pronounced the name—"will be given to the Rogets."

Brig rounded on his grandmother. "And where will you put Jessie? All the other bedrooms are much smaller."

Elizabeth's back stiffened, and she rose from behind the desk. "It's as good a time as any to bring the subject out into the open. Jessie Howard will have to find a place down in the ranchería."

Howard? Jessie stood stunned, listening to Brig and Elizabeth argue as if she were not present.

"What?" he thundered.

"Even then," Elizabeth continued calmly, coolly, "it is only because of my goodwill that Jessie is fortunate enough to have a roof over her head. If it weren't for my promise to your father, Brigham, I would see that she never set foot on Cristo Rey again."

Brig went to stand before the old woman. A muscle jerked in his temple. "Good God, Grandmother, have you taken leave of your senses? Father would never hear of it!" His fist slammed against the desk. "And I won't either!"

Elizabeth looked at Jessie for the first time since the argument began. "No," she said, "I haven't taken leave of my senses." A faint smile twitched the withered lips. "I am at last tying up the loose ends. Your father is dead, Brig. And he appointed me as administrator of Cristo Rey until you reach twenty-five years of age. And even then I will still hold half the interest in Cristo Rey. So my decision, my authority, is irrevocable. I want the bastard child out of the Stronghold today—immediately!"

Chapter 28

JESSIE leaned low over the pony. Its tail streamed behind, blown by the wind, as was Jessie's own mane. She laughed, exulting at the exquisite feeling of flying over the earth, of pacing the man made machine—the train that bellowed and snorted as it raced along the narrow-gauge railroad track beside her. But she knew she would win; she would reach Cristo Rey's southern boundary

Camp Huachuca, first because she could take the short cuts the New Mexico & Arizona train could not.

The watering hole, banked by a copse of acacia and ironwood, came into sight, and Jessie pulled up short, almost setting her calico on its haunches. She watched the train, its black smoke rising to faint white puffs in the sky, diminish in size as it edged its way around a bluff and chugged toward Nogales. Then she wheeled about and began the long trip back to the Stronghold's ranchería.

She rode the pony bareback, like an Indian, with her skirts hitched up above her knees, exposing the long, smooth line of calf and the bare feet sandaled in huaraches. She could no more imagine riding sidesaddle, as had her mother, than she could imagine living anywhere but Cristo Rey. She loved its vibrant colors and drastic change of landscape, as she loved the people— the Papagos and Mexicans she worked and lived with—as she loved Brig Godwin.

She wondered sometimes that it did not show—the wild, sweet stirrings when he came near her, when their hands touched as she served him food when he ate with the other cowboys. He spent more time at the ranchería than he did at the Stronghold. She liked to believe it was to be near her, though she knew the problem of getting the cattle ranching back on its feet demanded much of his time outside the Stronghold.

And she knew that she was only fooling herself, hoping that he could ever love her, for he had become engaged to Fanny two months before, in June. Fanny and her mother were gone now, escaping the summer heat by shopping in New York for the trousseau for the coming fall wedding. And Hugo had opened an office in Tucson, from which he directed his various mining ventures that included the gold and silver ore taken out of Cristo Rey's rich earth. Elizabeth had achieved everything she had planned.

Thinking about the woman, Jessie dug her heels into the calico flanks more roughly than she intended. She had always known the old woman detested her. But now, only as she neared her seventeenth birthday, did she realize the reason for Elizabeth's enmity all those years. Elizabeth feared to lose Lorenzo Davalos's half of Cristo Rey to his daughter.

The woman was possessed by Cristo Rey, made mad by her

love of it. Jessie knew she would never have made any claim to the land. As long as she could have lived there, could live within sight of Brig, it would have been enough. But for Elizabeth to declare her illegitimate in order to retain control of Cristo Rey—that put Jessie beyond Brig. For how could he have ever come to love or marry a bastard?

A bastard. She had not even known what it meant when first she heard the name on Elizabeth's tongue. Now she carried the name as a *penitente* did his flagellum. Once more a mat was her bed and her hands were reddened and roughened with work.

She knew Elizabeth was lying yet knew no way of proving it. She knew of no one who had witnessed the ceremony between her mother and father.

And Brig, what did he think? How did he feel? If whirlwinds twisted deep inside, no hint of emotion played across his face that had these days the cold stillness of sculptured stone. There was no swashbuckler bluster in Brig. He thoroughly and efficiently carried out all the tasks of actually running Cristo Rey.

She could not help but ask herself if he carried out so thoroughly his courtship of Fanny those months she lived in the Stronghold. Had he kissed Fanny on the long rides the two had taken? Jessie could remember counting the hours until she saw the two ride back through the Stronghold's gates. And always the ravishing Fanny looked . . . slightly ravished.

Damn her red hair and big bosom!

Jessie kneed the calico into a gallop. The pony crested a catback hill that overlooked the Stronghold and its ranchería, slid down the pebbled sides to the Cienega's sandbar crossing, and streaked for the outbuildings.

Her eyes searched among the cowboys gathered about the corral, but she did not see the one man she was looking for. Neither was he in the mess hall later that afternoon when she and old Marta served the hands their lunch. When Elizabeth had banished Jessie from the Stronghold, Brig had asked the old Mexican woman to take Jessie in. Marta had given her work to earn her keep and in return served as a substitute grandmother.

Halfheartedly Jessie joked with the cowhands as she spooned the red beans over the fry bread. She passed by Red who threw a beefy arm about her waist. "Jessie, tell Slim you're my sweetheart."

She struck Red's arm with the wooden spoon. "The only sweetheart who'd have you, Red Mahoney, is that sow sleeping in the mud out back."

The men clustered about the long table punched each other in the ribs and winked. A few openly laughed at her sally. Although Jessie Davalos was an eye-catching wild beauty, not one of them dared approach her on any but the friendliest terms. The boss had made that clear the day the scrawny kid had moved out of the Stronghold. Whatever stigma of bastardy rumor had it Jessie carried, Brig let it be known that as far as he was concerned she was his cousin and therefore lived and worked at the ranchería under his protection.

But sweet Jesus, some of them thought as they watched her move out of Red's encircling arm, a man could withstand only so much temptation. And Jessie Davalos was a young woman grown now, sweet and ripe for the taking.

From the mess hall's screen door Brig watched the scene in progress—the men admiring Jessie's golden beauty and Red's arm about her waist. The door slammed shut behind him as he stepped inside, and whatever jest Red might have made to Jessie died on his lips. Talk turned to other subjects, and the men nodded respectfully as Brig made his way to Slim.

Jessie's heart galloped as she watched Brig pull out a thin yellowed sheet of rice paper and roll himself a cigarette while he talked to his foreman. Slim was a man twice his age and twice as leathery-looking. Long hours spent in the sun had only lightly tanned Brig's skin below the Stetson, but the rough range work had molded the tall, slim body into sinewy strength.

He said only a few words and was removing his spurred boot from the bench to leave when Jessie gathered her courage and took the initiative. "Want some lunch, Brig?"

When the intense blue eyes fell on her, she did not see the usual gentleness in his gaze. Suddenly she felt a stranger to this man with whom she had grown up, who to her was more than a stepcousin. His lids drooped, curtaining his expression. "No, Jessie, I lunched at the Stronghold. I'll just have a cup of coffee."

She had to refrain from smiling, for Brig had never drunk coffee at the Stronghold out of deference to his father's Mormon leanings. He himself had once confessed to her as they sat before the door of Marta's *jacal* watching fireflies that he had his doubts

(*173*)

about the revelations his namesake had experienced. Since she had not been raised in a church, she had never given the subject of religion any special thought other than a passing curiosity for the *retablos* hanging on her grandmother's bedroom walls.

When Jessie returned with the cup of coffee, she found Brig's eyes studying her. Her steps slowed, and she could not help the pleasure she took in the way his gaze ran from her sloping neckline above the peasant blouse down to the short length of calf and bare ankle that peeped beneath the full skirt. A surge of heat leaped out like tongues of fire through her stomach.

It was not the first time this had happened. She could be alone in the *jacal* she shared with old Marta, and the thought of Brig crushing her against him in a passionate embrace could cause the same aching feeling. But this was the first time he had looked at her like that—a look that made her knees go weak as water, so that when she passed the cup her hand trembled and the coffee sloshed over her wrist.

With a gasp she dropped the cup. It shattered on the table, splashing scalding liquid on Brig. He shot to his feet. His plaid flannel shirt was soaked. At once she began to rip open the shirt. Buttons flew everywhere. "Brig, Brig," she murmured over and over, "I'm sorry. I'm sorry."

"It's all right," he reassured her, but already large red welts roped across the chest that was forested with dark curling hair.

Once the cowhands realized no real damage had been done, they returned to their eating and raucous conversations, sounding for all the world like magpies. Beneath the noise she persuaded Brig to at least let her give him a clean shirt as she led him out of the mess hall.

"I have several laundered shirts left over from the washing," she told him over her shoulder, pushing open the plank door to her quarters. In one corner of the darkened room was a large woven basket, and she knelt beside it as she dug through the mound of clothing. "Here," she said, rising and crossing to Brig. "This should fit just about right." She held up the shirt to his shoulders, measuring their width. In the darkness she did not see the probing gaze he directed at her.

She began removing his own now-tattered shirt, saying, "As long as you've gotten your shirt off, Brig, you might as well leme apply some salve to those welts." Nervously, she crossed to the crude cupboard and returned with a tin of balsam of myrrh.

Brig stood watching her. His muscle-corded arms hung limply at his sides, but as she approached him she noted the way his thumbs rubbed against clenched fingers. She stopped within inches of him, feeling the tension that erected a glass wall between them. Brig's face froze into marble as she scooped the unguent from the container and touched his chest. The muscles beneath his feverish skin reacted visibly to her touch, twitching and flickering like a muleskinner's whip.

She glanced up into the rigid face. He was looking beyond her at nothing in particular. Hesitantly she massaged a small area where the burn was the worst, then moved on to the next red patch, always acutely aware of the pale smooth texture of his skin beneath her fingertips. Almost absently her fingers entwined with the short, wiry curls that tufted the skin about the small, hard nipples, then followed the dark thatch that swept down the center of the ribcage and taut stomach to enwreath the navel.

Her hand halted its progress. The seconds ticked off like staccato beats of an Indian cottonwood drum. At last Brig grasped her wrist in a painful grip. She raised her eyes to meet the eyes that burned in their sockets like cholera's raging fever. "Jessie," he grated.

She gasped at what she saw in his eyes, and the breath seared her throat. "Brig . . ."

His lips cut her short. Like a newborn blindly seeking nourishment too long denied, he covered her lips, her lids, her temples with soft, nipping kisses. Her head lolled backward. Her body trembled when his lips followed the graceful line of her throat down to the rising globes of flesh exposed above her blouse. She gave herself up to his ravishment, not even feeling the hands that bit into her arms with the agony of having something too long withheld.

"Jessie," he murmured, his breath hot against her skin. "You're just a child. Too young. My cousin."

"A stepcousin," she cried out as he moved to set her from him. Her hand grabbed at his and brought it up against her breast, forcing him to feel the furious thudding of her heart. "Feel me, Brig! I'm not a child any more! I'm a woman—with a woman's needs!"

"Good God," he groaned, closing his eyes. "Jessie, I'm getting married next fall. This can't happen."

She wouldn't let him pull away. "I think I've loved you since I was a child, Brig. I'm not going to give you up. You can't make me stop loving you!"

His lids snapped open. "I have to marry Fanny, don't you understand! There's Cristo Rey to—"

"Damn Cristo Rey!" she rasped and stood on tiptoe to claim the full mouth, her hands cupping his head to pull it down to hers.

Sunlight flashed through the shadowed room. *"Chiquita,"* Marta's voice began, "there are the dishes to do, and—" the old Mexican woman's words dropped off like falling stones as the couple broke apart.

Brig's fingers dug into Jessie's arm, as if he wished to transfer his agony to her. Then he spun away and stalked from the room.

Marta stepped aside as the tall young man strode past her. She looked at Jessie who stood like a statue. *"Dios ayudate,"* she said, sadly shaking her head, "for you need all the help God can give you, *chiquita.*"

She crossed to Jessie. Her horny, gnarled hand lifted the young girl's chin. "Even if Señor Brigham loved you, do you think La Señora Elizabeth will let him marry you? Not only are you a *bastarda*—and I say this because I love you like my own, and you must understand the truth—but Cristo Rey needs the Roget money. No, Señor Brigham could never marry you, *chiquita.*"

Chapter 29

FROM over the clothesline that stretched between the two big cottonwoods Jessie's gaze followed Brig's slim, sinewy figure as he strode from the Stronghold's open gates down to the smithy. The stocky man, bare-chested and aproned, listened respectfully to whatever it was Brig told him.

It had been two weeks since that afternoon Brig kissed her

She questioned how any human could want another one so much that it could cause physical pain; yet, watching his lithe, graceful movements—a gesture of his hand, the tilt of his dark head, his authoritative stance—she felt the knotting of her stomach, twisting and coiling inside her like some serpent out of Eden.

Brig, Brig, Brig. I love you. I want you.

As if the unspoken words had reached his ears, Brig's head turned slowly. His gaze moved past the bunkhouses, the *jacales* where brown children played, the blindfolded burro whose circular plodding ground the corn into meal, and finally to the cluster of wash kettles and caldrons. He glanced only briefly at Marta hunched over the scrub board. His eyes narrowed as he found the young girl's figure silhouetted against the white muslin sheets. He felt the flame rise in his groin.

A child. How old was Jessie now? Old enough to have the monthly flow. His fingers dug into his palms. God, but he was being torn asunder! The want of her warred with his notions of right and wrong. He could think of half a dozen reasons why he shouldn't touch her. She was his stepcousin. She was still a child. He was engaged to another woman.

And all the reasons faded into oblivion at the sight of those smoldering eyes—eyes like green fire—and the provocative smile that was still so childlike . . . and trusting. Shit! If he had to have a woman, why not Juanita or Carmen or any of the other women at the ranchería who flaunted their willingness at him?

Jessie turned away from the gaze that locked with hers to dig a shirt from the laundry basket. She would not go to Brig like some Indian squaw. She would will him to come to her. She was Jessica Davalos, regardless of what Elizabeth Godwin said or anyone thought.

When she straightened to jab the wooden clothespins on the shirt she held, Brig was stalking toward a far corral. Her hands clung to the line as her head drooped forward with despair.

Brig did not come at all to the mess hall now, and three days crawled by before she saw him again. It was her chore to rise before dawn, and, with Marta, see that breakfast was ready when the hands filed into the mess hall after sunup. That morning the air was still cool when she made her way through the predawn darkness to the well, where the churned butter was kept against the heat of the day.

As she pulled up the crock the clank of a spur behind her warned her, and she whirled. The rope slipped through her fingers, and the crock slid back into the well. Brig's pale face, ravaged with torment, loomed out of the dark. He reached behind her and drew up the crock, holding it out to her.

"I can't sleep at night for thinking of you, Jessie," he said quietly. Anyone watching the two of them would not have suspected the longing that flowed between them like an electrical current.

She took the crock, careful not to touch his hands. "I know." Her eyes met his. "And you won't, Brig. Your soul will never rest again until we belong to each other. You'll never know happiness with Fanny Roget."

His hands shot out to grab her upper arms. "Damn you, don't say that!" He began to shake her. "Don't make it worse than it already is!"

The crock slipped from her grasp to shatter at their feet. The pinkish-yellow butter with its separated grease seeped out to flow between them like an unfordable river. Brig flung her from him. His chest heaved with the effort he made to contain himself. "I'll find a way to have you—forever. Cristo Rey—my grandmother—I won't let them stand in my way."

At the mention of his grandmother, hopelessness washed over Jessie, and all her resolve to win Brig dissolved like the greasy butter in the sand. "She'll never permit it," she whispered, almost afraid the woman was so omnipotent she could see them, hear them, now. "She'll find some way to stop you."

"Not this time. Not this time! Next week when I go into Tucson, I'm going by Roget's office and break the engagement with his daughter."

Jessie bit her bottom lip, not really believing what she was hearing. She was still dreaming. Brig loved her, wanted her!

"I'll make Cristo Rey keep going," he continued. "If nothing else I can reopen the mines. I can cut back on expenses—though God knows, there's so little to cut back on. But some way or another, Jessie Davalos, I mean to have you. Nothing will stop me."

"Your grandmother—"

He reached across to catch Jessie's waist and pull her into his arms. The tension had gone from him, and she could feel his lips soft, tender, against her forehead. "My grandmother's not God, Jessie. She's an old woman." His thumb tipped Jessie's chin up so he could see her face. "Come to me tonight. I need you, Jessie . . . I love you."

She searched his eyes, seeing there the love. At last she asked, "Where, Brig?"

"At the storehouse . . . just before midnight."

The afternoon's hours took forever to tick away. Once her chores were finished, Jessie forsook her riding to bathe. Several trips were made, bringing the water from the well to heat it at the *jacal*. Marta, hobbling in from the cornfields, caught Jessie standing in the wooden tub which was little more than a cask sawed in half. Beneath the folded lids, her eyes ran over the tall, slim girl who held the large scrap of rag before her, shielding her nudity.

"*Jabón?*" Marta asked, espying the lye soap. "And hot water? Something special goes on, *chiquita?*"

"No, Marta." Jessie turned her back on the woman and began to furiously scrub her neck and arms. "It is only that it has been a long time, and the dust is beginning to bake on me like glaze on pottery."

Marta watched her lather the yellow hair until the unruly curls shone like newly minted gold. Afterward Jessie dried off with the skimpy patch of terry cloth and donned the red flowered skirt and drawstring muslin blouse that she had worn that day. "There is no young man among the vaqueros?" the old woman asked. "You are becoming a young woman—and it is time for a man, no?"

Still bending from the waist as she brushed her damp hair over her head, Jessie paused and looked at Marta. "No, there is no man for me among the worthless cowboys."

Marta began to dig at one of the few teeth she had remaining in her gums with a straw. "*Posibilimente un indio, eh?*" she asked, closely watching the girl.

Jessie straightened and smiled. "No, no Indian either. Have you ever heard the Anglo saying, 'Curiosity killed the cat'?" Then, laughing, Jessie tossed her wildly curling hair back over her shoulders. "There is no one, I tell you. I simply wanted to bathe."

"It isn't the señor, is it?"

Jessie blushed. She pulled the skirt over her head, mumbling, "Nor Brig either."

That evening, as she served Marta's tamale pie to the hungry men, she shrugged off their flirtatious remarks with a fling of her head. She was well aware that they all watched her more closely than usual and knew that it was because she had knotted her hair atop her head, making her look older than her nearly seventeen years.

"*Hola, princesa,*" Juan Jesus called out from the far end of the table. When Jessie glanced toward him, he rose and bowed. "You have a crown on your head, no?"

She took the remark good-naturedly, as it was meant. A waggish smile curved her lips, dazzling the men and making them her subjects. She made her way along the length of the bench until she reached Juan Jesus. "And you," she said sweetly, "are wearing a bump for a crown," and she brought the spoon down with a light thump on his head.

Laughter reigned through the rest of the dinner, and she was kept occupied until at last the evening meal was over. After a last lingering cup of coffee, the men one by one drifted off to their own *jacales* or bunkhouses. She finished washing the dishes and was free.

Sunset lacked an hour, and she whiled it away in the privacy of the *jacal* reading her much-thumbed-through Latin text, *Julius Caesar's Crossing of the Rubicon.* Marta sat nearby, darning a pair of cotton hose. The old woman finished and looked up at Jessie. "*Lista para dormir?*"

Jessie closed the book and shook her head. "No, I'm not sleepy. You go on to sleep. I think I'll go for a walk."

"Aha! Someone's courting you!" Marta cackled.

Jessie rose and pinched out the candlewick. "The only suitor I have is the old man in the moon," she teased back, shutting the door behind her.

There was no moon, and she counted her blessings as she made her way through the *ranchería,* careful to skirt far around the bedrolls of the cowhands who sought some relief from the heat of the July night.

She knew there would be other lovers seeking each other's arms that hot night, but none went to such a forbidden rendezvous as she—the *ranchería* bastard and the Stronghold heir. Far in the distance a summer thunderstorm was in progress, its lightning writing across the sky forebodingly, and Jessie paused in her steps to shudder. Yet she knew that foolish premonitions would not stop her mission . . . nothing would keep her from Brig.

The storehouse, a solid, windowless one-story adobe, rose before her. Here slabs of bacon and ham hocks were hung from the ceiling rafters along with white cotton sacks of sweet but hard cured meat. On the floor stood sacks of green coffee to be roasted and ground as needed, dried fruit, potatoes, and onions. In the corners were stacked cases of canned goods—pickles, tomatoes, and shellfish.

Jessie took the storeroom key that Marta had allotted her when she began to help out in the mess hall and opened the door. Shadows of sacks and crates filled the room. Hardly a bridal chamber. At the sound of footsteps she whirled back to the open door. Brig stood there, filling the doorway. "I thought the sun would never set, Jessie," he said huskily and stepped inside. He shut the door behind him, and total blackness blanketed the room.

Above the musty odor of stored, dried food, she caught the faint scent of his cologne, and then Brig's muscle-roped arms encircled her waist, drawing her against him. His mouth ground down on hers, bruising her lips so that they gave way and parted. His tongue thrust inside and violated her mouth. She stood helpless under the onslaught, shocked and numbed by the brutally passionate action.

At her quiescence, he released her. Her fingertips went to her lips. "You've never really been kissed before, have you?" his voice asked quietly out of the darkness.

She shook her head and realized he could not see her. "No. That is how people kiss?"

"Sometimes. Didn't you like it, little Jessie?"

"I don't know. No . . . yes."

He laughed softly. His hand caught hers, pulling her somewhere. Then she realized he was tugging her downward onto the sacks—sacks of green coffee, if the pliancy was any indication of their contents. His arms enfolded her against him so that she was half reclining along the length of his body. A little frightened at this side of passion he had shown her, she trembled.

As if sensing her fear, Brig brought her hand to his lips and tenderly kissed the palm. "I will never hurt you, Jessie," he whispered. "Let me tell you how you've been on my mind since the first day Father brought you home." He proceeded to tell her about the skinny little girl with wide frightened eyes the size of silver dollars and hair the color of corn that escaped the braids by springing into curls. "You were enchanting. But I don't think I began to love you until the day the centipede dropped into the tureen at dinner."

She laughed now, relaxing. "I don't think your grandmother was as appreciative of the incident."

"Nor do I. As I recall she was quite indignant about the way you calmly scooped the thing out with your spoon and squashed it on the floor with your heel. Jessie, Jessie . . . you're such a strong little female. I don't think even my grandmother frightens you as she does other people. She just has to look at them."

Jessie settled deeper in the crook of Brig's arm, her head nestled against his chest. "I don't know, Brig. Growing up as I did—wild—I always thought I wasn't afraid of anything. But loving you—it's my Achilles heel. Elizabeth is shrewd . . . I'm afraid she'll find my weak spot."

His hand slipped inside the blouse to caress her bare shoulder. "Our love will make us stronger, Jessie. After I end the engagement with Fanny, we'll go to Grandmother together. She loves Cristo Rey, and we'll make her see that you love it, too . . . that together we'll make it into the empire she has always dreamed of. But with or without her blessing, I intend to marry you."

Little nameless apprehensions still chipped away at her bedrock of assurance, but when Brig's hand slipped farther inside her blouse, moving down the slope of her chest to cup one breast, she forgot all else. She lay motionless while his fingers sought her suddenly turgid nipple. Her lids drooped and her limbs eased in languid abandon at the pleasant sensation.

"Kiss me," she murmured. "The way you did before."

His mouth closed over hers, and her lips parted for the entry of his tongue. When he pulled the drawstring on her blouse, loosening it so that it slipped down over her shoulders, she made no protest but began to work at the buttons of his shirt.

Her feverish fingers reached the buttons of his pants, and his hand caught them, halting them. "I don't think you know what you're doing," he said, pulling away. Perspiration gathered at his brow, and he brushed it away with the back of his hand.

She caught the hand and held the palm over her bared breast.

"I love you, Brig, and you love me . . . this love between us can't be wrong."

"No, Jessie, it's not. But I'll not have anyone calling our child a bastard. I'll not have them going through what you have." He put her from him with a gentle kiss on her forehead and a wry grin. "What I need now is a long walk in the cool air."

It was a week of deliriously ecstatic moments. Jessie lived for the sight of Brig. After breakfast when he shared a cup of coffee with the men, their hands surreptitiously touched as she passed him his cup. Sometimes he even managed to break away and ride to meet her at some preassigned rendezvous. And then there were the wild evenings of passionate kisses that were beginning to tell on her and Brig.

The need to consummate their love was like the raging vortex of a dust devil—disorienting her, so that she moved through the day as tensely as finely strung barbed wire. She was certain the ranchhands could sense the electrical tension that flowed between her and Brig whenever they were within sight of each other.

She was just as certain Elizabeth had to suspect something. The absence of her grandson every night would surely give her a clue. Perhaps she believed Brig was seeking his masculine privileges among the ranchería's Mexican and Indian women, falling back on the ancient *droit de seigneur,* the privilege of the master.

That she would overlook. But the mistake of marrying a bastard—Jessie knew it was a mistake Elizabeth Godwin would never allow.

Brig tried to allay her anxiety that last evening before he left for Tucson. "Jessie," he said, taking her firmly by the shoulders, "you're giving my grandmother too much credit. There is nothing she can do to keep me from marrying you. Do you understand? Nothing! You must trust me."

Reluctantly Jessie nodded, then gave herself up to Brig's demanding kisses.

Chapter 30

AT best, Roget was outraged," Brig said, smiling down at the young woman who so anxiously searched his face. "It's over, Jessie." He took her face between his hands and lightly rubbed the tip of his nose against hers. "If you're ready, we'll go up to the Stronghold."

She pulled away and took a deep breath. "I'm ready." She wished she had a mirror in the *jacal*. She would feel better prepared to meet Elizabeth if she knew she looked her best. As it was, the pink gingham dress was not that bad, but the bare feet encased in leather huaraches detracted from the desired effect.

Brig touched the pink ribbon that held back her wealth of curls. "You're beautiful," he said, and she knew he had perceived her feminine uncertainty and was grateful for his reassurance.

She let him lead her out of the *jacal* that had been her home the past four years—back to the Stronghold. Elizabeth had banished her from the Stronghold once, but she would not do it again, Jessie told herself, holding tightly to Brig's arm. Despite the evening's relative coolness, nervous perspiration broke out on her upper lip.

Brig looked down at her as they passed through the gates. He patted her hand. "The next time you pass through these portals, you'll be coming home as my bride."

A sudden thought occurred to her. She abruptly halted, pulling him around to face her. "Brig, you're not marrying me—just to set everything right? To make sure I receive my father's share of Cristo Rey?"

He saw the worry blanch her already pale face. "Dearest Jessie," he murmured, "I think it is absolutely beautiful the way justice will triumph in the end—but, no, this is certainly not a solution I would undertake if I did not love you." His fingers brushed away the tendrils of hair that escaped the ribbon to curl about her face. "You have a hold on me, my little wild thing, and I know that I shall never be happy without you."

Together they entered the house. At the parlor doorway Jessie paused, her gaze actually passing over Elizabeth in the Queen Anne armchair to fix on the empty space above the rock fireplace. The painting of Doña Davalos that had been there as long as Jessie could remember was gone. There was only the lighter, faded blue rectangular outline to mark that it had ever been there.

Elizabeth halted in carding the wool at the sight of the couple at the doorway. No flicker of surprise at seeing Jessie in the house crossed her face. In fact, Jessie thought, there was a placidity in the finely seamed wrinkles, as if she had been expecting to see the two of them together . . . and this unnerved Jessie.

It had been four years since Jessie had last stood before her, and Jessie expected her to screech invectives and have her thrown out. Nevertheless, she drew back her shoulders and let Brig lead her forward to sit on the sofa. She took a small amount of pleasure in the fact that she was once again in the Stronghold— true, as a guest only . . . but one day she would be its mistress.

Elizabeth put the finely spun wool away in the basket at her feet and folded her hands before her. "Hello, Jessica. It's been a while since last I saw you." She looked at Brig, who sat next to Jessie but leaned forward, his hands clasped between his knees. "Did you put in the order for the mine's boilers while you were in Tucson?"

"Yesterday, Grandmother. But mining obviously isn't what I wanted to talk to you about. Jessie and I are getting married. We want your blessing."

Elizabeth closed her eyes and opened them to fix the stonelike irises on Brig—as the albatross must have fixed its gaze on the ancient mariner. "Dear God, I had hoped it wouldn't come to this."

Brig's brows met in a straight line over the bridge of his nose. "I know you don't approve of the possibility that Jessie is illegitimate—a possibility which you cannot prove in fact. But—"

"And you cannot disprove it," Elizabeth reminded him.

"But the fact remains that I love Jessie and"—he paused and

took Jessie's icy hand between his large warm ones—"and she has agreed to become my wife."

Elizabeth rested her hand in one hand, shielding her eyes. "How far has this . . . love . . . gone?"

Her voice was so low that Jessie was not sure she understood the question. Brig asked, "What exactly do you mean?"

Elizabeth removed her hand. The gray eyes were like marbles, Jessie thought. "I mean, exactly, has this affair been consummated?"

Brig shot to his feet. "I don't like the word 'affair,' Grandmother. And I don't think it's any of your—"

The old woman's eyes glistened as if she were about to cry. It startled Jessie. "Dear God, I wish it weren't my business. But it is—more than you both realize."

Brig glanced at Jessie with a puzzled frown before switching his gaze back to the grandmother. "What are you talking about?"

Elizabeth looked at Jessie. Sadness seemed to droop the corners of her mouth and etch deeper furrows in her brow. "You, Jessica, are my son's illegitimate daughter. Sherrod told me as much before he died."

Jessie rose slowly to her feet, propelled by the fury boiling in her like a volcano about to erupt. "I don't believe you!" She almost strangled on the words.

Elizabeth sighed and looked down at her folded hands. "I'm sorry, but what I'm telling you is the truth. Brigham, Sherrod knew the truth would kill your grandfather, so he had to let society accept Catherine Howard's version of Jessica's conception."

Elizabeth looked up to meet her grandson's wild-eyed glare. "You two are brother and sister, Brigham. And if you go through with this, you'll be committing the unholy act of incest."

"No!" Brig roared. "No!" His fist swept out in a wild arc, striking at anything to refute her statement, and happened to hit the lampstand. The crystal globe crashed to the floor. Sudden darkness filled the parlor. A loud silence followed, broken by Brig's anguished bellow. "You had to win, didn't you, Grandmother?"

Jessie stretched out her hand in the dark, groping for Brig, and found his arm. "Brig," she frantically pleaded, "don't listen to her! Don't you see, she's trying to separate us. She's a lying evil old woman! I know. I overheard your father and her arguing the day he brought me here. I remember him saying I was Lorenzo Davalos's child and deserved to live here as much as you or Abigail!"

A scratching sound pierced the darkness, and lights flared again as Elizabeth settled the globe back on its stand. The light shone up into her wrinkled face, casting demonic shadows. "My poor grandson," she said, sorrow weighting her voice. "Don't you realize that Jessica will tell you anything to gain back what she thinks belongs to her?"

"Don't believe her!" Jessie cried out.

Brig slowly withdrew her hand from his arm. "Don't you see, Jessie, every time we kissed . . . every time we made love . . . we would be doing so beneath the weight of a horrible sin. We'd never know," his voice cracked, "and we'd never find happiness."

Incredulously Jessie watched him swerve away and make for the doorway, heard the slam of the front door. Elizabeth said, "He'll get over this infatuation." As did my husband with the Davalos woman, she thought bitterly. "So will you, Jessica. For Brig's sake . . . if you love him . . . leave."

Jessie was shaking. A deep, red-hot anger seethed in her, bubbling, boiling. She did not know anger could be tangible. But it was there inside her . . . a living thing. As tangible as her blood or bones. Her voice came in a tight, harsh, almost inaudible whisper. "You haven't won yet, Elizabeth Godwin. No matter what Brig said!"

At that moment Jessie knew she was strong, as Brig had told her. As he was weak. Blindly she turned and sought the doorway, grateful for the things her hands touched for support—the back of the couch, the wooden hallstand. When her hand felt the ironwork of the door's handle, she half turned. "Somehow, someday," she told the formidable woman who stood in the parlor doorway, "I *will* win. I will have the Stronghold!"

Chapter 31

*F*ROM the mesquite-stubbled hillock the young woman sat astride the calico pony, looking down at Tombstone. The raw mining boomtown in no way resembled its sleepy sister town of Tucson. To the young woman it looked more like an antbed of activity.

Within the year that Ed Schiefelin found his silver lode and named the claim for his friends' predictions that he would only find his tombstone in that Apache-infested country, the sudden gathering of tents had leaped in population to become the largest town in Arizona territory—fifteen thousand people, all caught up in the silver dream.

Heavy ore wagons drawn by sixteen mules, two abreast, came and went from the mines that ringed the four-year-old town. Wagon trains loaded with lumber rumbled in from the sawmills in the Chiricahuas and Huachucas. Rustlers were arriving from the San Pedro Valley. Sheriff's posses clattered out on the trail of stage robbers. Stages and Wells Fargo coaches were departing, shotgun messengers on the box beside the driver, for Benson, Bisbee, Tucson, and mining towns across the nearby Mexican border. Cowboys mounted on horses and soldiers out of Fort Huachuca mixed with the cabs and barouches that swarmed the streets.

Tombstone, Arizona Territory, was the first sign of civilization that the young woman had seen in five days . . . five days of aimlessly wandering through the basin and low desert ranges of southern Arizona, of sleeping on a saddle blanket beneath the summer's silver sickle of a moon and eating the remnants of the cheese and dried beef Marta had urged on her.

But then Jessie had not really been hungry, only utterly tired, wishing to sleep forever. The furnace heat of the day drove her on, kept her moving. She feared not for her safety, cared not if the next moment she drew her last breath. Once, as she paused in the shadow of a ravine's striated walls, she had seen a string of Indians riding single file, their heads bobbing in and out of sight among the rolling hills.

For a fleeting second she thought about charging into their midst. The swift flight of an arrow would put an end to the agony of living and thinking and feeling. Only the knowledge that the Apaches sometimes let their victims live to sell as slaves south of the border prevented her from so rash an act.

The thirst for vengeance was greater than her death wish. Because of Elizabeth's treachery . . . despite the disillusion of Brig's weakness, she had to go on living. And the wild, raw Tombstone—it matched her own wild nature—seemed as good a place as any to mark time until she found the way to avenge herself.

She kneed the pony's barrel and let it slowly make its way down a beaten path into Tombstone's outskirts of tents. There she joined the throng of people surging into the town proper. Her gaze studied the names of the establishments she passed—Addie Bourland's Millinery, Fly's Photography Gallery, Vogan's Bowling Alley, Kerney's Drugstore. None of these businesses displayed "help wanted" signs.

Passing through the district housing businesses of ill fame, she then reached the town's center, where saloons and theaters jostled for elbow room with restaurants and hotels. The old man at the Dexter Livery and Stables where she left her calico looked at her strangely, and only then did she realize what a sight she must look—her hair hung in rats' nests, her brown serge skirt was mud-splattered, and its matching jacket was ripped at one shoulder seam.

Regardless of her unkempt appearance, she determinedly set out down Allen Street, carpetbag in hand, chin held high, as though she were one of the Eastern society matrons who had come to the area for its mineral baths rather than a bedraggled, homeless sixteen-year-old. At the corner of Fifth and Allen she paused on the boardwalk outside the first gambling establishment— the Crystal Palace Saloon.

It was a two-story gray frame building with well-designed French windows and doors and overhanging eaves that protected lolling inhabitants from the summer sun. It looked the most luxurious of the saloons and gambling houses as she compared its facade with the others that fronted Allen Street—names like the Oriental Bar, Hatch's Saloon, the Alhambra, the Occidental, the Arcade, and the Dragon.

For a moment she lost her pluck, realizing how little she knew about life in towns, how naive she was. Then she drew a deep breath and squared her shoulders. One thing she did know was how to play cards. Four years among the Cristo Rey's cowhands had taught her well. She marched into the Crystal Palace.

Inside she stood goggling. The walls, covered with colorful eagle-bedecked wallpaper, were resplendent with oil paintings and gilt-framed mirrors. Even at that time of day the gambling tables girding the walls were surrounded by men of every nationality. Monte tables were stacked with gold and silver. Faro was played in feverish silence. The little ivory ball danced capriciously over the roulette wheel's red and black numbers.

She hesitated, not knowing whom to approach for work. Behind the long mahogany-and-brass bar three bartenders in white aprons hustled furiously. An old vacant-eyed black man in a battered derby played a tinny piano. At last she turned to the thin wiry man sitting as a lookout in the high chair near the door. Beneath the straw sombrero his eyes were as hard as the six-shooters buckled about his waist. "I would like to speak with the proprietor, please," she said, using her most prim voice.

She realized he could not hear her above the noisy rattle of the dice in the chuck-a-luck boxes and the call of the roulette dealers. She repeated herself, this time in a louder voice. The cold orbs slid down over her and back up to her face. "Diamond Dan is in the cage—his office," he said at last in monotone syllables.

She followed the nod of his head. At the rear of the room was a barred window and a door. She did not even bother to glance at the guard again. "Thank you," she said and began to make her way through the gamblers elbowing for positions at the green-baized poker tables. Her first hesitant knock on the door brought no response, and she rapped more loudly.

The door swung open, and a blowzy woman of maybe thirty stood before her in a low-cut red satin dress with once-matching slippers now dirt-stained. Black net hose showed a full five inches above her ankles. Jessie had never seen a dance-hall girl before, and her lips parted in an O as she surveyed the castle of dyed black ringlets atop the woman's head, the black beauty patch on the chin, and the paint above the eyes and on the high cheeks. "Yeah?" the woman asked.

"I'm looking for the proprietor—Diamond Dan."

"Let the woman in, Mary," a deep voice spoke from somewhere behind the girl. Virgin Mary stepped back, pulling the door wide with a grimace, and Jessie saw the owner of the voice—or the back of his head, to be exact.

He sat at a notched and battered black desk, head bent. When Mary closed the door behind Jessie, he swiveled around in the chair. His dark eyes narrowed as they met Jessie's. The visual contact slammed against her with a sexual impact. Beneath the pencil-slim mustache the lips curled slowly in a sensual smile. He was not as extraordinarily handsome as Brig, but there was a devil-may-care expression in his eyes and lips that demanded attention. His raven-black hair was parted in the center and smoothed back with the aid of a pomade. Apparently he was a wealthy man, for stuck ostentatiously in the lapel of the finely tailored gray pinstriped suit was an enormous diamond stickpin.

He rose, crossed to her, and took her hand. He bowed low over it, and Jessie's own eyes narrowed, mistrusting the dandy. His gaze had most certainly taken in her disheveled state, so why the elaborate politeness? When he straightened, saying, "Daniel O'Rourke, at your service, ma'am," she jerked her hand away, thinking he was making fun of her.

"In that case," she said frostily, "if you are at my service, you may employ me."

One of O'Rourke's finely delineated brows arched. His practiced eye scrutinized her more closely, from her huaraches, past her dusty, wrinkled—and too small—traveling suit, to her birdnest hair. "You wish to work as a . . . dance-hall girl?"

"No. As a dealer."

Striving not to, the solemn lips gave in and curled upward in amusement. "I see. But dealing cards calls for a certain amount of dexterity—uh, skill, Miss—"

"Flora," she improvised.

"Flora?" His lips twitched again. "Just Flora—like the Spanish 'flower'?"

"Just Flora."

"Well, Flora, a woman dealer, while not unheard of in San Francisco or Dodge City, would be most unusual here in Tombstone."

"Nevertheless, I am quite—dexterous," she mimicked, "with playing cards and would like a job as a dealer."

O'Rourke glanced at Mary, who stood, hands on hips, surveying the scene. She rolled her eyes. "The only thing she can do, Dan, is rob you blind."

"All right," he said. "Do you have anything more—appropriate—for the Crystal Palace than what you have on?"

Jessie took a deep breath, gripping the carpetbag. "No."

"Any money—a place to stay?"

"No."

O'Rourke pulled out a cheroot. "Mary can get you a dress that might halfway fit if it doesn't swallow up those—" He saw her face color and amended what he had been about to say. "If it doesn't hang on your bosom. And we can give you a room upstairs. Of course, it'll—"

"No."

He blinked. "No—what?"

"No, I don't need a room here, thank you."

The man threw back his head and laughed, a soft chuckle that seemed to caress the skin. "So that's it. A real virgin, eh?"

She blushed. "I'll find a place to stay," she said stiltedly, though she knew until she was paid her bed would probably be the ground and her pillow her saddle.

"All right, perhaps it's just as well. I've a feeling you'd put my girls out of business."

Mary put her hands on her hips. "That ain't likely, unless the men have the sweets for boys. Then they might go for her type."

"That's enough, Mary," O'Rourke said mildly. He jammed the cheroot back between his teeth and surveyed Jessie with a critical eye again. "The name Flora—it hasn't got class. We'll give you the name of a flower. What'll it be, Mary? Any ideas? Maybe a yellow flower for the yellow hair."

Jessie felt foolish, standing before the two, who eyed her as if she were a piece of horseflesh. "Daisy?" Mary suggested.

O'Rourke waved his cigar in rejection. "No, no. We want something exotic."

Jessie fidgeted beneath their intense stares. "Look, it's not exotic, but it *is* yellow—and it does fit me . . . the desert primrose."

"Jeeminy!" Mary derided, rolling her eyes again.

"No, wait—the girl may have something. She certainly could be called a prim desert rose. The Primrose," he said, testing the name. "Yes, I think it'll go." He pulled the Albert watch from his checkered waistcoat's pocket and glanced at it. "Be back tonight at eight, Flora—er, Primrose."

"Thank you, Mr. O'Rourke," she said. "I'm very grateful for the opportunity you're giving me."

Mary said, "Don't be too grateful, honey. This Irishman always collects."

He flashed Jessie an intimate smile and flipped her a gold piece. "And get something to eat."

Jessie spent part of the gold piece at the New York Coffee Shop, one of the more reputable-looking restaurants along Allen Street. At a table opposite her were two dowdy women in black who pursed their lips at the sight of Jessie's rumpled appearance. She ignored them, leaving them to drink their tea—their lips still puckered as if tasting something sour.

She scanned the menu, which listed such delicacies as *pasas*, half-dried grapes, from El Paso and honey from the Tía Juana Ranch in Lower California. She decided to be extravagant and ordered the shrimp, which was freighted on ice from Guaymas. After a five-day fast, the seafood, followed by a compote of fruit, was delicious but too much for the already full stomach.

The Mexican boy who waited on her directed her around the corner to a two-story adobe building known as the Russ House. Nellie Cashman, who operated the boardinghouse, surprisingly asked no questions of Jessie. Though only in her late forties or early fifties, the horse-faced Miss Cashman was partially deaf and thus practically screamed her directions to Jessie.

"Now, remember, Miss Primrose, no men in the room! And the rent's due on the first!"

Jessie replied that would be fine, and Miss Cashman held the ear trumpet to her ear, shouting, "What's that you say, Miss Primrose?"

Jessie repeated herself and escaped to the privacy of the room. It was more than she had expected, certainly more than the *jacal* she had lived in at the ranchería—a bed with an iron-grilled headboard and a washstand and a mirror, no less. The crude clothespress looked wasted with only the pink calico and the peasant's *camisa* and red flowered skirt to hang on its pegs. Without even bothering to remove her clothes, she stretched out on the bed, falling asleep immediately.

The room was in darkness when she awoke, and she hurriedly straightened her traveling suit and vainly tried to tuck in the unruly curls into the knot of hair at her nape. Unfortunately, there was no water in the pitcher, and, as much as she disliked it, she had to return to the Crystal Palace Saloon in the same state of disrepair.

She nodded to the guard on lookout, a different man this time, and moved past the milling men to the bar, where Virgin Mary sidled next to a middle-aged man in specs and a bowler who hugged a case in one hand and a glass of gin in the other; obviously he was a huckster. He ogled her as she approached Mary. "Won't you introduce me to your lovely . . . friend?" he asked Mary in a thick, fuzzy-tongued voice.

"She's going to work here," Mary said tartly. "See you later, Frank." She patted his sloping chin and cast Jessie a withering glance. "Come on along . . . Primrose."

Jessie followed her up the carpeted stairs and into one of the rooms that did not really have much more furniture than the Russ House bedroom—but it did have a large painting above the headboard of a nude woman shielded only by a huge ostrich feather. Jessie's eyes riveted to it in shock.

At a ruffle-covered dressing table a young girl who was maybe two or three years older than Jessie sat before the lamp-illuminated mirror. At the sight of Jessie she stopped applying the bright spots of rouge to her cheeks. "A new recruit, Mary?"

"No, a dealer," Mary told the girl, whose hair was a dull washed-out yellow. "Dutch Annie—meet the Primrose."

Annie smiled now, and her blue eyes did not look so old in the waxy face. "Nice to meetcha," she said congenially. "Come on below when you're ready, and I'll show you the ropes."

"Here you go," Mary said, pulling a plum-pink satin dress trimmed in black from the clothespress. "There's hose and slippers in the trunk. And do something with that haystack on your head," she added before closing the door on Jessie.

Alone now, Jessie shed the dusty clothes, shedding her past

life like a snake shedding its skin. In the new clothes she donned another personality. She took a seat before the dressing table and began to brush out the matted hair. She used the satiny rose pin perched in the low V of her gown to anchor her hair atop her head in a wreath of braids. A pot of rouge sat on the table, and she lightly touched the greasy pink cream to her suntanned cheeks. When she was ready to leave, she did not recognize herself in the mirror.

Slowly, hesitantly, she descended the stairs to the saloon below, her heart pounding in her ribcage like a blacksmith's hammer. Gaze after gaze, like the rippling fall of dominoes, rose from the dice and cards on the tables to fix on the incredibly lovely apparition. Even old black Beauregard at the piano let his fingers fall silent on the keys.

In the sudden hush of the room she made her way to the cage. From inside came Dutch Annie's voice, arguing. "My God, Dan, she's only a kid!"

And O'Rourke's voice: "So were you, too, Annie, when you first started."

Jessie opened the door. O'Rourke and Dutch Annie stared at her in disbelief. Coming to his feet, O'Rourke held out his hand to Jessie, and she placed her hand in the palm of his. "The Primrose has arrived," he said, his eyes never leaving hers.

Chapter 32

H I ya, Rose!" a drunken voice called out.

"Hey, it's the Primrose!"

More gamblers took up the call until the room almost reverberated with the shout: "It's the Primrose! It's the Primrose!" Old Beauregard launched into his nightly tribute to her, the Irish "The Rose of Tralee," which was as true as any of the rumors that circulated about her, she thought as she passed by him and patted his arm in a fond gesture. If one could ignore the Mexican half of her ancestry.

It had been the same every night for six months when Jessie descended the staircase to work at the tables . . . the shouting, the ogling, the applause as she took her seat at one of the tables. Some nights she perched on the high stool behind the blackjack table, swiftly dealing the cards out and raking in the money for the house. Other nights she managed the roulette table, the monte table, and, on occasion, the fan-tan table.

But whatever table she presided over, it was always immediately crowded and stayed that way until she took the ten-o'clock break and then refilled with patrons once more on her return until the end of her shift at four in the morning.

It was not just the innocent beauty, childlike yet provocative, that intrigued the men. It was the education, the pseudonym, the mystery about her, the reserve that ran beneath the polite words she exchanged with each man who visited her table. It was because she knew each man by name and within a short period of time was familiar with each man's tide-of-woe story; it was because she seemed to listen as if she really cared. Yet she never divulged a word about herself—and this captured their adoration just that much more.

She distributed her warm smiles impartially among the men. She listened to the old prospector, Tumbleweed, tell his story over and over about the strike he was going to make one day or Curly Bill lament that he was forced into a life of robbery because he had a dying mother to support.

The men tried to press money on her, but she would not take it. She had never wanted money. She wanted only one thing . . . one man. And without him, without Brig, nothing else held interest for her. The Crystal Palace was merely a means to an end, a way to earn a living until one day she had her revenge.

The four bagnio dance-hall girls who also worked the bars and tables, and sometimes the beds—if they were lucky and the miner was old or very drunk or both—at first watched the newcomer, the Primrose, with suspicion that bordered on jealousy. But the Primrose did nothing to fan their dislike.

She refused to take the tips the men tried to press on her at the gambling tables—leaving them to spend their tips at the bar on the women. And she never took a customer to bed, departing instead at half past four in the morning for the Russ House, chaperoned by the Palace's patrons who were almost as formidable as the United States deputy marshal, Wyatt Earp.

Only Dan O'Rourke did not seem to fall beneath her spell. But then he never fell beneath any woman's spell. And, of course, he knew something about the young girl who dealt the cards. If nothing else, he knew her first name—and he knew she was running.

Running from herself, most likely, he figured as he watched her agile fingers riffle the cards before distributing them to the five men who were lucky enough to possess the chairs at her table. One day, he knew, she would want to leave, but before that day came he would know her story . . . and her weakness. And perhaps he would bind her to the Crystal Palace.

He came up to stand behind her now. Her fingers flittered over the deck again with rapid dexterity. The house had twenty, and Jessie leaned over to rake in the silver pieces and 'dobe dollars. When she straightened, Dan's fingers toyed with the loose tendril of hair at her nape. "How's it going, doll?"

She pulled away a fraction of an inch. "As usual," she murmured. Dan withdrew his hand. He would not force his attentions on her, though as her employer he would not have been doing anything out of the ordinary. But he suspected Jessie would give her notice as easily as she had appeared, no doubt to seek employment at one of the other saloons.

Word was out that Earp, a part owner in the Oriental Bar, had appealed to her to come to work for him. Evidently she had demurred, as Dan knew she would. As long as she was free to come and go, he knew she would remain at the Crystal Palace.

He leaned over her shoulder and said in a low voice, "Rose, tomorrow's your day off. How about dining out with me and then taking in the acts at the Bird Cage Theater? Lotta Crabtree's playing there."

Jessie glanced up at Dan, her eyes narrowed in suspicion. But the dandy's face was guileless. True, for six months she had been nowhere but back and forth between the Russ House and the Crystal Palace. And Dan had yet to make a dishonorable pass at her. "All right," she said slowly.

* * *

"I save it for special occasions," Dutch Annie said, holding up for Jessie to admire the black beaded and laced two-piece dress with the white lace around the low, square neckline.

"Yeah," Mary said from the dressing table, "like two minutes before she strips for bed."

Annie shot the older woman a venomous look and said, "Go on, take it, Rose. With your golden good looks, you'll set the men on their heads."

The evening dress had an enormous bustle and a long train, and when Jessie looked in the mirror, she had to admit it was stunning. "You'll need gloves," Mary said in a simulated bored voice and began to rummage in her trunk. "This oughtta do it." She produced a pair of long black silk gloves that had to have at least twenty buttons on each arm.

A tawdry, aging woman with henna-dyed hair who went by the nickname of Salome draped a sable boa around Jessie's shoulders. "From the good old days, dearie," she said in a nostalgic voice. "When gold ran like water in California."

"All you're lacking is a hat," said Belle, an ample woman with frizzed bangs. She sat a large leghorn with a black ostrich feather at a tilt on Jessie's head.

The four dance-hall girls stepped back to look at their creation, satisfied smiles settling on their faces. Jessie said, "You four look like fairy godmothers, and I feel like Cinderella."

"Just make sure you come back the same way you leave, Cinderella," Mary said dryly. "A virgin."

The evening was far more exciting than any of the times Jessie had visited Tucson. Tombstone had plenty of money to spend—and spent it in these boom times. The men at the Maison Dorée would have looked at home in a metropolitan club. The women in attendance kept abreast of the styles and the fashion edicts of the Rue de la Paix as set forth in the *Tombstone Epitaph.*

The Maison Dorée's owner, a portly man with a triple chin who went by the name of Julius Caesar, smiled and bowed as he welcomed Dan and Jessie into Tombstone's most prestigious restaurant. "What epicurean delights do you have to offer tonight, Julius?" Dan asked.

The rubicund little man rubbed his hands unctuously. "The quail on toast is magnificent, Mr. O'Rourke."

And it was, she thought. French wine from Guaymas in a silver iced champagne bucket was followed by ripe strawberries and cream and a demitasse of *pousse café* while Dan regaled her with stories of the town's wildness and even spoke a little of his own life.

"I was born during the potato famine," he said as he lit up the after-dinner cheroot. "My parents were terribly poor and did any kind of demeaning labor in order to survive. As I learned to do. Any kind of labor but work in the mines. You won't find the superstitious Irishmen going in those black holes."

After dinner they took a cab to the Bird Cage Theater. There was a bar at the front of the Bird Cage, but it was the theater behind it that was packed. Wooden benches filled the lower floor of the theater, and a horseshoe of curtained boxes flanked the upper walls. At the front the glare of kerosene-lamp footlights illuminated a vaudeville performer cutting capers on the stage.

Jessie, sipping on a mint julep, checked her playbill and found that it was Tommy Rosa, King of Comedians and Laugh Makers . . . to be followed by Professor King in His Wonderful Suspension Wire Act. In between performances, beautifully painted ladies in scanty costumes sang touching ballads of home and mother on the stage and then hurried to the boxes, where, by their voluptuous charms and soft graces, they swelled the receipts of the downstairs bar and received a rakeoff on every bottle of beer they persuaded their admirers to buy.

Dan's box was on the same side as the boxes of Doc Holliday, the Earp brothers, and Bat Masterson. Opposite, the boxes were filled with Earp's enemies—the Cochise County sheriff, Johnny Behan, and his men. The story went, Dan said, that every night the two factions faced each other with grim eyes—and that one day soon there was certain to be an eruption of gunplay.

In another box Russian Bill swaggered and postured. Remarkably handsome, with yellow hair that tumbled about his shoulders, he dressed in cowboy regalia, complete in every detail from white sugarloaf sombrero to high-heeled boots with immense spurs. "It's rumored that the man's actually a Russian prince," Dan told her. "Of course, no one can prove it one way or another, but it is known that he has been paying twenty-five dollars every night for his box over the last year and a half."

In between acts, Jessie took delight in studying the people. She could spot the professional gamblers at a glance by their immaculate clothes—their silk shirts, dandy crutch sticks, and headlight diamonds. At first she had classified Dan as one of those who succumbed to the fascination of faro, for over the months she noted that his diamond pin disappeared at intervals, as did he for two or three days at a time. But she never once saw him touch cards or dice.

"Having fun, Flora?" he asked warmly, taking her hand in his when the lights were turned up between acts.

"Very much, Dan." She let him squeeze her fingertips, then withdrew her hand.

"We'll do it again," he said, louder now that the crowd began to applaud Lotta Crabtree's appearance.

Jessie leaned forward to study the beautiful redheaded woman with the tiny figure. Lotta had a charisma that came through on her simpler songs like "The Pink Lady" and "She's Only a Bird in a Gilded Cage," which was written about the fallen angels who serviced the boxes, or cages, at the Bird Cage Theater. The song was very popular now in the States. But it was when Lotta began to dance her famous—or infamous, depending on the viewpoint— "can-can" that she took the theater by storm.

When the tassled red velvet curtain closed on the last performance, the benches were moved against the walls, and the crowd began to dance "until the sun peaks over the Dragoons," Dan said. Not everyone danced. Jessie noticed some of the couples from the boxes entering the small hatch door under the stage.

"If the beds beneath the stage could speak," Dan said, following her gaze, "the *Epitaph* would be chocked with scandals." He raked a brow. "Want to see what's going on?"

She laughed. "I'm sure whatever happens is not much different from what goes on upstairs at your place."

He leaned across the small candlelit table and kissed her cheek. "That's what I like about you, Flora. Your innocence. Let's get you back to the Russ House before I decide to drag you below the stage."

When the barouche halted before the boardinghouse, Dan drew her into his arms and kissed her—a soft, searching kiss. "You really should leave Tombstone and go back wherever you ran away from," he said huskily before he released her and instructed the driver to go on.

Chapter 33

DAN'S hand went to his flower-brocaded vest to withdraw the watch fob. "It's about time for you to go off duty, isn't it?"

Jessie handed over the deck with a small smile. "I'm ready, Dan. Tonight seems longer than usual."

"It's the heat. Get yourself a glass of scotch. It'll cool you off." But, of course, he knew she would not get anything to drink from the bar. She never did. Instead she brought a jar filled with sarsaparilla by Nellie Cashman.

Jessie made her way to the cage and kicked off her satin slippers, laying her head against the back of the scrolled chair while she slowly fanned herself.

At that moment she could think of a hundred places she would rather have been. Even the excitement of the Bird Cage Theater was beginning to pale now. Dan had taken her back several times to see such acts as Fatima's Little Egypt, the Famous Human Flies, and a group of minstrel players. But there was a void in her that no amount of entertainment could fill. Nothing could drive the thoughts of Brig from her mind for long.

Tonight was no different. She willed her treacherous thoughts to other things . . . to the man who sat at the fan-tan table earlier that evening. A Chinese, she guessed, although, with the exception of the slanted eyes and the saffron-colored skin, he certainly did not resemble the other Chinese.

In lieu of the long pigtail, the queue, his ebony hair was scissored off neatly about the nape. In place of the loose, quilted cotton jacket and trousers, he wore the canvas dungarees of a miner and a clean plaid shirt. But what was so unusual was the Oriental's build. Admittedly he was on the slender side, but he was tall—as tall as Brig, yet with muscles that twisted about the arms, bulging the veins of the forearms. And then he did not cross the Crystal Palace Saloon in that trotting walk typical of the Chinese coolie, but rather his long legs seemed to eat up the board floor.

For a few minutes she had been fascinated by the Oriental, by his deft movements with the cards, by the stonelike countenance that revealed nothing. A true poker face, she would have said of the slitted eyes and immobile lips. He was the first person—of all the strange, assorted men and women who drifted in and out of the Crystal Palace—to hold her interest for any length of time. But even then the apathy that had its hold on her like a boa constrictor tightened, and her mind had gone blank to all but the colors and numbers on the cards.

Listlessly she tossed her fan on the desk and picked up the *Epitaph.* Her eyes inattentively scanned "Death's Doings," which occupied more than half the paper's columns. The door opened behind her, but she only half heard the amplification in the noise from the outer room as her gaze moved over, then swept back to one small column headlined "Godwin—Roget Wedding."

The paper began to rattle in her hands as she read about Brig's marriage to Fanny two weeks earlier which "united two great families," John Clum, the editor, wrote.

Two arms encircled her and took hold of her hands. "Whatever you read," Dan said from behind, "sure has ruffled the Primrose for a change."

Her fingers gripped the paper in a monumental effort to halt the shaking. "It's nothing. Just all the deaths. You get tired of reading about such depressing things." She folded the newspaper meticulously and laid it on the desk. "Guess I'd better be getting back to my station."

Dan took her arms and turned her toward him. His gambler's keen eyes searched her face, but she had learned after six months to wear the dealer's impassive facade. Her seventeenth birthday had come and gone, but she felt eons older now. "Are you sure everything's all right, Flora?"

"Sure," she said and brushed past him, anxious to escape his scrutiny.

In the outer room the smoke-cloud haze and the din of noise—Beauregard's piano music, the whoops of the flirtatious dancing girls on stage, and the bark of the dealers—served to cover her flustered state. But her hands did not as easily conceal the earthquake that rumbled and surged and cracked her interior. She half expected fissures to erupt on her surface so that she looked like a china doll that had been dropped.

Twice in a row she misdealt the cards. Another time she forgot to rake in the house's winnings. Most of the players were too far gone in drink to notice the mistakes, but once she looked up to find the Oriental sitting directly before her, his oblique eyes studying her with the unwavering gaze of the fox.

This shook her even more. She signaled to the lookout for a replacement, and a small baldheaded man threaded through the crowd to take her place behind the table. Unheeding of the friendly calls the men made as she passed, she groped her way to the bar. "Give me something, please, Ollie," she told the bewhiskered bartender. "Anything."

The protuberant eyes blinked in surprise. "Never thought I'd see the day you'd be lifting a glass, Miss Rose."

"I didn't either," she said grimly, wrapping her hand about the empty glass he sat before her.

"Pour Rose a whiskey," Mary said, coming to her side. "And none of that cheap rot-gut either, Ollie."

Jessie downed the glass's contents in one swallow. Her breath caught in her windpipe like a cork, and a deep flush engorged her skin a bright crimson. Her eyes watered. For this, at least, she was thankful. The potency of the drink disguised the real reason for the tears that coursed down her cheeks.

"What is it, honey?" Mary asked as Ollie poured another drink at Jessie's direction. "One of the men here do you wrong? They're all heartbreakers, you know."

Jessie's stony gaze met Mary's in the mirror behind the bar. "They're weak bastards." She tossed off the whiskey as if she had drunk all her life and spun the glass away. "Good night," she rasped and began what seemed like a long journey toward the saloon's swinging doors.

Somehow she found her way to the Russ House, though she would have sworn her befogged mind played tricks on her— mischievously echoing footsteps behind her that belonged to the night's darkness and the hill's ghostly breezes. She thought for certain she would pass out and sleep away the misery that writhed inside her like a parasitic worm. But her lids were glued open. Her pupils stared unseeingly at the water-stained ceiling while her pulse hammered out the word *Brig* seventy-two times a minute, four thousand, three hundred and twenty times an hour.

Her blood sang of Brig's betrayal. Her heart collapsed and expanded in the cyclic rhythm of the pain that besieged her. Visions of Brig and Fanny twisted together in passion stormed her brain. Her fingers knotted about the chenille spread beneath her still fully clothed body.

It would have been better had she known that Brig loved Fanny. But as it was, he had sold his love for Jessie for thirty pieces of silver . . . and gold and copper and whatever riches from Godwin property the Roget mines produced.

And how long before Fanny produced? she wondered in her agonized stupor and began to laugh in small hiccough-like gasps.

Sleep finally released her from her torment, and she did not awaken until past noon. One look in the mirror at the swollen eyes and still-flushed cheeks—and the thick, fuzzy feeling of the caterpillar tongue—replayed the events of the night before. She left the boardinghouse early to spend the afternoon walking in the fresh air, hoping to clear the whiskey cobwebs from her mind.

She made a stop at the Company's Bank, depositing her wages for the week, window-shopped at Schuenfeld and Hayman's Furniture Store, and stood beneath the striped awning of Seamans and Sons' Jewelry Store. But she wanted neither furniture nor jewelry. Her desultory footsteps took her by the Assayer's Office—the Office of Heartbreak, it was called. A humorless smile curled her lips. That was where she should be working.

At last she made her way to the Crystal Palace. "You're early," Salome said, looking up from the mirror as she applied the carmine lip rouge from the cosmetic pot.

Jessie began to change into the black satin spangled costume, careful to keep her back to Salome and the mirror, for after all that time she still had not adopted the careless attitudes of the other women. She still suffered embarrassment when disrobing before the others. "I left early."

Mary came in and surveyed her, hands on hips. "You look worse than you did last night. Come on down and have a drink before you go on duty."

Jessie consented but found the drink no better than it had been the night before. There was nothing, she thought, that could alleviate her misery. The suffering she experienced was as real as if she had taken a barber's razor and slashed her wrists. She left the glass three-quarters full and took her place at the monte table early.

At first she was able to concentrate. Then her thoughts began to drift and slide like the cards beneath her fingers. At one point the jack of spades turned up Brig's face as she fanned out the cards. The evening became a blur as she moved from table to table. She thought about going back to the bar for a drink after all. She wanted to wipe her mind insensible with alcohol.

Tumbleweed was not at any of the tables she presided over, but it seemed the Oriental waited for her at the fan-tan table, watching her. Her hands became more unsteady under his scrutiny. She wondered if he could see her weakness. She hated herself for her weakness. Yet she could not help herself . . . nor her hate.

When break came at ten, she went to the bar. The men made way for her, shouting good-naturedly down its length while the nearer ones claimed her attention with either tales of woe or stale jokes. Vacantly she listened, smiling at the times when it seemed a proper response was in order. Ollie reluctantly poured her three straight drinks of bourbon. "You're gonna be sick, Miss Rose," he cautioned *sotto voce.*

"That'd be wonderful," she told him, never looking up from the dark liquid in her chipped glass. "Then I wouldn't feel anything else."

However, she did not become sick, and the last half of her duty that evening seemed to go easier with the drinks to drown out all thought but the cards before her.

Still, as she wended her way back to the boardinghouse at five that morning, her numbed brain picked up the sound of footsteps that dogged her own.

Chapter 34

WHATEVER sorrows you're trying to drown in that alcohol will only keep popping to the surface like a cork, baby."

Jessie looked up from her glass into the mirror above the dressing table. Dan stood in the doorway behind her. "I'll be sober enough to deal the cards by eight." It was true, for over the past few weeks she had learned to "hold her liquor," as the men at the bar termed it.

The Irishman pulled up a chair and sat next to her. He turned her face toward the mirror. "Look. Look at yourself, Flora. There's no happiness in that face. No laughter in the eyes. No smile curving the lips."

His forefinger reached out to outline the bow of her upper lip. "If you're determined to forget whatever it is that's bothering you, there is something better than alcohol."

She frowned in an effort to focus and understand what the saturnine face was saying. Her lids narrowed. "Just what is it you're talking about, Dan?"

"When you go on break, meet me at the cage," he said, rising. "And bring your shawl."

She gave the conversation little thought after he left. But curiosity and her dislike for the taste of liquor—and her utter misery—prompted her to go to his office when her break came. He took the shawl from her cold hands and placed it around her shoulders. "Where are we going?" she asked.

"Not far. Over to Hop Town." He opened the door and ushered her out through the crowded saloon.

She knew by now that Hop Town was Tombstone's Chinese community. As many as five hundred Chinese, legacy of the railroading-building era of the previous decade, inhabited this downtrodden area, a place even more depressing than the tent cities scattered about Tombstone's outskirts. Hop Town comprised a little over a square block of twisting, dividing back alleys. A depression hung about it like acrid smoke. She had even heard tales that a tunnel, part of the Mountain Maid Mine, snaked its way beneath the settlement. She hung back now, and Dan said, "It's all right. We're safer in Hop Town than drinking before the Crystal Palace's bar."

The shanties in Hop Town all looked alike—all windowless weather-beaten frames that seemed to lean together for support. At that time of night the streets were empty but for two or three Chinese males who scurried in pigeonlike gaits to some unknown destination. She was reminded again of the Oriental who came into the Crystal Palace every night to play fan-tan at her table, though he was so unlike these small inconspicuous men of Hop Town.

Dan paused before one shabby structure that looked just like the rest and knocked softly. The door cracked. Small eyes peered out at them. "Ling Chuey," Dan told the man.

The eyes disappeared, like the Cheshire cat she had read about as a child. An uncomfortable feeling seeped through her skin, and she shivered despite the almost balmy March night. Dan put his arm about her. "It's warmer inside."

It was more than warm inside when they entered, the door's tinkling brass bell chiming their presence. A stifling, cloying warmth pervaded the room and made her feel as if her lungs had collapsed. She drew deep breaths, looking about her. By the colored lanterns suspended from the low ceiling the room did not look as dilapidated as its exterior. Black-and-red carpets decorated with dragons and serpents that seemed alive covered the walls and floors. Scattered about were fringed cushions and small, oblong tables with exquisite ivory carvings or small boxes enameled with jade.

From a doorway partially shielded by a green silk screen a small man in a black silk robe and cap glided into the room. His yellow skin, like parchment, was stretched tightly across the high cheekbones. The small eyes of jet regarded her closely before he bowed, his hands concealed in his bell-like sleeves.

"Ling Chuey," Dan said in a respectful voice she rarely heard him use, "I have brought a friend who would be interested in the Golden Dreams."

Ling Chuey nodded. "A thousand celestial pardons, but—the woman is worthy of your trust?"

"Absolutely."

The Chinese bowed once more. "Then come with me, please. The House of the Golden Dreams would be most honored to entertain one of your friends, Mr. O'Rourke."

Jessie followed the Chinese down a narrow, dimly lit hallway and through another door that opened onto a descending staircase. Tallow candles in tin sconces on either side of rocky walls illuminated the three wooden steps. It was much cooler inside the tunnel, and as she followed Ling Chuey down the sloping passage, she could feel the uneven and rough walkway. Every so often a candle lit the dampness that clung to the walls and low ceiling.

Ling Chuey abruptly veered into an offshooting passage that opened into a large room whose walls were banked with tiers of platformlike bunks. Thirty or forty Chinese males reclined on these, since there was scarcely space to sit upright. Their heads lolled, their eyes rolled back; they seemed to Jessie in a state of semiconsciousness. Some mumbled in a singsong chant. Others lay with a snakelike tube running from drooping lips to filigree bowl. A few glanced at her without curiosity.

Here and there she counted maybe four or five beautiful Chinese women, as small as children almost, who appeared to be heating the pipestems over black-and-gold-filigree burners or molding some claylike substance between nimble fingers before passing the bowls back to the smokers.

She stared unbelievingly about her before Dan tugged at her arm, bidding her to follow him and Ling Chuey, who passed through a doorway almost hidden between the tiers of bunks. "It's all right," Dan whispered at her ear. "The Chinese emigrants are relieving their miserable existence with opium. Ever hear of it?"

She shook her head negatively as she followed the little man ahead of her along the short passage. In a much smaller room whose walls were covered with gold brocade was a low black enameled table encircled by red and green silk-tasseled pillows. On the table a stick of incense burned low in its jade container. Dan directed her to sit opposite him at the table. With a bow,

Ling Chuey vanished, and Dan began to talk in a soft persuasive voice as he lit the wick of the filigree burner.

"Opium relieves your pain, my dear girl. Eases the misery in the most pleasant of ways. It's like . . . floating." His gaze penetrated her. "Would you like to try?"

The palms of her hands began to perspire. Each day it seemed she sank deeper in her depression. Anything that would help . . . and something that actually felt pleasant . . . could it be any worse than the burning alcohol she imbibed?

Still, there was something furtive about the place. As if he sensed her hesitancy, Dan said, "If there was anything repugnant about opium, I certainly would not smoke it. It's frowned upon by certain segments of our society because they're simply afraid of it. Those people are afraid to experience anything beyond themselves." All the time he talked to her soothingly, quietly, until the sweet tang of the incense filled the room.

Sitting with her legs folded to one side, she carefully watched as he inhaled the substance. He tipped his head back and closed his eyes. "Most pleasant sensation, Flora."

After a moment he passed the pipe to her. She stretched out a tentative hand, wary, but wanting something that would take her beyond the emptiness that assailed her. "Draw in on the pipe," he instructed. "Like a man does a cigar. Try to feel it here, expanding in your chest. Then slowly let the smoke rise out of your body. Whatever pain or sorrow or suffering you have, Flora, I promise it will drift from your body like the smoke."

She sensed what she was about to do was forbidden, dangerous, and for that reason, she was intrigued all the more. For a precious few moments something was drawing her outside her misery, if only curiosity. What did she have to lose?

With the pipe's tip at her lips, its tubing coiling about her like a serpent, she could smell the deep sweet vapors. Slowly she inhaled, as Dan had instructed. At first she felt nothing, then the scratchiness of the smoke as it exploded into her lungs.

Her breath wheezed through her windpipe, and a small smile curved Dan's fine lips. "Try it again," he prompted. "The next time will be easier . . . and much more enjoyable, I promise you."

She raised a brow and experimentally drew on the stem once more. The smoke surged into her lungs, abrasive, yet after the initial contact, softening. A serene, silky sensation webbed its way through her mind after a few moments, and, gratified, she sank into the pillows, passing the pipe back to Dan. Exhilarating feelings wafted through her, leaving an afterglow of warmth as they passed.

Through the wisps of redolent smoke, she watched the recumbent Dan across from her, the drooping lids, the slack mouth, and she knew that he was experiencing the same depths of pure, exquisite sensation to which she was succumbing. Yet he seemed to withhold himself on some plateau that she was quickly verging past.

She did not care why he only partially experienced the pleasures of the pipe. The fact was he had introduced her to something far better than she had known in all her lonely life . . . in all her life of loving Brig.

In addition to her visits with Dan to the opium den, Jessie now escaped once or twice a week on her own. Ling Chuey politely took the bills she passed him at the door and escorted her to the small chamber. She knew she was safe through the morning's early hours with those strange people—that come noon Ling Chuey would gently remove the pipe from her lax fingers and send her on her way to the boardinghouse.

The fresh air and the bright sunlight would restore some clarity to her head on the walk back to the Russ House, and she slept off the last of the drowsy effects before going to work in the evenings. Now the steps that dogged hers no longer frightened her, for she knew they were a product of the heavenly opium.

Miss Cashman never mentioned her late-afternoon arrivals, but a frown of concern would crease the New Englander's long face. "You feeling all right, Flora?" she sometimes shouted, and Jessie would have to shout back into the woman's ear trumpet, for everyone in the boardinghouse to hear, that she had never felt better.

After a while Jessie sensed that even Dan seemed concerned for her. One evening he called her to his office after she had gone on break. "Ling Chuey tells me you often go alone, Flora. Perhaps too often."

She arched one brow. "I can take care of myself. Besides, I might point out you haven't cut down on your visits."

"Ahh, but I know exactly where to stop," he said, exhaling on his cheroot in much the same manner he did on the opium pipe. "I know how much my body will take."

"Why do you smoke it—the opium?" She tilted her head to one side. "What are you running from, Daniel O'Rourke?"

He puffed quietly on the cheroot, and for a moment she thought he was not going to answer her. Then he said, "From myself. You see, Flora, the golden smoke makes me forget the desire I have for men . . . an unnatural desire, my provincial parents thought. Are you shocked? No, I thought not. In some ways the opium elucidates . . . makes you see things as they really are—oneself included."

In spite of Dan's words of caution, she continued to visit the opium den. She realized she was courting danger, but she cared not. Sometimes she even wondered if she did not actually enjoy the duel she played. Over a period of time she came to know more about the mysterious operations of Hop Town.

Behind the facades of the Chinese restaurants, Soo Sin's Parlor & Games of Chance, the laundries, the bakeries, there existed a darker underworld of child slavery, prostitution, and, of course, the forbidden opium dens. Now she knew why Dan disappeared for days at a time—and where his diamond pin went.

Through the opium den's underground doorways she occasionally overheard the rattle of the dice and the triumphant exclamations of the Chinese gamblers. Occasionally she would glimpse a small child, stooped with the burden of the trays of food she carried, scurrying down the darkened halls like a mine rat. Dan explained that in order to feed all the hungry mouths in the household the impoverished Chinese were sometimes forced to sell a child to the Westerners who trafficked in child slavery.

Walking through the town—seeing the thin, yellow faces of the children, the bent shuffling figures of the women with their bound feet, the hopelessness that stared out of the eyes of the men— she would cry out inside at the injustice, the injustice of one race to another, of one human to another.

And then she would think of Elizabeth Godwin—and Brig— and she would hurry on to the House of the Golden Dreams to find her oblivion.

Chapter 35

*T*ARO Shima bowed low before Ling Chuey, who made the same traditional greeting, then straightened. He had to look down at the wily Chinese who in effect actually controlled the lives of Hop Town's inhabitants.

"You are most welcome to my humble establishment, Taro Shima," Ling Chuey said, speaking in English.

Taro inclined his head in acknowledgment. His stone-carved face never once betrayed surprise that Ling Chuey knew who he was. Ling Chuey knew everything and everyone, or soon would, who rode in and departed from Tombstone. "I seek to enjoy a game of mah-jongg," he responded, likewise in English.

"So good, Shima-san," Ling answered politely, his small eyes probing behind Taro's smooth facade. "The white man's poker and the Mexican's monte do not offer the challenge of the Oriental game."

Taro followed the man along the long hall and down the wooden steps into the tunnel. He ignored the bodies sprawled in drowsy abandon as he passed through the main stope to another smaller room bathed in a yellow light from a filigreed oil lamp suspended from the ceiling by a gold chain. About a low, square black table, a *kotaku,* sat three men, all middle-aged though they appeared eons older.

Like virtually all the men of their race living in the United States' Western territories, they had signed on in China as youths to work in the Land of the Golden Mountain, as America was known there. Soon they were disillusioned, realizing that the wages they had hoped to send back home were needed entirely for survival. They were outcasts, spit on and reviled by the round eyes. But there in the mah-jongg parlors, in the opium dens, and in the cribs of prostitution they were the great lords they had hoped to be.

The three men rose and bowed, palms on knees, as the stranger entered with Ling Chuey. A foreigner, they knew, but obviously not of the round-eyes.

Taro crossed the tatami floor mat and took a place on one of the *zebuton* cushions. The mah-jongg tiles of bone were distributed among the players, and within minutes a Chinese girl dressed in a white cotton jacket and black trousers slip-stepped into the room to set china cups of pungent tea before the men. After the expected pleasantries were exchanged, the game commenced, and Taro concentrated on the complicated scoring system so that he was able to vanquish his opponents within the hour.

As if Ling Chuey knew the exact moment of the game's termination, he rejoined the men. New cups were placed on the *kotaku,* this time filled with rice whiskey, sake. One by one the other three men departed, being sure to politely leave a small amount of sake in the cup. Now there were only Ling Chuey and Taro Shima left to face each other.

The two men began to speak, keeping to light subjects—the price of tea in the territory, the problems of growing the mulberry trees for a silkworm industry, the lack of respect the young people of the round-eyes displayed toward their elders. "There is no *enryo*—modesty—in the presence of one's superior," Ling announced with a heavy sigh.

Taro nodded, politely agreeing with his host. He knew he would have to be patient. Ling Chuey no doubt correctly suspected why he had come and in time would broach the subject. At last, when the cups were refilled with sake a third time, Ling said, "It is so sad that the *ha-ku-jins,* the round-eyes, do not know how to enjoy the worldly pleasures with moderation. The bars of Tombstone are an excellent example, are they not? The men have no self-will—cannot put aside their glasses at the right moment. The same holds true for the poppy. Even now a young woman, a round-eye, who has visited my establishment for many months lies drifting in another room on the poppy's vapors."

"That is too bad, Ling Chuey. The Westerners have no sense of decorum. How long has the girl been dreaming?"

Ling paused, as if counting. "Three days this time. Maybe four.

She no longer returns to her place. And there is no money left to pay for the poppy." He shrugged his shoulders elaborately. "Such is the life of a businessman. He takes chances. Now, for my generosity to this woman, I must lose."

"What will happen to this round-eye?" Taro asked with apparent indifference.

"Most likely I will have to bear the burden of her keep. If I keep her supplied with the poppy, I can use her as a concubine. The bachelors who have contracted marriages back in the old land would take her to bed for relief. But, of course, after a while the poppy will render her useless. And then . . ." He sighed fatalistically. "We all die . . . but such a painful death in the throes of the poppy. Yes, it is such a shame the woman could not have used more good sense. Such a waste."

"Does no one miss the foolish woman?"

"Ahh, yes, Taro Shima. There is her employer. He, likewise, enjoys the poppy dreams. He has seen her. Yesterday, I believe. He realizes the woman is an addict—too far gone for him to help her. No, the best I can do for the unworthy woman is to let her have her dreams to ease the way to death. The bachelors will be grateful and kind to her."

Her employer. Taro knew of him. Understood him and his kind far too well. The innate sensitivity, the appreciation of beautiful things that Taro's race had refined to such a high degree, could be sensed, though at a much lower level, in Daniel O'Rourke. Like O'Rourke, Taro could find pleasure in the beauty of every living creature . . . the male sex as well as the female. But for Taro that appreciation had come to be in most cases something remote, an appreciation through the inner senses. An appreciation that he found more often those days through meditation.

But the round-eye woman's extraordinary beauty had captivated him. To experience her gift of love, the gift he knew she was capable of giving, was something that few human beings ever experienced. For that kind of gift he would dedicate his life.

Slowly Taro swallowed all but the last dregs of the sake. "Such a shame," he agreed at last. "For you especially. As you have pointed out, she will not last long on the poppy dreams—and you, Ling Chuey, will not recoup your loss."

"I could perhaps auction her off, but none of the men who

(214)

frequent the House of the Golden Dreams has the kind of money it would take to make up for what I have spent to keep her."

"You could, of course, use the round-eye as a wager in a game of fan-tan," Taro said, setting down his cup. Did his voice sound too anxious, betray too much his concern?

"Ahhh, yes. But, likewise, who could equal such a stake?"

"The round-eye is not worth a high stake," Taro pointed out. "A woman, an addict—who would want her? Still, in honor of my host, I would offer a wager that would not insult you . . . the claim to the Lotus Land Mine."

Ling Chuey nodded sagely. "It is said the Lotus Land Mine has been a moderately successful enterprise."

"People's words give it too much credit," Taro said modestly.

"But the evaluation scales at the Assayer's Office do not lie. Some silver has poured forth from your mine, Shima-san."

Taro was not surprised that Ling Chuey knew of the mine's productivity, no doubt to the exact dollar the silver yielded each month—though it was not as much as it could have been because of the primitive methods to which he was forced to resort.

Ling Chuey poured out more sake, an indifferent look in the black lacquered eyes. His whole demeanor as he sipped the whiskey bespoke a man giving casual consideration to a matter that did not interest him greatly. But Taro knew Ling Chuey's reputation and knew men like Ling Chuey in Japan. Greedy, avaricious men. He knew the man who controlled Hop Town would like to add the Lotus Land Mine to his holdings. And so Taro did not partake further of the sake but sat cross-legged, focusing his energies inward, as if Ling Chuey's decision to stake the white woman was of no consequence to him.

And yet it was of great consequence to this aesthetically oriented male. When he had first seen her at the Crystal Palace, she had riveted his attention. She was unlike any woman he had ever known—not the helpless and meek, submissive Japanese females nor even the other white women with whom he had come in contact since landing in San Francisco four years earlier. She was neither the painted harlot of the saloons nor the pale fish-belly woman of the frontier who soon withered like the sage.

There was her extraordinary coloring . . . the sun-spun hair that actually curled of its own volition, giving the illusion of a separate entity. And then there was the vibrancy beneath the dusky gold skin. An aliveness that sheared the breath, like a quick sweep of the samurai sword, despite the dullness of the jade eyes . . . stones that needed polishing to restore their original beauty, he had often thought.

Only the wistful curve of the lips gave any indication there existed a vulnerability to the willful woman, a vulnerability that could endanger her—and, as he had feared, trailing her as he had those many nights, *had* endangered her.

Ling Chuey set his cup aside. Instantly the Chinese girl was there to refill it, but at the almost imperceptible shake of his head she lifted the tray and was gone, leaving the two men alone. "I have thought much on your offer, Taro Shima, and am highly honored. I feel much embarrassment that I have nothing of greater value to place as a stake except the worthless female, but if you will accept such a wager I would be more than delighted to participate in a game of chance with you. It has been such a long while that I had a challenging opponent. As the host, I will defer to your choice of games."

Taro nodded. "Perhaps fan-tan. The round-eyes seem to like it well enough."

And he had become quite proficient himself in playing it at the Crystal Palace. He had rarely gone into town, preferring the isolation of his mountain fastness, but sometimes the overwhelming need for human contact drove him down to the dens of civilization—drove him into the empty arms of a Chinese slave girl or the more devouring ones of the round-eyes, dance-hall girls who seemed to find him diverting, different from the bleary-eyed, unshaven souls who lumbered to the beds of paid-for passions.

He smiled thinly when he thought of the Western males who never took time to show their partner the many pleasant diversions of the sexual act. Perhaps that was why the dance-hall girls had ceased to charge him after the first of his occasional visits.

The game began with each player intent on ridding himself of the cards in his hand. It was a tedious game to the onlooker, as tedious as chess, with many decisions to be carefully thought through and plotted. Taro never once let it cross his impassive face that he held all four nines and three of the fours, unlucky numbers for the Oriental, indicating death or misfortune.

But then he had left behind in Japan the superstitious lore of

his people when he signed on to work in the pineapple planta-
tions of Hawaii. He had been chosen, along with ninety-three
others, because of his strength and willingness to work. The other
Japanese men who had come over in the stinking hold of the
steamer had reluctantly left the famine-stricken land only temporarily in hopes of sending their wages back to starving families
and of returning themselves one day to their homeland.

Not so Taro. His parents and his younger brother had yielded
to starvation's scythe. He had no reason to return, no land to
claim, since his father had leased the earth they plowed. Lately,
though, that desire for immortality that at one time or another
teases every man had caused Taro to ponder making a marriage
contract, a *miai-kekkon,* with some young woman back in Japan.
He had enough made to send for a Japanese bride now. But
curiously the idea receded, ebbing and waning like the tide
moved by the moon . . . like a man moved by the sight of one
certain woman.

He shook himself from his thoughts. It was not wise to dwell
on the round-eye now. He would need all of his concentration to
overcome the hazard of chance—and Ling Chuey's own skillful-
ness with the cards. He never permitted himself to consider the
possibility of what it would mean to lose the mine—that it meant
more than just the wealth the mine promised. It was the land
itself. Having grown up in a country where land was scarce,
reserved for the war lords and the samurai warrior class, owning
his own land had become paramount for him, something akin to
the religious fervor of a Buddhist priest.

One by one he rid himself of the unlucky nines and fours until
all he held was a three of clubs. His turn came, and with an inner
sigh he placed in on the tableau. Ling Chuey's sigh was more
audible. With a bland face, the host clapped the flats of his hands
against his knees. "So, Shima-san! You are a most worthy opponent! I wonder if you will find the stake you have won as worthy
as your skill at playing?"

Chapter 36

*T*ARO followed as Ling led him to the place where the white woman was kept—through a tunneled maze and into another stope guarded by an iron-scrolled gate. He had to bend his tall frame almost double to enter the low, timbered doorway.

"I took the precaution of removing the woman from easy accessibility to the men," Ling explained, as he entered into another low room—this one richly draped with black velvet curtains embroidered with whorls of gold design. There was a gold enameled table topped by an exquisite porcelain vase containing an artful arrangement of dried dandelions. A delicate rice-paper screen partially concealed a bed covered in black velvet matching the drapes.

"You see, Shima-san," Ling Chuey said, moving now to the bed, "I did not wish for the woman to give up the only bargaining power a female possesses."

Half propped on tufted cushions in gold silk lay the woman, one arm stretched out, the lax hand holding a pipestem whose flame had long before burned out. Taro's gaze locked on the ravaged face. A pallor had settled over its skeletal contours. The lips, dry and cracked, moved softly, inanely, so that spittle ran from the corner of the mouth. The irises were faded, lifeless half-moons. And the hair—it was matted with filth.

Taro's sensibilities were revolted by the stench and sight of the thing on the bed, and he wondered that he had chanced the Lotus Land on the pathetic creature.

His burro's hooves wrapped in cloth to obscure the trail, Taro began the arduous journey home. Before him he cradled the round-eyed woman, Rose—a name that did not befit her, for she had the wild loveliness of the sacred lotus.

A scant burden she was for the burro and the man, her flesh wasted away by the seemingly harmless poppy. Indeed, her pale skin, made waxy now by the effects of the opium, resembled the lotus. The shrunken flesh was pulled tightly across her bones. The cracked and split lips concealed the once haunting beauty. But there still remained a semblance, an aura, of the vibrant good looks that had set her apart from all other women.

He halted twice during the night's trip to trickle water into the slack mouth. More often than not the water ran back out the corners, but he was persistent, and when the few drops had been swallowed, he resumed his journey.

The sun's first tenuous shafts brought Taro into the canyon of his Lotus Land Mine and illuminated his home, a plank-and-log structure clinging like an eagle's nest to the steep side of a juniper-stubbled reddish-brown mountain. The burro, a jenny, took its two passengers easily along the narrow pebble-strewn path that twisted upward over precarious ridges to the small house.

Upon arrival, without resting, he set about restoring the woman's fragile health. A soup, *miso-taki*, made from the vegetables he cultivated in the small patchlike garden—chickpeas, ginger root, and onions were boiled along with vinegar, beer, and soy sauce in a black cast-iron kettle over the native stone fireplace.

Behind the cabin he constructed a rock domelike cave, no higher than three or four feet. It resembled the sweathouse the native Americans, the Indians, used for purifying the body, which was what he intended—to purify the woman's body of the drugs over the long days and equally long nights that were to come.

Throughout the morning the man heated stones and toted them to the dome in large ore buckets suspended from a pole he yoked over his broad shoulders. By noon he had his bathhouse ready. He went to the woman, who lay unconscious on the straw-woven mat in a darkened corner of the room. His fingers began to work at the fastenings of the sweat- and vomit-stained clothing. First the myriad buttons of the high-necked blouse that followed the smooth line of the woman's backbone, then the heavy, wrinkled skirt and underskirt, the long corset and attaching wire-frame bustle. Lastly the Cromwell shoes, the ribbed cashmere stockings, and the camisole.

He sat back on his knees with a grunt. Not even the Japanese woman's kimono, which took two people and forty-five minutes to don, entailed so many needless garments. The woman's almost lifeless body lay exposed to his gaze, but he neither noted the ribs and pelvic bones made prominent by lack of nourishment nor the soft, firmly rounded breasts faintly streaked with blue veins. His culture had taught him that for the ritual bath neither sex actually acknowledged the sight of the nude body. The bath ritual was set apart from the sexual desire—it had to be in his land of little space and privacy.

He easily lifted the woman and carried her to the sweathouse. For a moment he hovered over her as the dry heat enveloped the two of them. For a moment, despite the thousand years of assimilated culture, he let his gaze move over the woman in something that was other than impersonal . . . not necessarily a gaze of sexual assessment but one of intrigue.

He was intrigued by everything about her—the coloring of the tawny-gold hair, the peach-lustered glow of the skin that lay just below the waxy surface, the shape—so obviously feminine in spite of the fact that she was taller, with longer legs, than his countrywomen. Just for a moment he willed her lids to open—to see there the green-eyed gaze. The lashes fluttered, then fell motionlessly on the high sweep of the cheekbones. He moved away to hunch outside the sweathouse.

Nearly half an hour passed before he judged it time to remove the woman. Wrapping her in a woolly blanket, he carried her back to the house. But he was not yet finished with her. With a cool rag he sponged off the perspiration that beaded her skin, and for the first time she made a noise, a half-moan, half-whimper. He continued despite the moans that, had they carried more strength, would have been protests. He let her sleep then, exhausted as she was from such little administrations to her body.

Later that afternoon, when she stirred, he began to patiently spoon the *miso-taki* into her mouth. After several spoonfuls passed her throat, he was rewarded by seeing her irises. Yet he was not lulled into relief. Too often he had seen the signs of an addict, and the path to recovery was not so easily traveled. The eyes had the dull cast to them so that the irises were more a flat pewter than the deep meadow green . . . which alone told him so much.

He let the woman rest while he attended to the chores that had accumulated in his absence. But within the hour, before the evening's darkness had even covered the deep gulch below, he took up his task of restoring the woman's health . . . a warm bath administered by hot towels, followed by a vigorous massage that took in handfuls of muscles running from fingertips to toes. He used the *shiatsu* finger-pressure method that was an art in the old land.

When he concluded, the woman collapsed like a doll that had had the stuffing removed. Barely audible grunts and whooshes and groans emitted from her, and a slight smile crossed his generous mouth.

For the day he was finished, and he retired to the meticulous washing of his own body as golden-hued as the woman's and incredibly muscled by the years of working with the pick and ax. That night, as in the nights that followed, he placed his own tatami floor mat next to hers so that instantly he was there when she began to mumble or moan.

And moan she did over the days that came and went as slowly as the shadows across a sundial, days and nights punctuated by the woman's belligerent shrieks and agonizing screams. He neglected his work at the mine, his garden, everything but his determination to save the woman.

At times she was lucid, and she would look about her, never speaking, never moving—only the eyes that had that old-young look in them. After a few minutes, minutes that grew into hours as the days passed, the woman would ask for the opium, softly, persuasively at first. "I must have it, don't you understand—whoever you are? It makes me feel better, you know."

Taro would shake his head, sadly, it seemed to her, and a new tactic would begin. Her hand would slide up to cup one of her breasts suggestively or rub sinuously at her pelvic area in a pathetic attempt at seduction. "If you will get the opium for me," she would ask in a voice made hoarse by her intermittent screams, "I will give you myself—and no man has had me."

He saw the sudden uncertainty of her last statement pass across her face, and he repressed a smile. "I could easily take you without getting the opium for you," he pointed out.

It seemed to her he was impervious to her agony—and her tricks.

And her screeching would begin again. Vile curses and crude, coarse language echoed in the cabin—obscenities that she must have picked up at the saloon, for despite her dissolute surroundings, he felt she was unsullied. The nights and days he had trailed her, watching her—guarding her—she had never taken a man to bed that he knew of. And always he would ask of himself that final question, did it matter if she had?

Although her lucid moments were punctuated with salacious phrases, the other times were even worse. Taro was forced to straddle her and pin her arms to the plank floor as she tossed and bucked, clawing at her own skin in her torment. If he had to leave the cabin for any length of time, he bound her hands and feet with rawhide so that she would not injure herself. If she was awake while he tied her up, she shot volley after volley of bawdy oaths at him, which he ignored, as he did the furious glares.

One morning early, before the sunlight had barely dappled the floor, he was gifted with the first genuine smile. The woman looked at him, studying him as he lay near her.

"Yes?" he asked, turning his narrow-lidded gaze on her.

"Why have you done this—why have you cared for me?" she asked in a voice that was no stronger than the spring breeze outside.

"I would not see something of beauty die," he replied simply.

Chapter 37

AGAINST the harsh light that invaded the room each day the man's slender figure moved about like some ghostly presence. A benevolent one, though, Jessie thought, as she tried to separate reality from the nightmares. For in the fog of serpents and rodents and, of course, the incredible pain, there was the man . . . and his hands. In all that time of drifting and sliding and writhing she subconsciously had wanted only the relief of the opium, and if not that, then the man's hands.

She covertly watched him now from beneath the veil of her lashes as he moved quietly about the room, and she realized his slender physique was deceptive. Below the three-quarter-length sleeves of the black ceremonial tea robe he wore, his forearms rippled with sinewy muscles, and she remembered the strength in his hands. The shoulders were broad, the chest deep. She smiled, thinking how the description better fit a stallion, and he said, "Your smile lightens my home."

So, he had known all along that she was awake, watching him. She blushed, bringing the first glint of color to the long-deprived skin. As if sensing her embarrassment, he turned back to the hot liquid he poured in china cups. "Where am I?" she asked him.

He crossed the room, carrying the two cups on a tray. Only then, as he sat before her, legs crossed, did she realize the man was the Oriental who had so often played fan-tan at her table. "In my house," he replied as he passed her one of the cups. "Have you enough strength to drink on your own now?"

The cup, beautifully fired with tints of flat green and black, had no handle, and Jessie held it in both hands as she struggled to support herself on one elbow. She had not realized how weak she was. Past the man, through the open wooden shutters, she could see the scattered juniper and scrub oaks and, beyond, tips of distant mountain peaks. "But *where* is your house? And exactly who are you?"

Taro smiled. "I can see you are better. Drink your tea, and I will answer all your questions."

She raised a questioning brow. "All of my questions?"

"Whatever you wish to know." He set the cup aside, and she was momentarily diverted by the grace of his movement—smooth, fluid, liquid—so out of character with the rough, clumsy men who frequented the gambling saloons.

"I have brought you to my house, which is in the Mule Mountains south of Tombstone, because you were very ill."

"From the opium," she stated more than asked, wondering about Dan—if he knew what had happened to her. But then in his own way he had become just as addicted to it, so that he cared for little else. He had only controlled his intake better.

"Now drink your tea," Taro told her, "unless you have any more questions."

She had many, but she was afraid she knew the answers. He alone had to have undressed her—and seen her nudity. She blushed again, crimson spreading across her face to the roots of her hairline. "I did not take unfair advantage of you," the man across from her stated quietly. "You are as you were."

"Not quite," she said sadly, her gaze falling on her hands that clutched the cup like bird's claws. "Perhaps you should have let me die. I wanted to."

"And you will want to again, many times before your karma dictates your wish, but you won't—so you must make the best of living until that time comes."

She looked up into the granite-smooth face with the undecipherable gaze. "That sounds pretty much like a speech."

He smiled, showing the teeth that were whiter than pearls. "I have labored long for your life. Therefore you cannot so lightly regard it, for it belongs to me now. You must excuse my excess of words. But I . . ."

She belonged to him? What a quaint thought . . . and a disconcerting one! "Who are you?" she murmured.

"I am Taro Shima, from the southern prefecture of Kumamoto, Japan."

"Then you aren't Chinese? But who are you? I mean, it is so odd to find a person like you—here—in the middle of nowhere."

"You still have not drunk your tea," he reminded her.

The tea was excellent, much better-tasting, she decided, than the sarsaparilla-root tea Nellie Cashman made. Taro Shima began to talk to her. Quietly he told her how he had come to the United States four years earlier at seventeen. "The steamship that brought me from Japan was unable to dock in Hawaii because of a plague raging the islands," he explained, "so the steamship was forced to transport myself and the other ninety-two Japanese laborers to San Francisco. When it arrived, thirty-seven of the laborers were dead—from ill treatment."

He spoke of working on the railroad as a gandy dancer and rail layer to support himself; of keeping his money until he had enough to buy the land the Lotus Land claim sat on. The softly spoken words, the mesmeric gaze of the those slanted eyes, soon lulled her into a deep sleep unmarred by the hellish dreams.

When next she awoke, she found the man was kneeling over her. A soft darkness enveloped the two of them. His long fingers pressed in concentric circles at her temples. "What are you doing?" she whispered in a nervous croak.

"You were having unpleasant dreams. Your hands beat at your head. The headache—it is gone now?"

She remembered now the pain that had throbbed in her head like a sledgehammer, threatening surely to crack open her skull. But now beneath the gentle pressure of the man's fingers the intense pain had miraculously subsided. "Yes." She sighed. "The headache is gone, Taro."

Her lashes fluttered closed, her mind drifting into the netherworld once more with the nebulous thought that she should be afraid, alone with the man. But somehow, with his fingers massaging her temples, her mind, it did not matter. Nothing mattered.

"You are ready to eat something today?" the voice asked.

Reluctantly Jessie forced her eyes open to the clean, sunlit room and to the man who stood over her, seeming taller than ever. Slowly she nodded, for indeed the flavor that wafted by her nostrils was tempting.

"Good," Taro replied. He set the tray he carried on a low table that he moved between Jessie and himself.

She looked at the fluffy brown food in the bowl. "What is it?" she suspiciously asked.

"*Ochazuke*. Rice with tea poured over mushrooms. And these," he said, passing her two wooden sticks with blunt tips, "are *hashi*."

She watched, fascinated as the man began to eat, deftly moving the two sticks with the fingers of one hand. Then she tried, but the rice kept sifting through the awkwardly held utensils. After a few moments, Taro said, "You will have to use your fingers until you master the *hashi*."

"Oh, but I won't be here that long," she protested.

He said nothing but continued to eat, and she asked, fear rasping her voice to a whisper, "You will let me go, won't you?"

He set down the bowl of half-eaten rice. "You are free to go at any time, Lotus Woman. But wherever your footsteps may take you, your soul belongs to me, now . . . and always."

A rose-scented candle burned low, casting dancing shadows. In the hush that fell she could see only his face, the jet eyes that held her as truly as chains.

* * *

Another hour. Another day. She could only measure the passing of the time by the slow inching of the sun's slanted rays across the plank floor, by the curious but tasty meals that Taro prepared for her, and finally by his comings and goings. The intervals he was away became longer as she grew stronger—strong enough to get up, though she was still unsteady on her feet.

He was unfailingly kind, unfailingly polite in her presence. Still, she blushed each time he entered the cabin, his tall, slender frame dominating the small room. She recalled the intimate tasks he had performed for her—changing the straw mats, leaving them outside to air, when, in the deeper throes of withdrawal, she had been unable to control her bodily functions; then later he had seemed to know and unobtrusively provided a porcelain chamberpot.

With him gone from the cabin her thoughts seemed to linger on him more than when he was present, and she decided that there could be nothing more unromantic than what passed between the two of them; yet each time he entered the room she instantly knew it, though she might be asleep, by the way the air seemed to crackle—as if charged, like the electrical storms that lashed the deserts and canyons, sending the wind howling up through the mountains' saddlebacks and fissures.

She was coming to know the cabin as thoroughly as a prisoner his cell. It was a spare, austere, but immensely peaceful room. There were the immediate things—the rough-textured mat beneath her, the porcelain jar of Indian paintbrush that wafted of spring sitting on the low black lacquered table nearby.

Farther away stood the ornately carved chest with gold handles. In it she had glimpsed exquisite ivory carvings, golden bowls, and jade vases. In a corner on a raised platform stood a large cypress tub. A bamboo bird feeder hung in the open window, rendering the occasional sight of a hummingbird or a fragmentary song from the mockingbird.

That afternoon, when Taro at last returned, his arms burdened with chopped wood, she felt for the first time really alive. Isolated as she had been, her senses picked up things that went unnoticed before—from the sighing of the breeze outside as it winged its way down through the interlocking gulches to the pungent taste of the green tea she drank.

"So that's where you go every day," she murmured.

He began stacking some of the logs in the fireplace. "Not always, Lotus Woman," he said as he added small chips of kindling. "There are other things which need my care besides you."

She tilted her head to better study the man whose profile was to her. He held a bamboo match to the chips, and the wood caught fire. He looked directly at her then, and she caught the slightest curve in the carved lips before he turned back. "There are the burros to be fed, the garden to be tended to, the mine to be worked."

"I'm a lot of trouble to you, aren't I, Taro?" she asked in a teasing voice.

He stood and crossed to her, looking down at her recumbent figure. "Your presence gives me great pleasure. My house will be empty when you leave."

Before she could consider some sort of reply to his solemn words, he left her to bring in two large buckets of water, which he poured into a great caldron suspended from the spit in the fireplace. "It is time for a complete bath for you," he explained when he saw her quizzical look.

Once a week she had used the boardinghouse's public tub located in a room back of the kitchen. It had been a hurried necessity that accomplished little more than the surface cleaning of the dust from the skin and hair, a routine that she often thought more trouble than it was worth, especially struggling to rinse the soap's film from her tangled mass of hair. Her daily ablutions had consisted of a quick sponging from the basin of tepid water in her room.

But watching Taro as he moved about the room preparing for her bath, she began to realize his motions took on the aspects of a ritual. On a short wooden stool he placed a dried gourd, a small lava rock, a wooden bowl of what she learned was wet rice bran, and a large porous washcloth.

After emptying the hot water into the tub and replenishing the caldron over the fire, he came to kneel at her side, hands flat on his thighs. "I am ready to bathe you."

She clutched at the neckline of her robe. "Well, I'm not," she said fiercely.

"Do you think I will see anything I have not already seen?" he asked patiently.

Her lower lip thrust out petulantly. "It's not that."

"Then do you think what I shall see will stir in me desires this time that I did not feel the first?" Without giving her an opportunity to consider, he continued. "A person who cannot control his mind as well as his body is weak. What I do for you is an impersonal service. Please think of it as no more."

When she made no reply, he scooped her up in his arms and carried her across to the tub, sitting her on the stool, which had been cleared of its bath utensils. He began to talk to her, explaining what he did, as if he sought to ease the tension between them. "The geishas are women in Japan who are hostesses— entertainers—and they devote much time to daily bathing."

"Daily?" she asked, so incredulous that she was not really aware that he lowered the neck of the embroidered robe to bare her shoulders.

"Yes, daily." He smiled at her naiveté. "And it is the women in my land who perform the task of bathing the men, not as I am doing for you. The same holds true of eating. It is the women who eat last and wait on the men and walk behind them."

"I don't think I would like your country," she snapped.

"But you like what I am doing, don't you?" he asked as he moved the wet, warm cloth across her shoulders, lifting the mass of her heavy, snarled hair to scrub the long column of her neck.

"Yes," she admitted in a whisper, wishing that she could divorce herself from the task he performed as easily as he seemed to do, for she was all too conscious of his nearness and her own near nudity.

Taro moved around in front of her, hunching on his heels, so that his face was even with hers. She was struck by the sheer masculinity of his features—the harsh planes and angles, the narrow-lidded eyes that seemed to smolder with black smoke.

His hands parted the robe, and, rewetting the cloth in the warm water once more, he began to run the cloth over her throat and shoulder bones. "You are as delicate as a hummingbird, Lotus Woman," he said in what anyone else would have termed an impersonal observation. But having been in close contact with him over the many days and nights, she would have sworn that a deeper, richer substance imbued his low-pitched voice.

The cloth slid down the valley between her rose-tipped breasts, around her ribcage, and up under her arms before moving lower to bathe her stomach. She began to tremble inside, like the slightest tremors of the earth that go unnoticed before a quake. What this man did to her was a hundredfold more arousing than all the nude paintings . . . even than Brig's exploratory kisses. She could not take her gaze from Taro's face, yet his countenance remained impassive as he went about his task.

His hand lowered to her thighs now and gently slipped inside before sliding down to cup her calves and ankles. For a moment her lids snapped closed in a reaction of sheer shock, then remained that way as she savored the pleasant sensation that followed. Even the soles of her feet, small and narrow, did not go unwashed.

"Why must you wash me before I take a bath?" she asked tremulously. "It makes no sense."

He rose now. "You would not wish to bathe your body in dirty water, would you?"

"But you just bathed me."

"No. You Westerners do not know what real cleanliness is." Then, "Forgive me if I have offended you. I'm afraid I make a very poor host."

"No . . . no, I . . . like what you are doing," she unwillingly admitted. "It's just that . . ." Her gaze lowered.

His eyes searched her face. "I know this must be very difficult for a Western woman such as yourself," he said slowly. "But you must understand by now that I would not bring harm or discomfort to you."

She could only nod her head.

He smiled. "Good. Now we will complete your bath. Then, after you have rested—for your body still needs much rest—we shall eat."

What followed was actually very enjoyable, once she closed the door on her thoughts and let herself relax and only feel. First he added the last of the boiling water to the half-filled tub of tepid water; then, to her amazement, he dropped orange slices in the tub—to scent it, he explained. And she could indeed smell the citrusy-fresh scent of the fruit rising with the steam. Lastly, he stood her on her feet, supporting her with one hand about her waist, and with her faced away from him, he removed her robe.

When he scooped her up, she wrapped her arms around his

neck. She could smell his own clean scent. With her head tipped back against his forearm, she looked up into the inscrutable face. He seemed totally unaware of her naked body held against him.

He lowered her into the deliciously hot water, and it surged about her breasts, distorting everything below. While she lolled in the tub, soaking, he went to the fireplace to return with two more pails of hot water, which he emptied into the tub. "Give me your foot," he instructed.

Languorously she offered up her right foot, and he began to rub its heel and sole with the lava rock. She closed her eyes and sank farther into the tub, letting her arms float to the surface in dreamy abandon.

He repeated his actions with the other foot, then took the dried gourd and scrubbed each leg, from ankle to calf. She did not find it particularly enjoyable, but he explained it removed the superfluous hair and dead skin. He began to apply the wet rice bran. "This is like a facial," he explained. "In my land the geishas use nightingale droppings."

She laughed, realizing both that it was the first time she could remember laughing in a long time and that Taro was attempting to make the bath easier for her by making her relax. At her laughter, his glance flickered to her face, then dropped as he resumed his task.

At last, to her disappointment, he leaned over her with a large soft towel and lifted her easily from the tub. Beneath her hands that she put around his shoulders, she could feel the ripple of the muscles. His face was just above hers, and she contentedly nuzzled her head in the hollow of his neck, dreamily wishing she could stay in that secure, fetal position forever. But too soon he laid her on the mat and released her.

As he knelt over her, roughly toweling her proffered body, her gaze clung to his face. She perversely wished that there was some way she could break through his self-containment. She sighed, somehow knowing that no one would unless he permitted it.

His dark gaze fell on her. "You enjoyed the bath after all?"

"Very much. Can we . . . you will bathe me again?"

A mask slid over the eyes. "Whenever you wish, Lotus Woman."

Chapter 38

DAILY Jessie's strength returned. The color returned to her skin and the shining life to her butter-yellow curls. She knew soon she would be strong enough to leave the cabin. But her soul was not yet ready to return to the dichotomy of her former life. And so she luxuriated in those lazily passing days of spring.

Taking up her perch on the narrow wooden arched footbridge that Taro had constructed over a nearby rivulet, she watched as the scrub oaks and piñon and occasional willow changed into their emerald garb. She learned to sit patiently, knees drawn up beneath her chin, while the shy mule deer or pronghorn antelope made its way down to the thin but deep ribbon of water. It was the mating season; even a flock of cinnamon teal proclaimed it from the cerulean sky with their gargled calls. A desert bald eagle swooped down into its mountain cranny where its mate waited, and the smaller birds trilled their love calls.

And Jessie waited, for what she was not certain.

Her life there in the mountains took on a comfortable routine, beginning with dawn when Taro woke and stirred the banked embers into life against the early-morning chill, for the altitude was nearly five thousand feet above sea level. After breakfast, usually rice and bean curd, which she was learning to prepare, he would leave for the mine, equipped with three candles, for his ten-hour day beneath the ground.

After his departure she would clean the dishes and then read some of the out-of-date newspapers he furnished her. Later she went to sit on the footbridge, enjoying the sun's life-giving rays as she had never thought she would. At noon she walked down to the mine entrance that was half-pit, half-cave and shared a picnic lunch with the man who had come to own a part of her, as he put it.

It was easy to talk with him, for he seemed interested in what she had to say, especially her earlier life and her education—something that the Japanese female did not receive. However, Taro surprised her when she learned that he had more education than she, for he told her the Japanese male usually had a full eight years of education unless he was of the *eta*—or the untouchable—class.

"There is a class system ruled over by the nobility," he clarified. "Below that is the warrior, or samurai, class; the agriculture class, from which I come; the mechanics and artists; and lastly, the merchants. Then there are the untouchables, which are not dignified with a class."

She admitted that there was a class system in the United States despite its egalitarian claim to democracy, the class being ruled by the Anglo. "Below that are the races of color. That I am partly one of color—Spanish—was one of the reasons I was considered unsuitable to marry Brig Godwin."

"The heir to Cristo Rey?" Taro asked carefully.

She nodded, and he said, "It is this then that drove you to the House of the Golden Dreams?"

She looked away from his probing gaze. "Yes, but what I feel for him no longer exists. I have come to see that he was not the man I thought he was. He was a weakling. A puppet!"

"And yet your soul is still not healed, is it?"

"Maybe one day," she replied evasively. *If you allow me to stay here long enough.*

Would he? Or would he make a bridal contract for some young woman he had never seen, as he had told her many of his countrymen had done?

The thought stung—not the thought of Taro's marrying someone else, but the thought of what would take place between him and his bride, something that she would never experience. Why, she was jealous!

And what would Taro think of her outlandish thoughts, coming as he did from a society where a woman supposedly had no thoughts? Yet he had been in the United States for four years, since he was only seventeen. In some ways he did seem to think as a progressive American would.

But what American male, she asked herself, would have done for her, or any woman, what he had?

Embarrassed as always by the direction her thoughts seemed to run, she would change the subject, asking Taro to tell her more of his strange homeland, so that daily she was becoming more familiar with the unusual man and his customs.

She learned to remove the funny shoes, the zori slippers, he had provided, really not so different from her huaraches of childhood, before she entered his house in the tabi stocks. And she always made certain the zori toes pointed away from the door. She acquired the taste for the furry green tea and learned the polite ritual of taking the thumb and forefinger to wipe the lip of the teacup when one is finished.

Such a simple custom, yet as she watched Taro perform the rite on her own cup, it seemed a terribly intimate gesture.

Sitting on the wooden slats that bridged the stream, she pondered the irony of the situation. At the Crystal Palace she had watched men nonchalantly slip their hairy paws down the low-cut fronts of the dance-hall girls' dresses and had felt only repugnance for what she saw. Yet there in the clean simplicity of Taro's home, she had only to watch the smooth slender fingers trace the rim of a cup and her stomach fluttered with the beating wings of a hundred Japanese nightingales!

Even now her breath seemed trapped in her lungs as her gaze fell on Taro moving up the boulder-cropped path toward her. Behind him plodded the burro that had brought her to the mountain refuge. She rose and went to meet Taro, feeling shy before the man with the memory of her thoughts about him still fresh on her mind.

What would it be like for his hands to touch her in a way that was not impersonal?

She patted the rough, furry hide between the burro's droopy ears. "How was your day?" she asked Taro, noting that the rawhide chests on either side of the burro were full.

"The silver is wearing thin, but I may have found a streak of copper."

She fell into step beside him as they moved toward the cabin. "Copper? Is it valuable? The men at the Crystal Palace talked of nothing but gold and silver lodes."

"It will be," he prophesied. "But maybe not soon enough."

They removed their shoes and went inside the cabin. Jessie crossed to the wall of staggered shelves to find the tea canister and prepare Taro a cup while he changed into a robe. She had been careful over the weeks to keep her head averted, her hands busy preparing the tea, but sometimes her eyes glimpsed a forbidden flash of gold-sheened, muscled flanks, and her stomach would lurch, as if she were falling.

The late afternoon was her favorite time of day. After the tea, she and Taro would bathe, first him, then herself. Though he no longer performed the intimate task of bathing her, since she was strong enough to do this herself, she still found the bathing a sensual rite.

Afterward they would eat and spend the hours of the evening talking—he perfecting his English, which she thought was as good as or better than hers, and she learning smidgens of Japanese. Sometimes she would help him pack the dynamite blasting caps with black powder. At other times she would simply sit and watch, entranced by his liquid movements, as he sharpened his pick or worked on his hand drill. Occasionally she sewed, one of her first projects his robe that swallowed her despite her tall frame, while he read Cooper's *The Spy* or Hawthorne's *The Scarlet Letter*—to learn more of his new country, he explained to her.

Taro seated himself now before the *kotaku,* and she noted how the ebony of his robe enhanced the deep, utter black of his eyes. She sat two cups on the table and took her place across from him. From experience she learned that the first few minutes of drinking the tea were reserved for savoring its taste.

After a few moments, Taro spoke to her, his jet gaze without expression. "Your afternoons in the sun have replaced the color in your skin. Now it has the color of a summer peach—the shade it had when first my eyes saw you."

Her gaze dropped before the intensity of his. "Why did you come each night to my table?" she asked, her voice barely above a whisper.

He put the cup to his mouth, letting the hot liquid flow over the beautifully delineated lips, and she watched, fascinated— fascinated by everything about the man. "You were like a burning bush," he said finally. "You were alive with color, except for your eyes. But the color inside you radiated, like an aura. Your body spoke to mine, Lotus Woman. And my body grieved when it noted your color was slowly fading, that your body was dying."

"I have never thanked you for what you did—taking me from that horrible place and . . . making me well."

"The light and color you bring to my house are enough."

He rose in a fluid motion and, taking the wild strawberries she had gathered earlier, crossed to the open window where hung the bird feeder. He began to talk as he mashed the berries' pulp into the feeder. "Within the week I need to return to Tombstone to renew my supplies—and, of course, have the assayer test my ore. Perhaps you would like to go with me?"

Her heart missed a beat, then double-timed to catch up. His back was to her. She could not bring herself to ask the gentle man the one question she wanted to ask. "If you wish me to."

He turned toward her. His back was to the sun, and she could not see that inscrutable face. "I wish to give you your freedom, Lotus Woman. There are no birdcages in my house, for the bird would never be mine if it were caged."

And am I yours? Was she reading too much into what he said? Would he think her too forward were she to reveal she dreamed erotic fantasies about him now? "Shall I prepare the bathwater?" she asked instead.

He nodded, and she took the kettle of boiling water that was kept continuously hot from the bed of coals and poured the water into the large tub while Taro brought in more water. This time, however, when the bath was ready, instead of retreating to another part of the room to occupy herself, she said, "You once told me that it was the woman who bathed the man in your country, yet you have not asked this of me. Will you not let me bathe you this time, Taro?"

Silently he studied her. "It has been a long time since a woman performed such a task for me. I would greatly appreciate it."

She retrieved another kettle of water while he shed the robe and seated himself on the stool. Carefully she poured the steaming water in the tub, then collected the cloth and dampened it. Remembering how he had gone about bathing her, she first washed the broad shoulders, noting the ridges of muscles that were crisscrossed by welts. "The scars—how did you get them?"

"The railroad supervisor was not pleased because I did not bow before him as did the Chinese coolies. Not too long afterward I left the railroad—the Chinese call it the Smoke Dragon," he added, smiling. "Then I began to work in the mines."

Her fingernail traced the corduroy line of scars, and she had the satisfaction of feeling his muscles flex beneath her fingertip. She left his back to wash his body precisely as he had washed hers. There was something tantalizing about the clean, smooth skin that covered the rock-hard muscles, the well-formed calves, and the strong line of the feet.

She thought about how reversed was the situation compared to that of the Anglo society. Here she performed the most personal of tasks for a man, and yet a sexual act was never culminated; but from what she had learned in the Crystal Palace, couples engaged in the sexual act and yet never once experienced true intimacy, she was certain.

She began to wash the arms now, not bunched with muscles but ridged in sinewy strength. Taro's lids were closed, and she enjoyed the chance to look upon the purely masculine face of tawny marble, wondering if she would ever have the chance to know the man, his thoughts. His eyes opened to meet hers. He said nothing, and she knew then he did know her thoughts.

Her throat worked, wanting to break the overpowering silence with words. Taro's fingers came up to rest on her lips. He moved his head in an almost imperceptible negative gesture, and she sensed he was telling her that it was no time for words. Puppetlike, her hands resumed the task of bathing the man. Carefully she kept her gaze averted from his genitals.

With his bath finished, she retired to a corner to discard her blouse and skirt while he donned his robe and prepared her bath. Sitting on the stool with only the robe thrown discreetly about her shoulders, she cleansed away the day's accumulation of dust and dirt before stepping into the tub to soak, her head resting against the cypress's edge. Taro did not watch her. Instead he worked on the primers and drillers that he would use in the mine blasting, but she knew that he was as aware of her as she was of him.

Later, they stretched out on their respective mats, his across the room from hers now that she was well. The candle was extinguished, and only the banked embers cast a faint golden glow over the room.

"Taro," she whispered.

"*Hai?*" he answered, reverting to Japanese, as he did more often now.

"The headache—it's bothering me again. Would you massage it away, please?"

"*Hai*," he said quietly and, moving as silently as the mountain cat, came to kneel at her side.

And his fingers took away the pain and brought the safety of sleep.

Chapter 39

*T*HREE days Taro had said he would be gone! And this was only the second day! Jessie sighed and resumed mending the robe's hem where a plank's splinter had torn it. She knew that the isolation was letting her imagination play tricks on her; yet she could not help but worry.

Would Taro seek out one of the Chinese concubines who she had come to learn existed in Hop Town? Or perhaps worse, would he partake of the pleasures offered by some willing Anglo woman? It was an absurd thought, for in the short time she had worked at the Crystal Palace she had learned that the Anglo prostitutes did not solicit the business of the Orientals . . . at least not openly.

The thought of Taro and another woman led her to ponder that at some time he would naturally take a wife, no doubt a contract bride from the old land. She knew she should leave soon; there was no pretext left for her to stay. The memory of the night before Taro left for Tombstone—the magical touch of his fingers—flooded through her, and she put aside the robe to pace the room in restless agitation.

Outside the summer sun floated lazily just above the orange-tinted mountain humps. In another half hour it would begin its rapid descent. Another lonely night, she thought, standing at the open door to catch any hint of a breeze. And how many more lonely evenings after she left the mountain refuge?

Then, incredulously, she heard a faint clipclop somewhere down the trail. Her heart began to beat in time to those unseen hooves, loudly there in the silence of the cabin. Her lips formed the word even before she saw the man astride the burro. "Taro!" she shouted and ran from the house across the footbridge to stand waiting in trembling anticipation.

Taro dismounted and, leaving the burro to graze on the short croppings, came to stand before her. He put his hands on her shoulders, felt her quivering beneath his touch. "You are cold?"

"No, Taro. I am warm inside. I am shaking because . . ." Could she match the honesty he had demonstrated? "Because I am so glad of your return. I've missed you very much." The words sounded so stilted in her ears. That was not at all what she wanted to say.

Taro nodded. He bent down, his arm slipping beneath her knees to lift her, cradling her slender body against his chest. "I have missed you, also, Lotus Woman. My thoughts have ever been of you. You have come to a decision?"

"Yes," she murmured, snuggling deeper in the warmth of his embrace. "I had made it before you ever left."

"*Hai,* this I know. But it was necessary you have this time alone."

He carried her across the footbridge into the house and laid her on the mat. But when he would have tarried, his hands tracing the curvatures of this strange woman he had come to love, she took them between her own. "Taro," she rasped, "I can't wait. My body has waited too long for yours."

An inarticulate gasp escaped his lips. His arms went around her, and she clung desperately, pressing herself against him as soft little sobs racked her body. He held her, and his own eyes filled with tears for her.

Then they fell upon each other, the need to consummate the desire that had been building between them overriding all thought. They tore at each other's clothing, anxious to touch one another, to share their love and lust and loneliness. She arched to meet and accept the muscle-striated torso that plunged into her.

Nothing she had seen or heard, either in the blunt discussions of the ranchería or the coarse descriptions in the Crystal Palace, had prepared her for the mind-shattering impact of the physical union with Taro. Wave upon wave of a pleasure too great to sustain inundated her. Even the small, initial pain had evolved into a pleasure.

Her mind reeled with the sensual attack of her body's senses, so that she was only half aware when Taro, still united with her, moved his head to one side to study her face, his own mirroring puzzled concentration. A frown marred the otherwise smoothly planed face. "You were a . . ." He paused, not knowing the equivalent to *mizu.* "You had not gone to the well," he murmured.

"The well?" she echoed, confused.

"*Mizu* means 'pumping the water out of the well,' " he explained. "It is used to mean when a girl is first initiated into the art of lovemaking."

The smallest of smiles curved Jessie's lips in her contentment. "Was I a virgin?" she said. "It seemed a minor point." Her forefinger traced the line of the lips that hovered above hers, then lifted to follow the sweep of one winged brow.

His hand caught hers in midmovement. "Still, it is great shame that I carry," he said, and Jessie, hearing the anger in his voice, realized it was directed at himself.

"Taro, Taro," she said softly, "there is no shame. I wanted you. You have made me a woman now, a happy woman."

Those slanted eyes drilled into her as if to read her thoughts. At last there came only the slightest nod before his slender hands closed upon her shoulders and his fingers began their mastery of her. "It's only just beginning, Lotus Woman," he whispered in a husky voice. "It is your time now to soar on wings."

She was stunned. She had not known that a man was capable of renewing himself several times within the night. The clientele of the Crystal Palace's dance-hall girls climbed and descended the stairs in such a brief span of time that she had hardly imagined anything beyond the simple, brief act of animal copulation.

And she had not known that the word "pleasure" in regard to the sexual act had actual meaning to the woman.

Yet throughout the night Taro brought her to a feverish pitch, playing her body as finely as a mandolin's strings, so that she quivered at his merest touch, fearing that she would snap if relief was long denied her. But his lovemaking, a part of techniques perfected over thousands of years, allowed her only moments of the splendid sensations to be followed by weak contentment before he brought her to the heights once more.

Low animal whimpers of delight danced on her delirious lips when his fingers exerted the slightest pressure on her body's intimate spots. "No more," she begged, yet still she opened herself up to his lovemaking, the ultimate in the art of love.

Even with the first shafts of dawn he was not finished with her but scooped up her limp body to place her in the tub of warm water he had moments before prepared. Her face, arms, and thighs were bathed with the tenderest care before he toweled her briskly, her skin shining with the attention, and laid her on her mat.

Her fingers entwined in his when he drew the blanket up over her and prepared to move away. *"Arigato,"* she said dreamily and was rewarded for her thanks by the soft smile that creased his beautiful face.

"If I had my way, I would keep you here with me," Jessie said drowsily from the mat as Taro shrugged into the hickory shirt.

"You purr like a contented cat," he teased. His gaze left her face, dropping to the swell of her breasts that showed just above the blankets she held across her nude body.

She knew he was enchanted with her breasts, so different from the "small acorns" of his countrywomen, he told her, yet lacking the pendulous droop of those of the Anglo women he had known.

This she did not let herself think about but instead shivered in delightful memory of what he had done to those breasts the night before. "If I do not leave now," he said, "it will be your body I explore and not the mine."

After he left, she pulled on the robe and padded about the cabin, putting away the food staples that she and Taro had neglected the evening before in their haste to seek each other's arms. She smiled to herself as she came across the coiled velvet length of ribbon, the color of persimmon. So, Taro had noted the string of rawhide she had confiscated to use as a tieback for her unruly hair.

She laid aside the new adz he had purchased and took up the folded newspapers to read before the fire's banked embers, humming lightly to herself. He had promised her before he left to find something more entertaining than the yellowed newspapers that were months out of date.

Hungry for the news, her eyes scanned the sheet, but miraculously enough the Crystal Palace escaped unscathed from John Clum's editorial pen. This was because the *Epitaph* devoted four full columns on the front page to a shoot-out at Tombstone's O.K. Corral.

"Three Men Hurled into Eternity in the Duration of a Moment," proclaimed the headline. As Dan had predicted, the Clantons, McLaury, and Claiborne had dueled against the Earp brothers and Doc Holliday for control of Tombstone, almost seven months earlier by the date of the newspaper, dated December of '83. And the Earp faction had won, as Jessie would have guessed, remembering the stern, leonine man who had offered her a job.

Reclining on the cushions, she thumbed over to another page, reading other news items until the name Godwin slid across the recesses of her brain. Her gaze darted back up a few lines to reread the paragraph.

> In conjunction with the birth of Mrs. Elizabeth Godwin's first great-grandchild, Franklin Godwin, she and Mr. Hugo Roget, the child's maternal grandfather, have announced the formation of the Cristo Rey Consolidated Mining Company. Estimates for the company's first week of production run as high as several hundred tons of silver bullion, which will be shipped weekly to the newly built stamp mill at Charleston. A welcome industry to southern Arizona!

The paper fluttered to the floor like a fall leaf from Jessie's lifeless hands. She stared unseeingly at the mandarin-orange flames that bowed and leaped in the fireplace. How foolish she had been to think she could forget Brig. What she felt was not the deep gentle love she had for Taro—how could she after Brig's betrayal? And now Fanny had given him a child.

There beat in Jessie's heart an enormous anger that combined with her years of bitterness. Yet the outrage was not really directed at Brig but at Elizabeth Godwin, who had taken Brig from her . . . who had taken Cristo Rey from her. The old woman sat in the Stronghold like a queen in her court while hundreds of her subjects danced attendance, while silver and gold bullion poured forth from her kingdom. *Her kingdom!*

It's my kingdom! Jessie's tormented brain screamed. "It's my kingdom," her lips spoke aloud, softly but firmly. And it was true, she knew. It was more her kingdom than ever that of Elizabeth Godwin's. At her mother's knees Jessie had learned the intriguing history of Cristo Rey, though at five years of age it had not seemed of monumental importance to her. And though she had loved her Uncle Sherrod, she knew that Cristo Rey originally belonged to Doña Dominica and was intended for her son, Jessie's father, before it had ever come into the Godwins' keep.

She picked up the newspaper now and fed it, sheet by sheet, into the greedy, licking flames. And as the flames destroyed the crackling paper, she swore she would destroy Elizabeth Godwin one day.

For now it was enough to float in the refuge of Taro's arms; to enjoy the simple pleasures—sitting on the footbridge in the late afternoon or performing the tasks that delighted him, preparing a completely Japanese meal, giving him a slow, luxurious bath, or even exchanging a few words of Japanese in her conversations with him.

As the summer months slipped into fall, and the scrub oaks donned their coats of reds and browns, she often wondered that she did not become pregnant, and from there her thoughts veered to what would happen if she were. Would Taro give the child his name?

She knew he loved her, but enough to marry her? He knew little of her background. She even suspected he at times found her uncivilized compared with those of his own race. And what if a child did come of their union? What kind of life could the child hope for—half Japanese, a quarter Spanish, and a quarter Anglo? It frightened her to the core when she considered what could await such a child—the Barrios Libres, the Hop Towns. Of what people like Elizabeth Godwin were capable of doing to such children.

As winter blustered upon Taro's eyrie and the cold weather isolated her and Taro from outside contact, her thoughts dwelled more and more often on the injustices of the fates and on

Elizabeth Godwin until her hatred for the old woman consumed her as the flame had the newspaper.

Her preoccupation did not escape Taro. One evening as she soaked in her bath, he came up behind her and caught her head between his hands. Cupping her face, he tilted it back to meet his gaze. "The bitterness in your heart will destroy no one but yourself, Lotus Woman. You must put what it is that eats at your heart like a cancer behind you."

She closed her eyes beneath the fierceness of his gaze. "You are wrong," she countered. "My soul will know no rest until Elizabeth Godwin's power is destroyed."

He sighed. Releasing her, he rose. He stood looking down at her with eyes that were narrow slits. "So that is it. Then do what you have to do to exorcise this bitterness. For you will never belong to me until you do."

Chapter 40

IN March, when the anemones, gentians, and violets suddenly unfolded on the slopes in a painting of riotous colors, Taro made his next trip into Tombstone. He brought back for Jessie a set of small men's clothing that she had pestered him for, saying, "This way I can help in the mine."

In addition, there was a short-barreled carbine in his pack. Knowing that he never carried a weapon, she looked at him inquiringly as she held the nickel-plated weapon. "You are often alone here," he explained seriously. "And more and more men now prowl the hills for the silver."

Her mother's smile curved her lips. "If I didn't know better, Taro Shima, I would think you cared for this lowly woman."

His smile matched hers. "It is only that I want to preserve your body to sell to some old Chinese man when I grow tired of you. I am certain I would get your weight in silver."

"That I shall never let you do—sell me," she said, putting down the carbine. She moved until she stood against him. Her forefinger went up to press against the soft inner rim of his lower lip. "I plan to keep you so occupied that you never grow tired of me."

Still his arms did not slip around her. "Show me," he ordered.

Her fingertips worked at the buttons of his shirt. "I will show you that I am much better at entertaining than those silly geisha women you're always talking about." Her hands slid inside his shirt, and though his expression never changed, she was gratified to feel the twitch of the taut stomach muscles beneath her fingertips.

A slow smile pirouetted on the ends of her mouth. She grasped his belt and tugged him over to the mat, pushing him down until he lay on his back. "I think it is time for the Chinese Rope Trick," she said with feigned insouciance, her fingers playing with the buttons of his pants.

Beneath the fringe of thick lashes she saw the flare of his pupils. "Where did you learn of such a thing?" he asked huskily.

"The Crystal Palace's ladies of the night," she tossed off airily. "Then I did not understand this trick with the rope and knots." Her lids drooped to veil her eyes and her lips parted seductively. "But now . . . maybe with your help, I can manage it."

He joined the act now, displaying only desultory interest. "We shall see," he said. "It is an art that takes much practice." He crossed his arms beneath his head. "But I would be willing to work with you. In time you may prove to be worth your weight in gold instead."

"I'm truly unworthy of your interest," she bantered. "And am such a stupid pupil that I must ask you to show me the technique."

"Get the rope—the slender one—from the saddle pack," he instructed thickly.

When she returned, she knelt at his side and did as he told her, knotting the rope in increments. The sun had set now and there was only the candle's flame to light the tawny-hued body of her beloved, to light the way for her hands as she performed the intimate task, to light the feverish concentration in her blushing, beautiful face.

She gasped when he gasped, sharing his ecstasy as the slipping passage of each knot triggered another peak of pleasure for him.

Then she knew she could wait no longer. Her body demanded its own release. "Taro, Taro," she begged, "take me now. Now!"

Jessie sifted through the newspapers Taro had brought back from Tombstone the day before. Some of the dates were more than three months old, but it made no difference. She was eager for any news. The *Epitaph* carried nothing about Cristo Rey or the Godwins. However, she did notice that one subject, the headlines varying somewhat, recurred in all the issues. "Benson-Globe Stage Robbed." Or "Wells Fargo Messenger Held Up."

Now she began reading more closely. Another one: "The messenger who was transporting boxes of payroll money to the Patagonia mine camp was waylaid by two masked highwaymen. Reward is being offered for . . ."

It was the printed word "mine" that jumped from the page into Jessie's imagination. For more than thirty minutes she sat staring at that one column. A plan slowly began to evolve in her head. There were risks to it, but as she considered it, tested it in her mind, she decided the odds were in her favor.

She knew the area between the Stronghold and Tombstone as well as Taro knew every darkened inch of the mine he explored. She visualized the road which the Cristo Rey ore wagons would take from the Whetstone mines—traveling south, skirting the northern stretches of the Canelo Hills, bypassing the Huachuca Mountains, it crossed the San Pedro plains eastward for the Dragoon Mountains and Charleston's stamp mill. The only road that could sustain that kind of heavy wagon traffic, it twisted mile upon mile through empty country with lava hills, arroyos, canyons, and mesquite thickets to provide hideouts.

Taro, squatting on his haunches across the *kotaku* from her, made no interjection but slowly sipped the tea as she eagerly explained her plan to him. "I will simply see that no wagonload of ore reaches Charleston's stamp mill. In six months' time I calculate that Elizabeth Godwin—and Company—will be defunct. Cristo Rey can no longer survive without the mines to support the floundering cattle empire!"

"For the first time there is the glow of the spirit in your eyes."

She blinked her surprise. "That's all you have to say?"

"What would you have me say? No—that I don't approve? I have no right over you—I cannot stop you."

"But how do you feel about my plan?" she persisted, leaning forward on the table. "I don't want to know what is right or wrong. Because I no longer believe in a world of absolute black and white, Taro. I simply want to know how you *feel.*"

He sat staring silently over the rim of his cup. At last he said, "I feel this is your karma I once spoke to you of." He shrugged. Beneath the ebony tea robe his massive shoulders rolled with the movement. "It is something you have to do. *Shi-ka-ta-ga-nai*—it cannot be helped or changed."

Anxiously her gaze searched his. "I can come home to you when it's over?"

He reached across the table and took her hands, pulling her to her feet with him as he stood. "You will never be gone from me in thought."

He took her to his mat then, and they lay together throughout the night. There was no need for either of them to demonstrate the love that surged like some gigantic, magnetic force between them. Sometime near dawn the plaintive, dismal yip-yip of a coyote filtered up through the maze of gulches, and Jessie shivered. She clutched Taro to her. "I'm afraid of the future," she whispered.

He kissed her cold temples, his lips lingering, his warm breath stirring her hair. "There is no other woman for me, Lotus Woman. Our karmas are intertwined. Whatever your future," he murmured, "I will wait to find you."

A day's journey on the back of a burro brought her into Cristo Rey territory. Dressed in men's clothing, she rode clear of the basin, keeping to the lava rock trails that bedded the far eastern side of the Whetstones. Higher up, where the juniper and piñon and scrub oak fuzzed the bald caps, she set up camp in a small abandoned mine.

She had thought she would be frightened, sleeping alone, or uncomfortable, but she enjoyed the challenge. Lying in the cold darkness, she thought about the confrontation the following day would bring and smiled to herself before falling asleep.

Halfway through the next day she discovered that her raids would have to be postponed until she studied the comings and goings from the main mine shaft. She had blundered in thinking that wagons left every day. It took a full seven days, watching through the field glasses from a position on a cliff above the mine, until she was able to establish a definite pattern to the movements of the men and wagons.

Once she thought she could make out Brig below, talking to three miners who wore the candle-sconced helmets, but she could not be sure. And she realized, to her surprise, that her heart no longer hurt. Only one thing mattered. She might never be able to prove that Cristo Rey was hers, but she would make certain that it became a millstone around the veined neck of Elizabeth Godwin.

Tuesday mornings and Friday afternoons, two or three wagons, hitched together and pulled by ten to twenty teams of mules, left the main mine and began their snaking descent to the Tombstone–Charleston road.

Carefully she studied the way a driver would handle his teams. Usually he rode the near-wheel mule. From his seat in the saddle he managed all the animals by a single jerk line attached to the near leader. The mules understood the jerks, short or long, and were thus guided. In addition to the jerk line, the driver manipulated the brakes of the wagons by another rope. Yet at the end of that first week Jessie thought she could master the technique—enough, at least, to accomplish her purpose.

When she thought she knew as much as was important to her plan of operation, she slid her carbine into the saddle's holster and left the brush-sheltered mine. With a bandanna covering the lower half of her face, she waited in the second of the mesquite-stubbled canyons through which the wagon had to pass. Long before the two wagons arrived at the bend, she heard the hoarse cursing of the driver mixing with the music of the chiming bells attached to the collars of the mules' harnesses.

Her throat suddenly went dry, and the pulse began to pound at her temples. She realized she was about to embark on what could well be a disastrous undertaking. Yet she knew there was no alternative for her. It was her karma, as Taro said.

As it turned out, that first robbery was absurdly easy. When the two ore wagons rolled around the bend, she rode the burro out of the mesquite thickets onto the road. The musical "Whoop—whoop, haw!" broke off as the driver, this one an older, stoop-shouldered man, jerked back on the reins at the sight of the masked rider.

"Get down!" she ordered as gruffly as her voice would lower.

The driver's hands shot up. He slid off the mule as if it were a greased pig. "You don't plan to use that, do you, kid?" he squeaked.

"Nope, not as long as you keep walking back where you came from. Now get those boots a-movin'.'"

The old man hastily complied without even a backward glance, and she felt shame lap at her feet for the fear she had seen in the rheumy eyes. Perhaps he was from the ranchería—one of the people she would have been feeding, ironing and washing his clothes. Her thoughts moved on to Marta. Was the dear old woman still alive? Jessie would never be able to return to the ranchería to find out.

For a moment the triumph was driven from her victory. Nevertheless, she quickly set about her course of action. The mules were unharnessed, and a smart slap on the rump sent them scattering. The brake was released. Slowly, inch by inch, the wagons began to roll forward. A full five minutes passed before they gathered sufficient speed to be termed runaways.

The two wagons, joined like mating cattle, careened their way along the rutted road, bouncing off boulders. They came to the curve bordered by the deep gulch Jessie had marked earlier and missed the turn. Seconds later the splintering crash of the wagons fifty-five feet below echoed up the canyon.

Jessie smiled to herself and returned to the mine to await her next foray. Two days later a lone ore wagon began its descent, but this time with an armed guard. She reassessed her plan and waited until the wagon passed, then fired a shot into the air.

The driver tugged desperately at the reins to keep the mules from spooking. The guard whipped around his shotgun, scanning the thickets behind him.

"Drop the firearm," she shouted from her concealment.

The sombreroed guard complied. This time she had both men unharness the mules and scatter them before she sent the two employees walking back to the Cristo Rey mining camp. They had to dodge as the wagon began to roll rapidly backward. The bluff it sailed over was a mere twenty-five or thirty feet, but she believed the wagon's contents, the precious ore, were lost to the swift flowing creek below.

She made two more raids over the next seven days, each time

surprising the guards and drivers. But her supplies ran out in concurrence with a sudden instinct urging her to let a few weeks pass until Cristo Rey relaxed its guard once more.

And she needed the time, too. The triumph of her raids faded at night, leaving her lonely, empty; and it was with rising excitement that she rode the day's journey back to the Mule Mountains and Taro.

He was still working at the mine when she arrived, and she took the opportunity to enjoy her first bath in over two weeks. Imagining how she must look—and smell—dressed as she was like a man, she had to laugh as she shucked the dirt-encrusted clothing and slid into the tub. The hot water steamed away her weariness with the dirt.

Later, the delicate woman wrapped in a yellow silk ceremonial robe who knelt serenely before the *kotaku* bore little resemblance to the wiry young bandit who plagued the Cristo Rey Consolidated Mining Company. When Taro entered, she bowed her head to the floor, touching her overlapped hands with her forehead and murmured, *"O-yasumi-nasai,* good evening."

Taro removed his boots and crossed to the young woman. He took her hands and pulled her to her feet, his own hands cupping her shoulders. His dark eyes glided over her face, always returning to her eyes as if he sought to find her in their depths. "You have been ever on my mind."

She stood on tiptoe to brush the lips that had showered passionate kisses, bringing life to her body so that it blossomed as a desert flower beneath the spring rains. "I need you," she whispered.

His fingers slipped down to part the robe, exposing her slender, supple beauty to his touch. His hand slid around her waist and crushed her to him in a savage kiss. There was no patient journey to the culmination this time but a frenzied seeking, a fiery explosive renewal of their love.

Taro's teeth cast tiny love marks into Jessie's smooth, sleek skin, and her nails welted his muscles in crimson half-moons. They came together again and again throughout the night, as if they would never have enough of each other—as if they feared there might never be another time.

Sometime toward dawn they withdrew from each other's arms long enough to have tea and a cold dish of rice and vegetables.

Over the meal, Jessie recounted to Taro her successes, giggling like a girl as she told of the bearlike driver who had soundly cursed her one moment, then yelped like a dog when she fired a shot into the air to send him galloping on his way back to the mines.

Taro listened, a faint smile on his lips. When she finished, he rose and crossed to the black lacquered chest. He withdrew a folded newspaper. "You went into Tombstone?" she asked, taking the newspaper he handed her.

"My concern was too great. It would seem that Elizabeth Godwin does not share your amusement at your success."

Jessie's eyes scanned the print. Then, "Godwin Family Offers $2,000 Reward." The small article went on to note the bandit's description, a young male, and listed two of the four robberies she had made.

She would have tossed the newspaper aside but for the even smaller notation in the "Condolences Column." Her eyes burned as she read of Brig's year-old son's succumbing to some fatal childhood malady. She knew it could have been their child who had died.

"You will destroy Brigham Godwin along with his grandmother," Taro said. "You realize that, don't you?"

She shrugged, trying to hide the old hurt she suddenly felt . . . a pain for what was lost to her and Brig, a pain for what could have been. "Brig doesn't covet Cristo Rey as his grandmother does. She will stop at nothing to keep it. And I will stop at nothing, Taro, to take it from her."

Chapter 41

WHEN Jessie returned to her role as highwayman, her first two robberies were easy enough. Apparently Taro's strength and love had renewed her. With the two-week interval the miners—and Elizabeth Godwin—must have believed she had disappeared from the area, for the wagons which Jessie watched from her perch on the bluff no longer carried the guard.

She chose a different location each time, and her method worked so well that after three weeks of her relentless attack the ore wagons, with a double guard now, left the mines only once a week.

At night she lay alone in the darkened mine shaft, shivering from the cold, wishing she could build a fire. But that day she had sighted a band of men and knew they were scouring the countryside for her. Hands behind her head, she silently questioned why she continued, why she did not return to the man who gave her the only peace she knew in her life.

But her love for Cristo Rey and her hatred for Elizabeth were bound together as tightly as barbed wire and fence post. She knew she would never be able to claim the land as hers, but when Elizabeth's gray head was bowed in defeat, then she would cease her attacks. When Cristo Rey went up on the auction block she could return forever to the haven of Taro's arms.

With the guard now doubled, she knew she had to be more resourceful, more careful. She chose the next site of her attack at a most unlikely place—clear of the canyons on the open range. It would be there the driver and guards would be most lax.

She waited at the bottom of a draw that angled near the road. As she had foreseen, one of the guards had even propped his shotgun, butt down, on the wagon floorboard. The other guard had his shotgun lying carelessly across his knees.

Her plan went smoothly, the guards yielding their firearms—and boots—and, cursing her, beginning the long walk back to the Whetstones and the mines. Disposing of the wagonload presented more of a problem this time. Though not as strong as the driver, she was able to manage the mules and maneuver them off the main road. She drove for perhaps three hours across the range. She judged that initially the wagon's trail would be easy enough to follow. But once far enough away from the road there would be other wagon tracks crisscrossing the grass—those of the Indians who did not keep to the main road of the white man's civilization.

By late afternoon she was whipping the four-mule team wagon into the small but wild outlaw hideout of Charleston. She joined the other ore wagons that crossed the bridge to the stamp mill. Its stacks belched great plumes of gray smoke twenty-four hours a day. When it came her turn for her wagon's ore to be dumped into the hopper, she pulled her sombrero down low and mumbled to the smelter superintendent a fictitious name.

"The Hellhole Mining Company?" the potbellied man asked, his pencil poised over the notebook. "Never heard of it."

"We've just started up."

"Well," he grunted, "give me a box number where your payment can be mailed."

She rattled off some box number with a Tombstone destination and hurried away. The sight draft would sit in the Tombstone post office's dead-letter box for months, with any sort of luck.

Over the week that followed she was both triumphant and wary. Not one wagonload of ore left the mine. Once she walked close enough to view the mine through her field glasses. Work was still going on, but with fewer men. She would wait for the next wagon out, she decided. The loss of its ore should be enough to break Elizabeth Godwin.

For this last robbery she was most meticulous in her planning. She dressed in her old skirt and blouse and the sombrero. The driver and the guards would not be expecting a woman. Her face she left uncovered, judging that the floppy hat would make it difficult to later identify her accurately. It should be the easiest of all her forays.

She waited just beyond the site of her first attack, her carbine hidden in the folds of her skirt. Within minutes after stationing herself on the road, the chimes of mules' harness bells could be heard. The wagon rumbled over the porcupine ridge into view. At once the two armed guards snapped up their shotguns into position. In spite of the fact that she was a woman, both kept the sights trained on her until they pulled alongside. The Mexican driver, a short stocky man with yellow-brown teeth, whistled, and the guards grinned when they saw the pretty face.

The guard closest to her spit a brown stream of tobacco juice into the dust and said, "You're on the right road, miss, if you're headed for Tombstone, but you oughtta be a sight more careful. There's a bandit working this road."

She dimpled a smile. "I'm visiting the McPherson ranch and somehow got lost. Can you tell me how to find my way back?"

His wariness allayed, the nearest guard sat his shotgun down and pointed to the northeast. "Just keep to that dirt path veering off over them hills there, ma'am. You can't miss it."

At that moment her carbine came up from the fold of her skirts. She smiled again. "Thank you, gentlemen. Now, all three of you will toss your guns over the side—and your boots, too. Please."

The trio uttered gasps at the realization that this dainty female was the bandit. Amazingly, no words were exchanged as they grunted and groaned in removing their boots. The two guards climbed down from the wagon in obvious disgust, but the driver said, "Guess you've duped us, senorita. But one day—pronto—your pretty neck's gonna swing at the end of a hangman's noose."

She repressed a shiver. It was not what the Mexican said, but the way he said it, the certainty, that suddenly frightened her.

She told herself she must not let him shake her and proceeded with her usual plan, dispatching the men on the hike back up the hilly road. When they were too far away to be of danger, she boarded the wagon, only to hear the sudden drum of hooves. She whirled to see a dozen or so men descending on her in a flurry of dust. Her hand went to the shotgun on the floorboard, and a shot rang out, its whoosh sizzling past her ear.

Instantly she knew there was no hope of holding the posse off. She crouched low in the wagon seat and snapped the lines over the mules. Their ears pricked up and they broke out into a trot—a slow one, hampered by the wagon's load.

Too soon the men drew closer. She realized it was stupid to try to outrun the horses. Her shoulders drew back in a surge of pride, and she tugged on the reins, pulling the mules to a halt. She drew a shuddering breath and turned to face her enemies. A dozen guns trained on her as the posse cantered up to the wagon.

Two men rode forward, one wearing the badge of Tombstone's new U.S. marshal, John Slaughter—who had replaced Wyatt Earp. The other wore a brown Stetson, but she recognized him immediately. "Brig!" she breathed.

For a moment he did not say anything. His gaze moved disbelievingly over her face. He reined in next to the wagon and lifted the hat from her head. Her wild golden curls tumbled over her shoulders. "Oh, God," he rasped. "Why, Jessie?"

She met his tortured gaze. "You need to ask?"

"String her up now!" a voice in the posse shouted.

Hands grabbed for her, yanking her down from the wagon. Her head cracked against the sideboard. Simultaneously she felt the sharp pain along with the warm blood that streamed down the side of her face.

"Wait!" Brig's command was lost among the babble of the men. A gunshot went off, and all turned toward the marshal. "This here is no lawless vigilante committee," the sun-leathered man said.

She shook loose the hands that held her arms and looked up into Brig's face as he came to support her.

"You're not setting her free?" a cowboy demanded heatedly. Several men stepped forward with bellicose snarls, only to face the sight of the rifle Brig trained on them.

"No," Slaughter said, coming to stand at the other side of her. "But she will have a fair trial."

Her gaze swung back up to Brig's face, and she saw there the same great sadness she felt for what might have been.

Jessie sat in the courtroom, handcuffed. She stared about her at the rabid faces who had come to see her trial, all hoping to see the first hanging in the territory of a woman.

There were so many faces, yet she felt as if she knew each of them intimately after the three days of testimony . . . damaging testimony. There was the old man on the jury who looked to be at least seventy-five and who sat whittling each day, never once looking up. Only that morning, as the testimonies reopened, she realized he was carving a hangman's gallows. There was the fat woman who brought a picnic lunch each day so that she would not miss getting a front row seat. There were the many righteous faces that became more indignant as each witness took the stand.

And there was Elizabeth Godwin, who sat in the back, dressed all in black. Her Victorian-proper face was starched with her noble long-suffering. Beside her sat the vividly beautiful Fanny and a granite-cast Brig.

Each day as the deputy led Jessie from the jailhouse into the courtroom, it was Brig's face she sought. Only his face held out hope. Her eyes would meet his, and she would see a spasm of the muscle in the jaw.

This morning would bring the last of the prosecutor's witnesses. Jessie had hoped that Brig would testify in her behalf, but the small, balding lawyer told her it would be out of the question— not just because Brig's own grandmother was bringing the charges against her but also because his testimony could be made damaging by only a few adroit questions from the brilliant prosecutor, brought all the way from New Orleans by Elizabeth Godwin.

Elizabeth was the first to be called to the stand this morning. "Jessie Howard was a bastard child of my stepson's," she said with a despairing shake of her head. "I did everything I could to give her some sort of a home. I even saw that she received an excellent education. But she was a wild sort of thing I never knew which of our cowhands she might be . . ." Elizabeth paused and coughed discreetly.

"We understand how difficult this is for you, Mrs. Godwin. That will be enough."

"Do you want to take the stand?" Jessie's lawyer, John Pate, asked.

What would be the use? She shook her head negatively. The prosecution was doing its work well.

The prosecutor, a tall dignified gentleman with a kindly face and a shock of silver hair, next called Dan O'Rourke. For the first time Jessie was shaken. The dapper man had not changed, except perhaps he was even more slender. She marked his eyes, the distended pupils. He was caught up in the poppy's spell after all.

"Yes," he acknowledged, "that is the woman who worked for me, except we knew her as the Primrose—Rose."

"Besides dealing the cards, Mr. O'Rourke, did this lady have any clientele—er—in the rooms above?"

Every head jutted forward in anticipation. "I don't promote that sort of—participation—in my establishment, sir."

"Of course, we realize that. There are two types of women, we all know. But usually a certain type of woman works in a gambling house."

Dan glanced at her, and she caught a flicker of concern before the lids drooped over the pupils. "What Rose—Miss Howard—did in her spare time I could not tell you."

"Miss Cashman is my next witness," the prosecutor announced smoothly.

Nellie Cashman made her way to the stand among the buzzing of the crowd. "We understand that Miss Howard roomed at the Russ House."

Nellie put her trumpet to her ear. "Eh?"

"Was Miss Howard one of your roomers?" the prosecutor repeated, louder this time.

"Yes, yes," she answered, nearly shouting. "And a good one, too, always paid her rent on time."

"Just answer the question, please, Miss Cashman. Did any men come to visit her."

"For the pity's sake, no! I don't allow such goings-on at the Russ House."

"But you'll admit there was something unusual about her?" the prosecutor prodded.

The woman fidgeted. She looked at Jessie anxiously. "Yes?" the prosecutor demanded, leaning against the witness stand's wooden railing, practically atop the nervous New England woman now.

"Well, one of my boarders, old man Stevens, claimed he saw her making her way to Hop Town several times."

Pate jumped to his feet. "I object, your honor. Old Hiram is as blind as a bat, and everyone knows it!"

"Objection overruled!"

"And you think Jessie Howard was involved in the opium dens

there?" the prosecutor continued, like a hound dog hot on the scent.

"Oh my, no, I wouldn't know anything about such goings-on!"

"But you will agree, Miss Cashman, that Jessie Howard did act strangely whenever she would return to the Russ House—like she was in a daze, maybe?"

"Well, yes, but she did have to keep late hours."

"And then she just disappeared, didn't she, Miss Cashman? Never returning for her clothing or to pay the back rent."

"What's that you say?"

"Witness dismissed. The prosecution rests its case."

The jury adjourned to an upstairs room to go into deliberation. The deputy had taken Jessie's arm to lead her to a room on the other side when she saw the tall Oriental standing at the back of the courtroom. "Taro," she whispered. For the first time in all the horror of the testimonies, tears came to her eyes.

Taro threaded his way through the crowd. He said nothing but simply took her hand. Yet it was enough for her. Just his touch gave her the strength she needed. "I guess this is the karma you talked about," she said, a slight smile curving her tremulous lips.

His hand went up to cup the side of her face, but the deputy grabbed Taro's shirt collar and began jerking, even though the two were of even height. "Listen here, you chink, you have no business in a white man's court. This whore may mean something to you, but as far as—"

The deputy's words broke off as Taro's hand neatly clipped him on the neck. The man slumped to the floor at Jessie's feet. Pandemonium seemed to break out. Men roughly hauled Taro out the double front door. Jessie screamed, afraid they would kill him, but she was quickly ushered into the small anteroom.

She hurried to the one window, hoping she could see Taro, but the window opened onto the courtyard . . . and a chilling view of the hangman's gallows with its thirteen steps.

Mr. Pate walked in, and she ran to him. "What will happen to Taro?" she demanded.

"The Chinaman?"

"He's Japanese."

He shrugged. "They all look the same. Marshal Slaughter is putting him behind bars for the night—for the man's own safety.

He'll be turned loose before dawn," he reassured her. "Did you meet him in Hop Town?"

She went back to stand at the window. "I guess you might say that. He saved my life there."

The deliberation took less than an hour—which lent her little hope. Obviously every member of the male jury, with their wives sitting in the audience, was already decided against her. She looked at each of the solemn twelve faces as they led her back into the courtroom. One by one, as she filed past them, they turned their gazes away from her.

"The foreman will render the verdict," the judge said.

She held her breath, feeling that when it did come, she would shatter.

The beanpole of a man rose. "We find the defendant . . . guilty."

PART
3

Chapter 42

1928

AMANDA Shima was drawn to her enemy from that very first meeting, there in the time-eroded foothills, the *bajadas* of the Huachuca Mountains. She was only a child at the time of that meeting, perhaps ten or eleven. But sometimes at that age things stand out more clearly in the memory than at any other time in one's life.

And the memory of Nick Godwin was etched in her mind forever, as indelible as the Indian hieroglyphics on the rocky walls of Arizona's Casa Grande.

Thinking back over her childhood, she supposed that it was inevitable she would meet Nick, for she often wandered the boundaries of Cristo Rey. She was a loner, preferring her own company to that of the snobbish families of the soldiers stationed at Fort Huachuca. But then, she was different. Everything about her was different.

For one thing, unlike the other children at the military post, she had no mother. Her mother had died soon after her birth. The post doctor said that at fifty-one her mother had been too old to bear a change-of-life child. But Amanda thought it was more than age. It was the many years, six to be exact, that her mother had spent in the Yuma Territorial Prison.

A shocking fact, for only one other woman, Pearl Hart, had ever been sent to that infamous jail. Fortunately, it was so long ago that not too many people ever recalled the sentencing of Jessie Howard for highway robbery.

Amanda sometimes thought that after her mother was paroled she must have welcomed the isolation of Taro Shima's cabin in the Mule Mountains and the refuge his love offered her. And that brought about another reason Amanda was different.

Her father was Japanese.

She could remember his telling her one night as he prepared dinner at their post quarters how he and her mother journeyed into Tombstone to get married. "The justice of the peace refused to perform the ceremony, Amanda, because it was against the Arizona state law for a Caucasian to marry an Oriental."

Taro smiled then, and Amanda thought how handsome, how gigantic, her father was. "But your mother's adamant statement that she was Mexican, which was only partially true, and therefore not fully under the Anglo jurisdiction, finally persuaded the old man, and the ceremony was performed."

When the Lotus Land Mine eventually played out and there was no money left to support Taro and his wife, he was forced to sell the Lotus Land and seek employment. The Tombstone mines had flooded, but the mines at Bisbee, twenty-five miles to the south, were bursting with untapped copper. Yet Amanda thought her father realized that her mother would never be happy in the hustle-bustle of a booming mining town.

Instead he accepted the job at the Fort Huachuca military post as cook, which Amanda sensed must have been demoralizing to such an independent person as he. It was at the post she was born. Her father, whom she came to realize possessed unsuspected depths of humor and who was himself born in the Year of the Tiger in the fourth moon, claimed Amanda was born in the Year of the Villa Raids, 1917.

However, it was not the stories of Pancho Villa's raid on the Arizona border, twenty miles southward, that occupied Amanda's inquisitive mind. It was the stories of the Ghost Lady. Of course, all the children at the fort had heard the tales of the woman who rode horseback over Cristo Rey, whose borders were only some miles distant from the fort.

But Amanda had more than a vague interest invested in the Ghost Lady. From the time she had been old enough to ask questions, her father had explained patiently about her mother, her past, and her heritage. He spoke quite candidly, without bitterness, but she suspected her mother had to have been bitter. The legendary Cristo Rey had been Jessie's, and she had been cheated of it by the Godwin family.

Oh, Taro Shima never stated the fact as such. Nevertheless, some uncanny instinct told Amanda otherwise. Though she had never actually seen the Stronghold, she had seen photos of it in an article *Arizona Highways* had done on the famous villas of the state. She had found the thumbed-through magazine in the post's stables trash barrel, and as she leafed through it the words "Cristo Rey's Stronghold" had jumped out at her.

She would hardly have called the mansion in the photo a villa. But it certainly was imposing—a majestic combination of territorial adobe and Gothic castle. The castle, the magazine said, was added during the early years of the twentieth century, copied after the robber barons' baronial mansions at Bar Harbor and Newport.

Falling in love with it at once, she tacked the magazine's photo above her bunk. And from that day on the image of the Stronghold danced through her dreams at night—taunting and teasing her with its Babylon-like gardens inside the compound, the wide marble staircase that both blended with and complemented the older heavy-beamed ceilings and ornate wrought-iron grillwork, and the tasteful and elegant furniture and accessories.

From that one impregnable, fortified adobe had risen, growing bigger and more beautiful over the years, that vital and magnificent work of architecture which became an obsession with Amanda. She could even more now understand her mother's loss. And as her mother had sought her revenge, she knew she also would one day, though she did not know how. But she did know that her vengeance would be more clever, more subtle.

How arrogant, how presumptuous are the young! In those early years of formation she had not met her adversary. Not until her tenth summer did she chance upon Nick. At that time she had wangled the privilege of riding some of the older cavalry mounts by working in the stables in the heat of the afternoon after school let out.

She figured she must have had some of her grandmother's, the Ghost Lady's, love for riding, for it was only when she was astride a horse, galloping across the grassy rangeland or boulder-sheltered canyons, that she felt really free . . . free of her past and free of the taunt of her peers.

That particular sun-baked August afternoon she left the gray two-story earthen barracks behind her and struck out for the sycamore-shaded canyon that emptied via a sagging section of barbed-wire fence into the rich Cristo Rey lands.

Once inside its borders, she came alive. She tossed back the straw hat so that it flopped against her narrow shoulder blades, held by the rawhide ties, and let her hair—long and as black and tangled as the mane of the bay she rode—blow free. She would have quite readily shed her overalls and khaki shirt and ridden buck naked but for the fear of being sighted by some of the post scouts.

The scouts still patrolled the border, more to intercept the Mexicans and Chinese who continued to flow across the international boundary than to guard against Apache attacks. The last one Amanda recalled had been some three years before in '24.

It was fortunate that on that day she did not strip down, for she didn't see the Ghost Lady she'd feared and hoped to encounter but a boy not much older than herself. When she spotted the horse dancing in the shadowy grove of Joshua trees her mind shouted, for just a fleeting second, *It's the Ghost Lady! She really does exist!*

So great was her disappointment when the magnificent steed cantered out of the grove and she recognized the rider as a mere boy that if a glare could kill, the boy would have been roasted. "That's a dumb stunt!" she reproached in her best imitation of a sergeant's dress-down. "You could have spooked my horse!"

Whatever quelling effects her haughty manner had on the post children, it did not produce the same result with the boy, who looked to be twelve or thirteen. He boldly edged his larger horse near hers and looked down at her with such careless insolence that the urge to hop him like a cat on a June bug was overpowering.

Those cool blue eyes raked over her, and his mouth damn that mouth it actually curved in amusement. "That's a pretty dumb stunt—riding a nag like that in this kind of country."

"Nag! And just who do you think you are, the landowner or something, to tell me where I should ride and shouldn't?"

"More or less," he replied indifferently, leaning forward, his palms on the cantle supporting his bulk.

"More or less what?" she asked, not having actually anticipated a direct answer.

"More or less the owner. You know, for a girl, you sure aren't much, are you?"

Coming from a boy, she thought it most likely a compliment. But she was too stunned at that moment to give the statement much consideration. *She had to be facing her archenemy, some-*

one she had never expected to encounter face to face. "You a Godwin?" she asked cautiously.

"Nick Godwin. And you?"

"Amanda Shima," she replied, knowing the name would mean nothing to him. Would it have had significance to him if she replied, "Amanda Davalos Shima"? She wasn't to know, for at that moment another horseman rode into view.

"My stepbrother, Paul," Nick said, noting the direction of her gaze.

Curious if this was the man who controlled Cristo Rey, she studied the rider as he loped his mount toward the two of them. When he was near enough she could see he was an old man, maybe thirty-five or forty she judged from her limited experience in such matters. He had none of Nick's black arrogance; yet there were the classic patrician looks about his face—a slim face with dark hair already gray at the temples. He bestowed a somewhat vague smile on her. "Lost, little one?"

"Hardly," she retorted. "Since this is my land we're on!"

Brows shot up in both of the brothers' faces, and they flashed each other questioning looks—about her sanity, she was sure. But she did not wait to explain. Instead, she whirled the bay about and heeled her into a gallop (as much as the horse's bony body would take) back toward the post.

Thereafter she saw Nick Godwin several times, and each time was as charged with current as a live electrical wire. Sometimes she thought it was as if the two of them were expecting to chance upon one another, though their meetings were certainly irregular and covered a span of two or three years.

One spring—she had to have been going on twelve—she happened upon him as he watered his horse at Canelo Springs. He acknowledged her with an indifferent nod of his head. Chagrined, she said with acid sweetness, "Mind if I water my horse on *your* property, Nicholas?"

He removed the dust-stained hat and knelt to dip it in the stagnant water. "Name's not Nicholas," he said, swashing the water about in its crown. "It's Dominic—for Dominica Davalos."

Rage exploded through her. Before she realized what she was doing, she leaped from her bay onto Nick's back. Unaware of his peril, his head was bent to drink from the hat. The two floundered in the water. She pummeled his face and chest. He cheeks streamed with water that had nothing to do with the springs in which they sloshed.

"Whoa, you little jackass!" Nick yelled out, finally gaining control of her flailing fists. With a deft roll he came up on top, straddling her small, slender body. "What's got you so fired up?"

Her eyes, their mint-green color a legacy of her grandmother's, narrowed to slits. "Get off me, you—you—" No words would come that seemed vile enough. But it did not matter, for Nick's attention had left her face to slide down to the burgeoning rosebuds that thrust imperiously against her wet, clinging shirt. She felt the sudden tightening of his thighs about her boyishly slim hips and saw the blue eyes cloud over like a violent summer storm.

His dark gaze swung up to meet her puzzled one. "You could get yourself in a lot of trouble," he said, his voice sounding a timbre deeper to her, "riding alone like this and—everything."

"I can handle myself!" she began, then clamped her lips together as she realized she was in the weaker position. "Well, I can if I don't let my anger get the best of me."

"That wasn't exactly what I was getting at," he said dryly and rolled from her to stand above her in one fluid movement. He retrieved his hat and swatted it against his thigh, beating out the water.

Looking up into his face, she thought how strong the features were—so unlike the baby-roundness of the boys she knew at the post. But then he was somewhat older; maybe that accounted for the squared-off jaw and arrogant jutting nose. Only the shaggy brown hair that fell across his forehead lent a boyish cast to the promise of the coming virile features.

He reached down a hand and yanked her to her feet. "What got you so riled up, anyway?"

"That's none of your business," she said with a toss of her head. She pulled her hair, heavy with water, over her shoulder and began to squeeze out the excess, coolly disdaining the look of irritation he turned on her.

"Next time you might not be so lucky," he warned. He swung up into his saddle. Looking down at her, her fist knotted at her hips in a belligerent stance, he said, "I'd better not catch you on Cristo Rey land again."

"Try and stop me!" she shouted after the departing figure.

She ran into him several times after that, and, curiously enough, he fell in alongside her mount each time with a simple "Howdy." Together they would ride a spell over the Huachuca foothills, never exchanging a word, until she would decide to return to the post. He would nod desultorily and swing his horse off in the direction that she imagined the Stronghold must lie.

She often thought their relationship odd, for Nick seemed to accept her, as the post children did not. As she was different in other ways, she also was in her looks. But Nick seemed not to notice her tawny-gold skin or the eyes with the slightest suggestion of a slant.

Yet on their last meeting, she thought maybe he did notice her more than she realized. They had dismounted to sit beneath the shade of a mesquite, and she leaned back, inadvertently tangling her hair in a cat's-claw. Her pained "Ouch!" brought his deft, sun-browned hands to free the snarled strands from the bush's thorny twigs.

For a few brief seconds she was able to study the face as he concentrated on her hair. She could have almost sworn she saw admiration in those sharp eyes; admiration for her hair's blue-black silkiness—her one feminine vanity.

Of course, Nick did not know, as did the post children, that her father was Japanese, part of that "yellow peril" that threatened Anglo society. Yet neither could she say that his attitude toward her was one of casual acceptance.

They both watched each other warily, like circling bantams. On her part, the hatred for the Godwins was so great she could not deal with it and simply had to let it simmer within her until she one day found the vent for it.

During those times she was with Nick she castigated herself for not avenging the Davaloses. But to do something like throw a rock or spook Nick's horse so that he would be left mountless in the middle of nowhere would have been too easy and have accomplished too little. The few times that her mind turned toward the darker side, that of actual murder—perhaps stealing one of the post rifles and ambushing him—would have put too swift an end to her revenge.

And on Nick's part . . . what did he feel? Whatever he felt, he concealed it well behind that controlled countenance. Yet she sensed that he could not help but be aware of the turbulent flow of feelings that ran between them like a flash flood through a desert draw.

There was the constraint on her part, for she could never let herself forget that their grandfathers had been stepbrothers, that Nick Godwin possessed what was rightfully hers.

Overriding the constraint was the more powerful, unidentifiable feeling which to this day she could find no accurate description for . . . a sort of grim bondage of the souls that nothing that side of heaven or hell could sever. Whatever it was, it had a mesmeric effect on her that transcended the bounds of mere fascination.

Chapter 43

AMANDA was not to see Nick again for nearly four years, for soon after that last meeting on Cristo Rey the country sank into the miry depths of the Great Depression. Employment was scarce, and the men in the area resented that her father had employment at the post, though he worked for less than anyone else. He was still an Oriental, and the cook's job should go to a Caucasian. Officials bowed to pressure, and her father had to look for employment elsewhere.

She could recall her father's face, remarkably unlined for his advancing years, when he told her they were moving to Bisbee, that he might be able to find work as a muck in its copper mines (he was still an incredibly strong man). An unutterable sadness dulled those loving eyes. It was not just the appalling working conditions, the fact that one never saw the light of day—that one literally breathed, ate, and eventually was consumed by the insidious dust. It was also the living conditions to which he knew he would be subjecting his daughter.

Amanda tried to explain to her father that she really did not mind the move. "Life at the post was getting to be humdrum," she told him, as she sat his teacup on the *kotaku* and took her place opposite him.

Her peers, who found her outrageously independent, would have been surprised if they had known she followed the Japanese custom of submission in her father's home. Yet to this man who had bestowed on her mother and herself such undemanding love she freely gave loving servitude.

"What is this 'humdrum'?" he demanded, as he did whenever she slipped into slang, for he expected faultless English from his daughter. But his black-lacquered eyes did sparkle. They sparkled for the daughter whom he loved so dearly, for the daughter who was a reflection of his Lotus Woman.

Lotus Woman had granted him that rarest of gifts, if only mankind could know or understand. She had granted him immortality. And she had permitted him to be a participant in the truest sense of the word in life's performance of perfect loving. He wondered if his daughter would ever know or understand the exquisite type of loving, of giving, that had existed between him and her mother.

"Boring, monotonous," Amanda answered now in Japanese.

He shook his head. "I do not like it. I shall be working until nine or so at night, and you will be alone after school."

"Then I will quit school and get a job. Fourteen's old enough."

Taro shook his head brusquely. "No! You will finish your schooling."

She reached across the table to cover his muscle-veined hand with hers. "Father, I know your fathers set great store by education, but you know that we will need the money," she said calmly. "And if I work, I won't be alone at home then, and we can go home together."

Taro was adamant that she would not work, and she was just as determined she would. In the end they compromised, and she worked after school.

However, those first few weeks in Bisbee were ones of difficult adjustment. The anachronistic town of thirty thousand or more was crowded onto the steep hills of Mule Pass Gulch, and it seemed to Amanda that the little frame shacks had to be glued to the canyon sides to keep from slipping.

Its Brewery Gulch section was a wide-open den of gambling, prostitution, and careless killings. The housewives with their handkerchief-size gardens hid inside houses separated by mere inches. And there was none of the orderliness, the spit-and-polish cleanliness, found at the Huachuca military post.

Still, there was an excitement that was almost tangible in the Bisbee mountain air, and Amanda wanted to be a part of it. Its hillside setting and robust activities made it an inland replica of early San Francisco. In that popular mining town, she was not set apart, for few realized she had a Japanese father. Because of her fierce pride, she had been more often than not on the defensive at the military post. In Bisbee she went about for the most part unnoticed.

Unnoticed, at least, until she began to mature into a woman. For four years she had been fortunate enough to work in the Victorian Copper Queen Hotel's elegant restaurant, first as a dishwasher, then as a waitress. All the waitresses wore the same uniform of long black skirts and white cotton blouses with the ruffled white cap and apron. At first glance the waitresses all looked vaguely alike. But at nearly eighteen, Amanda was still different from the others.

Many men whispered compliments on her enchanting beauty as she laid out the blue-checked tablecloths or poured the flagons of wine into the crystal glasses. She suspected it was because she was different from the other waitresses, girls who were mostly of Slavic origin. Instead of the standard blue eyes, hers were green— but tilted, though they did have the Caucasian's double fold. The Slavic waitresses were short and stocky with pendulous bosoms, while she was tall and slender with smaller breasts that she thought looked like tiny muskmelons beneath the starched blouse, nothing at all to excite the men whose flirtatious gazes followed her movements.

The patrons of the Copper Queen were of the wealthy class— the stockholders of the mines, the resort visitors seeking the healthy climate, and the great landowners—for during the Great Depression there were only the very poor and the very rich, the middle class having been almost wiped out in the country's financial devastation.

It was a gentleman of the latter she noted on a sunny afternoon in October—the day she turned eighteen. The gentleman's gaze followed her as intently as the others; yet the fierceness of that gaze communicated itself to her, and she unaccountably set down the tureen of *pot-au-feu* before the matronly woman and the pompous old man and turned to face the room of crowded diners, searching for what it was that disturbed her so.

Her gaze moved beyond the nearest tables to the veranda, where the sidewalk tables were set up for the lunch hour. Her breath cut short, as if from a jujitsu chop at her windpipe. Beneath the shade of the umbrella her gaze encountered the smoldering one of Nick Godwin.

Chapter 44

*I*T seemed she stood looking at that arrogantly masculine face for an interminable length of time so that she burned each separate feature into her brain to recall many times later . . . the careless ruffle of hair the color of old cork, the mocking tilt of the full lips, and the eyes—as blue-hot as a flame's center. They seemed to strip her naked there in that crowded, noisy dining room. It was a handsome face in a homely way, if one defined power as handsome.

Did Nick Godwin remember the tomboy who had challenged him so often, or did he merely stare at her, as did the other males, because of her unusual beauty?

"Miss. Miss." the old man at her table snapped his fingers impatiently. "A refill of the coffee."

She broke the snake charmer's spell Nick seemed to hold on her and turned back with murmured apology to fill the old man's cup. The availability of jobs shrank every year, and she could not afford to lose hers.

She refused to look again in the direction of Nick's table, but when her duties carried her near the veranda, she could hear his low laughter mixing with that of his three companions—another young man and two very pretty young women who had, as did Nick, the look of college imprinted on them, the V-neck sweaters and pleated flannel pants and wool skirts that whispered of casual elegance.

The college boys often drove their dates down from the university of Tucson to spend the day at Bisbee, which with its narrow streets twisting up and down the mountainside (so different from Tucson's flatness) and its population of Finns and Swedes and Slavs held a decidedly European flavor.

It was so easy for her to resent the rich college youths who so carelessly accepted the privileges wealth afforded them. The desire to attend college burned in her almost as greatly as the hunger for revenge. She knew she would never escape the poverty of the mining towns or the stigma of her heritage unless she could make something of herself.

True, she had completed high school the previous spring, a rare accomplishment in that mining town, but there was no money for college that fall. It took all that she had earned working part-time and the meager salary her father made to pay the rent on their shanty and furnish food and clothing.

She was immensely relieved that the veranda was not her serving section that afternoon. Somehow it would have been too demoralizing to wait on Nick Godwin, to serve him and his elegant companions when she foolishly fantasized making him grovel at her feet, ruining him financially, and ultimately taking Cristo Rey from him.

When a lull in the afternoon diners occurred, she allowed herself to dart one furtive glance toward the veranda. She was disappointed, rather than relieved, to find that Nick and his companions had left. She had in a way looked forward to a confrontation.

Unexpectedly she had the opportunity to confront Nick the following Saturday when he returned, this time alone. He took a table in one of her sections, as if he had known beforehand which tables she was working.

She stood behind the latticework divider, staring at his back as he scanned the menu. Her hands were clammy, twisted together. *Since when have you ever been afraid of anything?* As a child she would have taken on anyone who looked at her the wrong way and especially anyone who was foolish enough to taunt her about her father. But at that moment the effort it cost to cross the oakwood floor and speak to Nick was beyond her capability.

"Ssss!" the floor waitress hissed at Amanda, jamming her thumb in Nick's direction.

Reluctantly Amanda acknowledged her cue with a nod and somehow managed to traverse the room to Nick's table. "May I help you?" she asked in her most efficient wooden voice. She tried to keep her gaze just below the level of the blocklike chin, but her peripheral vision picked up the amused quirk of his lips, and her whole body prickled beneath his bold stare.

"Is it true?" His voice had deepened even more over the intervening years. What was he now, twenty, twenty-one?

Caught off guard, she glanced up to meet the laughing eyes. Was he referring to her Japanese heritage—or had he finally discovered that she was a claimant to Cristo Rey? "Is what true?"

"Is it true you won't date?"

This she could handle, had often handled. "What would you like?" she asked stiffly, her pencil posed over the pad.

"You, Mandy."

Her face flamed. So, he remembered her. Then a small smile played on her lips, as she enjoyed the brief moment of power he had inadvertently accorded her. "I'm afraid I'm not for sale. I'll have someone else take your order, sir."

She moved to signal the floor manager, but Nick's hand hooked her wrist, stopping her. "I'd really like to talk with you," he said, serious now. Then his eyes crinkled in a grin. "I've never forgotten the girl who could wrestle like a boy—or have you forgotten the boy?"

Dumbly she looked at him. Didn't he know how she disliked him? But why would he? He had no reason to suspect that she was anything but a young working woman he had known in his childhood. An easy mark for his kind. A weekend tumble in the hay that whatever girl he had pinned in Tucson would never find out about.

Finally she found her tongue. "I'm sorry, I don't have time to talk." She fled to the rear of the dining room before he could detain her further and summoned another young waitress, Anna—a plump strawberry-blonde who was only too glad to wait on him.

Still, Nick did not let Amanda escape. At six, when her Saturday shift ended, he was waiting for her at the back steps of the Copper Queen Restaurant. Thumbs hooked in belt loops, he leaned negligently against the fender of a sleek metallic-blue

Duesenberg convertible coupe which had to have cost a cool twenty grand.

When he saw her freeze, he came to his feet with a wicked grin. He had not forgotten the girl with the swaggering manner and biting tongue. Nor had he forgotten that devastating smile that she had flashed all too rarely. "You didn't think I would give up so easily?" he asked.

He was not that tall, maybe two or three inches under six feet, and with her own height she was almost eye level with him; yet there was the essence of power stamped on him—in the authoritative set of the brawny shoulders, the unyielding mouth, and sharp, shrewd eyes. It certainly was not a handsome face—but a strong one that proclaimed vigor and forcefulness.

She held her ground. "I thought you would have the good taste to recognize a rejection."

He grinned and took her arm, steering her toward the car and ignoring her resisting footsteps. "No one ever accused me of good taste." He deposited her in the front seat with little gallantry and went around to the driver's side.

"I don't guess it ever occurred to you," she said when he slid behind the wheel, "that I don't like you."

He chuckled and maneuvered the car out onto the cobblestoned street. "Sure," he said, "but I don't let little things like feelings stand in my way. Feelings can be altered."

"Not in this case, Mr. Godwin."

He pulled out a pack of Chesterfields and offered her one. She shook her head. "Where do you think you're taking me?" she demanded, though she was not really worried yet.

"I hear Chichuahua Hill Road is a great place to take a date."

"I'm not your date!"

"A girl you want to take with you, then," he amended.

She folded her arms. "Whatever you want to say to me, you can say now."

"Oh, no." He flashed her a grin in the dimming evening light. "I want to concentrate my full attention on you."

The challenge of the confrontation excited her, but she said nothing and stared with a set expression out her lowered window at the musty hotels with rusted grille balconies and the miners' old weathered boardinghouses they passed. Against her will she even enjoyed the ride, for it was the first automobile she had been in, if she did not count the vintage World War I bus that had brought her and her father from Fort Huachuca to Bisbee.

The luxurious automobile whipped up the curving road at a high speed in eerie silence. Nick halted it on top of the bald hill. Below them the tiered city was lighting up against the night. He turned to her, putting his arm on the back of the plush leather seat, and she instantly felt diminished by the sheer force of raw power that was like a blast of dynamite.

"All right, then," he said, no longer smiling. "Tell me why you dislike me."

She wished he were not smoking, because the smoke enwreathed his features, so that she could not tell what he was really thinking. Yet she had the feeling her thoughts did not go so easily undetected by those keen eyes. She looked away, to the twinkling lights below. "You don't know, do you?" she whispered. "You never guessed."

"I don't have the damnedest idea what you're talking about."

She reeled on him. "Our grandfathers are stepbrothers, Nick Godwin. And the Stronghold is rightfully mine!"

His gaze drilled into hers. "I see," he said, grinding out the cigarette in the ashtray. "Tell me about it—the whole story."

"You don't know anything about the Stronghold's history?" she asked, incredulous.

"I want to hear it from you."

Tersely she began to relate her grandmother's story. "So you see," she concluded, "the Stronghold rightfully belonged to the Davalos heirs, but Elizabeth Godwin made certain that your grandfather and father inherited it. She let nothing stand in the way, to the point of driving my mother from her home and eventually seeing that she was imprisoned."

Finished, she slumped weakly in the seat. Whatever reaction she had expected from Nick (perhaps prejudice upon learning of her Japanese heritage?), it was not one of amusement. He threw back his head, and deep laughter rolled out of that barreled chest. "My God, Mandy," he said at last. "That's the reason for this grudge—a silly family feud?"

She snapped upright. In the darkness her eyes blazed their wrath. "That's easy enough for you to say, isn't it—as the king sits in his counting house, counting all the money!"

She heard his dry chuckle. "The truth is, Mandy, I'm penniless."

"Try again," she retorted. "This car isn't a Model T Ford."

"To be exact, the Duesie's borrowed from a friend. I had to find some way to get down to Bisbee, didn't I?"

She heard the humor in his rumble-pitched voice but did not respond to it. "What about the Godwin fortune?" she demanded.

"It all belongs to Paul—my stepbrother."

"Your stepbrother?" she asked, her eyes narrowed suspiciously.

"Paul is the direct heir," he replied patiently, while his gaze boldly roved over her. "His father married my mother after Fanny, Paul's mother, died."

"But . . . but the Stronghold," she stuttered. "You live there!"

"Wrong again, honey. I only visit. Oh, Paul's very generous. He's tried every way in the world to convince me I ought to live there. God knows it's big enough. Of course, if Paul and his wife, Arlene, never have any children, I'll inherit that monstrosity and the wealth that goes with it. But fortunes can be won and lost and won again. It's life's game and not the cashing in of the chips that holds all the fun." He caught one of her hands that lay knotted in her lap and pulled her across the seat to him. "Does that destroy the barriers you've erected?" he asked softly.

She tried to yank free, but he held her fast. "No!" she hissed. "You're still a Godwin, and the Stronghold is still yours if you want it!"

"Then maybe this will destroy the barriers," he said, impatient now, and crushed her against him in a furious kiss. His mouth ground down on hers, smothering her protest so that it came out like a moan. She tried to push him away, but he was like a boulder. Then she went rigid as his tongue thrust inside her lips and stroked the roof of her mouth. After a moment he withdrew his tongue and, still holding her against him, kissed her lips again. His tongue lightly caressed the soft inner edges where his teeth had cut the first time.

She tried to bite his lips, and he jerked away. She lashed out at him then, her palm resounding in the silence of the night.

He shook her violently. "Damn you!" he exploded, his jaw smarting. Who did she think she was, sitting there with such a haughty flash in her eyes? Royalty? His fingers itched to bury themselves in the blue-black hair that swayed halfway down her back, to yank her head back until she yielded her lips to him. He swung her from him and switched on the engine. Their anger filled the car, making it difficult for either to breathe normally on the trip back down into town. "Where do you live?" he snapped.

"There," she mumbled tersely. "Below Castle Rock." It was a miner's typical clapboard shack perched on naked stilts to escape the floods that deluged the canyon after a summer cloudburst.

He halted in front of the wooden steps, and she sprang from the car. "Your company leaves a lot to be desired!" she gritted and slammed the car door. She heard the car screech off as she rushed up the steps. Once inside, she leaned against the door, breathless . . . weak . . . and hating Nick Godwin more than ever.

Chapter 45

WHEN the following Saturday came, Amanda half expected Nick to return to the Copper Queen Restaurant and was so edgy that she dropped a plate in the kitchen and later spilled wine on a tablecloth. "What's wrong with you, Amanda?" Annie demanded, who was on break when Amanda rushed into the kitchen to get a clean tablecloth. She stubbed out her cigarette. "What's happened to Miss Cool?"

"Nothing," Amanda snapped, angry that she could let the thought of Nick unnerve her so, and hurried back through the swinging doors.

It was understandable, she told herself, that she would feel so helpless before Nick. Her childhood had been one of grandiose dreams—of revenge and possession. And none of them had come to pass. She was still a poverty-encircled girl from the wrong side of the tracks . . . and Nick Godwin was Nick Godwin. The Godwins' name in Arizona implied wealth—land, cattle, mines, the very substance of Cristo Rey and the state.

Even Lars, a giant of a Swede from Michigan, noted her

preoccupation. He waited each weeknight to walk her home after the restaurant closed at ten, a deed for which her father was grateful. If she had worked in the Brewery Gulch, where rowdiness was the order of the day, she would have been more worried about the walk, but the Copper Queen area was perfectly safe.

Lars caught her shoulders and turned her to face him beneath a streetlamp. "What is it, Amanda?" he asked in his thick English. "You don't even half listen to what I'm saying."

What *was* he saying? "I'm sorry, Lars. I guess it's been a long, long day."

He sighed. "Only what I been trying to tell you for the last year now."

She made her voice gentle. "I've told you before, I don't . . ."

Lars released her and jammed his fists in his pocket. "I know—you won't marry me because you don't wanna be poor the rest of your life. But tonight is different, Amanda. I was promoted today—to head foreman!"

His voice held such pride that it was difficult for her to dampen his excitement over his news. Like her, he had his dreams. He already held a position on the local International Union of Mine, Mill and Smelter Workers and planned to be mine superintendent one day.

And he had been awfully good to her father. When Phelps Dodge laid Taro off because he could no longer do a miner's full day's work, Lars had arranged for him to get a job in the shower rooms, laundering the soiled towels and clothing stiff with mine dust. The free showers for the workers and freshly laundered work clothing was another appeasement by the company to the miners' union.

She knew she could not lead Lars on, let him believe anything could ever come of their relationship. She laid her hand on his sleeve. "That's wonderful. I told you that you would make something of yourself one day."

He turned eagerly on her. "Then you'll do it—you'll marry me, Amanda dear?"

Slowly she shook her head. "No, I can't, Lars." She hurried on. "As much as you want to become something, somebody, I want to escape the mines altogether—the pollution, the hopelessness, the raw towns. I want to rise out of my hole, also."

He grimaced. "Is it I'm not good enough for you, for a Jap's daughter?"

She gasped. Lars was one of the few who knew, yet she had never expected prejudice from him. But then she had discovered that the Cornish looked down on the bohunks, and the bohunks on the greasers.

He saw the pain in her eyes and grabbed her. "I'm sorry, Amanda. I didn't mean it that way. But I want you so, and it's not fair. It's hell being so close to you and no ... is there someone else?" he asked fiercely.

She looked up into that Nordic face, usually so placid. "Has your candle been dimming?" she teased, hoping to lighten the mood. There was an old miner's superstition that if the miner's lamp flickered, his sweetheart was cheating on him. More than one miner suddenly hurried home, presumably ill, so great was the belief in the superstition.

An embarrassed grin twitched his lips. "I guess I play the fool, eh—*spela narr?* Come on, I best get you home, or your father'll start swinging the samurai sword."

He climbed the rickety steps to her shanty with her, and she kissed him lightly at the door. She knew he wanted to grab her and plant kisses all over her face, but he ducked his head shyly and retreated down the steps. Watching him, she felt a pang of pity for the hopelessness of their relationship. Mining was Lars's life; it consumed him as Cristo Rey did her.

Inside, she quietly crept through the dark to her side of the room, but her father's nagging cough told her he was still awake. He never did let himself sleep until she returned, although he rose every morning at four. "Have you taken your medicine, Father?" she asked through the darkness.

"That colored water? No!" She could hear the humor in his voice and did not chastize him. They both knew he had the miner's disease, every miner did, but neither she nor her father would mention it to one another.

Once she had mentioned it, the year before, pleading with him to see a doctor. He had looked right through her. Later, over dinner, he had said abruptly, "There is nothing to cure it"—"it" was his euphemism, for he would not deign to give the disease the power of a name. "I can quit the mines, but I shall nevertheless die. All of us die one day. So I shall work as long as my legs will carry me. Now do not mention this ugly thing again."

After she undressed and stretched out on her mat, her father asked, "Will you marry Lars, daughter?"

After a moment she said, "No, Father. I want more from life than what a mere man can offer."

Her father chuckled. "In some ways, Amanda, you're still immature compared to the other girls your age. They know more of men, understand better the opposite sex."

But it was mere men, Amanda thought bitterly, who two weeks later laid off her father because the union voted that no Orientals and no Mexicans could be employed. Lars tried to sway the workers against the ordinance but was unsuccessful. The emotional suffering her father experienced was greater than the occasional pain that nibbled away at his lungs. Taro, who had been so muscular, so strong and independent, who had taken care of her mother and raised herself, was rapidly showing and feeling his age.

He even had trouble using the chopsticks as skillfully on the rice she set before him. "Father," she teased, "you're going to be forced at last to eat like a Caucasian."

He smiled, but she could see the misery in his soul. She slammed down her own chopsticks. "We're not going to let this defeat us! We'll make the layoff work to our benefit!"

"You sound like your mother," he said quietly. "Her determination was both her rose and her thorn."

"But I am not my mother!"

She said no more, yet she could not help but think that she had let her emotions get in the way of what she wanted. She would not let her bitterness for the Godwin family or her love for Cristo Rey blind her to her priorities . . . climbing out of the mining society and making something of herself.

"What do you suggest we do?" her father asked later that night, and she knew how rare it was for the Oriental male to accept that a female could think beyond the realm of children and home—not just the Oriental, she reminded herself, recalling some of Lars's chauvinistic attitudes toward her independence.

"We're moving to Tucson, Father. It's large enough that I may be able to find some sort of secretarial job there to support us.

And I can begin classes at the university in the evening." She pressed on. "It'll be tough, I know. We'll probably live under worse conditions than here for a while, but at least we'll have hope in Tucson."

Taro's lips curved in a slight smile. "If you were anyone else, I would say you wouldn't have a Chinaman's chance. But maybe . . ." His stooped shoulders shrugged with his Oriental's fatalism. "Maybe there you will find your karma."

Chapter 46

AMANDA found a house for rent at the edge of downtown Tucson in the Barrio Libre—the "free neighborhood" where lived the Mexicans and Chinese. The adobe was not much better than the shanty in Bisbee, but it did have two rooms curtained off, and the outhouse was much easier to reach than the one that had clung to the steep incline behind the shanty.

Getting accepted into college was a little more difficult. She had an excellent transcript from Bisbee's Central High, but the university's counselor who reviewed her application wore a dubious expression.

"Is there a problem?" she asked the bespectacled man as his face furrowed further.

He looked at her and dropped his gaze back to the sheaf of papers he seemed to shuffle aimlessly. "Well, Miss Shima, you must realize we don't have very many Oriental students enrolled in our curriculum. And the fact that you are opting for a career in law, which really is a man's field, well . . ."

"What you're saying, Mr. Browne, is that I have two strikes against me already—my race and my sex?" she asked curtly.

"No—no. But you must realize that while you do have very high grades, we can accept only a limited number of applicants. And we have no proof that, uh, you can afford the tuition and cost of the education. If you drop out we will have wasted space we could give to another."

"I won't drop out, Mr. Browne, and I will have a job to support the cost of my education." (And support herself and her father, she did not add aloud.)

"You have a job now?"

"I *will* have a job."

Such a rash statement. In spite of the typing course she had taken in high school, she found that the offices where she applied for a secretary's position had just hired a secretary only hours earlier. After days of looking, she tossed the want ads in the Armory Park trash barrel and caught a bus back to the university, spending precious money for the fare.

When she reappeared at the counselor's door, Mr. Browne glanced up and sighed, looking as if he were facing his nemesis. She crossed the room to stand before his desk. "Mr. Browne, your bulletin board advertises part-time jobs for students, I want one."

"You won't take my advice, will you—go up to the State Teacher's College at Tempe?"

"No." There she was—a female Oriental, her stomach knotting with hunger, begging for a job—and trying to behave in an assertive manner. "It's only a two-year college, and I want a full education."

He sighed again. "Sit down, Miss Shima." He got up and closed the door. The poor man's shoulders were slumping when he returned to his seat. "As you said, you've two strikes against you. There's no use pretending that your race isn't going to hold you back. You and I both know it."

He glanced up from beneath the bushy brows that lay atop the wire rims of his spectacles. "But I'll deny making that statement if you quote me."

She sat rigidly, silently, and he continued, leaning forward on the desk, hands clasped. "If you'd be willing to change your last name and indicate that you're a Caucasian on application records, I can assure you I'd be able to find you employment somewhere."

"No. I won't be robbed of the only thing I have left."

His fingers clasped and unclasped. After a moment, he said, "There's a job available cleaning the dormitory bathrooms and toilets. Are you interested?"

The maid's job did not earn enough money to enable Amanda to remain in college and support herself and her father. "I shall become the proverbial Oriental and take in laundry," he told her with a wry smile as they counted out the last of their change they kept in a jade vase. It was only the beginning of her second semester at the university, and after she bought her books, there was simply no money left for food.

"No, Father, we'll sell the vase. That should keep us for some time."

"And then what shall we sell, my daughter?" he asked, his veined hand sweeping out to indicate the dismal barrenness of their adobe. "Since I left the mines my health is much better. There is no reason why I should not work. And I'd be much happier."

Although her father was approaching his seventy-second birthday, she knew he would be happier working. But getting started in the laundry business was slow. They scraped by. That winter things were so bleak financially that Amanda was reduced to putting a playing card in the bottom of one of her oxfords to cover the hole in its sole.

That same winter she and her father took a third member into their household—a burr-haired mutt who had been following her when she made the cleaning rounds of the dormitories and sorority houses. The dog would sit patiently outside each building until Amanda reappeared with her mop and pail of cleaning utensils.

"We'll call him Trouble," she told her father the afternoon she brought the mongrel home. "He looks as half-starved as we are—and will only mean more trouble. But I want him."

During those lean years, which seemed to get only worse when war broke out in Europe toward the end of 1939, Amanda would read in the *Arizona Daily Star*'s society page of how the decadent rich lived and think that it was like reading a fairy tale. There were the Little Princesses, Elizabeth and Margaret Rose, who appeared almost weekly in royal photos now that their uncle, Edward VIII, had abdicated the throne for "the woman I love."

Then there were the glittering publicity photos of New York's café society and titillating stories of extravaganzas thrown at the Stork Club, El Morocco, and 21 by such personalities as the

Red-Hot Mama, Sophie Tucker, and Elsa Maxwell. Did such a world really exist?

What the Arizona wealthy did for amusement—their balls and charities and scandals—afforded entertainment that was almost fictional for the poverty-stricken people of the state. They were tired of the depressing headlines chronicling the war in Europe or Roosevelt's latest New Deal agencies to combat the terrible times.

For Amanda the society columns provided something more, because occasionally she would read tidbits about the Godwins. Most of the new items dealt with Paul, president of the state's leading banking firm, and his wife. "Godwins Return East for the Summer" . . . "Arlene Godwin hosts ball at Cristo Rey for European War Effort."

Amanda thought Paul's wife looked older than he, maybe fifty or so, but later columns whispered of her cancerous illness. And Amanda was sorry, for she thought the woman looked like someone she would have liked.

Sometimes she saw Nick's name in print. Though Paul occupied the Stronghold, it was Nick and his arrogance that somehow represented all that Cristo Rey was to her. Once she read that he had escorted one of Tucson's debutantes to the Winter Ball and another time that he had graduated with the highest score on the Arizona bar exams.

She was not surprised. She knew he was shrewd and ambitious, as indicated by the young women she sometimes saw him with on campus . . . young women with expensive wardrobes and, of course, those all-American features—blond, bright-blue eyes and sunny smiles.

Once or twice she sensed he saw her also, though she could not be certain. It was only a feeling of sudden heat, like the hot flashes that swept over older women—and she would turn and find that he was near, usually walking in another direction with a couple of his friends. But with Nick off campus now, practicing law, she found it easier to concentrate on graduating and preparing for her LSAT exam. The day she received word of her acceptance into law school, she and her father quietly celebrated with a glass of sake.

Then, as 1939 slipped into 1940, both the Godwin brothers made headlines the same week. Tucson was surprised to wake up one morning and read that Roosevelt had appointed one of her sons, Paul Godwin, as his economic adviser. With the article was a photo of a handsome middle-aged man and the announcement that Paul would be leaving shortly for Europe to accompany Prime Minister Chamberlain in his negotiations with Chancellor Adolf Hitler over the German claims on Czechoslavakia.

Paul's appointment shared the spotlight with the younger brother, Nick, whose engagement to one of the Boston line of Warrens, Danielle Stirling, was announced three days later. The paper carried a photo of the bride-to-be (a stunning sultry blonde) and what Amanda thought was a nauseating recital of how the handsome pair met—"The divine Danielle and her mother visited the Double U Dude Ranch this previous winter and were introduced to Tucson's young lawyer through mutual friends. Mrs. Stirling informs us that her cousin, Arthur Sidney Warren, will give her daughter away at the wedding. We Tucsonians will have something to look forward to this fall."

Amanda felt she knew everything about Nick by the time she finished reading the various columns that appeared that summer detailing his courtship of "Warren's Niece." She swore she would not read another word about him, but it was as if he were an obsession with her, and so she would plow through another insipid column describing the novel "crazyjamas" Danielle Stirling wore to the Wild West Hayride Benefit for Crippled Children or the daring strapless gown she modeled at the Pioneers Ball— in order to linger over the sentences about Nick.

Eventually the length and number of those sentences exceeded those written about Danielle, for late that fall, after their wedding (with a last-rose-of-summer theme), Nick announced his candidacy for mayor.

"I will personally mount a campaign against him here in the Barrio," Amanda told her father as she slowly wadded up the *Daily*'s front page.

Her father set the coal iron on the board with a thud. "My daughter, will you never learn to accept things you cannot change, or must you singe your wings against the flame like a foolish moth?"

She scratched Trouble between the ears and with a shrug opened the hornbook she should have been studying. "Everyone must have a goal. And my education and triumph, however small it may be, over the Godwins are my goals. They are the only things that matter to me in life. And you, Father," she added quickly, lovingly.

"The first goal is commendable. The second is more than a waste of one's time, which is more precious than jade. It is self-destroying. There is no room in a heart for both bitterness and love. Like oil and water, they will not mix."

She wanted to cry out that his proverbs could not apply in a modern world gone mad, but her respect for him held her tongue. She cast down her lashes in the age-old way of the Oriental woman.

And in a way she knew her father was right. But it made it no easier when six months later Nick Godwin was elected by a landslide margin. She told herself it was the combination of the Godwin-Warren names and not the sweeping reforms Nick had promised to carry out.

His name appeared in print quite often after that. And there drifted rumors of the various fortunes he made wheeling and dealing with the bankers and businessmen who were always willing to back his ventures. In the *Arizona Businessman* he candidly and insouciantly admitted to losing a cool thousand every once and a while, but such as his gambler's devil-may-care charm that Amanda felt he could have been one of Hitler's cronies and the Arizona populace would still have supported him.

She reminded herself she had priorities over following Nick's charismatic career, and finishing law school and passing the bar exam were most important to her at that moment. Nick Godwin and Cristo Rey would keep. And there was the more pressing issue of finding some type of evening employment, for with only a year left for her LL.B., she was now forced to take the rest of her hours in day classes.

She was only too glad to give up the janitorial job and was lucky enough to find within the week an ad for employment at the Casablanca Restaurant—singing, no less. Since she had no vocal training, only a music-appreciation course in college, she was terribly nervous when she auditioned against two other girls for the final selection.

One was a slinky honey-blonde with a pompadour hair style and the other was a vivacious redhead her own age who belted out "Tutti Frutti" with such enthusiasm that Amanda's hopes sank to her toes.

When her time came, she sang a husky rendition of "Deep Purple." The crusty manager's expression never altered; if anything he seemed to bite tighter on his stubby cigar, tilting its smoking tip up closer to his pug nose. The young man at the piano handed Amanda back her sheet music. "Great going!" he whispered with an encouraging wink.

"But not great enough," she said, watching the manager amble on bandy legs toward her. Sorry, but you're not the type we're looking for—it would be the standard reply.

"You got the job, doll," he said without removing the cigar from between his nicotine-stained teeth. "Be here at six tomorrow evening—and with something that has a little more pizazz." He waved the cigar now at her one suit, a blue twill that looked more suitable for church than a supper club.

She could not believe her good luck. "Thank you, sir!"

"Mike's the name." He turned to the other two girls, saying, "That's it, kids. Sorry."

"Congratulations," the young man said and rose from the piano, closing the lid. "How about celebrating over a cup of coffee at the campus cantina?"

She knew she should catch the next bus back to the Barrio. Her father would be worried. But she did feel like celebrating. For so long it had been touch and go, doing without lunch, wearing shabby clothes. And now she had landed a good-paying job that would cover the expenses of the last leg of her education. "All right, I'd like that."

Over coffee in one of the cantina's wooden booths she learned that Larry Willis was a senior majoring in economics. "I'm lucky enough to have a CPA firm ready to take me on as soon as I graduate," he said. "How about you?"

He was a nice-looking young man with sandy hair and warm hazel eyes that made her remember that she was attractive, something she had forgotten in the rush from mops to books to laundry in the evening. "I'm going for my Bachelor of Laws," she told him.

"Business or criminal?"

"Neither—constitutional."

Larry's lips formed a soundless whistle. "You don't take the easy route, do you?"

She smiled. "It's something I've been wanting to do for some time now."

"In your spare time," he quipped. "If you aren't careful, Mike'll talk you into singing more than four nights a week."

She was caught up in the easy bantering; the time slipped away too quickly, and she had to leave. Larry walked her to the bus stop. In the dim light of the streetlamp, he took her hand, saying softly, "Goodnight, Amanda. See you tomorrow."

When she explained to her father that she had found a job, he was no longer so upset that she was three hours late. "You make me a proud father, Amanda. Do you see any of the other daughters of the Barrio's families going to college? No, they get married and then have babies."

"Or have babies and then get married," she teased, delighting in shocking him, although she knew she never really did despite his expressions of disapproval. After all, he and her mother had shared the same cabin without the benefit of marriage.

Still, Amanda found it difficult to believe that people then did not experience the same passionate love that young people now did. Obviously, from the stories about the Ghost Lady, her grandmother also knew of that all-consuming love. Maybe one day so would she, though she doubted it. Cristo Rey consumed her as if it were her lover.

"Things aren't all that great," Amanda suddenly wailed, remembering Mike's last instructions. "I've got to have a dressy costume by tomorrow, Father!"

She had nothing appropriate—all sweaters or blouses and short skirts, something her father deplored until she would halt him, reminding him she had a newspaper clipping with a drawing of her mother in men's pants and the caption "Female Bandit Masquerades as Male."

After Amanda rummaged through everything and was wringing her hands in despair, her father came from the front part of the house, holding something behind him. She tilted her head to one side and narrowed her eyes. "All right, Father, what are you hiding?"

He drew forth a bright shimmering red satin dress. "Father!" she breathed. "Where did you get that?"

A mystical smile flashed across his face. "It came like manna from heaven, as the Christians say, I believe."

Her hands went to her hips, but she could not help but smile. "All right, the truth."

He feigned a sigh of regret. "From one of our patrons. She isn't due to pick up her laundry until next week . . . but the Lord will provide something else by then."

Her father was neither a Buddhist nor a Shintoist, and she had never thought to hear him speaking or thinking in Judeo-Christian terms. She herself had been taught Christianity from the good ladies at the Fort Huachuca school.

From whatever providence she received the dress, she was able to keep it, for the Chinese family never came back to pick it up.

The dress was made for the smaller Chinese woman, and as it was styled to be loose-fitting, it instead hugged her high breasts and rounded hips closely. It was edged with black rickrack and had the high-neck mandarin collar with a split reaching halfway up her thigh. Contrasted with her blue-black hair and the shimmering stage lights of the dinner club, it created a sensational effect . . . sensational enough to catch the eye of Nick Godwin when he entered the Casablanca three weeks later.

Chapter 47

AMANDA certainly never expected to see Nick Godwin in the Casablanca. It was not the stuffy sort of supper club the mayor of Tucson would patronize but rather a small, intimate restaurant that had become the "in" place for Tucson's younger set.

The stage lights had not yet been turned on when Nick entered with his party, and she was leaning against the piano, talking with Larry, her back to the entrance. But she would have known that Nick was in the restaurant even if it were not for the sudden increase in muted conversation, whispers of recognition from the other patrons mixed with not a few low exclamations of admiration for the beautiful woman with him.

The hair at Amanda's nape prickled, the same as it had nearly three years earlier, when she had felt his presence in the Copper Queen dining room, and then again the myriad times on campus. She broke off in mid-conversation with Larry and slowly rotated to survey the room.

There at the largest table she found him. The candlelight illuminated the tough lines of his face as he leaned across the table to light his wife's cigarette. For only a moment Amanda observed her. She had seen her in photos that did not do full justice to the woman's beauty. The shoulder-length hair was arranged in the new rage—a peekaboo effect—and her complexion was a creamy pale against the fire-engine-red lipstick. Amanda knew the dress with the daring padded shoulders had to be a designer's creation. Everything about Danielle whispered of elegance, as everything about Nick thundered of power.

Amanda's gaze was inexorably pulled back to Nick, who, head inclined, seemed to be listening to what the elderly debonair gentleman on his left was saying. It was not just the power so evident in Nick's brash features that demanded attention . . . it was everything about him. His very presence dominated a room. Perhaps it was his roguish gambler's charm that made him appear handsomer than he really was, but every woman's head seemed to be turned in his direction. His body movements, restrained by the superbly tailored dinner jacket, announced the man's self-assurance—a rugged, brawny body backed by an astute intelligence. Oh, how she longed to crush that insolent assurance!

"Hey, Amanda, you're on," Larry muttered above the soft piano music he was playing.

The one overhead light brightened, and simultaneously Larry went into the opening number, a crescendo of "So Rare" before muting the last notes for sliding into Amanda's introductory song. It was one Judy Garland had made famous a couple of years before in *Broadway Melodies of 1938*. Larry and Amanda had run over the number several times that afternoon to make certain they had it down.

As she sang the words, *"You made me love you, I didn't want to do it, you made me want you, and all the time you knew it . ."* she could feel Nick's bold gaze raking her. Beneath its intensity her knees grew cottony, and she was grateful for the support of the piano she leaned against.

Of all the adversaries who could have been thrust on her, why the indomitable Nick Godwin? Anger at her own weakness raged in her so that by the song's finale she delivered it in such a way that applause reverberated through the small restaurant on her last holding note.

"Wow, Amanda, you sure know how to deliver when it's called for," Larry said.

She knew he was surprised that she had outperformed their rehearsal. She was surprised also—by the audience's evident approval—and somewhat embarrassed because she did not really take singing seriously. For those few moments of audience adulation she almost forgot Nick was out there among the people.

But as the applause subsided, the intensity that flowed between the two of them like magnetic needles on a compass regenerated itself, galvanizing her—causing her to tremble and leaving her breathless. It was all she could do to find the air deep in her diaphragm as she opened softly, slowly, beneath the muted lights with, *"Kiss me once, kiss me twice . . . kiss me once again. It's been a long, long time . . ."*

It seemed like a long, long time before her act was finished for the evening. She retreated to the small cubicle that was the dressing room, anxious to change and leave. As she quickly applied a sheen of lipstick before the small mirror, she told herself she was running away. Yet she knew she could not afford to do battle with her nemesis unprepared. One day the time would come, the right time. She would choose her own battleground—and one day vanquish the Godwins.

She did not understand why she chose Nick rather than his stepbrother, Paul, as the object of her antipathy. They were both Godwins, and it was truly Paul, and his wife, who lived at Cristo Rey when not in Washington. But Nick was more Amanda's age, and it was Nick she had associated with Cristo Rey since childhood.

And then there was that indefinable chain that seemed to bind them—invisible, intangible, but nonetheless as unbreakable as links forged of steel. Only such a powerful emotion as her hatred could have forged such a chain.

There came a knock at the dressing-room door, and Larry stuck his head inside. "Hey, guess who has invited us to his table?"

"Let me guess," she said flippantly, pulling her hair to the side so that she could slide into the three-quarter-length jacket of white silk with black braided frogs. "FDR and Eleanor."

"You're close—the mayor of Tucson."

She froze, never expecting Nick to go that far—to invite her to share the same table as his wife and friends. But then Nick *would* do that—flout convention. He was capable of anything. She looked at Larry's excited face in the mirror. "Give the mayor my apologies, but tell his honor I can't make it."

"You gotta be kidding, Amanda! This isn't an everyday occurrence."

She picked up her purse. "I've got moot court and a test over the Justinian Code tomorrow."

"Mike won't like it if he hears about it," Larry cautioned, still not quite believing she would turn down such an opportunity.

She shrugged. "I'm not getting paid to mix with the customers, Larry."

In an expression of hopelessness, he raised his brows and spread his palms. "All right. Wait up till I get my jacket."

After their show Larry always made it a point to walk her to the bus stop, waiting with her for her bus before he walked back to his fraternity house, which was not far. That particular evening she was more grateful than ever for his companionship as they skirted the dining room's still-packed tables, edging their way along the walls. She did not feel so alone in her defiance of Tucson's mayor.

They reached the small lobby, and Larry was tossing a flippant goodbye to the cute young girl in the checkroom when Mike stormed through the swinging door. "What's going on here, doll? You can't keep a Godwin waiting!" Then he saw her purse clutched under her arm and her coat. His eyes bulged. "You ain't thinking of leaving?"

She and Larry exchanged looks. " 'Cause if you are," Mike continued, "you don't have to worry 'bout coming back."

Larry rolled his eyes. "Aww, Mike, we were just stepping out for some fresh air, weren't we, Amanda?"

Both men looked at her. Damn! Thirty different thoughts barraged her like gunfire in that brief interval, but what it came down to, she decided, was a duel between her pride and the need to graduate. If the gentleman had been anyone else but Nick, she would have acceded a great deal more graciously. "Sure, Larry. I was just checking my purse."

Mike's cigar tilted upward with his grin. "Good going, kids. There's a tip in it for you."

Walking back into the semidarkness, she could not at first make out Nick's table. Larry took her elbow and maneuvered them through the maze of tables with Mike trailing behind. "Mayor Godwin," he said expansively, "Casablanca's two stars, Larry Willis and Amanda Shima."

Nick and the two other men at his table rose. He did not take his eyes off her as she took the chair her partner pulled out for her. He'd never meant to see her again—her with that hellfire temper. And that damned pride. Sitting there on those perfect hips as if she were some Far Eastern princess. But he had her number. An avaricious little wildcat who meant to have what she thought was her due. Sweet Jesus, but would he like to give her what *he* thought was her due!

"I believe we've met before," he said, addressing her alone.

"It seems you made the same mistake then also," she acknowledged coolly. "In Bisbee, wasn't it?"

Nick raked a brow, as if amused by her reply, but she turned her attention to the gentleman directly across from her, who began to make the introductions. She was wedged between Nick's wife and a stout matron with turquoise necklaces and pendants draped from an ample bosom. These people, of course, needed no introductions. Their names and faces were familiar in Tucson society.

The man across from her, Richard Attenberry, was the city's district attorney, and his wife, the turquoise woman, headed up the opera guild. The other gentleman, Allan Shriver, and his wife owned the city's largest department store, which rivaled that of Goldwaters in Phoenix.

It was Danielle who spoke first after the introductions. "You have a very good voice, Miss Shima. Is Shima an Italian or Oriental name?"

The way she inhaled on her cigarette, stubbing it out in an irritated gesture, told Amanda she did not really care about the answer. Through the swirling haze of cigarette smoke, Danielle watched her as closely as Nick, and all at once Amanda realized that Danielle sensed Nick's more than casual interest in her. For a man to remember a woman he allegedly had met only once three years prior said more than mere words to his wife.

"Shima is of Japanese origin," Amanda replied evenly.

Mrs. Attenberry asked, "Are you studying music at the university, dear?"

"No, I'm not," she replied, volunteering as little information as possible. She wanted only to finish with the pleasantries and leave.

Danielle raised a delicately arched brow. "Oh? Then this kind of—work—it's your . . . profession?"

"No, it's only a way to earn a living." On her left, Allan Shriver offered her a cigarette, and she declined but continued to converse with him, grateful to escape Danielle's patronizing conversation. Nick ordered drinks. She watched his hands light a cigarette. They were large and capable. Too capable.

The talk turned to the certainty of the coming war. "My brother's even signed up with the Army Air Forces, he's that sure we're going to be in it," Larry said, and Allan prophesied it would drive up the prices of commodities and shorten the supply.

"It's Roosevelt who wants us in," Richard said. "I lay ten to one. It's the only way he can carry through with his New Deal policies and get us out of the Depression. What does Paul think about it, Nick? Or does he say?"

"Whatever Paul thinks about it, he's certainly not allowed to put into letters—at least not to me."

"He and Arlene are coming home for a visit soon." Danielle put in. "You can ask him yourself at our party." She turned to Amanda. "And we'd love to have you and Larry come and entertain us. Wouldn't we, Nick?"

"I'm sure we'll be working through the weekends," Amanda replied. "But thank you for the invitation." Recklessly she tossed down the scotch and water the waiter set before her. She had done her duty to Mike and the Casablanca. She looked at Larry, who sat at the other end of the table. "I'd better go or I'll miss my bus."

Larry rose immediately, but Nick put a restraining hand on his arm. "We'll take you home, Miss Shima."

She met his hard gaze. Her eyes frosted over. "Thanks for the offer, but I'm sure my house is nowhere in the vicinity of yours, Mayor Godwin."

Larry came around to her chair and thanked everyone before ushering her out. "Well, was it as bad as you expected?" he asked as he helped her back into her evening coat.

"Worse. I felt like a freak on exhibit at a sideshow. Our society friends were only interested in seeing how the other half lives."

She inhaled deeply of the fresh air when they stepped outside. Larry caught her arm and turned her to face him. "I don't think so. I think, Amanda Shima, the mayor was interested in you—alone."

"Don't be ridiculous, Larry." She twisted away. "Mayor Godwin has a beautiful wife. And if he wanted another woman, I'm certain there are plenty of women all too willing to volunteer their charms."

Larry smiled at her obvious indignation. It was difficult to imagine that she was actually unaware of her incredible beauty. Like the renowned beauty of Eurasian women, she had inherited the same breathtaking qualities from her Anglo-Hispanic mother and Oriental father. Exotic features balanced on a tall, willowy frame. Heads turned wherever she went. And he was no exception.

"You underrate the power of your own charms, Amanda," he said now, catching up with her. "Hey . . ."

She stopped and looked at him, and he caught her against him. "Can't you tell the power of your charms has ensnared me also?"

Before she could move, Larry kissed her. At the noise of the people spilling out of the restaurant, he released her, and over his shoulder she saw Nick's raking glance.

Chapter 48

*L*ARRY nodded as his nimble fingers tapped their way across the keyboard. "He's out there again."

So, she wasn't the only one who had noticed Nick Godwin's repeated presence. Three times by her count in the past month— twice with business associates and once, surprisingly, alone. She would have bet her last supper that those were the only times

Nick had been out there among the Casablanca's patrons, listening as she sang. She would have known it had he been out there more than those three times—as surely as she knew the songs she rehearsed so often.

It was unnerving to sing when he was there, knowing he watched her, studied her, as no other male did. He was an animal! His presence served to remind her how quixotic were her dreams of revenge, of possessing the Stronghold. Dreams made more vivid by photos of the Stronghold that Larry had pointed out in *Architectural Digest* the month before.

She finished the song and signaled to Larry to cut her next number. "I'm leaving," she lip-synched after the applause, which was light, since it was a weeknight. Leaving early was something rarely done, but Larry never missed a note as he swung into "Love Walked In."

Mike caught up with her on her way to the dressing room. "The mayor's asking for you," he said, jerking his thumb over his shoulder. "You must have made some impression on him."

She looked beyond Mike to the shadowy people at the tables, then back to the manager. He had been around a long time, and that mug of his was street-wise. "I know what you're thinking," she said tightly, "but I've had nothing to do with Mayor Godwin. And I'm not going to."

"Hey, doll. I don't pass judgments. I leave that to the judge." As if he sensed the inflexible temperament that corraled her at that moment, his gruff voice became wheedling rather than demanding. "The mayor has the power to take away our liquor license, with us this close to the university and all. And then we'd all be without a job, wouldn't we?" He winked broadly. "Come on, it won't hurt just to go over and be sociable for a few minutes, eh?"

Only a year of school left until she got her LL.B. If it had been May a year later she could have spit in Mike's face—and Nick's. She whirled around and walked back into the dining room. It dismayed her to find her hands were knotted, her jaw tensed. Nick rose at her approach. She slid into the chair he pulled out for her. "Mike said you wanted to talk to me," she said curtly.

Above the flickering candle, Nick's square, almost homely features glowed with a saturnine quality. "You don't smoke, do you?" he said. He pulled out a gold case of what must have been his own personalized brand of cigarettes. It was a statement tha did not require an answer, and she sat across from him, lips clamped together in a stern line.

He bent his head near the candle's flame and lit the cigarette His eyes narrowed as he inhaled. He blew the smoke out slowly observing her, before he spoke again. "Your dislike for me intrigues me."

" 'Dislike' is a mild word. How about 'hostility'?"

"If that's what it is. But I think it's stronger than that, even— what I feel between us."

"As I see it, Mayor Godwin," she said, stressing his title, "there is nothing between us."

He quirked one of those thick brows. "You might deny it, bu you and I both know you're lying. Mandy—" He paused as the obsequious waiter hovered over him, inquiring if he wished to renew his drink order. Nick shook his head with irritation and the waiter backed away. "Get your purse," Nick commanded.

"I will not!"

His gaze lanced her. Damn her green eyes! He ought to give her what she was itching for. Everyone else probably was, includ ing Piano Fingers. That made him even madder. He ground ou his cigarette and caught her hand, jerking her to her feet. "I'm taking you home."

"No, you're not," she said, trying to wrench away from the clamplike grip with no success.

He grimaced impatiently. "You'll only make a spectacle, because you're going with me even if I have to call the chief of police and have you arrested."

She did not doubt he would make good his threat and let him pull her along beside him. At the checkroom he ordered the young girl to hand over Amanda's purse and propelled Amanda out the door toward the darkened parking lot behind the Casablanca.

"You're hurting me," she cried, rubbing at her wrist. Never in her life had she been subjected to such brutality. Her father had never raised his hand to her, for a quelling look from those gentle eyes had been enough of a discipline. "You're nothing but an animal!"

Nick laughed out loud and practically shoved her into the slee white Pierce-Arrow. "And what do you think you are?" he asked as he gunned the motor. "You, my fine pet, are a cow a-bulling."

Her fingers arched for his face. This time he caught her hand in midflight. "Oh, no, not again, you don't!" He yanked her to him, crushing her breasts against the buttoned jacket of his business suit. He slammed his hard, angry mouth over hers. His teeth ground against her lips, and her teeth were forced to part, opening the way for the assault of his tongue. His tongue shoved hers to one side, raking her mouth, laying claim to every intimate recess.

It was like—it was like what it must be to be raped! Worse even than that first time he had kissed her! Oh, the beast! His mouth fired hotter and hotter over hers. He kept kissing her—vigorously, thoroughly—until she felt herself catch fire from his own body heat. This was not the way it was supposed to be!

They kissed longer and harder. She wanted to hurt him, and he wanted to hurt her. They punished each other with their kisses. Then he shoved her away from him abruptly. "See?" he rasped. "I was right. A cow a-bulling! I can smell the scent on you. Doesn't Larry the Piano Man satisfy your animal lusts?"

"Oh? You disgust me!"

"I can say the same for you. You have none of the refined virtues of a lady, my dear!" He whipped the car out onto Park Boulevard. "Where to?"

"The Barrio," she bit out, not trusting herself to say more. Fury boiled in her. He was nothing but a savage who brought out the worst in her. She couldn't get out of the car fast enough, and when he maneuvered the Pierce Arrow down the Barrio's narrow dirt streets, her hand was already at the door handle. At that time of night, for it was nearing ten o'clock, all the lights from the mud *jacales* were out. Somewhere in the darkness a cat screeched.

She swung open the door, prepared to bolt, but Nick grabbed her arm. "You don't get off that easily," he snapped.

She turned on him. "What more do you want? Me?"

"Yes!"

It was her turn to laugh. She was afraid she wouldn't stop. "Oh, that's justice," she said at last, getting her breath. She brushed a knuckle along the outer corner of her eye to catch the laughter's tear. "It's a small measure of triumph, Nick Godwin, that I can say, 'Never!' "

His grip tightened on her arm, so that she was almost reclining across the car seat. His face was near enough that she could smell his cologne—and his man-scent. "Whatever revenge you're hell-bent on won't change what you feel about me!" he snarled.

"I feel nothing about you—except contempt!"

His mouth claimed hers, forcing her head down against the seat. Her hair spilled over its edge, and he trapped it with his thigh as he bent over her, kissing her savagely, brutally, burning her with the heat of his open mouth. His teeth bit into her lips. She clutched his head to hers so that he could not withdraw from the fierce attack of her own tongue and teeth, her fingers digging into his scalp, burying themselves in his thick hair.

They pulled away, gasping in deep audible breaths. "I hate you!" she whispered.

"You'd like to pretend that there isn't something between us," he grated. "But I'm not going to let you."

"I don't ever want to see you again!" She bounded from the car and slammed its door.

She was half afraid he would stop her, or worse, follow her into the house. But she made it inside and, with her back to the door, closed her eyes against the tears. She listened to the hum of his car as he drove off into the night.

Trouble whimpered at her feet, begging to be petted, but she was unaware. It's mine, her heart cried out in despair. The Stronghold should be mine!

Nick did not come the next day to the Casablanca, nor the next week or month, and Amanda thought she was able to forget the impact he had on her. Without him watching her, reminding her of their kisses, her life seemed to steer a steadier course.

Sometimes she read about him in the newspaper—"Mayor Godwin Signs Deal with Colorado River Authorities" . . . "Godwins Attend Fourth of July Gala" . . . "Godwins Host Party for Howard Hughes." Beneath the last was a photo of Nick and a gorgeous Danielle, swathed in a frothy crepe and organza gown, with the tall, slender Hughes in between the two. A caption told of the party held at the mayor's home in the exclusive Paseo Redondo section of Tucson for the elusive Hughes.

And then there was the smaller headline when Paul Godwin returned home from Washington to bury his wife.

Reading about the Godwins or hearing their names mentioned on the radio was like the discussion of a stranger. Surely Nick Godwin had never held her, kissed her . . . and she had never betrayed herself.

As long as she could put the Godwins and the Stronghold in the right perspective—names that meant nothing to her—then her life was as pleasant as it could be under the circumstances, rising at four to work on the laundry with her father, attending school until three, and singing at the Casablanca from seven until ten (or one o'clock on weekends).

In fact, that August of 1941, the month she turned twenty-three, held bright promise for her. She was entering her last year of law school. It had been three hard years, but it would be worth it when she could put up her shingle along "Lawyer's Row" that ran near the County Court House.

Her father often teased her when he would catch her poring over a law journal in the middle of the night. "I have raised a female Clarence Darrow!" But she knew he was secretly proud. A female lawyer would have been unheard of in his country.

Like the social unfortunates she hoped to represent, she had to believe that one day she would win her own struggle. Not just the struggle of prejudice—for some of the students had begun to avoid her when they realized she was part Japanese. With Japan on the Axis side in the war, her name was not a favorable one to have. Then there was the other struggle she had to believe she would one day win—her struggle for the Stronghold.

Yet the next time she saw Nick Godwin she knew she was facing a much more powerful adversary than mere prejudice. She was facing—no, battling—herself, her own conflicting emotions.

A late-summer dust storm raged through Tucson's streets the next time she saw him. She had just finished a class, and Larry waited to walk her to the corner bus stop. Together they fought the grit that abraded their exposed hands and faces. "Go on, Larry," she yelled against the whirl of the wind. "There's no use your getting coated with sand, too."

Larry pulled her to him, brushing his lips across her forehead. "It's worth the sandblasting just to be near you." Then, more earnestly, "Why won't you go out with me?"

"Because I don't have time in my life to be serious about someone. There's too much to do and not enough time as it is."

(299)

"That won't go, Amanda. People make time for what they want badly enough."

She reached up and brushed back the swath of toffee-colored hair that the wind whipped across his forehead. "And what would your parents say about your dating a Japanese?"

"But you don't look it!" he protested.

"Oh?" Hurt, she moved away. "If I looked Japanese, then I wouldn't be acceptable. Is that it?"

"That's not how I meant it!" He caught up with her. "Amanda, what I was trying to—"

A car pulled up at the curb, and, turning, she saw it was Nick's Pierce-Arrow. From the shadows inside his voice ordered, "Get in, Mandy."

It never occurred to her not to obey him. The door swung open, and she slid in. The car's interior crackled with the charge of animosity that inevitably fired the two of them. Neither spoke. For a fleeting moment she felt contrition at leaving poor Larry alone there at the corner, but the sheer power of Nick's presence eroded everything outside the two of them. "Where are you taking me?" she demanded.

For the first time he looked at her, those thick spiky-lashed eyes hard. "I've a council meeting in an hour—enough time to find out what I want to know."

She looked out the window. The office buildings had given way to occasional adobe homes as the car ate up the road toward the Santa Cruz River and the Tucson Mountains. "I thought you knew everything!"

There she went again, letting him get her all upset. Just being around him ignited her burners, so that her anger always seemed to get the best of her.

He ignored her sarcasm. "You said you never wanted to see me. I thought it would be easy enough. After all, I know what kind of a mercenary, sex-hungry female you are."

"Sex-hungry!" she screeched. "That's enough! Let me out! Here! Now!"

He grunted impatiently. "Not until I've said what I have to say!"

He eased the car off the pavement that paralleled the Santa Cruz River bed, which was as dry as dust, into a grove of cottonwoods that clumped precariously along the perpendicular banks. Outside the car the sandstorm isolated them from the rest of the world.

He sat looking straight ahead, but his knuckles were white on the steering wheel. "I thought I could forget you. But I see you in every woman, hear your rum-smooth voice at the most crowded party. My God, when I'm in bed at night, I sometimes think I can even smell that exotic perfume you wear."

What Nick was saying, the angry way he confessed it, as if she were some sort of demon he wished to exorcise, shook her—even more than his abhorrent kisses. "Are you certain it's not your wife's perfume that haunts you?" she snapped, trying to summon the image of the cool, delicate blond beauty as a defense to put between them.

"Danielle and I stopped sleeping together over a year ago. She doesn't want to be bothered with children."

Amanda didn't know what to say. After the moment of surprise passed, she retorted, "You two seemed made for each other—the Beauty and the Beast!"

But that wasn't completely true. Danielle seemed as cold and fragile as ice crystals, and Nick—he would burn like dry ice. At that moment she felt icy cold on the outside, with a fever raging within. "What do you want from me?" she whispered.

His smile was roguish. "I want you."

"That's something you'll never have! The Godwin name, all its money, all your political connections can't buy me." Perspiration broke out at her temples and on her upper lip. For all her defiance, she was shaking. If Nick reached out and touched her, she was certain she would shatter.

"I wonder," he said softly. "Everyone has a price, Mandy." He shrugged. "But that will come in time. Right now it is sufficient to enjoy the pleasure of your company."

She wanted to slap that mocking smirk off his homely face. "And what makes you think I'd give you even that?"

"You mentioned revenge once—I can think of no sweeter revenge of a woman on a man than to tempt him with what she'll never give him. Can you?"

Yes, she could. The idea took root to grow in the darkness of her soul. She was not sure how she would achieve it, but it was enough that she had at last found a path to that end.

"You mean you want to see me, be with me—and yet demand nothing more?" she asked with arched brows.

"Oh, I want more. I want you totally. But that is something you'll give on your own—tomorrow, next week . . . one day."

She knew it was a dangerous game she was playing. But the risk was worth it. "It doesn't bother you that my father's Japanese?" she asked, recalling her earlier conversation with Larry.

"Your father could be Hitler for all I care."

He revved up the engine. "I'll drop you by your house on my way back to City Hall."

During the tensely silent drive back, her gaze involuntarily strayed to Nick's hands, the deft way they handled the steering wheel. She could imagine the way they would manhandle her! Paws!

Nick caught her furious glance. "Good Lord!" he grunted. "What a relationship we're going to begin—you hell-bent on revenge and I intent on seduction. It'll be interesting to see which one of us wins."

Chapter 49

SHE did not know exactly what she expected from Nick. If the previous encounters were any indication, she could probably expect to be mauled. On the other hand, Nick had too much finesse for outright rape. He would enjoy the Machiavellian tactics of a chess master. She imagined him toying with her, leading her through his wily maze and, when she was most lost, maneuvering her into surrender.

After Nick let her out, she went into the house almost dazed. Thinking back over their conversation, she realized it seemed preposterous. No man calmly warns a woman he is going to seduce her and then sets about to do it.

Nick would.

She recounted the impossible conversation to her father. He continued to iron, saying nothing, until she finished. The steam drifted chimerically around him. "Play with passion, daughter, and you will get burned."

Startled, she broke off petting Trouble, who licked at her hands as if they were candy. She looked up at her father. Only in the last year had he really begun to age, and, watching him, she saw the tiredness in those eyes that were usually such a lustrous black. His shoulders were permanently stooped now. "I thought you would at least lecture me about seeing a married man."

He hung the suit jacket he had pressed on the hanger. "It is too late for me to lecture on that. You are old enough to know what you are doing. But to play at passion as if it —as if it were a game of mah-jongg ... more experienced people than you have played and lost. There are no winners in such a game."

"I'm not playing, Father. I'm very serious."

That night at eight a knock at the door brought her face to face with Nick. For a moment she was too stunned to say anything. She never expected him to actually come to her house to see her. But there he stood—imposing, dominating the doorway.

His gaze raked over her, taking in the petal-pink kimono she wore. "I've come to call on your father," he said casually, as if it were the Old World and not America, 1941.

She stepped back and opened the door. Dumbfounded, all she could think was that if seeing how a poverty-level Japanese family lived did not change his mind about wanting her, then her chances of gaining her revenge were better than she imagined. "You'll have to remove your shoes," she told him, trying to keep the derision from her face.

He slid off his wing-tips with indifferent ease and followed her into the back room. Her father, who sat before the *kotaku* drinking his tea, said politely, "Mr. Godwin, please come in and share some tea with us."

Nick folded his solid frame into the cross-kneed position of her father with a little more difficulty than a small slender Oriental would have had. "Thank you, Mr. Shima. I am honored that you will see me, and especially since I assume Mandy has told you already of my proposition."

Her father nodded solemnly before turning to her and saying, "Daughter, tea, please."

Conditioned to serve her father, she bowed and slipped through the screened-off kitchen for the tea service. From the outer room she could hear Nick saying, "I meant Mandy no dishonor by my proposition, Mr. Shima. I want to see her. If I were not married, people would find nothing to talk about. But I am married. A fact I cannot and will not change."

She went back into the living room and, kneeling between her father and Nick, set out the teacups, pouring fresh tea for each man. Her father tasted the tea, and Nick did likewise, seeming not at all discomforted by the silence between him and her father.

At last Taro said, "You have told me of your intentions. And I am honored that you have come to me. But if I were to tell you that I don't approve of what you intend, would that change your mind?"

From beneath lowered lids she saw Nick look at her before meeting her father's questioning gaze. "No. There is nothing this side of life that will keep me from your daughter."

Her father took another sip of tea. "My daughter—she has told you her intentions?"

Nick smiled. "It would seem we are at cross purposes."

"It would seem," her father said sadly, "that there can be then only one unhappy solution."

An entire week passed without Amanda's hearing again from Nick, and she often wondered if she had not fabricated the whole affair in her mind. Thursday, Friday, and Saturday she looked for him at the Casablanca, but he did not come.

Then Sunday she found herself looking at a newspaper photo of him and Danielle at what was supposed to be a private dinner party for the state's leading Democratic politicians. There had to have been at least fifteen or twenty reporters present by the coverage the party received. Governor Stanton was even quoted as saying he would back Dominic Godwin if the Tucson mayor agreed to run in the next senatorial race.

She wadded up the newspaper and hurled it against the dividing screen that separated the kitchen. At once Trouble pounced upon the balled newspaper. Her father poked his head around the screen. "Ahh, so you saw the articles?"

"Does he think he'll manipulate me so easily?"

"My daughter, you accepted his challenge with eyes wide open. He hasn't deceived you, has he? Did he promise you to give up his wife or his career for you?"

"You sound as if you're on his side!"

"No, I'm on yours. But if you expect to win, you can't let your emotions overrule logic."

Then Monday afternoon, crossing the campus, she saw Nick's sleek white Pierce-Arrow. "See you later," she called to Kathy, a brown-haired, pudgy girl who was the only other female in the law class.

Opening the door, Amanda slid inside the car. "I presume you wanted to talk to me?"

He creased a wicked smile. "Until your father gets phone service, this is the only way I can let you know I want to take you out—or have you changed your mind about engaging in a duel of wits with me?"

"You mean you want to take me where we'll be seen in public?" she asked sarcastically.

"I want to take you—period," he growled. He looked away from her as he steered the car through the traffic, saying, "And one day I will—'cause you can't wait for me to. You swish that tail of yours like a heifer in heat."

"Your arrogance is insufferable!"

"For now," he continued, smiling, "I'll settle for your charming company. If you think you can mange to act charming."

"With you it'll take a great deal of acting!"

He disregarded her biting retort. "Can you skip your classes tomorrow? I thought we'd go to the horseraces at Santa Anita."

"The Santa Anita Race Track?" she asked stupidly. "The one in California?"

"The same. We can fly up tomorrow morning and be back in time for a meeting I have at four-thirty."

Slowly she nodded her acceptance. It was difficult enough to try to outguess Nick. She certainly would not have thought that a stadium of forty thousand people would have been the place to choose for the first attempt at seduction.

The fact that Nick did not even bother to kiss her when he let her out at her house only infuriated her more. Apparently he thought he had all the time in the world to work his way with her!

It was an eerie feeling she had about the abominable man, and she indirectly asked her father that night about her feeling—if, like the Japanese Buddhists, he believed in life before birth or after death.

Her father, in his usually perceptive way, said, "Do you think you knew Nick before this life?"

She tied the sash of her kimono before replying, searching for her words. "No, not exactly. But I feel what's between us is bound by the past." She looked up at her father. "It all sounds absurd, doesn't it?"

"Quite." He smiled, and she glimpsed a vision of what a handsome man he must have been when he met her mother. "But then life is absurd. I set out from Japan for the West and my fortune. I found it, but it was not measurable in coins."

She heard the sadness in her father's voice and saw the terrible hunger in his age-ravaged face for the love that had passed beyond him. It was too powerful to look at, and she turned away to roll out their bedmats.

Nick showed up the next morning dressed in brown slacks and a sports jacket. Accustomed to seeing him in expensively tailored business suits or elegant dinner jackets, she found her gaze lingering longer than necessary. She could see above the open neck of the silk shirt where the dark hair cropped up. She was right; he was nothing more than an animal.

His sunglasses hid his eyes, but nevertheless she could feel the sweep of his gaze taking in her brown linen skirt that sheathed her hips and the tan blouse beneath the matching linen jacket that she purposely left open at the neck so that the slightest suggestion of cleavage showed. She wanted to see the same hunger in his face as she had seen in her father's for her mother. She wanted to see Nick suffer.

As usual, Nick surprised her. She expected to catch a commuter plane out to Los Angeles. Not so. At the Tucson municipal airport he had his own private plane, a Cessna.

"Ever been up?" he yelled above the roar of the engines as he ran them up, going over the preflight checkout of the instruments.

She shook her head. She had never set foot in a commercial plane, much less a private one. Aloft she lost all her fear as she gazed at the beauty of the tawny desert and brown mountainous terrain speeding by below her.

There was in the constriction of the tiny aircraft an enforced intimacy. It was difficult for her and Nick to speak above the engine's roar. He sat relaxed behind the half-wheel, yet she knew his eyes scanned the horizon constantly. And she knew he was very much aware of her, the way her skirt hiked just above her knees, so close to his; the way perspiration, brought on by the plane's heated cabin, sheened the valley between her breasts; the way the exotic rose and chrysanthemum attar she wore faintly scented the cabin.

The plane glided into a small dirt-strip airport outside Los Angeles that was only minutes to the racetrack by taxi. The stadium was already full when they arrived, and Nick ushered her directly to the Turf Club at the top, where there was a restaurant and bar—for private members only, of course.

"Ever bet on horses?" he asked as they slid into their seats and he pulled out a program.

"Another first." She leaned over his arm when he opened the program and checked off the horses as they passed by below.

"Some place their bets according to the horse's lines—the conformation," he explained.

"And you—how do you render judgment?"

He passed her the binoculars. "By the jockey. Look at their faces. Nervousness, fear, anticipation—all the human elements are stamped there. I look for the one stamped with greed. It's the one element that will win a race nine times out of ten."

"Oh, does that apply to politicians as well?"

He pocketed the race form and took her hand in his big one. Her breath sucked in at the mere contact. Dear God, if he had this kind of power over her, what would happen if she were ever foolish enough to let the relationship go beyond the simple limitation she had imposed—the flirtatious glances, a casual touch of hands or knees, perhaps even a kiss when she knew Nick was irrevocably hers?

"Yes, Mandy. There's a kind of greed in all of us. Without it, we wouldn't be driven to accomplish what seems the impossible."

The bright, gaudy colors of the jockeys, the auctioneer-like voice of the announcer blaring above the roar of the stadium, the precise beauty of the landscaped track—she stored away these assaults on her Oriental-trained senses for later.

The afternoon passed too swiftly. Nick and she placed their bets, and she had to laugh as she won almost as many times as

Nick. Every so often a waiter in a red jacket would come by their box to take their order or refill their glasses. Three boxes away Carol Lombard held hands with Clark Gable, and one time Amanda glimpsed Cesar Romero passing by with some beautiful young woman.

Throughout the afternoon Amanda was constantly aware of covert gazes trained on her and Nick. Sometimes she would turn her head to catch women, heads together, talking, as they stared. And a reporter snapped a picture of the two of them when they went down to the winner's circle.

The sun was rocking on the Tucson Mountain tops by the time Nick circled over the airfield and delivered her home. The day had been pleasant—but only because Nick had not put his lust-crazed hands on her!

However, by the time she reached the door, the tension she felt strangled her nerve endings so that her emotions were jagged-sensitive. Nick reached across her to open her door, and his arm brushed her breasts. She shivered, and he said softly, "Not yet, Mandy. It's not the right time."

"Not ever!"

He straightened, the corners of his mouth quirking a crooked smile. "I'm gambling you're wrong."

That night she lay silently on her mat, unable to sleep. She played back the mental tape of the afternoon, enjoying the flavors, sounds, and scents of the racetrack, believing she would never have the opportunity to see Santa Anita again.

She could not know she would be there within six months under conditions too horrifying to believe.

Chapter 50

*T*HE following week Nick's campaign manager announced Nick's candidacy for state senator. A grim smile curved Amanda's lips when she heard the announcement on the radio. Her triumph was going to be just that much sweeter.

The next Sunday afternoon, Nick showed up at her door again and informed her he was taking her out to dinner. She looked to her father, but he only nodded, giving her his permission, and returned to the radio program "Eddie Cantor's Camel Caravan," as if his daughter's going off with a married man were a perfectly normal and acceptable thing.

Once inside the car, Amanda folded her arms and asked in as ungracious a tone as she could, "Where are you taking me to eat?"

Nick flicked her an amused glance—as if he didn't buy her disgruntled act for one moment. His arrogance was too much. She couldn't be with the impossible beast five minutes and he had her steaming with irritation! "Nogales," he replied and returned his attention to the superhighway running south out of town.

"Nogales!" She sat upright. "The border?"

"Right."

She settled back in the plush seat, refusing to say another word. She could stay just as cool as he. But just being near him set off an itch. Now he didn't even look at her. Treated her as if she didn't exist. Her first impulse was to order him to take her back. But she kept glaring at those hands that seemed to almost caress the steering wheel. There was black hair scattered on the back of his hands. She shuddered with distaste. Only animals, and crude, coarse, vulgar men, had hair on their bodies. He probably had it running all the way down his stomach to . . .

Now how did such a revulsive image worm its way into her

thoughts? It was the ridiculous way he handled the car—as if it were an animate object, a woman . . . the same almost tender way he had treated the Cessna. And with her he was so rude and rough and overbearing!

The flat roofs of the American business buildings and the housetops on all the hills glistened with the last light of the afternoon. Nick halted the car at the customs house on International Avenue, and an officer waved him on through into the more vivid Mexican side. Once past the gaily colored curio shops and hotels with tiny iron-grilled balconies, Nick turned the car onto Calle Elias, which was bordered by pink, orange, yellow, and white adobes.

At that time of evening the street was filled by vendors hawking handmade leather belts, holsters, and bridles and children selling sugar-coated cigarettes or boxes of tissues. Mexican women wrapped in the folds of bright rebozos slipped quietly along the narrow walks. The Mexican men, as though conforming to a ritual, strolled up and down the sidewalks flashing flirtatious glances at the women passing in the opposite direction.

Nick opened the car door for her, and the pungent smell of Carta Blanca, Dos XX's, and other Mexican beers and liquors from the scores of cantinas assailed her. She wasn't prepared for the kind of restaurant to which he directed her . . . a cavern. La Caverna Restaurant was the only one of its kind for three hundred miles around, and Nick told her it used to be an Apache hideout. The restaurant's manager seated them in a secluded alcove lit by a candle ensconced on the cool, rough-textured wall. She had to admit grudgingly that the atmosphere was exotic, the Mexican food Nick ordered for her excellent, and the five-piece mariachi band dressed in black, silver-conchoed costumes most entertaining. Rather than a Mexican folk tune, Nick requested they serenade her with the currently popular "Green Eyes."

Even in that hideaway restaurant Nick did not go unnoticed. Halfway through their meal a tall, florid man stopped by their table to offer Nick his support in the upcoming senatorial race. Nick introduced her unabashedly. "Mandy—Jim Tyson, our railroad commissioner; Jim—Mandy Shima, a law student at the university."

After Tyson left, she rounded on Nick. "Won't your wife mind the gossip about us?" she snapped, annoyed.

"Danielle is very liberal-minded," he replied indifferently. He tasted the salted Margarita. "I'm sure she didn't expect me to become a monk when she set up another bedroom. She knows there have been other women, and she doesn't give a damn as long as she has all the power and prestige accorded the Godwin name. And as long as she behaves discreetly as a politician's wife—and a Warren—should, I don't care how she satiates her sexual appetite. If she has any."

"Has it ever occurred to you that not all women find you . . . appealing?" Amanda retorted. "You probably just . . . just rear up on them like a bull and—and force them into submission whether they like it or not!"

His grin was infuriating. "If you're curious, I'd be delighted to demonstrate my crude technique on—"

"I most certainly am not!"

"Well, I'm afraid then what I do with other women is none of your business."

"As long as you occupy your unpleasant attentions with other women and leave me alone, I couldn't care less!"

She could not wait for the evening to end and breathed a sigh of relief when Nick deposited her at her door without demanding even a kiss.

Three weeks passed by, too slowly. She was edgy, and everyone knew it—her father, Larry, even Kathy. "What do you expect from a married man? They're after one thing only. And if they don't get it, they move on to another claim."

Amanda did not say anything, and Kathy, still chomping on her spearmint gum, added, "But for a man like Nick I'd willingly give up my virtue." She cast Amanda a sidelong glance and grinned. "If I hadn't lost it already!"

That same night Nick came to Amanda's house. She and her father had already finished dinner, and she was studying for the approaching midyear exams while her father listened to the radio. At the sound of knocking, she rose and went through the darkened business portion of the house to open the door.

Nick leaned against the doorjamb, grinning at her. "Miss me?"

"We don't take laundry after business hours," she said and started to close the door, but he stepped inside, somehow managing to close the door with her between the door and him. He planted his hands on either side of her head. "I would have sworn your eyes were jade-colored," he teased. "But they're not. They're a cool mint green."

She turned her face away, feeling his hot breath playing on her skin. "I missed you," he said, an almost belligerent tone to his deep voice now. "That damned mysterious face of yours haunted me all my waking and sleeping hours. Doesn't that make you happy?" he demanded.

He grabbed her shoulders and slashed his mouth down against hers. His lips moved angrily across her lips, as if he wanted to bruise them, to leave his mark on her for everyone to see.

"Who is it, Amanda?" her father asked from the back room.

Nick kept kissing her. When she wouldn't part her mouth, he nipped at her lips. Her mouth flew open, and his tongue plunged into the intimate cavity in triumph before he abruptly released her.

She wiped the back of her hand across her lips. Her eyes blazed at him. She wished her gaze would burn the man to a cinder. "It's Nick," she called out at last.

Nick slipped off his shoes most naturally and, taking her hand, began walking toward the back room. "I would have been by sooner," he said, as if his visits were of any consequence to her, "but Danielle has become suddenly demanding—even to the point of sharing my bed. I think that like a cat she has scented my interest—beyond the usual—in another woman."

"God help her then!"

"Welcome to my house, Mr. Godwin," her father said.

"Thank you, Mr. Shima." Nick seated himself on the floor with all the ease of an Oriental now despite his solid frame. "I've come to ask you and Mandy to spend Thanksgiving with me—at the Stronghold."

"The Stronghold?" she echoed in an almost reverential tone. She could not have been more astounded had he said the White House. "You're serious?"

"Most." He looked at her father. "Your presence, Mr. Shima, will, of course, prevent me from compromising your daughter."

"And your wife?" her father asked.

"She's flying back east to be with her parents for the holidays."

Taro nodded slowly. "Tell me, Mr. Godwin, why do you want us to come?"

"I want your daughter near me. And since Mandy believes the

Stronghold should be hers, I can think of no better bribe than a weekend there."

"You would set her up as your mistress?" her father asked.

Nick's bold gaze met her father's steady one. "I detest that term, Mr. Shima. I would take the greatest care with your daughter, treasure her as you do. And permit no harm to come to her. I would offer her everything but my name."

"That is something I don't want!" she snapped.

"But you want the Stronghold. And as far as I'm concerned, it belongs to Paul—and his children, if he ever remarries. Yet the Stronghold is still the family home, and I want you there with me for the weekend."

He rose to his feet, towering over her father and her. "I hope I do not offend you, Mr. Shima. You are a man who appreciates honesty, I believe. I would have your daughter. But I am not setting the condition that to stay at the Stronghold she has to become my mistress. That will have to come of her own free will." He shrugged his heavy shoulders and looked at her. "Think about it, Mandy. You can reach me at my office."

"Would you come?" Amanda asked her father after she had deliberated three agonizing days over her decision. The desire to see the Stronghold warred with repulsion for Nick's overbearing masculinity. There was nothing delicate or tender about his lovemaking as she was sure there must have been between her mother and father.

"If I would not?" her father asked.

"Then I wouldn't go either. I wouldn't think of being without you on Thanksgiving."

"Sooner or later you two will have to confront each other— and yourselves. Perhaps Thanksgiving will be the time."

She called Nick from the Casablanca. It was not yet five, and only a few customers were beginning to trickle in for the first show. From the piano Larry watched her, curious. A switchboard operator answered and transferred her call to Nick's private secretary. She gave the efficient young voice her name, and the secretary put her through immediately to Nick.

"Hello, Mandy." She heard the sound of victory in the low thunder of his voice and wanted to slam the receiver down then. Agreeing to go to the Stronghold was an admission of surrender to a certain extent. And Nick would chip away her defenses little by little until she gave herself to him. If she had her way he would go on wanting her the rest of his life.

Taro closed his laundry on Wednesday afternoon and found a neighbor to care for Trouble in their absence. Amanda arranged to have the Friday and Saturday off, though Mike was not too pleased at the idea. But after a year she had built up a following, and she knew he did not want to push her into quitting.

Nick came by for her and her father Thursday afternoon. It was one of those perfect Indian-summer days. The Empire foothills were alive with fragmental shades of autumn—oranges and reds and browns. The Pierce-Arrow covered the narrow winding road in rapid time. As far as the eye could see, Nick told them, was Cristo Rey. The Huachucas, Santa Ritas, and Whetstones served as its boundaries. Amanda kept thinking, this could have, should have, been mine.

Cristo Rey's ranchería was a mass of crumbling ruins, but Amanda could truly say she was not disappointed when she saw the Stronghold. As stately mansions go, it did not compare to some of the elegant Victorian homes found in the Paseo Redondo section of Tucson. But it was imposing—as Nick was. She saw it first silhouetted against a magnificent sunset of pinks and purples. Her breath caught. Nothing could be more beautiful!

Yet by the time they drove up to the gates the Stronghold was even more beautiful—incredibly beautiful, lit up as it was with a thousand lights to contrast against the sudden black velvet of evening. Nick allowed her that one tantalizing view, then drove on through the wrought-iron gates, telling her they had replaced the heavy timbered ones that had rotted away. The earthen-walled castle that reared up behind the original adobe fortress had been added by Elizabeth Godwin, he told her dispassionately, after her grandson, his father, Brigham, went to Tucson to live with Nick's mother.

Nick took them on a brief tour of the castle turrets and cathedral room with skylights that spanned the original adobe and the castle. He pointed out the billiard room that was *de rigueur* for the wealthy in the years after the turn of the century. Then there was the enormous library and the conservatory to see. Despite Paul Godwin's absence, a wealth of servants unobtrusively kept the Stronghold going. And the stable of thoroughbreds and garage of roadsters and Rolls-Royces testified to his occasional visits.

For Amanda it was like coming home. A sense of belonging pervaded her, especially when she walked through the fortress's courtyard to her great-grandmother's bedroom. It was an austere room, almost like a nun's and cool and musty from disuse. Religious tin paintings graced the walls, and a bed and hand-made bureau occupied the otherwise bare room. She could imagine Doña Dominica waiting there for Don Francisco, as Catherine must have waited for Lorenzo.

Nick did not seem to find it strange that she wished to stay in that room rather than in a much nicer guest room provided in the castle proper. When she and her father joined him for Thanksgiving dinner that night in a dining room that would seat at least fifty, it seemed completely right to her that she should be there.

After dinner a retainer, an old Mexican man, served liqueur in the parlor that housed Paul's growing art collection. "He brings a painting home from almost every country Roosevelt sends him," Nick said, adding grimly, "which are becoming fewer in number as Hitler's armies march across Europe."

He paused and looked at her father. "That brings me to something else I wanted to talk to you about. Eventually we will become officially involved in the war. I'm sure you've already experienced some anti-Japanese sentiment. But it could—and will—get much worse. I fear for Mandy's safety."

Her father set his cup on the round marble-topped coffee table. "I also, Mr. Godwin. But there is nowhere we can run and hide. And this is my country now."

"If war comes, promise me you'll accept my protection—promise me, Mr. Shima, that you'll bring Mandy here."

Her father rose. "No, that I cannot do. I submitted to this one visit to Cristo Rey, Mr. Godwin, because I hoped to quench my daughter's unnatural thirst for the Stronghold. I am hoping she will see that it is only a pile of rock and wood that with time will be nothing but rubble."

He left the parlor then, his stooped shoulders carried with dignity. Nick crossed to her and took her cup from her trembling hands. He set the cup on the coffee table. "Your father is right, you know."

When he pulled her to her feet, an intense urge to flee the room that was dominated by his presence swept over her. But he

(*315*)

held her tightly to him. "Isn't this what you wanted? To tempt me, to make me half mad with wanting you?"

She tried to push him away, but he ground his fingers into the soft flesh of her buttocks and pulled her against him. "Can you feel what you do to me?" he asked thickly. He jerked one of her flailing hands down and pressed it against him, and the rock-solid bulk frightened her. She was no match for Nick. The balance of power could easily shift in his favor.

When she would have wrenched free, he lifted her in his arms and carried her through the *zaguán* out into the courtyard. He reached Doña Dominica's old bedroom and set Amanda down, pinning her against the door. "No!" she hissed. "Leave me alone!"

"It's my time now," he rumbled. His hand slipped down to the fork of her legs in a half-slap and half-caress that did not cease until he heard her groan. Then he released her abruptly. "Sweet dreams!" he snapped and stalked off into the darkness.

She hated him! Hated him! She rolled restlessly in bed from her right side to her left. The itch between her thighs was unbearable. Damn Nick Godwin! He had known, and she hadn't, that a man could make a woman burn like that! It was unfair—and cunning of him. Surely this hunger for what he could give her would leave her system. If she could just hold out against him.

At last she went to sleep and awoke in a vile, ruffled mood. Now she knew why the female scorpion stung her mate to death. She dressed in khaki pants and a beige cotton shirt and headed out to the stables that had been built after the old ones were torn down to make way for the addition to the Stronghold. Apparently Paul retained only three horses in his absence, but they all appeared to be thoroughbreds. She chose a stocking-footed chestnut that took her out to the Cristo Rey wildlands and away from Nick Godwin.

She rode southeast toward the Fort Huachuca military post— toward the craggy foothills and rock-strewn arroyos that her mother and grandmother must have often ridden. Her long hair blew out behind her, and though the early morning temperature was still cool, in the fifties, the sun warmed her face. Beneath her thighs she could feel the heaving barrel of the animal as it galloped unrestrained.

Once the friskiness was out of both the horse and herself, she settled her mount into an easy canter, always heading southeast. It was not as if she expected, at twenty-four, to see the Ghost Lady—as she had at six and seven. She did not scout out every lonely, twisted Joshua tree in some eerie expectation of an apparition.

Still, seeing the lone rider and horse loping toward her was like *déjà vu*. She pulled up on the chestnut and sat waiting for her past to approach. When the horse was close enough she saw that the rider was a man of perhaps forty-five or fifty—a handsome man, in a dignified sort of way, with silvery hair and mustache.

"Hello," the gentleman said, moving his black mount alongside hers. "You must be Amanda."

She canted her head, puzzled. Swiftly she scrutinized the ascetic features—the high brow, the contemplative eyes, and the refined line of the lips, so unlike Nick's more carnal, unforgiving features; yet she knew the man was his stepbrother. "You're Paul, aren't you?"

He smiled. "It seems we've met before—about fifteen years ago, wasn't it? You were just a—"

"Tomboy," she supplied, matching his friendly smile. "Yes. Though I'm surprised you would remember."

"Nick never let me forget. It was beyond his realm of comprehension that a girl like you existed."

"He talked about me to you?"

"He still does. And I must confess, Amanda, that I was prepared not to like you."

Her eyes opened wide. "Nick's description was not flattering, I take it?"

"On the contrary, he's quite infatuated with you." Paul leaned forward on the saddle horn. His eyes swept over her with the practice of a man who has met and entertained many women. And yet there was a sadness in them, and she instantly guessed he still mourned his dead wife. "Shall I be blunt?" he asked.

"By all means."

"I envisioned you as a homewrecker. Oh, I know Nick's had other women in his life since he and Danielle have gone their separate ways. But you're the first woman he ever brought to the Stronghold. When he called Washington and asked me to fly down to meet you over the Thanksgiving weekend—well, I was

(317)

quite prepared to dislike you. In fact, I had almost decided not to come and only at the last minute changed my mind."

She bristled. "What's between Nick and myself is not quite what it seems."

Paul chuckled. "So I've learned. Nick informed me—in his most irritating manner, this morning—that you have no interest in becoming his mistress. At first I marked this as a feminine ploy calculated to snare my stepbrother. Then Nick told me that you believe your grandmother was the rightful heir to the Stronghold."

"Not *believe*—I *know*." She shrugged. "But there is no way I can prove it."

"So you will settle for tormenting Nick?"

"To match your bluntness, yes."

"Marvelous. My stepbrother deserves to have some of his male arrogance deflated. And you seem to make the perfect adversary. I'm going to like you very much, Amanda Shima."

Chapter 51

AMANDA and Paul rode back to the Stronghold together, friends now, talking of trivial things. Nick was in the stables checking out the shoe of the third horse. At their approach he set the hoof down and rose, brushing off the dust and hay from his jeans. The way they hugged his hips, the way the plaid cotton shirt stretched tautly across the enormous bull-like shoulders, was too much. His raw masculine virility was blatant, overwhelming.

He raised a brow when Paul helped her down from her mount. "So she's beguiled you also?" he asked his stepbrother with a half-grin, half-sneer.

"So much that I'm setting myself up as her protector."

Nick glanced at her but only said, "Watch out, Paul. She stings." He took the saddle from the stable railing and slung it over his mount. "Either of you want to join me?" His mocking look challenged her, and she was relieved when Paul answered first. "Not me. I've got some briefs I've got to cover before Monday."

"I need to check on Father," she hedged.

Paul retreated to the library that was in the Stronghold's new addition, and she played a game of chess with her father before he retired to his room for a nap. The rest of the afternoon she spent exploring the Stronghold. Her hands ran lovingly over the pockmarked walls, and her eyes committed to memory the tree-shaded courtyard and the old one-eyed adobe ovens. One did not see those reminders of an Old World's Shangri-la any more.

Nick found her in the kitchen looking over the copper and wooden utensils that had to be almost a hundred years old. "Did the Bible warn against idol worship?" he asked gruffly.

She whirled, and he trapped her against the butcher-block counter, hands at either side of her hips. "Isn't that what you're doing—making an idol of this place?"

"And what did the Bible have to say about adultery?" she snapped.

The door opened, and Paul stuck his head inside. "Oh, pardon me. What I was going to say can wait until later, Nick."

"No, that's all right," she said. "Go ahead, Paul." She glared at Nick. "We're finished."

Paul saved dinner from being an uncomfortable challenge between Nick and herself by keeping the conversation on light topics. Only once did he become serious, when he addressed her father on the war.

"I think you should know, Mr. Shima, though it is still highly confidential, that the United States is imminently prepared to enter the war against Japan. Even at this minute our forces are on standby alert at Clark Air Force Base in the Philippines. Japan has been building up her arsenal in the Pacific. I think you can appreciate how this could affect you and Amanda. Nick and I've talked about the results here in the United States—about what a declaration of war against Japan could mean to you—but Nick tells me you refuse to accept his aid."

"That is so," her father said.

Nick sat opposite her, saying nothing. The smoke from his

after-dinner cigarette veiled his gambler's eyes, but she knew that he watched her. What had prompted him to speak to Paul? Or was Paul speaking purely out of his own concern now?

Paul leaned forward, his handsomely aristocratic face set in solemn lines. "I hope you'll reconsider, Mr. Shima. Nick is here close by, where he could do something immediately if the need arose."

"We appreciate your concern," was all her father would say. She knew he was too proud ever to accept help. And then again, she did not think he really believed—nor did she—that anything could occur in America so catastrophic as to reduce them to begging for help.

Nick and Paul lingered over after-dinner liqueur to talk, and she and her father excused themselves to retire for the evening. She thought for certain she would have no trouble sleeping. Lying in bed, she wondered how her grandmother had kept warm during the winter months when the weather happened to be harsh, for there was no fireplace in the room. She snuggled deeper beneath the comforter, though it was not really cold.

She could just imagine a warming pan at the bottom of the bed, or maybe even a hot brick or hot-water bottle . . . just as she could imagine the footsteps of Law Davalos passing outside her grandmother's door . . . as she suspected Nick's would.

But the footsteps never came, and the hours ticked by. She was wretched. It was Nick's fault for pounding this feeling, this miserable, debilitating desire, into her.

At last she bounded from the bed and stormed out of the bedroom without even bothering to throw on the rose-pink robe that matched her pajamas. The nippy night air cleared the cobwebs from her mind but not the heat from her body. Overhead the sky was studded with diamonds. Yet she cared not, nor did she notice the fragrant scent of the oleander that mixed with the fecund odor of the warm earth drifting from the courtyard.

She stalked down the open portico to Nick's room and rapped on the door. It opened immediately. The room was dark, but she could still make out that he wore only his jeans. His bare skin glowed where the black hair did not whorl about his chest. He stood back, saying nothing, and let her pass by him. Closing the door, he flipped on a dim lamp.

She whirled on him. "I came to tell you that it's not worth it! Staying here at the Stronghold is not worth putting up with you! I want to leave—first thing tomorrow morning!"

He looked at her beautiful face framed by the sleek midnight hair that brushed the curve of those ripe buttocks. He ached to pick her up and put her on the bed. He hurt with the need to burn his way inside her, to set her aflame as she did him. How could any woman fire him up the way she did, standing there in those damned virginal pajamas? She could!

He turned away and sat down on the edge of the tumbled bed. "All right," he said, as he removed first one boot, then the other. "Paul'll take you back tomorrow."

He stood up and began to unzip the jeans. She froze. That terrible gnawing was still between her legs. Dammit, why did she have to want him every time she was around him? He made her behave just like the animal he was. Well, she had more self-control. She'd show him she was stronger, more civilized! She refused to move while he stripped out of the jeans. Then she audibly gasped in the tense silence of the room. He wore no undershorts! He was exposed, engorged!

He never took his eyes off her the entire time. "I know why you came," he grated.

She pivoted and streaked for the door, but he reached it with her, trapping her. Too proud to scream, she stood rigid as his hands divested her of the pajama top. It dropped to her bare feet. He scooped her up and crossed to the bed, dumping her on it. She glared up at him with eyes that would have slashed him to ribbons had they been stilettoes. He jerked the bottoms off and stood looking down at her naked body.

She knew she should spring up now, run, naked, from the room while she still had a chance. "You beast! You damn rutting bull!"

He ignored her and mounted her, tearing into her. A soft moan escaped her lips as the pain winged through her. She tried to shove away the torso that plunged and hammered at her. But there was no halting it. And then she didn't care. The pain was gone, and he was giving only pleasure. It was all wrong, but it didn't matter. Not at that moment. Only the intense, breathtaking sensation. The terrible need. He drove into her and pulled back, and she followed, not wanting to lose him. And then he would slam against her again.

She hated him! Hated him! Still, she could not help herself. Helplessly she followed his lead. Had to. The whole room was afire with their savage battle of desire. She was afire. Only he could quench it.

Nick felt her explode, tightening about him, drawing him into her. And he exploded. "Dear God," he whispered, his breath hot against her face, "it seems like I've waited forever—for eternity—for you."

She looked up at him—at the strength in the contour of his bones, the roughness in the shadowy stubble of his jaw. Nick Godwin was very real, a very powerful force out of the present, not the past. Yet it was the past that had bound her to him.

She rolled away from him and sat up. Her hair curtained her perfect breasts, but her nipples, still aflame with passion, thrust through the silky strands. "You've raped me," she said tonelessly.

The tender look that had eased the harsh lines of his face faded. His muscles bunched, but he only said, "Did I?"

She rose to her feet, standing as proudly as a high priestess. "I warned you I would have my revenge. Now I shall."

The eyes shuttered over. Once more they were the politician's unrevealing eyes. "Oh? How so?"

"Do you seriously think you can take a mistress and not have it affect your political career?" she raged. "The public would never elect to the legislature a married man who's keeping a mistress. And I plan to let your constituents know that I've been your mistress! I'll tell every nauseating detail!"

The smile that slowly creased his face frightened her. "That is where you're quite in error, Mandy. The public couldn't care less if I keep a mistress. What they would never countenance is my making the mistress my wife. That is a social *faux pas*. And you would never be anything but a mistress, my dear, because you can be bought. Your price is high, but you can be bought."

Chapter 52

AMANDA was miserable. Unlike the spider, she had entrapped herself in her own web. She wanted Nick, needed him, as much as her mother must have needed the opium when Taro rescued her from Ling Chuey's. But this was a physical need, Amanda told herself, that could be satiated with the consummation.

The hunger of her soul for the Stronghold was something else. And throughout the long, lonely night in her great-grandmother's room she damned the Ghost Lady and her own mother for bequeathing her the hunger for something that would never be satiated.

The next morning Nick was already gone—riding, Paul told her. He himself was leaving later that morning to catch the next flight out of Tucson for Washington. Apparently Nick had said nothing to him of what had happened the night before, because at breakfast he said, "You have shadows under your eyes, Amanda. Didn't you sleep well last night? This old house gets drafty at times."

"I sometimes expect to meet a ghost whenever a draft does sweep through," she joked as she spread marmalade on her biscuit. She looked up to find her father watching her, and she could tell, despite his usually inscrutable expression, that he suspected her nocturnal visit to Nick's bedroom. She blushed, wondering if Paul also suspected.

She set her knife across her butter plate. "The fact of the matter is," she said, looking first at her father and then Paul, "Nick and I are making each other miserable. We each want what the other cannot give. Paul, can my father and I ride back into Tucson with you?"

Surprisingly, she thought she detected a look of admiration pass over Paul's face as he replied that it would be no problem.

She was anxious to be gone before Nick returned from riding. She did not want to face him. He was as formidable an opponent as Elizabeth must have been. Amanda feared his strength of will over her more than his physical or political power. If she was not careful, he would easily dominate her, her very thoughts, her soul even.

The admiration she had seen in Paul's eyes could not compensate for the deep ache that writhed inside her on the trip back into Tucson. As if sensing her agitation, Paul said, "You mustn't think too harshly of Nick. His life hasn't been that easy."

"I don't think of him one way or another," she lied, looking out the car window. Dammit, there was another one of those Joshua trees. Ugly, eerie things, no matter how romantic the tales told about them.

"Amanda," her father reprimanded from the back seat of Paul's rented Packard. "Your rudeness is—"

"No, please, Mr. Shima," Paul said. "My stepbrother's directness can be abrasive sometimes, which somehow seems to appeal to his constituents.

"But in his defense I must say something about his life—well, really about my great-grandmother. Elizabeth was awfully disappointed when my mother kept bearing children who died in infancy. Elizabeth wanted an heir. By the time Mother gave birth to me, I think she was—worn out. And, quite frankly, I think she knew my father never loved her. I used to hear their arguments, though I never understood what they were about. And then every once in a while I heard my father arguing with Elizabeth. Good Lord, she had to have been at least eighty or more, but even then she was a domineering old woman.

"Then, when I was a freshman in college, my mother died. The day after her burial my father moved out of the Stronghold and within six months married a widow carrying a posthumous child—Nick, or Dominic, as he named him. I think in honor of the original owner, your great-grandmother."

"A small bit of retribution," Amanda said thinly.

"Anyway," Paul continued, "my father and his second wife, Nick's mother, Laura, were killed in a senseless auto accident when Nick was three or four, I don't remember exactly. I was in France fighting." Paul flashed her a small smile. "World War I, so that should tell you how much older I am than you."

He returned his attention to the road. "The courts sent Nick to live with Elizabeth at the Stronghold. When I returned from the war to finish college, I drove out to Cristo Rey whenever I could to visit Nick. It was obvious the old woman barely tolerated him. Oh, she saw that he was fed and clothed, as stipulated by the courts, but love—I don't think she knew how to give it. Occasionally I took Nick into Tucson for a movie or a ballgame. But I don't think Nick ever forgot the horror of his dependency on her. I think that's why he's determined to climb his way to the top. You know, when Elizabeth finally died, Nick refused to come with me to the funeral. For that fact, not many people did. Not even her granddaughter—my Aunt Abigail. My father's sister hated everything about the Stronghold."

Paul glanced at her. "Perhaps I'm stepping out of bounds, saying all this. But I feel it needed to be said. I don't want anything standing in the way of our friendship."

Amanda expected her life to return to normal after that. Resolutely she put Nick from her mind and concentrated on her studies, which had suffered some in the time she had been seeing him. She had a letter from Paul the week after he returned to Washington, telling her how much he enjoyed meeting her and her father and that he hoped all was well now. She tried to read between the lines, but, of course, Paul was probably too much the diplomat to reveal anything other than the polite exchange demanded of a social letter.

She did not see or hear from Nick, with the exception of his name on the radio or occasionally his photo in the newspaper. And then anger at him and her own weakness would flood her, and she would switch off the radio or flip the page of the newspaper. At least the arrival of her period brought the good news she was not carrying the brute's child. But that damnable hunger for Nick persisted, a burning thing that was difficult to ignore.

Then early in December something happened that wiped all thought of Nick from her mind. She was fixing Sunday dinner—mashing the potatoes—when the radio announcer interrupted "Kaye Kaiser's Music Hour" with the report that Japan had destroyed the naval and air bases at Pearl Harbor and Hickham Field in Hawaii.

When the news commentator, H. V. Kaltenborn, reported minutes later that the battleship *Arizona* had been sunk in the bombardment, she dropped down on her knees next to her father. The news of the sneak attack by Japan continued to cut in on regularly scheduled radio programs the rest of the day. She and her father remained rooted to the radio cabinet. Each time an announcement was made, they looked at each other ominously, saying nothing, feeling only a great sense of shame.

Immediately after the attack on Pearl Harbor, newspapers blared out that the FBI had arrested selected enemy aliens, including 2,192 Japanese. She secretly hoped that would be the extent of the government's operations against the Japanese in America.

But the peace that was supposed to come with Christmas died out by the year's end. After that things had the quality of a nightmare that began in fear and continued in hysteria.

At work Larry showed her a copy of the *Los Angeles Examiner* in which a syndicated Hearst columnist, a Henry McLemore, had written, "I am for the immediate removal of every Japanese on the West Coast to a point deep in the interior. . . . Let 'em be pinched, hurt, hungry. Personally I hate Japanese. And that goes for all of them."

Very few Japanese lived in the Tucson area, although there were quite a few Japanese farmers outside Phoenix. She and her father began to hear and read about department stores, gasoline stations, and restaurants refusing to serve Japanese. The Chinese even took to wearing buttons proclaiming, "I am Chinese."

Then the next week the Arizona legislature passed a bill forbidding Japanese to buy anything but food, not even a bar of soap.

She experienced little trouble with the prejudice because she did not look Japanese; however, on campus, where her identity was known, she several times heard calls of "Buddhahead!" Once someone threw a tomato that splattered at her feet. But there were so many students around her when this occurred that she was never certain who was responsible. It made no difference; it did not bother her. But she did worry for her father.

She knew that he would be refused service if he ventured outside the Barrio Libre. Inside the Barrio, life continued as normal, as normal as could be expected under the wartime's abrupt conditions ... the gas rationing and belt tightening, housewives lining up for ration coupons and their sons standing in queues outside recruiting stations. In the Barrio, though, there was no racial prejudice, and she, therefore, assumed her father was safe from persecution.

Then, on February 19, President Roosevelt signed Executive Order No. 9066, authorizing the Secretary of War to establish military areas in the West Coast area and to exclude from them any and all enemy aliens. Her father, an issei, a Japanese emigrant, had never qualified for citizenship, since he had been too old to serve in the armed forces in World War I. He was therefore an enemy alien!

The "enemy alien" edict could have meant Italians, Germans, or Japanese. But then came Public Proclamation No. 1.

She sat in the campus's cantina, shaking her head as she read about it on the front page of the *Arizona Daily News*. General John DeWitt, as western defense commander, had set up the western half of three West Coast states and the southern third of Arizona as a military area—from which all persons of Japanese blood were to be removed, even those American-born, known like herself as nisei. This applied to anyone having as little as one-eighth Japanese blood.

At first she was enraged. Not the Americans of Italian or German ancestry, only the Japanese! Kathy and Larry were just as angry. "They won't do it," Kathy assured her. "A hundred and ten thousand Japanese on the West Coast—where would they put them all?"

"It has nothing to do with the war!" Larry said. He hit the table with the flat of his hand. "It's those California pressure groups!"

"You know how they feel about the cheap Oriental labor, that it threatens them," Kathy tried to console. "Not everyone feels that way."

"Really?" Amanda asked bitterly. "Listen to how Governor Clark of Nebraska feels. 'The Japs live like rats, breed like rats, and act like rats. We don't want them in our state.' "

She knew that for the most part, what Larry had said was true. In California, 1942 was an election year, and the labor unions and the various farmer associations were putting pressure on the politicians.

To her dismay at least one politician spoke out on the mass

evacuation of the Japanese. A small paragraph quoted Nick as saying, "The Japamericanese are just as much American citizens as those whose ancestors came to this country via the *Mayflower*."

She knew that one paragraph would probably be the only communication she would ever have again from Nick. They had both made it clear they wanted nothing further to do with each other; yet Nick was supporting her and her father indirectly.

Living in the Barrio as they did, and with her lack of obvious Japanese features, she figured she could manage to avoid being interned in one of the fifteen assembly centers appointed to house Japanese aliens and citizens until war relocation centers (or concentration camps, as she heatedly called them) could be constructed.

But her rage slowly altered to fear as little by little over the next few weeks the world began to close in on her father and her. It began with Mike's announcement that he would have to let her go. "It's not that I want to, you understand," he said, looking everywhere but at her. "But, doll, word's gonna get out we're employing a Japanese, then we're gonna be in trouble."

Fine! she thought. No money, no food. What her father made in his laundry business was not enough to feed and house them and keep her in college. She would have to draw out a portion of her meager savings to tide them over until she found another job—using an alias this time!

She left the Casablanca and walked the three miles to the bank she used. She waited what seemed an inordinate amount of time for the teller to return. At last the young woman returned. Her face was flushed. "I'm sorry, Miss Shima," she mumbled, "but the Treasury Department has frozen your account."

At that moment Amanda ludicrously thought that the teller's face had to have looked more stricken than her own. She was simply stunned. Slowly she treaded back to the nearest bus stop only to halt zombielike before a poster affixed to the brick wall of a building.

INSTRUCTIONS TO ALL PERSONS OF
JAPANESE ANCESTRY LIVING
IN THE FOLLOWING AREAS

Dazed, she read on.

A responsible member of each family, on Friday,
May 2, between the hours 8:00 A.M. and 5:00
P.M., will report to the Civil Control Station where
they will be:
1. Given advice and instructions on the evacuation.
2. Provided service wtih respect to storage or
other disposition of property.
3. Transported with a limited amount of clothing
to new residences.

Riding home through the darkened streets, she vowed she
would not report to the Civil Control Station to be penned like a
cow—or war prisoner, which was what she actually would be—in
a concentration camp.

When she walked in the door that night her father's face told
her that he had already heard about the latest mass-evacuation
order. She did not have the heart to tell him about their frozen
bank account right then.

"We must keep our faith in the ultimate good of American
democracy," her father counseled, unable to hide the deep sorrow that clouded his eyes. "By voluntarily complying with these
orders we will prove beyond doubt that we *are* loyal American
citizens."

She turned on him, forgetting he was her father. "Next you'll
be believing that they're incarcerating us for our own good—to
protect us from public sentiment!"

She grabbed up the newspaper and held it out to him, her
hand trembling with her anger. "Look! Do you think the U.S.
government truly gives a damn about us? Read what General
DeWitt feels about us. Read it!" She began reciting the statement
attributed to the General. " 'A Jap's a Jap, and their American
citizenship is only a piece of paper as far as I'm concerned.' "

"If you still have faith in American democracy, you're a foolish
old man," she cried.

For the first time in her life her father struck her, slapping her
cheek. They faced each other, tears streaming down both of their
faces.

Chapter 53

AGHAST at her own behavior, Amanda apologized to her father, throwing her arms about his emaciated body. He seemed smaller to her, or was it that she had only imagined him so much larger in her childhood—a giant with muscles like the rocks he shattered.

As the weeks passed in tense despair she realized her father was slowly wasting away. True, he coughed little more than before, but it was as if their argument had driven him to a point of apathy.

Two days before the May 2 deadline for registration for evacuation, her father came down ill with a cold that made simple breathing a labor for him. At any other time she would have gone for a doctor. But now not only did they not have the money but there were, of course, no doctors inside the Barrio, and she was reluctant to seek a doctor outside for fear he would report them to authorities if her father required treatment past the deadline for evacuation.

The only consolation for her father's illness was the fact he was not able to register as the head of the family when May 2 dawned. As a nisei—a first-generation Japanese born as an American citizen—she could be considered the head of their family. Yet she knew she would never register. She would never willingly submit to being interned like livestock.

Her father required her constant attention those next few days, but she made plans as she sat with him or worked on his customers' laundry. She would change her name (why had she been so stubborn with pride before?) and move them to the East, where there was no mass Japanese internment. Maybe New York, where a large colony of Japanese lived. She would worry about money for the move and her father's acquiescence to the move when the time came. At the moment she was only concerned with getting him well again.

Trouble's agitated barking warned her they had a visitor even before the knock came at the door. It was late, past nine, and she knew the visitor would not be a laundry customer. It briefly crossed her mind that it might be Nick, and she suddenly had as much difficulty breathing as her father did. Realizing what she must look like—the curl she so painstakingly put in her hair wilted by the iron's steam; her hands chapped and reddened from the laundry lye—she reluctantly made her way to the front door.

It was not Nick but a man of the same solid, muscular build. He was dressed in a business suit. "Miss Shima?" he asked.

She nodded.

He held out his hand, palm up, and she almost shook it when she noticed the black leather wallet. "FBI, ma'am," he said as politely as if he were one of their laundry customers.

She was Lot's wife turned to a pillar of salt. When she was unable to reply, he continued, "I'm sorry, but I will have to talk with you and your father. May I come in?"

She blinked, finding the situation akin to some horror tale of the Gestapo suddenly appearing at the doors of Jewish homes across Europe. "I don't have any choice, do I?"

He shook his head wordlessly. For a moment she thought she detected embarrassment in his nice-looking countenance. "It's either here or at headquarters."

She led him through the curtained doorway to the back of the house. His eyes assessed the small partitioned room in a professional manner. If he was surprised or appalled by what he saw—the bareness of the room, her father lying weakly on the mat, her dressed in a kimono—he gave no indication.

He introduced himself to her father—John somebody, she couldn't remember later—and proceeded to inform her father that he was with the FBI and was there to inquire why they had failed to register for evacuation.

"Because it violates the Fourteenth Amendment," she snapped behind him. "All persons born or naturalized in the United States," she recited bitterly, "shall not be deprived of life, liberty, or property without due process of law; nor be denied the equal protection of—"

"Amanda!" her father thundered. "I'm sorry," he told the agent. "Please continue."

The man shifted to the other foot but made no effort to defend her accusation. "It will be necessary for you—or your daughter, if you are unable—to come down to the Civil Control Center to register for evacuation first thing tomorrow morning. If you don't, I'm afraid things could become much worse than they are."

It was not a threat but a simple statement.

"My father's a sick man!" she protested.

"There'll be doctors at the assembly centers and the camps who'll give him excellent attention—most likely Japanese doctors," the agent assured her.

"I will be there," she said shortly and showed the agent to the door.

At eight-thirty she reported to the First Methodist Church, which was designated as a Civil Control Station. Soldiers were standing guard at the entrance. There were several staffed desks inside. With no registrants, the clerks were buffing their nails or reading the funnies.

The woman who interviewed her told her she would be appointed the head of the family unit of two. Their family name, Shima, was reduced to No. 24553. She was given several tags bearing their family number. At another desk she made the necessary arrangements to have their household property stored by the government. She was instructed that she and her father could bring with them only what they could carry in two hands. They were to bring bedding and linens for each member of the family, toilet articles, extra clothing, sufficient eating utensils including plates, bowls and cups, and work clothes suitable to pioneer life (boots and dungarees). Lastly she was told no pets of any kind would be permitted.

On the way back to the Barrio she stopped off at the university. She was supposed to graduate with her Bachelor of Law degree in three weeks. When she asked the counselor if she could get her diploma early, he looked at her regretfully. "I'm sorry, Miss Shima. Really, I am. But it would be breaking the rules. You might petition your local congressman."

If Nick won the senatorial election the coming November, she would be petitioning him—something she knew she would never do. She had to grit her teeth to keep from screaming at what seemed the injustice of it all. "No, thank you, Mr. Browne," she managed to say pleasantly.

The bespectacled man looked almost as unhappy as she felt, and as she reached the door, he said suddenly, "Miss Shima, I can possibly arrange for you to finish the term through a correspondence course. Would you be interested?"

She turned, blinking back her tears. Not everyone was as prejudiced as she believed. "Yes, yes I would."

Enthused by the possibility now, he continued, "And maybe, with a lot of luck, I can get you admitted to the bar when you finish—'on motion.' That's without examination. It's not often done, but all I can do is promise you I'll look into it."

She crossed to his desk and bent over to plant a kiss on his shiny forehead. "Thank you, thank you very much, Mr. Browne."

She told herself that with a lot of luck, as the counselor had put it, she would be the only practicing lawyer in a concentration camp.

After she left the blushing counselor, she found Larry at the cantina. "It must be bad," he said when she sat down opposite him.

She nodded. "I registered for evacuation today."

"Ohhh. It is bad then." He reached out to cover her trembling hands. "If it'll help any, the Casablanca's business is off now that you're not there singing."

She tried to smile. "Thanks, but it doesn't help any. In addition to all the other inflictions, we're not allowed to bring our dog with us."

It seemed as if everything she was experiencing was nothing compared with the simple act of giving up Trouble. She supposed the relinquishing of the dog represented the culmination of all the traumatic events in the past weeks. "Would you keep him for me, Larry? Until I return?"

He smiled. "I now consider myself the proprietor of one mongrel dog."

She worked feverishly the rest of the day, buying work boots and jeans, trying to find duffel bags—which the stores had long since sold out.

Her father seemed better when she returned home. While she sorted out the things they would take with them into two different piles on spread sheets, her father delivered the last of the cleaned laundry to his customers. The remainder of the night the two of them finished packing what would be stored in government warehouses.

Her father worked alongside her, though more slowly, saying little. She knew he would never complain, but it must have been difficult leaving. Yet he had voluntarily left his home in Japan as a boy of seventeen—so perhaps she had underrated her father.

Throughout the night, even as late as two in the morning, neighbors would drop in to say goodbye as word spread that the Shimas were leaving. Each time her father would halt his work and graciously offer hot tea. She did not think any of the Hispanics had ever acquired a taste for the green tea, but they just as graciously accepted a cup and drank the bitter brew without betraying their distaste.

The next day, before Amanda and her father presented themselves at the church's Civil Control Center, they stopped outside the university's Student Union Building, as she had arranged with Larry. Within minutes he appeared, greeting her father awkwardly. Then he bent down to scratch Trouble's ears. "So this is to be my roommate for the next—" He broke off clumsily, realizing that none of them really knew how long the Japanese would be interned.

Amanda knelt and rubbed her cheek against Trouble's soft muzzle. "Goodbye, boy." Her voice broke.

Together, she and her father trudged away with Trouble's lonely, confused yelping filling their ears and hearts. At the Civil Control Center she and her father were handed two train tickets. Only then did she discover their destination—the Santa Anita Race Track.

Chapter 54

SANTA Anita Race Track. Incredible! Impossible!

Amanda and her father were processed in the same large room (now known as the Intake Room) from which she and Nick had watched the race the year before. After they were processed, along with two thousand more weary Japanese who came in that day, they were assigned to Barrack 15, Stall 5.

She stood before the empty stall, not really wanting to accept the fact this was happening. Although two army cots had been installed, horse manure still covered the floor. A single bulb hung from the ceiling. "There is a lot we must do," her father said phlegmatically at her side, "and not much time before the ten-o'clock curfew."

She had not thought to bring a broom, but her father had packed a whisk brush. Tediously she swept the board floor while he packed the two mattress tickings they had been given with the hay provided in one corner. When the stall was as clean as could be hoped for and their beds made with the sheets and blankets they had brought with them, they collapsed on the cots, their backs against the low wooden partitions. In the glare of the naked light they looked at each other—Amanda's face stunned, her father's sorrowful.

"Shall we hit the hay?" she asked in a woeful attempt at humor.

From all around came the crackling of the straw as others settled in their stalls. On either side of them was the murmur of conversations. The entire stables seemed to echo with rumbling snores, babies' crying, and the grinding of teeth. As she lay in the darkness, listening to the sounds of human habitation, she thought nothing could be worse.

The reality of the next day was. Roll call was held at 6:45 A.M. and again at 6:45 P.M. by the house captain of each barracks.

And always there existed the "queue-ups"—for mail, checks, showers, meals, laundry tubs, toilets, clinic service, everything. And in between there existed only the boredom.

To pass the time until they could be transferred to the more permanent settlements now under construction, people made victory gardens, knitted, read, or played cards. But as Amanda ambled aimlessly about the track that first day, she noticed that many people, mostly the issei from the old country, sat idly, even sleeping in the open beneath the grandstands. Detained in a camp, life held no promise. Daily existence was desultory, monotonous, and worse, self-defeating.

She was determined she would not let this apathy happen to her father. The next week she organized *goh* and *shogi* tournaments—Japanese games somewhat similar to the American chess and checkers. Her father and a lot of the other issei men particularly enjoyed these matches and showed up every night in the mess hall after dinner. By the end of the second week the supply of game boards was exhausted, and she had to appeal to the camp director to order more boards from the Sears catalog—this time the American chess and checkers.

About that same time, to her delight, her correspondence courses began to arrive. With something to keep her busy, she did not find herself with empty time on her hands as did many of the other women. Day in and day out she plowed through the law journals until her eyes hurt with the strain.

Her father sometimes drilled her through the course's questions, but she noticed that he looked as tired as she those days. She compelled him to visit the camp clinic. There were no facilities for testing for tuberculosis, but one doctor, an overworked young Japanese, agreed with her opinion that her father had the disease.

"Almost all the war relocation camps are located in the desert areas," he told them while his fingers massaged his bloodshot eyes. "There—on the desert—I feel your condition will not deteriorate, Mr. Shima, and may even improve as it did when you lived in Tucson."

The doctor offered hope. More than that, he offered romance, or Amanda supposed she would call it that. He began to stop by and visit with her and her father once or twice a week, ostensibly to check on her father. But more often than not the doctor talked with her.

Bob Niiyama was of medium height and slender; and attractive. Like herself, he spoke Japanese fairly well but could not read or write it. His manner was gentle and courteous, and, as they talked of different things—philosophy, religion, education (but never the war)—she found that Bob reminded her of a younger Paul Godwin.

Sometimes she and Bob would attend the motion pictures which were shown weekly in the grandstand, elbowing for a place on the floor alongside the other patrons who brought blankets and pillows. At other times they would play a game of *shogi,* and she won almost as often as he did, which did not seem to bother his Oriental's masculine pride.

All her life it seemed she had known but one man, that like a homing pigeon she knew only one direction—Nick's. She thought of it as a hate/lust relationship. Thus when Bob's fingers sought and curled about her own in the darkness of the makeshift movie theater, she let herself take another man seriously for the first time.

That was the way it should be, she told herself. She had been trying to fit in a world where she did not belong. She was not of her father's old world, nor did she belong in Nick's Anglo world. Bob, a nisei like herself, understood that netherworld.

She alone joked with him. "The least the war relocation authorities could have done was to run the horses once a week. It would relieve the tedium and"—she smiled at him—"add some money to my pockets. I was getting to be a pro at betting on the horses."

"You've been here before?" They were walking along the infield at sunset, holding hands. Bob stopped and looked at her, really looked at her, his warm brown eyes moving slowly over her face. "There is so much about you I do not know, that you do not say. I want to know all about you—what you were like as a child and how you grew into such a beautiful person."

"I was a tomboy," she replied curtly and changed the subject.

It was bad enough that the thought of Nick tended to crop up without her summoning him, but worse was the occasional sight of his name in the newspapers to nag at her the rest of the day like an unrelenting fly.

In addition to the political notes the newspapers carried about Arizona's most colorful politician, there appeared innuendoes in the gossip columns. "What roguish mayor from the Grand Canyon State was seen in Hollywood escorting a very lovely (and quite married) actress to the Brown Derby?" asked Hedda Hopper. Walter Winchell said, "The old-world custom of dueling may soon return to Hollywood if a curtain rakish politician out of Arizona continues his 'love em and leave em' courtship of Hollywood's top film stars."

When Amanda and her father had been at Santa Anita a little over two months, she received a letter from Mr. Browne. Inside was her Bachelor of Law certificate and a congratulatory note confirming that the State Bar Association had confirmed his "on motion" in her behalf.

Bob showed up that evening with a jar of real oolong tea. "All you lack is the swearing-in," he told her, "and you are a full-fledged lawyer."

While she poured the black tea into tin cups, Bob talked to her father. "I have come not only to celebrate your daughter's achievement, Mr. Shima," he said, bowing low, "but also to request your permission to marry her."

A Caucasian female would more than likely have been surprised, and perhaps chagrined, that her suitor had not consulted her first, but Amanda, like Bob, had part of the Far East in her blood. The three of them sat on the two cots—her father and she on one and Bob opposite them.

Bob continued to speak, earnestly but in a low voice, for there were always ears to hear. "Mr. Shima, your daughter is everything I have ever hoped for in a wife. Beauty, intelligence, warmth. She is good for me; she makes me forget for a few hours the conditions here—the people and the burdens they carry. She is what my soul has been waiting for. I would like to take her as my wife."

"Assuming that Amanda feels the same," Taro said, "I would deem it an honor to have you for my son-in-law."

Bob held out his hand to her, smiling tenderly. She swallowed the lump that was lodged in her throat. She put out her fingers to touch his, but her hand fell limply on the mattress. "I—I'm sorry," she incredulously heard herself say. "But . . ."

"But what?" Bob asked patiently.

She could not speak for fear of crying. Her father said, "I believe, Dr. Niiyama, that as your soul has been waiting, so has my daughter's . . . and it has not yet found what it is it waits for."

Bob looked down at the cup of tea he held in his interlaced hands. "Love, honor, justice," he said slowly. "They are only abstractions. They can be dealt with. But the searching of the soul . . ." he let his voice trail off.

Setting aside the cup, he rose and bowed low once again before her father, then took her hands, which lay lifelessly now in her lap. "Amanda, I will not easily forget you. I hope we will continue to be friends."

For a few more weeks they *were* friends. She even began to assist Bob in the clinic with the other nurses, but at the end of the day she left the clinic on shaky legs and with a queasy stomach. The gashes, the diarrhea, the vomiting—apparently nursing was not in her blood.

Bob was always grateful for her assistance and politely attentive, and every so often she caught those intelligent eyes watching her wistfully. Yet their friendship did not and could not return to the same easy one it had been before he declared to her father his desire for her to be his wife.

Thus it was almost with relief that she received the news that she and her father would be among the first of five hundred shipped out to one of the newly completed war relocation camps.

She knew that Bob must have been aware that they were among those leaving, but he never mentioned it. When the day arrived for their departure, he was conspicuously absent from the clinic. She thought about searching for him. Instead she picked up her duffel bags and made her way toward the line of gleaming luxury buses waiting to take away the five hundred evacuees and the fifty military policemen. Bob knew what he was doing . . . a goodbye among friends was sometimes better left unsaid.

Her last glimpse of the Santa Anita Assembly Center made her smile. Some of the evacuees had climbed to the stable roof and were holding up large bon voyage signs while others waved. She saw Bob among them, waving. "He is a good man," her father said.

Quickly she blinked and turned her face back to the window as she blindly waved goodbye.

The trip by train was miserable. The aged engine creaked rather than chugged. Inside, dust covered everything. And the gaslights did not work most of the time, leaving the passengers in total darkness because of the rule that all shades were to be drawn and no one was allowed to look out of the windows.

Some of the Japanese became trainsick and vomited. These were people who had never traveled farther than the walk required through the Japanese ghettoes of San Francisco or Los Angeles. On the aisle across from Amanda a woman nursed her five-day-old baby. The infants cried incessantly, and the older children were restless.

At last, after a day and a half, the train halted. More buses waited to transport the evacuees through nineteen miles of greasewood-covered desert. The last half of the distance was over rough, newly constructed dirt roads. Straining to see through the alkaline dirt that the line of buses kicked up, Amanda gradually realized that the relocation project—their home indefinitely—looked, if possible, worse than their temporary assembly center had.

Desolation stretched out before them with only the hundreds of tar-paper black barracks marching row upon row to relieve the landscape. Barbed wire, about which soldiers could be seen patrolling the area, encircled these barracks. Every quarter mile or so were formidable watchtowers. A few telephone poles stood like sentinels to remind her that a type of civilization did exist out there.

There, according to the large sign over the guarded gate, was the Poston, Arizona, War Relocation Camp. The buses halted one by one to disgorge the evacuees into the mess hall, which served as the induction room. It was a scene of confusion as clerks (both men and women), stenographers, interviewers, guides, and baggage carriers wove their way among the tables.

Amanda looked about her, feeling a great sorrow for the sweating people who clutched at their children's hands and held onto bundles as they tried to assimilate what was next happening to them. While they waited to be assigned barracks a whirlwind rotated through the camp, spraying clouds of alkaline dust into the mess hall and sending papers flying in all directions.

Her father began to cough violently, and one young Caucasian lady was nice enough to point out the row of cots in the rear of the room. There another young girl gave him icewater, a salt tablet, and wet towels. "I'm all right," he reassured Amanda. "Return to your place in the line."

He closed his eyes wearily. She was reluctant to leave him but knew the sooner they were assigned a room the sooner he would be able to rest.

The female interviewer asked her about her former occupation, and Amanda learned that they were all to be assigned jobs—with the unskilled workers receiving twelve dollars a month and the professional and highly skilled qualifying for sixteen to eighteen dollars.

Since practicing law was out of the question, she was assigned to the local newspaper, the *Poston Preview,* receiving sixteen dollars a month. Her father requested a job, despite the fact he didn't need to work, and was assigned a position as cook for twelve dollars.

Finally they had their fingerprints taken and were trooped out across an open space and into another hall for housing allotment, photographs, and a cursory physical examination before being loaded onto a truck with their hand luggage and driven to their appointed barracks.

She and her father were assigned to Block 9, Barrack 11, Room G. They discovered there were six rooms to a barracks and twelve barracks to a block. Every block had its own mess hall, recreation hall, and combination laundry, showers, and toilets. The two of them trod to Room G and were left to survey a room ten by twenty feet with bare boards and beams and knotholes through the walls. In that space as many as three to five people were to live indefinitely!

It was completely bare, furnished only with a ceiling light, a closet space near the door, and three army cots. But they did have two windows. A two-inch layer of alkali dust covered the Masonite floor. They were told each room was intended for three and that they would soon be receiving a new member to their "family."

Forty-five minutes later the third member knocked at the door. Amanda opened it to confront a middle-aged, stout man with broad features and a large handlebar mustache. To her he looked exactly like a sumo-tori wrestler.

He introduced himself as Sam Tsuruda, a keibi—an American citizen who had been educated in Japan. After he settled his luggage, he began a nonstop discourse, telling them he was a widower from Portland, Oregon, who worked as a salesman for a wholesale produce company and going on to tell how he later operated berry farms in Washington.

But always as he talked Amanda could feel his eyes sliding

over her, assessing her. She knew that the next day she would appeal for another member to be selected for their "family."

For that night she had to be content to string a blanket, sectioning off her and her father from Tsuruda's ogling eyes.

Chapter 55

AMANDA, you got that column ready yet?"

She looked up at Betty Yasaki, the copy editor of the *Poston Preview,* and shook her head, sighing. "After the administration staff sees this, I may find myself looking for another job."

The young woman smiled and pushed her rimless glasses back atop her head. "The worst that can happen is they'll haul you out of the barracks in the dark of the night and shove you before a firing squad. Here, let me see the column."

Amanda took a deep breath and handed it to her. For three months she had been writing the "Poston Patter," an innocuous column that kept the residents informed about the center. Her duty consisted mainly of collecting the suggestions and news items turned in by each of the barracks' stringers she had delegated and combining the news into a twice-weekly gossip column.

But Thanksgiving was the following Thursday, and she had decided that a special column was in order. Perhaps reading of Nick's election to the state senate two weeks before spurred her on. For three days she had agonized over each word of the column. She knew the words by heart.

> The precious freedom of which we Americans are so proud is not stolen from us in the sinking of the *Maine* or the riddling of Pearl Harbor, for this only fires our patriotism to greater effort. Our freedom is forfeited inch by inch through such innocent words as "compromise" and "convenience,"

and "it's not that important." Then one day we find that our freedom has evaporated. Not only in the small daily things we do but, shockingly, in the spirit of our lives.

"I see what you mean," Betty said. "I feel censorship hiding around the corner. You want me to take it on over to the administration offices with the rest of the columns, or do you want to appeal to the administrators in person?"

She shrugged. "I think my appeal would make little difference."

Surprisingly, the Poston administration offices chose to run Amanda's column. Thanksgiving Day she was stopped many times in the mess hall and congratulated. And that evening people living in their barracks came by to thank her for expressing their own feelings about patriotism. For actually, most of the interned families were very proud of being Americans.

Privately, Amanda often wondered how they could feel so, especially when two weeks later a family in Betty's barracks received word their son had been killed in action in Italy . . . while they were still behind barbed wire. A mass meeting was held the following Sunday for a memorial service to honor the Japanese-American soldier. All the faiths were represented—Buddhist, Shinto, Christian—and even some former members of the American Legion participated.

About this same time Sam Tsuruda began to make trouble for Amanda. She had been able to persuade administration that if her father and she had to share their quarters with another member, they preferred a woman. Tsuruda's dignity was highly affronted, and he moved out his belongings in a huff. As it turned out, the young woman the administration offices assigned to their room had just married three weeks before the evacuation in April. Less than two weeks after she settled in their stall the red tape was processed, and she was happily on her way to join her husband at the Topaz relocation camp in the Utah desert.

The affair with Tsuruda was not so happy. For the first few months Amanda merely felt uncomfortable in his presence. But then, toward October, he was appointed their barracks house captain. It was the house captain's duty to make the rounds once a day and report the roll call held every morning and evening at curfew. Amanda began to notice that Sam lingered longer in their room, supposedly checking their quarters for, as preposterous as it seemed, weapons or communications apparatus. For a while she and her father managed to ignore him.

Nick, it seemed, she could not ignore. Once Betty caught her reading an article in the *Saturday Review* about a business deal Nick had syndicated between Howard Hughes, the government, and several minor investors. "The business coup of the year will mean a Hughes Aircraft Company site near Tucson and more jobs for Arizonians," announced the *Saturday Review.*

"Why the sudden interest in Howard Hughes?" Betty asked, reading over Amanda's shoulder.

"I know the gentleman," Amanda said curtly. "Nick Godwin—not Howard Hughes."

"Wow!" Betty breathed. "Isn't he the owner of that palatial estate near Tucson—the Ironhold or something like that?"

"The Stronghold," Amanda corrected, smiling. "Yes, I guess you might say he's more or less the owner," she said, repeating a phrase Nick had used at their first meeting.

Christmas Eve day she rose earlier than usual in order to get a shower before the stampede began to the combination laundry/washroom. Like everyone else, she wore only pajamas and robe as she made her way to the washroom. The winter wind was terribly cold and strong sweeping down across the open desert, and she was in too much of a hurry to reach the warmth of the washroom to look where she was going.

She was thinking how grateful she was for her homemade *getas,* the traditional wooden clogs, because they were built high enough to clear the mud puddles that swamped the area about the washroom. Next she looked up to find Sam Tsuruda blocking the washroom door.

"You're out early, Miss Shima."

She shivered as the wind whipped around her, blowing her robe high. "No earlier than you." She made to move around him, and his stocky body stepped between her and the doorway again. "You're breaking curfew law," he said, leering.

How she wanted to tear that greasy smile from his face. "At six forty-five the curfew is lifted—ten minutes, Mr. Tsuruda. I can't imagine administration throwing me under lock and key for taking a bath ten minutes early."

His protuberant eyes slimed their way down the length of her body, fastening on to the way the wind-whipped robe clung to her curves. "They wouldn't have to know about it, would they? They wouldn't have to know about extra rations of clothing or extra portions of food."

"Mr. Tsuruda, I am cold! Now are you going to let me pass? I don't intend to freeze standing here arguing with you."

"I can keep you warm," he muttered. His arms went about her in a bearlike hug. Together in the semidarkness of dawn they struggled. "This is ridiculous!" she raged, helpless as his hands fumbled at her robe ties while his mouth groped across her twisting head for her lips. She tried to scratch him.

Somehow, in the jostling, he slipped in the muddy water, splashing mud over both of them. She lunged for the door, more to keep her balance than in hope of the refuge it offered. She looked down at Tsuruda, who looked so silly sprawled face down in the mud, and burst out in laughter. He staggered to his feet. A drop of mud clung to the broad tip of his nose.

"You dare to laugh!" he roared like a bear.

Quickly she stepped inside the washroom, leaning against the closed door as she gasped with laughter. By the time a birdlike old woman arrived to do her laundry on the washboards, Amanda had recovered her aplomb. The outlandish incident was over as far as she was concerned.

When she returned to her quarters, her father was still in bed, which was unlike him. He was coughing, trying to sit up. She put one arm about his waist and the other around his shoulders and maneuvered him into a sitting position. She hurried for the cough medicine the clinic doled out and poured a teaspoon. The clinic kept saying he would improve more visibly after the winter was over.

But the cold at Poston seemed far worse than the winters in Tucson. Their rooms froze at night, and Amanda would take their extra clothing and lay it over her father. "It's no use." He smiled at her as he swallowed the vile-tasting medicine. "It's my bones that are frozen, daughter."

"We shall take care of that," she said, smiling. With the little she had saved from her monthly salary she had ordered a sheet-iron stove through the community cooperative. That night, Christmas Eve, her father would be warm for once!

She put him back to bed and tucked the blanket from her bed

around him. "I'm going to help decorate the mess hall for Christmas," she told him, kissing his still-smooth cheek. "And I shall be back soon with some breakfast."

She was in and out the rest of the day, checking on her father. By dinnertime he felt well enough to go with the rest of the evacuees to the mess hall. Christmas seemed forced as they trooped inside for the special dinner. Some of the younger men and women concocted a drink of grape jam and lemons, but it took a great deal of imagination to pretend it was the real thing.

More than one time during the Christmas Eve celebration she caught Tsuruda's weasel eyes on her, lingering over the way her jeans hugged her derrière. For once she wished the grape drink was inebriating. The gloom of the camp and her father's worsening condition combined with Tsuruda's blighting presence depressed her more than ever.

Later that night she lay awake, listening to the man and wife in the room next to theirs as they made love. The whispered words, the gasping pants. She thought about Bob. Should she have married him? But as the woman's soft cry of ecstasy reached her ears, it was not the thought of Bob that burned like a fever in her thighs and the pit of her belly. Her legs twitched. She tossed on her stomach, then on her back again. She pounded the moldy pillow with her fist and flopped it over, trying hopelessly to fluff it.

"You're not waiting up for Santa Claus?" her father teased from the other side of the room.

"Hardly." At dawn, just as she was getting to sleep, her father began to cough again, and she gave up and rose for the day.

On New Year's Day two events occurred—an ominous forecast of the year to come, she thought. She was leaving for the mess hall again, this time to help in the making of *mochi,* a special kind of rice used in celebrating the traditional Japanese new year. But as she put on the shabby coat, her father began to cough. This time blood spittled the handkerchief that he tried to hide from her. Even the black stove warming the room from the corner had not seemed to help.

Reluctantly she went on to the mess hall. She barely heard Betty as the young woman ran on about the special guy she was interested in who lived in the bachelors' quarters. Amanda's mind agonized over her father as she pounded her wooden mallet into the rice.

Betty, working the sticky mass into rounded cakes, said, "I have told Tim about you, and he is very much amazed that you, a female, are a lawyer."

"Not quite," Amanda replied dryly. "If I had already been sworn in, you can be sure I would have challenged the whole constitutionality of the evacuation."

Betty's fingers halted in shaping the cake she held. "How?"

Amanda smiled. "No need to be impressed. It's not that difficult. I'd file a writ of habeas corpus, contending that the War Relocation Authority has no right to detain loyal American citizens who are innocent of all the various allegations the Army used to justify our evacuation."

But her smile faded. It *was* difficult—impossible—without her Certificate of Admission to the Bar. Less than two or three months and she would have been eligible for the swearing-in and her certificate! She smashed the mallet down on the boiled rice with a satisfying thud.

She left the *mochi*-making early, anxious to get back to her father. Outside the room's flimsy door she could hear his hacking cough. When she entered, he smiled, but she could see the strain of his illness written in the shadowy eyes and the skin that was far yellower than his natural coloring. "We're going to get a doctor," she announced firmly, trying to hide her fright.

Her father caught her wrist. His bony fingers still held a surprising amount of strength in them. "Amanda, a few hours either way isn't going to make much difference. It's New Year's. Let the doctors celebrate. Tomorrow will be soon enough."

At first she refused to return for the New Year's celebration, but her father insisted. Knowing he would only wear himself out in trying to make her go, she acceded, though she did not plan to stay long.

As it happened, she never made it to the mess hall. Since she was late leaving their quarters, everyone was already at the mess hall. She hurried along through the shadows, clutching her coat around her. Suddenly a gorillalike figure loomed before her. Mistakenly, she judged it best to keep walking rather than show fear. She began to veer to the lighted portion of the dirt street. The shadowy figure lumbered across her intended path, and now she saw the face. Sam Tsuruda.

"What do you want?" she asked, forcing a calmness to her voice her pounding heart did not feel.

"*Inu!*" he growled. "Bitch!"

She took a step backward, prepared to run. "You are a silly woman," he hissed. "You do not know the proper respect that a true Japanese woman should show!"

"I am not a Japanese woman." Another small step backward. "I am an American."

Tsuruda's hamhock hands grabbed for her. "You are a traitor who must be disciplined!"

She dodged, but his hand caught her coat. The buttons gave way at his yank. She tripped and went sprawling in the mud.

"No!" she screamed. She kicked out and must have struck his groin, because he released her immediately and doubled over with a bellowing grunt. She scrambled to her feet and ran. In her ears she could hear her frightened panting, but she was afraid it was the footsteps of an infuriated Tsuruda closing in on her.

The door to her room gave way under her panicky hands. Her father turned from where he lay on his side and looked up at her. "What is it?" he demanded.

She crossed to her cot and sat down, shaking. "I don't know. I—I suddenly didn't feel well."

"Your coat—"

"I was hurrying back and stupidly didn't watch where I was going. I—I tripped over that barbed wire around that septic-tank hole and tore it."

She did not think her father was thoroughly convinced, but at that moment he was probably feeling too bad to investigate further. She lay there on her cot, staring throughout the night at the skeleton roof of the ceiling and listening as one by one their neighbors returned to their quarters, laughing and singing.

Their festive spirits annoyed her. She could not seem to think logically. Everything seemed so bleak. She kept telling herself that at night—in the darkness—things always seemed worse than they actually were. But the next morning, gray and overcast with another approaching cold front, the state of affairs seemed no better.

Sam Tsuruda continued to hound her, although as yet he had made no further overtures. Her father's situation was even worse. One morning six weeks later, when he did not feel well enough to rise from bed, she knew something had to be done.

She went to the mess hall to get some breakfast for her father, hoping she would not run into Tsuruda. He frightened her almost as much as her fear for her father's health did. She vacillated over reporting Tsuruda to administration. But Tsuruda was a barracks captain and carried considerable influence, while administration was well aware of her discontent with its policies. She doubted she would get much sympathy from them. She could, of course, request a transfer to another barracks, but that would hardly assuage Tsuruda's wounded vanity.

After she fed her father, she went to the clinic. The doctors— there were three to serve Poston's twenty thousand people—told her that unless her father was dying, she would have to bring him to the clinic to be checked.

"He is dying," she told the oldest doctor, who looked tired himself. Dr. Niosha glanced through her father's file, which noted only a moderate case of tuberculosis. But she was persistent.

The doctor ran his fingers through his graying hair. "I'll come over to your barracks at lunchtime then."

Taro agreed apathetically to let the doctor check him. The two old men bowed low after she introduced them, but her father immediately sat down again, weakened by the small effort.

Dr. Niosha took his stethoscope from his black bag and, after ordering her father to remove his shirt, began to listen to his wheezy breathing. After taking his pulse and temperature, he turned to her, saying, "The tuberculosis is, of course, degenerative, but it's pneumonia I'm concerned about right now. It seems to be a mild case, but it needs to be watched carefully. We'll have to move your father into the clinic, where he can receive immediate attention. I'll make arrangements at once."

That afternoon she watched the camp ambulance halt in front of their quarters and load her father into the back. She held his hand before they took him away, telling him she would be by to see him as soon as she finished work.

But she did not go to the newspaper's office. She walked the three miles through the freezing wind to the administration offices, a white two-story frame building. She knew that she and her father had to leave. It wasn't just Sam Tsuruda's threatening presence. She would not let her father die inside a concentration camp.

Taking a number, she waited her turn to see the project

director. He was an older man, a Caucasian, with salt-and-pepper hair and a kindly face that gave her hope her request would be granted. "Yes?" he asked when she took her seat before the desk that was mounded with papers.

"I have been told that the WRA is permitting a few Japanese families to leave the camps if they are sponsored by reliable persons on the outside."

The project director folded his hands before him. "This is true. But it often is difficult to find sponsors that the WRA will approve. Usually a church or even a large company, like Goodyear or Westinghouse, guaranteeing housing and employment, is what the WRA looks for. And right now we have very few such offers and a long line of waiting families."

"I realize that. But I believe I can present a sponsor for my father and myself who will more than satisfy WRA's requirements for sponsorship."

"Oh? Who?"

"Senator Nick Godwin."

Chapter 56

"*I* will not have you obligating yourself for me," Taro declared vehemently as Amanda began to pack their things. "We must all die sometime."

She continued folding their few belongings into the duffel bag. "True. But you are not going to die in a concentration camp. And I am not obligating myself."

Knowing the emotional war that existed between her and Nick, her father was most reluctant to leave Poston despite the wire Nick had sent immediately in response to the project director's wire of inquiry. Nick informed the project director he would be most happy to serve as sponsor and assured the WRA that housing would be found for her father and herself as well as employment when Taro Shima's condition had stabilized.

The last thing Amanda did before they left Poston was to give the highly prized sheet-iron stove to Betty. The two women hugged each other tearfully. "As soon as I put out my shingle," Amanda said, blinking back her tears, "I'll represent you in court. We'll get you out yet."

A passenger train was to take them to Phoenix, Arizona's capital, where Nick and Danielle now resided. Her father found it wasteful that an entire sleeping coach should be reserved for the two of them. Amanda tactfully remained silent during the trip. Looking out the window as the train puffed to a wheezy halt in the Phoenix depot, she wondered just exactly when Nick would demand compensation for his benevolent gesture of assistance.

If there ever was a blackguard, it had to be Nick Godwin. He had waited, warmly ensconced in the capitol building, biding his time. He knew that sooner or later she would be driven to surrender. The only thing that would probably save her from being attacked right there in his car would be her father's presence! Would even that stop a determined man like Nick Godwin?

When she and her father descended the coach's steps, a brown-uniformed man of perhaps fifty years greeted them with a wheelchair. "Miss Shima?" he inquired politely.

She nodded, puzzled, and he said, smiling, "Senator Godwin told me I would recognize you by your hair. He has sent me to bring you and your father to his house. He apologizes for not being able to meet you personally, but he is in a committee session right now."

Nick's limousine edged its way through the capital's noon traffic and out Center Street past the sparsely settled suburb of Scottsdale. She supposed she should not have been surprised to learn that Nick had leased a luxurious guest-ranch resort. A glistening white stucco one-story building with a red-tiled roof, it sprawled eleven miles northeast of Phoenix in the valley between the Camelback and Mummy Mountains. Nick had assured the project director they would be furnished housing—but a villa? What would Danielle think about Amanda and her father's coming to stay? Nick must have been out of his mind to actually bring her and her father to his house.

When the chauffeur halted the limousine in the drive that

encircled a large multi-tiered fountain, she leaned forward and said, "Is Mrs. Godwin in?"

The chauffeur's sun-wrinkled eyes darted a furtive glance in the rear-view mirror. "No, ma'am. Mrs. Godwin's in New York."

Oh, that was just great! Now there was no watchdog to ward off the beast!

Then, with watchdogs still on her mind, a large scruffy mongrel followed on the heels of a stout, aging woman who came down the flagstone walk to welcome them. "The housekeeper, Mrs. Rawlings," the chauffeur introduced.

But Amanda wasn't even listening. "Trouble! Father, it's Trouble!" she cried, kneeling to wrap her arms about the ecstatically yelping dog.

An enigmatic smile passed over her father's face. "It seems Mr. Godwin intends to be at his most persuasive while we're here."

Apparently Trouble wasn't the only surprise Nick planned for them. Both Amanda and her father were astounded to find a nurse in her father's room. The tiny old lady in white, who must have been as old as Taro, straightened from fluffing the bed's pillow. "Mr. Shima! I've been expecting you all morning." She practically bubbled. "I'm Nurse Haines, and Senator Godwin has hired me to look after you."

Taro bowed as much as could be permitted from the wheelchair the chauffeur pushed, but not before Amanda saw him roll his eyes heavenward. "I am a blessed man."

She ignored the frustration in his voice. "It'll be good for you to be pampered for a while."

"I'll help you out of those clothes," Nurse Haines said, "and we'll get you comfy-cozy."

Taro darted a beseeching look at Amanda as the woman began to work the ill-fitting coat off his shoulders. "Enjoy yourself, Father," she said, smiling. "I'll look in on you once I've settled in my own room."

After the small, chilly quarters of the camp, the room Mrs. Rawlings showed her was palatial. Warming sunlight streamed through the triple arched windows to fall on the large bed's hot-pink spread and the terra-cotta tiled floor. Luxuriant foliage of all sizes and kinds filled the colorful *mesetas* set decoratively in the room's corners and even in the private bath off her bedroom. Hibiscus, miniature orange trees, bougainvillea. Incredible. She had not seen any green vegetation in almost a year. How different was the bedroom from the barren cold room she had known at the post relocation camp; how different from the barren rooms she had known all her life.

After she unpacked and put away the few clothes she had in an immense rosewood dresser, she and Trouble wandered the labyrinthine corridors that emptied onto fountained patios and riotously blooming gardens. A view from the den displayed a nearby tennis court fringed with tall poplars and a kidney-shaped swimming pool landscaped with boulders, paloverde, and cacti. Farther off, against a backdrop of foothills, was what appeared to be riding stables.

The den was furnished in a Western pioneer decor—complete with a wagon-wheel light fixture, branding irons and coyote skins on the rough cedar-paneled walls, and leather-upholstered furniture. A warm, comfortable room, it even had a hand-carved bar of pine opposite the stone fireplace.

Mrs. Rawlings, who was passing through the den, told her that there were two other dens and twelve guest rooms.

"And Mr. Godwin," Amanda asked, "when do you expect him?"

"The senator usually returns anywhere from six to midnight, depending on how long a committee session may last," the woman replied, seeming not at all curious that her employer had a strange woman in the house. But then Nick and his wife no doubt entertained guests frequently.

Amanda hoped he would be quite late returning, because she felt unprepared to do battle with him. After she looked in on her father, who seemed to be resting comfortably (in spite of Nurse Haines—who sat in one corner reading a lurid detective story aloud), she returned to her room to take a bath.

She let a heavenly sigh drift upward as she settled in the sunken tiled tub, hair piled on her head. Jasmine-scented bubble bath lapped her breasts. How heavenly it would be to sleep the evening away in the tub.

Finally she emerged to change into the white kimono, the only item in her belongings that was not jeans or khaki pants. She had no perfume or cosmetics to play up her almond-shaped eyes or the childlike curve of her lips. Nick would have to take her as she was—as the lord takes his concubine, for had she not sold herself for a price?

At seven, with Trouble at her heels, she stopped by her father's room again, and Mrs. Haines was spooning broth between his recalcitrant lips. "Now, Father," she admonished him, "you'll feel much better if you do as Nurse Haines tells you."

He sighed and dutifully opened his lips for the determined old woman. Satisfied that her father seemed to be doing better, she went on into the dining room. It was dominated by a large rectangular dining table of oak and a long buffet near the jalousie doors.

She took a seat at the nearest end of the table, feeling lost in the huge, empty room. Recalling the mess halls, often crowded with as many as five thousand people, the loud interchange of conversations mingling with the shout of children made unruly by the lack of discipline, discipline that the families were unable to administer under such conditions, she shuddered. Yes, she would sell herself again if need be to take her and her father out of such a place.

Mrs. Rawlings served the gazpacho soup first with a rosé wine, then, as she brought in a sizzling steak (real beef, Amanda thought, dazzled), Nick entered the room. He stood in the double doorway, jacket slung over his shoulder, watching Amanda. Slowly she lowered her wineglass. Her stomach somersaulted as he walked toward her and pulled out the chair opposite her. He did not say anything at first, but the way his gaze traveled over her was almost like a physical assault.

When Mrs. Rawlings left, he said in that low rumble of his, "So, you didn't marry while you were at Poston. There was a doctor courting you, but that was at Santa Anita, wasn't it?"

"You knew?" she gasped.

He began to loosen his tie, his sun-browned fingers working at the collar of his La Costa silk shirt. "I told you, Mandy, you're a part of me." He stated it dispassionately, not as a romantic declaration but rather as a simple fact. "You don't think I'd ever forget what's between us, do you—or let you be interned in some hellhole?"

"But you did!"

"No, you let yourself. But I wanted to be there when you needed me, so I kept track of you. By the way," he said carelessly, "your columns were quite good. You should be a journalist instead of a lawyer."

Mrs. Rawlings entered with a bowl of gazpacho and another wineglass. When she left, Amanda said, "So you knew. You even went as far as getting Trouble back for me. Why?"

"You need to ask? I want you, and I'll buy you—bribe you—in any way I can."

She ignored the wicked gleam in his smile. "What must everyone here think about your installing me in your home? And what will Danielle say?"

He tested the soup. "They'll think just what I told them—that you're a distant cousin." His eyes twinkled. "You are, aren't you? And as for what my wife will say, I really don't care. She's not happy out here in the desert and has taken up residence in New York."

Mrs. Rawlings brought in a steak and set it before Nick. After he thanked her, he said, "I've made an appointment for your father to see a doctor tomorrow—depending on how he's feeling after the train trip. The doctor is the best in Phoenix. He'll run X-rays, a battery of other tests, and—"

"You didn't have to do that. I can arrange for my father to see a doctor and take care—"

"You forget, Mandy—"

"Don't call me that!"

" 'Amanda' doesn't fit your looks." Her beauty staggered him. In her was refined the best of the American and Oriental characteristics. But it was more than just the high cheekbones, the jet-black curtain of hair, the seductive shape of the green eyes—it was the tremendous combination of the Western drive and daring and the Eastern spirituality that almost created a tangible aura about her person.

"And it's your exotic looks that the WRA has made my responsibility," he told her now.

"Just what does that entail on my part?"

He set his fork on the plate's edge. His angry gaze slashed into her defensive one. "Nothing." He sighed and resumed eating. "Was it bad—the camp?"

She shrugged, not wanting to weaken her defenses with the kindness he seemed to be showing. She must remember he wore the facade of the smooth-tongued politician. "It could have been worse. We had food and clothing—and a roof over our heads."

"You're thinner. And you're looking tired."

It unnerved her the way his gaze ran over her, seeming to note every feature as if he possessed her. He did possess her. "I could say the same for you," she retorted. "You looked tired." Yet he certainly did not look thin. His powerful build dominated the room.

He set aside the steak and took up the wineglass. "It's been a long day. I'm bushed."

Watching his lips touch the rim of his wineglass, she knew what he was hungry for. She saw it as her gaze met his and his pupils blazed. She saw the way his gaze dropped to play on her lips, then slid lower to her exposed cleavage. It seemed to actually caress her, to peal back the folds of the kimono and bare her breasts. Her skin took fire. She shifted agitatedly in her chair.

"I—I can't just stay here!" she cried out, breaking the sensual tension in the silent room.

He raked a brow. "Why not?"

"I—I've got to have something to do!"

"Why?"

"It'd be worse than Poston. The boredom destroys your nerves." She fixed her eyes on his watchful ones. His intentions suddenly dawned on her. "You want to destroy me, reduce me to groveling, because you can't buy me?"

He flung his napkin to one side. "I have bought you! When will you realize that?"

"You're despicable!" she cried and, throwing her napkin on the table, ran from the room.

Only as she heard the water thundering in the shower an hour later did she realize that she and Nick must have connecting rooms. As she lay in the large bed, she could envision his rock-hard body, the way the water cascaded over the broad chest, catching in the tangle of hair, and then sluicing on down to be damned up by the thick wiry patch below his navel.

And she could too vividly imagine other things—the way he had seared into her, hammering at her until she was at last depleted. He alone set off the fire, he alone quenched it.

The shower stopped, and she heard the click of the glass door as he stepped out of the shower stall. She held her breath. Surely he did not dare to force her. Not with Trouble lying at the foot of the bed. She would fight Nick with every ounce of resistance she had left.

Then she heard the opening and closing of the door to his room. She lay stiffly through the dark hours of the night . . . expecting . . . waiting . . . and haunted.

Chapter 57

*N*ICK drove her and her father to the hospital the next day and waited patiently in the outer office while she paced the floor. The battery of tests took all morning, and at one point Nick left and reappeared with a paper cup of coffee.

"Drink it," he told her when she shook her head. To argue seemed to require more energy than she had at that moment, and she obediently swallowed the acrid liquid.

The doctor, an older man (had the United States armed services taken all the young ones?), informed her he wanted to keep her father in for a few days more while he ran additional tests.

"Is it bad?" she asked Nick as he drove her back to the guest ranch. "Do you think they've found something wrong with Father—other than the tuberculosis?"

"I think your father's condition is weakened by the pneumonia, but the doctors probably want to clear him of any other illnesses before they make a final diagnosis." He glanced at her tightly interlocked fingers. "Relax, Mandy. You're doing everything possible for your father."

She dragged her gaze from the window to Nick's homely but powerful profile. "And you . . . why are you doing all this?"

"You're going over old ground again," he said flatly.

She turned her gaze back to the dairy farms that were interspersed with the growing number of office buildings on Center Avenue.

With her father in the hospital, Nurse Haines was discharged until she would be needed again. Mrs. Rawlings lived in a cottage separate from the ranch house. After she served dinner and retired for the evening, Amanda was left alone with Nick. Nervously she picked at the roast beef and broccoli. Any moment she expected Nick to order her to strip and spread herself naked on the dining table. One would expect such a thing from a barbarian like Nick.

But he talked lightly of the Axis surrender in North Africa and what it would mean to the war and the new Davis-Monathon Air Force Base that was in construction southeast of Tucson. He made no effort to touch her. Damn him, he was playing with her as a cat did with a mouse!

After dinner he suggested a game of chess. "I—I have a headache," she said. "I think I'll go on to bed."

He rose from the table as she moved past him, and she could feel his eyes on her. When she reached the dining-room doors, he said, "Do you think husbands really believe that old excuse?"

She pivoted to face him. "You're a husband. Talk to Danielle about it!"

He was out of the chair like a cannon ball, the force of his anger almost knocking her against the doorframe, though he came to a halt only inches from her. "I'm asking you!" he gritted.

"And I'm not your wife, thank God!"

The smoldering embers banked in his eyes suddenly ignited into furious flames. His eyes scalded her from head to toe, as if he knew beneath the kimono she was naked. The heat of his anger pinned her to the door. Her breath came in deep fearful gasps. Then, abruptly, he swung from her to stalk away.

She grabbed at his arm, holding on. "It's true, isn't it?" she demanded, her anger now leaping to meet his. "You married Danielle gambling that her Warren background assured your ticket to political and financial success! You can be bought, too, Nick Godwin!"

"So?" he asked in a dangerously quiet voice. "At least Danielle was enough of a lady not to sell herself for anything less than a wedding ring."

Amanda's hands clenched at her sides. "So much of a lady that she found bedding with an animal distasteful!"

Nick's face took on its meanest look. He made a grab for her. She dropped his arm and spun away, running toward her bedroom. She could hear him behind her. She quickened her speed, running down the maze of arched corridors. Then she realized he was only loping behind, with Trouble following him.

Nick caught up with her as she jerked open her door. His arm closed about her waist, lifting her from the ground, and he slammed the door shut with an enraged kick of his foot. Outside Trouble whimpered.

In two strides Nick was at her bed, tossing her on it. She rolled to a sitting position, holding her ground. "Well?" she demanded impatiently, as he stood over her, glaring at her. "Go ahead, rape me! Isn't that what you wanted?"

He yanked her to him, so that, kneeling on the mattress, she was forced to look up into the strong, homely face. "Dammit, Mandy, that's all you understand, isn't it?" He shook her. "I don't want some sacrificial virgin!"

Her head was bobbing like a rag doll's. "But you want me!" she managed to get out triumphantly.

"And you want me!" His mouth landed on hers. Her lips opened beneath the force of his. His tongue burned her lips like a red-hot poker. She moaned as his kiss devoured her mouth. Her head fell back when his mouth at last released hers. His kisses laced the hollow of her throat while his hands slid the robe from her shoulders.

"No . . . no," she tried to protest, but the words came out in a gasp as his hand cupped the weight of one bared breast possessively and his mouth kissed the other, tugging, pulling on the nipple, then nipping at it with his teeth and flicking it with his tongue. Would he never stop the sweet torture?

Somehow she was sprawled on the bed and he was kneeling over her, stripping himself of his shirt and pants while his hot gaze ravaged the intimate swells and recesses of her body. Then he was straddling her. But he withheld himself. "Tell me," he prompted in what was almost the menacing purr of a panther. "Say it, Mandy! Say you want me also!"

She met his fierce gaze. Her lips clamped shut. He warned, "I won't have your accusing glare afterward."

Enraged silence.

He made to rise. She gasped angrily. "Yes! Yes, damn you!"

He slid over her then, like a knife seeking its sheath. He took her with smooth, rapid strokes. She met his pounding torso, raising her hips to receive him. She hit back at him with her pelvis, afraid his savage taking of her would end before he had rid her of the plague that raged inside her.

Sweat bathed them until they were slippery. Still they clung to each other as if in fierce combat. He did not fail her. He drove into her time after time until she felt the knot of impatience and frustration explode in a glorious release, coinciding with his own explosion.

There was that heart-stopping moment that followed, the "little death," when her body lay lifeless, and then Nick gathered her against him. His thumb wiped the perspiration that glistened beneath her eyes and above her lips. "It was good, wasn't it?" he whispered. "The way it should have been before. The way it could always be."

She lay in the crook of his arm, her body delighting in the soft words he murmured into her ear, the light caressing of her battered flesh. Unwillingly she responded to the feathery touch of his coaxing hands and the velvet-rough tongue. Incredibly, he was taking her again. And she was opening to receive him.

He felt her grow hotter, moister. He saw her lids half close in the throes of sensual oblivion and her lips part in sweet abandon. Would she never understand what he was trying to show her? Would the Stronghold always stand between them?

The passion and the pleasure were longer in coming, but all the more tender, more gentle, so that when she reached the peak of unbearable ecstasy, she knew she never wanted the feeling to end. Nick cupped her to him and felt the tears that wet his chest. "Why?" he whispered.

She gulped back the tears. "Because it was wonderful. And because I know that I'll want you again, dammit!"

He laughed softly, and she turned to him. "Do you love Danielle?" she asked in the darkness, glad that he could not see her face.

"I thought I did when I married her." He moved away a little and laid one arm across his forehead. "Oh, I was honest enough to admit to myself that the Warren name helped. But, yes, she was dazzling and delicate, and I was fascinated by her."

"Yet the fascination with her didn't stop you from wanting me?"

"No."

"Good," she said tersely. "Now get out of my bedroom."

He rolled back to her, half-pinning her to the bed. "Not yet, Mandy." His smile was roguish. "The night's not over yet."

Chapter 58

AMANDA lazed by the pool. Her hand floated languidly in the water. On the pool's far side, beneath the dappled shade of an ironwood, Trouble dozed, panting.

The noon sun beat down on Amanda's exposed back and panty-clad derrière. The gravel-studded cement was warm and rough against her bare breasts. She really needed to see about finding something to wear. If that sex-crazed man had his way, she would go naked.

The pool's chlorinated water, inches away, steamed up into her face. She heard footsteps and looked up through her veil of hair to see Nick standing over her. He was dressed in an expensively cut gray business suit. One hand held his brief case, the other his tie.

He cocked a lazy grin. "If you're not careful, you'll grow susceptible to the easy life of the wealthy. Then you'll have no choice but to live here."

She shrugged, throwing her hair over her shoulder and rolling over, her arms crossed before her breasts. She took great delight in seeing the sudden hunger leap like a flame in his eyes. Recalling the night before, she felt the warmth spread upward from the pit of her stomach. "Nothing could keep me here if it were not out of necessity."

His brows rose. "You mean if it were not for governmental red tape, your father's illness, the state of the nation, and a host of sundry problems, you would be gone from here immediately?"

"Precisely."

"Well, at least I'm benefiting in some way from the world war," he said dryly. He dropped the tie on the umbrella-shaded table and began to shrug out of his coat. When he unbuttoned his shirt and his hand went to the zipper of his trousers, she said nervously, "What are you doing?"

"Stripping," he said, never taking his eyes from the nylon panties that clung to her damp skin, revealing more than they concealed. "Can't I go for a swim in my own pool?"

She gasped and sprang to a sitting position at the same time the telephone shrilled, as if in her defense. Nick sighed and went through the opened jalousie doors to the den. Three minutes later he returned with a glass of water. He hunched at her side. "Here, take this." In his palm glistened a pink capsule.

"It'll relax you. Take it."

"I don't need to relax," she protested. "I feel just—" Seeing the grim lines about Nick's white mouth, she broke off. "It's Father!"

Nick deftly slid the capsule between her parted lips. "Yes. Swallow the water."

Mechanically she obeyed him. "What's happened?" she demanded.

"A heart attack. It felled him."

"No," she rasped. "No!" She began to sob hysterically, and Nick picked her up, muffling her cries against his chest as he carried her down the hall. In his bedroom he laid her on his bed. When she tried to scramble free, he pushed her down against the mattress. "Ssssh, honey," he said. He lay down beside her and pressed her head in the hollow of his neck. "I'm not going to bother you. Just try to forget right now."

At that moment she did not want to forget. She only wanted to rush to the hospital. Feebly, she pushed against the rock that entrapped her. Great paws held her wrists so that she could barely twist about. At last lethargy subdued her and her body began to drift. She could remember the wiry hair on Nick's chest tickling her face and the musky masculine scent of his skin filling her nostrils like an anesthesia before she lost consciousness.

A slow darkness descended over her, and when she awoke, pinpricks of stars filled the sky outside Nick's wide bedroom windows. She shot up in the bed. A figure rose from the corner, and Nick materialized out of the shadows. "My father?" she asked, hoping that what she remembered was some bad dream.

Nick went into the bathroom and came back with a glass. "I've arranged for the funeral the day after tomorrow," he said. "Your father—would he have wanted a Buddhist or a Shinto ceremony? I never heard you or him mention religion, so I arranged for a simple memorial service."

Then it was all true. She shook her head numbly. "No, he was of no particular religion. A memorial service will be fine."

Nick passed her the glass with another capsule. "It's over," she said. "The hysterics. I don't want anything."

"The hysterics, maybe. But not the memories that crowd in and keep you from sleep. You'll need all the rest you can get the next few days. Come on, Mandy," he coaxed, "don't be so damned stubborn for once in your life."

It was the old Nick speaking, and this she could cope with. She reached out and took the pill, quickly swallowing it. He placed the glass on the nightstand and turned to go back to the chair he had occupied. "I'm keeping you from your bed," she said, embarrassed. And only then did she realize she was beneath the sheets and spread, still nude but for her panties.

He sprawled in his chair. "It's not the first time you've kept me from sleeping, Mandy," he said with a wry smile.

She sighed. "Well, you certainly can't expect to get much pleasure in taking advantage of a drugged woman, and the bed's big enough for both of us."

Already the pill was beginning to have its effects, and she was only vaguely aware as the bed eased beneath Nick's solid weight and the warmth that enveloped her as he pulled her into his arms.

Nick stood behind her as the first of the earthen clods was shoveled over her father's casket. There were no attendants, only the two of them to mourn her father's passing. A large wreath from Paul sat at the head of the open grave.

Head bowed, she prayed silently that her father had found his rest, that he had found her mother.

"Let's go home, Mandy," Nick said, his hands cupping her shoulders from behind.

"Home?" she whispered. She turned around to face him. "I have no home!"

He looked into her eyes, as if trying to gauge the grief that suddenly unleashed her angry words. "Your home is with me,

Mandy," he said in a gentle voice which he had never used before.

"As your mistress?" she sneered.

"It cannot be any other way." He sighed. "We've been through this before. I will not divorce Danielle."

She shrugged. "It would make no difference if you did," she lashed out, hurt. "I would never marry you!"

"Did I ever say I would ask you?" he said, propelling her toward the limousine.

"No," she replied, tired now, her grief a dull ache in her heart and mind. "You never promised me anything."

"Mandy," he said, taking her cold hands between his. "I once promised your father I would take care of you. And I will, if you'll let me."

Never once had he mentioned any words of love. She pulled her hands away. "It doesn't matter. There is no reason for me to stay. My father is dead."

"And where will you go? Do you think I'd let you leave so easily? I have only to make one call and the FBI would arrest you."

She turned on him. "Then make the call. I'll go back to Poston before I become your mistress!"

He stood before her, the flaps of his jacket pulled back, his hands jammed in his pants pockets. "It's the Stronghold, isn't it?"

"The Stronghold is as important to me as your career is to you, Nick Godwin!"

His gaze burned over her face. "You're free to leave at any time!" he said and turned to enter the limousine.

The chauffeur dropped him off at the capitol. When Nick disappeared up the marbled building's steep flight of steps, she told the chauffeur, "Take me to the train depot, please."

He looked in the rear-view mirror with startled eyes. "Er—your luggage, Miss Shima?"

"There is none." There was so little that was actually hers at the ranch that it would make no difference. There was Trouble, but until she could find a place to stay, until she could take care of herself . . . yes, the mongrel would be better off with Nick. Still, after the loss of her father, giving up Trouble again was pain that actually twisted like a blade in her heart.

Chapter 59

AMANDA had hoped to find memories of her father in Tucson. But she was wrong. After the brief hour train trip, she caught a taxi to their old house in the Barrio Libre only to find it boarded up—confiscated by the Federal Bank.

She felt that she was worse off than when she had been incarcerated at Poston, for at least there she had had a roof over her head and food. And a job.

A job.

She went to the nearest restaurant, the Cushing Street Diner, bought a newspaper, and sat down with a cup of tea to look for jobs. The new Goodyear Aircraft plant at Litchfield Park outside Phoenix was advertising for women to work as riveters on the Navy plant assemblies. And the Civil Service advertised it was hiring personnel for the newly expanded Army base at Fort Huachuca. But she had no references, and she was Japanese.

An utter gloom descended on her. She drank the remainder of her tea, barely tasting it, barely seeing the newsprint before her . . . until the sentence "Judge Craymore to Preside at Elks Banquet" jumped out at her.

Why not? Why not have a judge swear her in? Unless Nick reported her to the FBI there was nothing to keep her from practicing law . . . unless she counted the money it would take to set up an office, to establish a practice.

She set her empty cup down with renewed determination. There was much to be done. First, a trip to the Pima County Courthouse.

Judge Craymore's secretary told Amanda the judge was still in court but should be through within the hour. Amanda took a seat in one of the wooden chairs. Every few moments she shifted uncomfortably. What if the judge refused to swear her in? Worse, what if Nick had already alerted the FBI?

Some time later, a small man in black robes swished through the outer office, and the stern-looking secretary grabbed up her pad and pencil and followed him inside the inner office. After a few minutes, she reappeared. "Judge Craymore will see you now, Miss Shima."

The old man was shrugging into his suit coat when the secretary ushered her in. "Miss Hoeffler tells me you wish me to administer the formal ceremony of admission to the bar. You have all your necessary requirements and certificates?"

"No, your honor. My Bachelor of Law certificate is—packed away. And I was not required to take the state bar exam. But Mr. Browne, the counselor at the university, can bear witness for me."

"I see," Judge Craymore said, rubbing his chin as he looked at her thoughtfully. Could she blame him for not believing her? "Shima . . . is that a Japanese surname?"

Dear God, would it all begin again? "Yes, your honor. For the past year I have been in a war relocation camp. That's why I've been unable to take the oath of attorney. But I have recently been released on sponsorship."

She stood straight now before his desk, bracing herself for another refusal. The judge leaned back in the large leather-upholstered chair. "You've got grit, young woman.

Was that a negative or positive statement? The palms of her hands turned clammy. The judge leaned forward now and picked up the telephone. "Get me the dean at the university," he told his secretary.

"Have a seat, Miss Shima," he said, replacing the receiver. "I hope I'll have the confirmation within a minute."

Even the minute seemed like an hour, and she jumped when the telephone shrilled through the office. "John!" the judge said heartily. "Glad to talk to you! Need you to verify a Miss Amanda Shima's law credentials for me."

She closed her eyes, her heart barely beating as she held her breath in suspense. The judge cradled the receiver. "Raise your right hand and repeat after me, Miss Shima."

Her hand slipped up. She could not quite believe it was really happening to her after all these years. "I, Amanda Shima, do solemnly swear:

"I am a citizen of the United States, and owe my allegiance thereto; I will support the Constitution of the United States and of the state of Arizona; I will maintain the respect due the courts of justice and judicial officers; I . . ."

There was more, but she could not remember it all as she left the county courthouse in a daze. With her swearing-in her bitterness at the War Relocation Authority fell behind her. There had been too many people who had helped her to let what happened at Santa Anita and Poston stand in her way . . . Mr. Browne, Larry, Kathy, and now the judge.

She stood at the corner of Pennington and Church streets, where once had risen the adobe wall that fortified the Old Pueblo, and tried to think what next. She was an attorney now . . . without an office.

And that was next. She took a bus to her old bank and asked to see a loan officer. The balding man looked askance when she informed him she wanted to borrow some money. "I'm sorry, Miss Shima, but certainly you must realize that we cannot just hand out money without some sort of collateral."

She smiled sweetly. "How about the two hundred and thirty-seven dollars of mine which your bank has frozen and the household furniture and the laundry equipment the federal government has stored in a warehouse?"

The loan officer gulped. "Well, you see . . . uh, governmental policy forbids us to touch any such—confiscations—until the orders are listed."

He was as uncomfortable as she was frustrated. "But that is my money! And my belongings!"

But, of course, the man was right. She might as well be jobless, for all the good her admission to the bar did her. She rose from the chair, defeated. "I am sorry, Miss Shima," the man said to her bowed head. "If only you had some other collateral or someone willing to co-sign the note with you."

She looked up. "But I do," she said slowly, as the idea occurred to her. "Will the President's economic adviser do as a cosigner?"

"The President of the United States?" the loan officer croaked.

She had to smile. "His economic adviser, Paul Godwin."

(*367*)

The loan officer cleared his throat. "Can you be reached by telephone? It may take some time to get through to Washington."

She gave him the name of the Parkview Hotel, which had at one time been an opera house. It was near the courthouse, and she figured that since it was an older hotel, the cost of a room would not take too much from the twenty-four dollars she had remaining in her purse.

All night long she kept waking, expecting to see Nick hunched over her, expecting to hear an FBI agent knocking at her door. It was the longest night she could remember.

The next morning she stepped out of the shower to find the telephone ringing. Grabbing up a towel, she ran across the room, afraid it would stop before she picked up the receiver. "Miss Shima?" It was the loan officer.

She took a deep breath and closed her eyes. "Yes?"

"Your loan has been approved," he said, his voice awed and respectful. "We can have a check waiting for you whenever you're ready."

Amanda found a small, narrow office in an adobe structure on Court Street next to the old IXL Lodging House. In the 1880s the lodging place housed many business and professional people, especially attorneys, but now it wore a rather run-down appearance. Still, the single-windowed office she leased was inexpensive and was partitioned off so that she could put a cot and a two-burner hot plate in the rear, which would serve as her domicile until she could build up her practice.

She was able to purchase a desk and an old bookcase from a car dealer who was going out of business. In the bookcase she installed her reference volumes, the *Corpus Juris Secundum, American Jurisprudence,* and the *American Law Reports.* She was ready to begin practice—but had no clients.

Not true. There was Betty Yasaki, whom she had promised to represent in a suit challenging the War Relocation Authority. Knotting her long, heavy hair at her nape and donning the one suit she had, the blue serge one, Amanda set out on her first day of practice for the courthouse, feeling slightly elated.

It had taken twenty-five years of her life, but she had finally become an attorney. She only wished her father had lived to see the signman hang out her shingle before her office.

But what she wanted most to complete her happiness, the Stronghold, she did not have. And, familiar as she was now with the law, she dismally accepted the fact that her chances of ever taking her case to court and winning were nil.

At the courthouse she filed the writ of habeas corpus on Betty's behalf and filled out all the many legal forms that had to be signed. While she was there a blustering old man in overalls stormed in to protest the citation he had received for double-parking his produce truck.

"I would be glad to represent you in court," she told him.

The old man removed his battered straw hat. "You a lawyer?" he asked, his skepticism showing in his squinched eyes and jutting, gray-stubbled chin.

"Yes, I am."

He shifted his quid of tobacco. "A lawyer woman don't know how—"

"I shall easily win your case for you," she coolly pointed out, "because the city will erroneously feel that no preparation will be necessary against a female attorney."

The farmer's jaws halted their chawing. His squinty eyes ran over her as if she were an old mule he was about to purchase. "All right, gal."

Since she had no other clients, she spent every waking hour poring over her casebooks that next week. Her days took on a reassuring routine. She rose at seven, coffee heated on the two-burner hot plate, a sponge bath from the small porcelain sink; then, at eight, she opened the outer office and sat at her desk, studying until noon, when she broke for a sandwich and usually a stroll through Tucson's old streets. The evenings were the loneliest for her. She read until her eyes hurt and her brain was numb. Yet sleep was forever in coming as she tossed on the narrow, uncomfortable cot.

She won the case for the farmer on a minor technicality—the officer who had issued the citation had listed the farmer's commercial truck as only a pick-up. But from that one case she received two more—the farmer's sister-in-law, who wanted a divorce, and the parents of a student athlete injured in a football game, who wanted to sue the school district for damages.

She was busier now, and she liked it that way. She had no spare time to think. She fell asleep at night, exhausted. Her routine was broken as she went into her second month of practice by a telephone call. "Amanda?" It was Paul! "How is your practice going?"

"Fi—fine," she stuttered. "Thanks to you. Where are you calling from?"

"Washington. I've been wanting to call sooner, but as usual the President has had me on the run."

"Paul, I can't thank you enough for cosigning the note. I promise—"

"Amanda—it was a purely selfish reason on my part." He hesitated, then said, "There was another reason I didn't call sooner. When you were at Poston, I wanted to arrange your release, but Nick let me know he had staked his claim. I've been waiting to see if it was really over between you two."

"There never was anything between us," she said flatly.

"Amanda . . . I've got a weekend off coming up. Will you be free? I'd like to see you."

"That would be wonderful, Paul."

After she replaced the receiver, she sat looking at the telephone, trying to sort out what lay behind Paul's call. Could it be possible that Paul Godwin was interested in her?

She dressed carefully, for Paul had said he wanted to take her out to eat. She wore the same blue serge suit but softened it with a pale-blue frothy blouse she purchased out of her first wages as an attorney. And rather than knotting her hair, she let it hang sleekly, framing her face in a very feminine style.

When the doorbell rang, her stomach dropped in nervousness. She opened the door. Paul stood there, tall and striking, with that dignified manner he had about him. She held out both hands to clasp his. "Paul," she said warmly. He had always been kind to her.

He took her hands and pulled her to him, kissing first her forehead, then her lips, softly, gently. The kiss left her stunned. Paul wasn't a big brother. He was a man. He put her from him. "You're beautiful, Amanda."

She smiled, suddenly shy. "I don't want to hear about me. It's not often a commoner gets to talk with someone of the hierarchy.

I want to hear what Eleanor wears to bed and if FDR truly has a mistress, and—"

"Good grief, you really don't think I know what Eleanor wears to bed?" Paul laughed.

Their banter set the mood to cover what they both were thinking about and continued after they got in the car Paul had rented. It was only after they passed the city-limit signs and left the lights behind them that she realized they were not going to a restaurant—at least not one in Tucson. "Where are we eating?" she asked Paul.

The smile lines about his lips eased as he sobered. "I suppose the President would say I hedged on you, Amanda. I *am* taking you out to eat. But not to a public restaurant. I know how you feel about the Stronghold, so I thought it would be the perfect place to eat tonight."

He turned off the main highway, and the final thirty-minute stretch of the trip through the Empire foothills was made in pleasant conversation. But beneath the lightness of her words her heart thumped in anticipation.

She was going home!

The lights from the Stronghold's many windows blazed like beacons against the darkness of the night. A table was already set with candlelight. The same old Mexican retainer stood waiting at the dining-room door to serve them. Paul pulled out a chair at the long table and seated himself across from her. She reached out to touch his hand. "Nothing could have been better," she whispered, affected by his thoughtfulness.

"And nothing could be better for my aging male ego than to look across the table and see a beautiful, warm, and intelligent woman whom I care for very much. No, more than that, a woman whom I love. Does it shock you for me to admit it, Amanda?" His long, slender fingers gripped hers with a strength that surprised her. "Shall I take you in my arms as the impetuous man I once was and tell you I've been half in love with you since you were a child—when those large green eyes of yours challenged both Nick and myself?"

Slowly she shook her head. "No, I've had enough of that, Paul." She looked down at the slender, capable fingers that interlaced her own. She knew they would be tender, patient, and loving with her . . . never demanding, never brutal.

"And how do you feel—how do you feel about marrying a man twenty-two years your senior? I feel positively selfish and just a little senile asking you to marry me, Amanda, but I really think I could make you happy. I know I'm too old to generate the wild passion that only the youth can, but I can love you. Let me love you, Amanda. Let me make you happy. Let me marry you."

He released her fingers and picked up the wineglass beside his plate. "You must believe I'd try to make you happy, dear. You haven't had much happiness in your brief life. Say you'll give me the chance."

The world reeled about her as if she were on a merry-go-round. Wordlessly she picked up her own glass and touched the crystal rim to his. As much as she had wanted Cristo Rey, no, lusted after it, it had never actually occurred to her that she would ever have it. There had lived in her only the madness for revenge. But now Paul was offering her not only Cristo Rey but an end to the revenge that had eaten at her soul.

Chapter 60

WITHIN the week, stories of Paul Godwin's engagement to Amanda were plastered over the front pages of newspapers across the nation, accompanied by separate photos of Paul and her. She shuddered when she recognized her photo as one taken at the Poston War Relocation Camp.

It made a fabulous story—"Millionaire Diplomat to Wed War Camp Cinderella." She feared the photos taken of Nick and her at Santa Anita would crop up, but they never did, and she could only guess that Paul, the wise politician, saw to it they did not. There was only a short paragraph in the *Arizona Daily Star* about her release from the Poston War Camp—"through the efforts of the Godwin family."

Paul could not get free for the wedding until May, another two months away, but he insisted that she take the time to shop for her trousseau. He was even arranging to have a refugee couturière trained at one of the well-known French houses design her wedding dress. "No *haute couture* could do justice to your golden-skinned beauty," he told her, taking her in his arms before he boarded his private coach on the train.

His mouth closed over hers in a kiss that began softly but increased in its urgency. She could feel the heat emanating from him. There was nothing soft about the body that she was pressed against . . . a slender, sinewy body, she knew, that would take her slowly, patiently, along the route to love's passion.

Her previously quiet life changed after Paul's departure. People were constantly streaming into her office to congratulate her, total strangers—some of whom became her clients. She was a celebrity now. Occasionally some newspaper photographer snapped her picture as she left the courthouse or entered City Hall. And once an interviewer for "Jimmie Fidler's Hollywood Gossip" shoved his shiny wagon-wheel microphone before her face as she left the university's law library.

Constantly in the news as she was, the story of Paul Godwin's long-distance courtship of her appeared in the *New York Daily Mirror*. She was forced to purchase a new wardrobe—tailored dresses, finely cut business suits, and a few casual clothes that breathed of elegance. She even splurged and bought a John-Frederic chapeau for sixty dollars; but then, with her increased clientele she could afford to appear better dressed.

Paul called her every day, and she looked forward to hearing his voice, to talking about her cases or listening to him describe the intricacies of the political debates waged at Washington's social gatherings. "The nation's policies are formulated there—and in the bedrooms, Mandy, not in the Senate chambers or the Oval Room."

"As long as you stay out of the bedrooms," she teased, "I don't care how you formulate our national policies."

One day she looked up from her desk to see Larry and Kathy coming through the door. "I don't believe it!" she said, rising.

"And we didn't believe it," Kathy said. She hugged Amanda, then stepped back, saying, "My husband, Larry!"

Larry smiled sheepishly. "The girl didn't give up on me."

"You two married? How marvelous!"

"And how marvelous the things we hear about you," Kathy said. "Not only did you manage to get your law degree, which I gave up on, but we've been reading everywhere about your engagement to Paul Godwin."

"Who would ever have thought . . ." Larry began and broke off with a smile. "How about going out to lunch with us?"

Amanda knew he had been about to mention Nick's name and thought better of it. "I'd love to! Living and working in the same place makes a wreck out of you."

In the weeks that followed, Kathy, bored being a housewife, stopped by quite often for lunch or invited Amanda for dinner on the weekend. Between Amanda's expanding professional career and the new demands on her social life as Paul's fiancée, her time was fully occupied, which was how she wanted it. She should have been happy, but there came the visit from Nick to change her euphoria.

It was nearing eight o'clock one evening, and she had just finished washing her hair in the sink. She only had time to slide her panty-clad body into a robe before she hurried through the darkened front of the building to answer the door. "Mind if I come in?" Nick asked and walked on past her before she could reply.

She shut the door and turned to face him, her arms crossed. "Well?" she demanded, hoping that her voice did not betray her inner trembling.

"Just wanted to congratulate you, Mandy. You're a smooth lady. Paul called earlier this week to get my blessing."

"I can well imagine what you told him!"

"Actually I told him nothing. If he doesn't already know the kind of woman he's marrying, he soon will. Scheming bitches, they call women like you."

Her hand slashed upward, and he anticipated it, catching her wrist in a brutal grip. A white-hot current ignited the chemistry that had always been between them. "Temper!" he growled, pulling her against him. Then she smelled the liquor that warmed his breath.

"What's wrong with what I'm doing?" she demanded. "I can make Paul happy. And he loves me."

"And in return you can have the Stronghold. What a marriage of convenience! Just like the Old World."

"Don't you dare judge me, Nick Godwin. You arranged your own marriage of convenience for that damned career of yours. Your wife and your mistress came second!"

He shoved her from him and pulled out his case of cigarettes. The match he struck briefly illuminated the darkened office and his strong, homely face. "That was the problem, Mandy," he said, exhaling. "I couldn't make you come second no matter how hard I tried. Your image kept crowding in on my thoughts, demanding of me what I had no right to give! Even after Paul told me he was going to marry you, I kept waiting, kept hoping that you would change your mind . . . that I was wrong about you. That you couldn't be bought."

"Get out!" she said. "Get out!"

She promised herself she would not let his visit interfere with her future happiness. She was to be wedded to a man she dearly cared about. The fact that she was to gain the Stronghold would only make her marriage that much happier.

The remaining weeks before the marriage whirled by with the last-minute tasks. Paul called two or three times a day now or sent telegrams the week he was in London. Every Friday a delivery boy arrived at her office with a vase of roses or chrysanthemums or maybe an orchid corsage, so that the tiny place looked like a greenhouse. She spent many hours on the telephone with Paul's secretary in Washington coordinating the wedding arrangements. Then there were the fittings of the wedding dress, the caterers to be hired, the invitations to be sent.

Kathy pitched in and helped, seeming to enjoy the excitement of the demanding hours of work. But Amanda dragged to bed each night. Still, she could not sleep. And often she felt ill. She could not eat, though her stomach churned with hunger.

Then as the last days of April slipped into May, she made an appointment—an appointment she dreaded keeping. She sat in the doctor's office, waiting. It could not be possible, she thought. Just when she had finally achieved what she wanted from life. But the doctor confirmed her fear.

She was pregnant with Nick's child.

"I take it you are not pleased with the news, Mrs. Willis?" the doctor asked, as he set aside his rubber gloves.

It had been Kathy's idea to use her married name. For once her voluble friend closed her mouth and did not ask who the father was when Amanda revealed her fear that she was pregnant.

"No," Amanda answered woodenly now. "I'm—I'm not ready for a child yet."

The doctor sighed. "Too often that happens these days. The woman's boyfriend comes home—a soldier on leave—and returns to the war front, leaving his girl with the burden to bear . . . no pun intended."

His graying brows lowered over the peering eyes. "In situations such as these I can sometimes arrange for . . . the removal of the fetus. Purely a minor surgical process which takes place in my office. Expensive, you understand, due to extenuating circumstances. But if you find that you cannot go through with this pregnancy, I can make the necessary arrangements."

"I . . . I don't know."

"Well, take your time, my dear. This is something no woman should be pushed into. You still have two weeks before you go into the danger zone. After three months I just won't risk the woman's life or my reputation in such an operation."

"No . . . no, please. Go ahead and make the arrangements. I'll need to rearrange my schedule, but I can be ready."

Where before her feet had dragged to the doctor's office, she practically ran out. She was in a hurry to get it over with. She was in a hurry to get married. Tuesday, the day of the operation, came at last. She could not get to the doctor's office soon enough. Quickly, quickly, her brain demanded. Nothing must prevent the wedding from taking place.

Kathy sat in the outer office with her while she waited for the nurse to announce her name. Around her sat half a dozen or so obviously pregnant young women, their expressions nigh beatific as their hands occasionally and almost surreptitiously gently touched their beach-ball stomachs. For one unguarded moment Amanda's thoughts wistfully drifted as she imagined the child inside her—a daughter, a son; the babe nuzzling against her breast; later those tiny dimpled hands latched onto her fingers as the tot balanced precariously on two small feet.

Amanda closed her eyes, shutting out the sight of the pregnant mothers' blissful faces, and shutting out the tears that threatened to spill. She forced the image of the Stronghold, its impregnable walls and splendid castle rooms, to the front of her mind. The Stronghold. After almost a hundred years it would be returned to the rightful heirs. It was justice! It was retribution! It was what the Ghost Lady would have wanted, wasn't it?

The nurse called her into a sterile anteroom, a terribly cold place it seemed, where she was told to remove her clothing. She felt as if she were in a butcher's locker room as she slid into the backless gown. Another nurse came for her, the woman's face an impassive mask, and led her through a back door that led to what appeared to be just another examination room, though there were many more gleaming instruments spread across its counter and the overhead lights were brighter—glaring, illuminating globes that seemed to leave her no privacy, no decency.

"If you'll just lie up here on the table." The nurse began to maneuver the valves of the oxygen tank. "Now the doctor will be in shortly to give you a last examination before we begin the . . . procedure," she explained in a brittly cheerful voice. "If you'll inhale a few whiffs of the oxygen, it'll make you light-headed, like a couple of good stiff drinks, so that the ether won't make you so . . . uncomfortable. Later, if you need it, you'll be given more."

When the mask descended, all Amanda could think of was the thing within her inhaling the nauseous ether as she did. Soon she would be rid of its presence. It was all that stood between her and the Stronghold. It *would* be Nick's child! Nick had always stood between her and the Stronghold. Nick's child.

A child.

She began to twist and shove at the cup that covered her nose and mouth. "The child!" it seemed she screamed, though it could not have been more than a faint cry through the mask's cup. She kicked and flailed her arms before the cup was mercifully lifted from her face and she fainted.

When next she awoke, Kathy was hovering over her. "Am I . . . did the doctor . . ."

Kathy shook her head, and her tight sausage curls bobbled. Amanda was afraid to hear her answer. "It seems you wanted the baby, and the doctor was afraid to go ahead for fear of a lawsuit."

"Thank God," she breathed.

"Did you want the baby?" Kathy asked, leaning over her in puzzlement.

She managed a weak smile. "I suppose so. Yes, yes, I do, Kathy."

Her friend shook her head in wonderment. "The baby's not Paul's, is it?"

"No."

"You know what this baby'll do to his career—and yours? I don't have to tell you, do I? You sure you don't want to reconsider?"

"No. I'm not going through with the abortion, Kathy. And I'm not going through with the marriage."

Her penciled brows knitted. "I don't understand, hon. You realize what you're giving up—the Stronghold and all? A person'd have to be a fool to give up marriage to a famous man like Paul Godwin and all that money!"

"How about going out drinking tonight, Kathy?"

Chapter 61

GO on to lunch without me, Kathy."

"You're not eating?" her friend asked. "The doctor would throw a tizzy, if he knew."

Amanda smiled. "But he doesn't, does he?"

"You're not upset, are you—over that photo of Paul and that Washington party hostess, what's her name?"

She sighed. "No, I'm truly not. It's just that I always seem to be sleepier these days, and it takes me longer to get everything done. Bring me back a sandwich, will you?"

Kathy hesitated at the door. "You know, when Nick Godwin came by our house for Trouble earlier this year, I thought he might be the one, but I seem to be wrong about both the Godwin brothers."

Amanda managed a smile. "If you see any good-looking soldiers on leave, grab one for me. The baby needs a father."

Kathy laughed and left. Amanda sighed. She didn't know why she pushed herself like she did. There really weren't that many clients pounding at her door, though she had enough to keep her reasonably occupied. When word of her broken engagement reached the newspapers, a great many of her "social clients" dropped off like flies in winter's first freeze. And she was certain that as word spread of her pregnancy, she would lose many more clients, regardless of how successful she had been in the courtroom.

At five months pregnant, her growing abdomen was almost impossible to hide now, especially on her otherwise slender figure. And the tent dresses she wore weren't really that becoming to a professional woman.

Soon all of Tucson would be gossiping, asking who the father was. Only Larry and Kathy and, of course, Paul knew, though she had never mentioned Nick's name when she told him she was pregnant and breaking off the engagement.

"I still want to marry you, Amanda," he had told her. It was his first evening back in Tucson since his proposal, and they were eating at the Westward Ho, one of the many guest ranches that had sprung up in Tucson's Santa Catalina mountains.

She looked away from the handsomely distinguished face. Her eyes shimmered like Tucson's night lights stretched out below the restaurant's panoramic window. "It wouldn't work, Paul."

"Why don't you give it a try?" he asked gently.

She looked back at the face that was etched with tender concern. "Like my grandmother," she said, managing a faint smile, "I seem to be caught up between two stepbrothers."

"It does seem a strange parallel," he mused. "As I recall the story of the Ghost Lady, in the end she had neither stepbrother."

"So a version of the story goes," she whispered, still clinging to her inane smile. "So why change what's fated to be?"

They parted that night, vowing their friendship, though she knew that Paul felt more. She swore Paul to silence about her pregnancy. "You don't want Nick to know?" he asked.

She nodded. "He'll know soon enough, along with the rest of the world. But the child's father I want to remain unknown." She raised her chin. "I won't have anyone feeling sorry for us."

"You promise you'll call me if ever you need me?" he demanded of her before he kissed her goodbye.

She knew she never would. Somehow she would make it on her own. There were a lot of mothers who had lost husbands in the war and were raising children by themselves, she reminded herself fiercely. She could not castigate herself for having given away her life's dream. Her hand descended to her stomach to the little soul that stirred there, and she knew that since she could not have both, she had made the only choice she could live with.

She returned her attention to a case outlined in the *United States Code Annotated*. The door opened, and she looked up to see Nick enter. She gasped and almost stood but then thought better of it. She could not let him see the gentle mound beneath her dress. When he was near enough she searched those cool blue eyes for the quick anger that seemed to be ever present when the two of them came together. But this time she could not make out what that gaze held.

He came around the desk and hunkered one thigh on its top, so that he looked down into that face that had hounded him for so many years. It wasn't just the tantalizing beauty . . . or the intelligent mind. Dammit, he had known from that first meeting at Cristo Rey that she had hooked his heart . . . if it was possible for a boy of thirteen to know and understand such a feeling.

It hadn't taken him long to find out that she was the daughter of a Japanese. Falling in love with her could only hold him back, and he had tried every way under the sun to deny his love. He had tried to go without seeing her. He had tried other women. He had tried replacing the love of her with the love of power. And he had tried calling the love for her lust. Nothing had worked. There was no magic potion to cure him of that Oriental sorceress's spells.

"Your friend Kathy told me you'd still be in," he said in that voice that was like low thunder.

She was afraid to speak. She had not the strength to face his anger as she so often had had before. "After I read that your engagement with Paul had been called off," he continued, "I kept hoping I'd hear from you. But I should have known your stubborn pride would stand in the way."

Her fingers clenched the book she held so that they would not reach up to caress the homely-handsome face she loved so much. He was her Stronghold. Had always been her heart's stronghold. "Nick," she whispered, "I can't go back to you."

His brows rose. "Then I'm wrong? No, I don't think so. What's between you and me, Mandy, I could never be wrong about."

Gently he took her shoulders and pushed her back against the chair. But there was nothing gentle in the mouth that claimed hers hungrily. Despite her determination not to, she returned the kiss, her lips following his lead. That same damnable itch that always plagued her when he was near began again in spite of the other changes motherhood had wrought in her metabolism. Nothing could ever change that burning knot inside her for Nick Godwin.

When his lips finally released hers, she realized his hand rested on her swelling abdomen. Her lids flew open. "You know?" she rasped.

"About our child?" He grinned. "Not until Kathy lit into me with a sermon. She hit me with both barrels right there on Pennington and Court. I think if she'd had her way, the police would have dragged me off to the old whipping post."

"I won't be your mistress again, Nick. I won't subject my child to that kind of life."

He leaned over her and began to nibble at her earlobe. His hand slid boldly beneath her dress's V-neck to caress one of her breasts, engorged now with motherhood. "Would you settle for marriage?"

Her lungs ceased to function. Nick's hand didn't. She pushed it away. "Danielle?"

He feigned a sigh. "Don't tell me that I'll have to forgo the delights of your marvelous body the rest of your pregnancy."

"Your marriage to Danielle?" she persisted.

"The night I came here I was going to tell you that I had asked her for a divorce."

"Oh, no, Nick. The destruction of your marriage—it could only hurt whatever it is between us."

His fingers were slipping back inside her dress, cupping one full breast, squeezing it gently. "They're delightful!" he murmured, his lips descending to burn a trail along the graceful column of her neck, while his hand loosed the buttons of her dress.

"You're not listening!" she cried indignantly.

"Oh, yes—yes, I am, love," he said huskily as he freed the golden globes.

Her hands tried to shield herself from his probing lips, and he sighed again. "Now listen to me this once, Mandy Shima, soon-to-be Mandy Godwin," he said, prying her fingers away from her buttons. "You are not responsible for my marriage's failure. Danielle's and my marriage has never been the kind it should have been. It was only after you left that I knew I couldn't continue the farce any longer."

"But your career—what will people say when—"

He chuckled. "Have I ever worried about what people said? I told you once before I'm a gambler and it's the game and not the stack of chips, or lack of chips, at the end that counts. Besides," he added, his hand slipping down to cup the weight of one of her breasts again, "with your drive and my gambler's daring, there's no way we can lose, love."

He bent his hand once more to tease the rose-tinted breast, and with a soft sigh she gave up resisting him. It was useless. She simply was not ever going to rid herself of the hunger for Nick Godwin. It tormented her like a plague.

Damn the animal!

And her hands slipped up to enfold him to her.

*A*S a grown woman with a child of my own, a daughter with honey-colored hair and dusky skin, I still return occasionally to the wilderness of Cristo Rey . . . only as a visitor, for with Paul Godwin's death, my husband, Nick, deeded the land over to become part of the Coronado National Park, which was as it should have been, I know now.

But that does not stop me from recounting to our daughter, Catherine, the stories of her great-grandmother, her namesake, the stories of the Ghost Lady. And when she asks if I have ever met the Ghost Lady, I tell her, "Only once, the day I agreed to become your father's wife."

At least I think I did. I realize that no one believes in ghosts in these modern times, but still I think . . . I think that the tortured soul of my Ghost Lady was at last returned to its resting place that day . . . to the chimerical arms of the lover long denied Catherine Davalos in life.

AUTHOR'S NOTE

A great many of the characters in *Deep Purple* are authentic people out of history. For those interested readers, Sam and Atanacia Hughes really did exist. Atanacia went on to have the fifteen children she wanted and celebrated her golden anniversary with her beloved Anglo, Sam.

I felt the Shoot-out at the O.K. Corral was an important part of Tombstone, Arizona, history, but in order to retain the continuity of the story, I had to date the event two full years later than it actually occurred, and I beg the reader's pardon for my literary license.

Lastly, I must thank both Lori Davisson and Bruce Hilpert of the Arizona Historical Society and Helen Weber and Gina Smith of the Lewisville Public Library for all their help.